Jason Apsley's Second Chance

by Adrian Cousins

... ...

Adriancousins.co.uk

Also by Adrian Cousins

Part 1

1

1984

Princess

"Fuck off, you fat bitch."

"Amy, there's no need for that kind of language. All I've done is help, and I've offered you more help if you need it." Jenny knew this was pointless because Amy really didn't give a shit as she stood and just repeated herself.

"Just fuck off, you fat bitch."

Jenny had worked for ten years in children's social care for Fairfield District Council. Overall, she enjoyed her job and had a great sense of satisfaction playing her small part in supporting those vulnerable children through their difficult early years. However, today was one of those days she truly hated, because delivering any child to Lexton House was nothing short of heart-breaking.

The car heater in her puce brown, eight-year-old Leyland Princess ticked and rattled like a Geiger counter, spitting out fume-filled smelly air, thus rendering it utterly useless on exceptionally cold days like today. Also, Jenny found manoeuvring the cumbersome beast of a car difficult. However, she wasn't in any position to moan as her father had given it to her when he'd upgraded his car a few years ago. How many times she'd asked her boyfriend to fix the heater, well, she'd lost count.

But, as always, she would just get Tom's usual response – *"Yes, yes, it's on the list!"*

Jenny suspected that bloody list of jobs must be significantly longer than the Magna Carta, and nothing got done. Well, only the stuff Tom liked to do. In fact, she really couldn't remember after nearly eight years why they were still together, which was somewhat depressing. There had been a time when she'd wanted to get married, not that Jenny could remember when that was, but now she just didn't care.

Jenny dreamed of owning the car that Barry, her boss, had; a brand-new Ford Escort Ghia in beautiful quartz gold with crushed velour mocha seats, sunroof, a built-in cassette player, and, unbelievably, electrically operated windows. Barry had banged on about it that much, Jenny now knew enough about the car and could probably explain the finer points of detail better than any Ford car salesman.

But for her, Jenny Lawrence, on her salary – even though she'd just received her annual pay review and had hit that magical four grand a year mark – that wasn't going to happen. Barry had paid nearly six grand for his new pride and joy, so a quick calculation in her head suggested if she didn't buy any food and then not eat for nearly two years, she could buy one. Also, she might lose a few pounds in weight that had piled on over the last two years, and then she could fit into those summer dresses that lay dormant in the wardrobe. That would be a bonus, but would also involve starvation. However, in reality, those dresses were just waiting for the charity shop clear out when she finally accepted that size twelve was a thing of the past, never to be revisited.

She parked outside Lexton House – an imposing grey turn-of-the-century building that looked worse in winter, if that were possible. The Victorian, four-storey house, owned by the local Council, urgently required updating. However, in its current use as a children's home, there was no chance of any investment coming its way soon. The battered, arched, double-front door

10

with grey flaking paint was heavily dented, probably by tormented children kicking and screaming as they entered into their new depressing home. Centred in the front of the building above the door perched a stone balustrade that appeared in danger of imminent collapse and would crush her every time she walked towards it.

Flipping down the sun-visor, she checked her lippy was still in place, reapplied for good measure and grinned at the mirror to check her teeth. With a quick flick of her hair she was ready. Stepping out of the car, Jenny opened the back door so her latest offering to Lexton House could climb from the back seat. Amy scrunched up her face like an old man gurning, folded her arms and just stared ahead, not moving.

"Come on, Amy, get out of the car. It's freezing, and I can't stand here all day. There are other children who need my help; it's not all about you, you know."

Jenny knew she was being hard on Amy, but this was the final stop on her pinball journey from foster home to foster home and back. As Elton John had sung, *'He's a pinball wizard,'* and Amy was the ball.

Out of the Princess – and nothing regal about her in any way – this was it for Amy. At the tender age of eight, and after six failed attempts to place her with a loving family, Lexton House would become her home for the next ten years. After that, Jenny suspected that she would disappear into the lowlife world that many of the kids had when the system failed them, although she'd tried so hard with Amy, and was determined not to blame herself.

Delivering any child to this depressing place could only be described as a failure. That said, Jenny had to accept she couldn't win with all her cases, because sometimes some of those kids were no-hopers. Amy was one such no-hoper – top of the class, degree level and Olympic gold medal status in hopelessness. She'd come out of the same mould as her half-brother who'd travelled the same route some years ago.

It's fair to say Amy wasn't blessed with any discerning features. Her greasy-blonde hair, slapped to the sides of her face, had missed the attentions of a brush. An old beige corduroy skirt hung awkwardly from her thin frame, mismatched with a pink and grey hooped jumper that had seen better days. She wore ridiculously large Doc Martens boots that she insisted on wearing, although Jenny suspected they were her only footwear.

Assessing those boots, Jenny thought they'd be good for kicking that grey door. Alan, her much younger brother, had owned a similar pair about six years ago, and Jenny recalled that he'd scrawled in white gloss paint *'Never Mind the Bollocks'* on them. Their parents hadn't been best pleased – not only regarding what they perceived was a pair of mutilated boots – but also, the ruined new tin of paint which had been stirred up and left open with the brush and their father's favourite propelling screwdriver gunked-up in the custard-like skin.

Amy had accepted her fate, and Jenny believed she was okay about it. Her disruptive nature in all six foster homes was, she guessed, by design so that she could end up here. Moreover, Amy was a loner and unable to show or share any love, so Lexton House was better than some *'do-good-family'*. Well, that's what she thought Amy believed.

Amy spent the first four years of her miserable life in a typical, grim, damp, filthy two-bedroom flat on the Broxworth Estate. The estate had been, for many years, a police no-go area controlled by drug gangs and the Gower family – nothing happened on the Broxworth Estate without the Gower clan's approval. The police just seemed to accept this, although there were very few police available these days as many were drafted up to Nottinghamshire to help with the miners' strike that now had, unbelievably, hit its eighth month. Her brother, Alan, who'd joined the police three years ago, was now creaming it in, securing at least thirty hours of overtime a week – he was loving it. However, it did concern Jenny that Alan seemed to enjoy the daily confrontation with the miners far too much.

The estate still exhibited all the evidence of the riots of three years ago, which started in Brixton and spread out to other towns and cities. The rioters had trashed the once vibrant community centre that now remained in position, burnt out, with all the windows smashed, the roof felt ripped up, and the walls covered in graffiti. Once the hub of the estate, the derelict building stood as a monument to that one night of riots back in 1981.

Amy entered the care system at the age of four. Her mother was alcohol and drug dependent, and the last in a long line of hideous boyfriends had abused Amy. Then, for the first time in her tragic young life, her mother did the right thing and called the police to report him. David Albert Colney was arrested for child abuse, and the pathetic criminal justice system deemed eight years and three months as an acceptable time at Her Majesty's pleasure. It was one of the first serious cases Jenny had been involved in, and it shook her to the core. He should have been hung, preferably by his balls. She'd often daydreamed back then that all she needed to do was jump in a time machine, slip back a few years, and perform the ball-hanging procedure herself before he had a chance to abuse young Amy.

Jenny marched Amy into Lexton House, with the customary glance at the balustrade, just to check it was safe to pass and not get crushed. Glancing up, it seemed to be moving, although it was the clouds drifting across the sky, an optical illusion. However, she played safe and increased her speed through the final few steps to the door. Amy also passed through safely and without the customary boot to the flaking grey paint.

Paperwork and formalities would have to be completed. As always, the assistant manager, Sue, was there to perform the necessary. Although once an attractive lady, now in her mid-forties, Sue appeared gaunt and worn down by the system. The live-in role afforded her limited 'Sue time', always opting for the same jeans and jumper combination and never bothering with make-up. Anyway, the shockingly low pay her public sector job offered thwarted any opportunity for shopping trips to improve her wardrobe. She smelt the same as the house, as if the walls had oozed out the smell of disinfectant mixed with old trainers, transferring it into her like a permanent invisible tattoo that randomly re-injected the air.

Jenny turned and looked at Amy to ensure she had her full attention. "Amy, you know my telephone number, and you can still call me whenever you like. I'm always here to help you – you know that, don't you?"

Amy just looked at Jenny with cold steel-blue eyes – colder than today's shit weather – a small green duffle bag of meagre possessions loosely held in her right-hand dragging across the blue linoleum floor and that gurning look again.

And that's when she said it.

"Fuck off, you fat bitch," was the response. Really nice coming from an eight-year-old girl, but it could have been worse, she guessed.

2

11th August 2019

Chernobyl

"Jason, can you make sure you lock the side gate while you're out there?" Beth bellowed from the top of the stairs.

"Yup, will do," I replied, as I ventured out for a cigarette before bedtime – my usual nightly routine.

I stood at the end of the driveway, pulling hard on my cigarette. Glancing around, it appeared no one was about at this time of night. Although I thought I could see Miss Redmond at the top of the close walking her chocolate-coloured Labradoodle, Frank, a bloody stupid name for a dog. She was a pleasant elderly lady and would always stop and talk, but the conversation was the same every time; apparently, I was the spitting image of a close friend from the '50s. Based on the fact I was a miserable tosser and didn't enjoy social interaction or was just crap at it, I skulked behind the hedge to avoid the repeated conversation.

The last six months had been super shit, and I knew my mental health was suffering. Beth had said go to the doctors and get some help, but what would I say?

"Hi doc, think I've got depression, or anxiety, or both. Oh yeah, and I suffer from obsessive-compulsive disorders as well. Can I have some pills, maybe different coloured ones for each condition?"

No, I had to deal with it myself. "Pull yourself together, Jason, sort yourself out for Christ's sake," I muttered.

An OCD affliction can apparently take root in your brain when triggered by an event in childhood. Well, my childhood was tough. The devastation of losing both loving parents at the age of seven could have been a trigger. However, after my parents had departed this world, my older brother, Stephen, and I were brought up by our maternal grandparents with a tremendous amount of love.

An additional trigger could have been attributed to certain beliefs I gained at a young age. I believe that whatever my grandfather said was unquestionably true, so I'm convinced some games we played contributed to this odd affliction. Although, that was a bit unfair because he was the most tremendous human being I'd ever known, and those games were just supposed to be fun. However, they affected my way of thinking.

I recall at the age of five, whilst staying at my grandparents, which Stephen and I often would for a week during the summer, holding my grandfather's hand as I accompanied him on his morning saunter down the steep hill of Milton Road to the newsagents. Fairfield Chronicle for him, and twenty Rothmans cigarettes for my grandmother.

My grandfather had never smoked and just didn't understand it. I could hear him saying, *"God would have put a chimney on the top of your head if we were supposed to smoke."*

On the other hand, my grandmother was rarely seen without a Rothmans poking out of the side of her mouth – the cigarette bouncing up and down, the ash hanging on for dear life as the force of gravity bent it down towards earth; all this, whilst holding a full-blown conversation over the garden fence with Vera, the next-door neighbour. Think of Les Dawson and Roy Barraclough as Cissie and Ada, and you'll have it clear in your mind.

On those walks to the newsagents, he would tell me, and I believed him unquestionably at the time—

"Stand on a crack and break your back; stand on a square, you'll turn into a bear."

I do recall my concern that I would wake up one morning covered in brown fur, as I never walked on the pavement cracks, and turning into a bear seemed a slightly more favourable option to breaking my back. I never did awake to the brown fur issue coupled with the feeling of the need to hibernate the whole winter, so I eventually stopped concerning myself about avoiding pavement cracks. However, the idea that certain stupid repeated rituals and routines would prevent or ensure events from happening stuck with me my whole life.

My OCD followed a clear rule, the more depressed and down I felt, the less stranglehold it had on me. What I mean by this is the repeated actions were there to ensure an outcome. So, when depressed, the OCD lost its tight grip as if its ivy-type tentacles were peeled away from the sides of my brain. Ha! Up yours, OCD, I would say. Conversely, when I was happy and looking forward to an event, anxiety took over, and then my OCD would grip tight, burrowing deep inside. I knew it could force me to perform and repeat a vast amount of ridiculous actions, as my dumb-arse brain was absolutely convinced that those actions would ensure continued happiness – yes, I agree, I was a total fruit-loop. This state of mind was akin to living in a bloody straitjacket, and maybe that's where I should have been. It was so debilitating and bloody time-consuming.

I'd started my nightly locking-up routine, and depending on my state of mind, that process could take a while. After I'd repeatedly checked the garage door handle was in the locked position, and performed in the set sequence that my OCD demanded, my next task was to check mine and Beth's car doors were locked, four times and twice, respectively. Failure to complete these actions in the precise order would cause my mind to believe that impending doom lay in wait. Often, I'd repeat the sequence to satisfy my OCD that I'd performed the tasks correctly – so, as I say, very time-consuming.

There were numerous other *'ticks',* as I called them, that debilitated my life. Although there are far too many to mention, here are a couple of examples so you get my drift. Absurdly, I always closed my eyes to turn off a light switch, fully believing failure to comply would cause blindness. If I failed to flick my cigarette butt through the third opening on the drain grill, I would suffer prostate cancer or hell, even my knob would fall off.

Although my slavery to OCD was spiralling out of control, I knew I wasn't alone with this odd affliction. I recall an old friend at uni years ago telling me his brother had mental problems, as he put it. Apparently, on one ludicrous occasion, his brother drove past the same lighting shop over fifty times, around and around the block, fearing that seriously bad things would happen to him if he didn't pass it when the displayed lights hung in the window had been turned off. Finally, at midnight, he realised that this wasn't going to happen and subsequently faced a real dilemma – continue forever circling until he ran out of petrol – or go home and await the impending doom.

As I pondered these thoughts, I knew I could no longer allow this debilitating condition to rule my life, now fearing there was a very real danger that I would slip into the same disturbing state as my friend's brother. The decision that I made tonight, I'd made a million times in the past, and every time I'd failed, usually straight after the decision was made. But, from tomorrow, a new start. No longer would I allow myself to be a slave to this controlling OCD – hell, even if my knob fell off.

After enjoying one last drag on this evening's pre-bedtime cigarette, I stepped up to the drain and positioned my feet as if preparing to squat on a toilet. It reminded me of our honeymoon in Turkey, where the hotel room sported a squat toilet. Lisa was so horrified she vowed to hold it all in for two weeks until we came home. There is, I know, real comfort in your own loo, like a bond with an old friend. After two painful nights of holding her stomach, Lisa could hold on no more. Then, for the next two days, the toilet became an official no-go area, with a Chernobyl-type exclusion zone, which wasn't a hugely romantic start to the honeymoon – setting the tone for our marriage.

Anyway, I took aim, nipped the cigarette butt between my thumb and forefinger and pinged it towards the drain – bollocks – I missed the third opening. Well, it didn't matter – or did it?

After twenty minutes, with my brain eventually satisfied that I'd completed all rituals, I could finally go to bed. However, as I passed Beth's bedroom, she called out again.

"Did you remember to lock the side gate?"

Oh, bollocks, I'd forgotten, I would have to start again. The set order of the routine laid out by my OCD couldn't be broken, so I had another twenty minutes of stupid, stupid, checking.

3

Pampas Grass

The next morning, I spent thirty minutes blindly stabbing at my phone every few minutes in a poor attempt to snooze. I'd settled on 'sonar' for the alarm sound some years ago, after spending hours going through the settings function on my iPhone. It sounded cool at the time, like a U-boat in a classic war film, but now it was just annoying the hell out of me. Concerned after missing the third hole of the drain grill when flicking my cigarette butt last night, I lifted the quilt and performed a quick rummage to check my knob was still in place. All good, still there, or was it prostate cancer for that one?

I slugged my way out of bed, ready to push through the repetitive morning routine. For the last few years I'd held down the same job, Sales and Brand Executive at Waddington's Steel, a sheet metal fabrication company. Basically, I led a team of misfits who persuaded other companies to buy sheet metal. I liked the executive title – always quoting it when asked what I did for a living – the snobby bit of me that I wasn't proud of. However, I had to keep ahead of that tosser, Mike, next door, with his constant showing off about his latest promotion in the banking world. *Tosser.*

Before performing my morning ablutions and after padding into the kitchen to flick the kettle on, I pondered what excitements today would offer – although my brain struggled to function without an injection of caffeine. Whilst slopping in a generous helping of soya milk into Beth's coffee, I mused how anyone could drink that stuff. As far as I was concerned, it afforded the taste and texture of wallpaper paste.

Plodding into Beth's bedroom, I popped the coffee on her bedside cabinet, convinced it would never be drunk and would end up joining the rest of this week's offerings lined up on the windowsill. All I could see of Beth was a mass of blonde hair poking out above the covers, the rest of her head and body cocooned in the quilt, all wrapped up and sleeping on the last six inches of a ridiculously large super-king-sized bed.

"Morning. Welcome to another day in paradise. Coffee for you. Try and drink this one before it gets cold," I mumbled. I was crap in the morning.

"Oh, ta. Morning, Mr Happy. Good to see you're your usual cheerful self. And that's a slur on my character. I always drink my coffee, thank you!" Beth babbled from under her quilt.

"Fridge stinks, something in there that needed to be surgically removed months ago. I don't have time to look properly, but I guess it's that lump of French Brie. If you don't get to it soon, it will grow legs and crawl out on its own."

"Yeah, yeah, whatever, try not to make too much noise, I'm asleep," replied Beth from somewhere under the quilt.

Leaving the house at my usual time, I was already sweating in the unbelievable August heat, even at this early hour. Beth's Porsche Carrera was thankfully still on the drive, so checking the door handle twice every night did work, as it would have been my fault if it were stolen. Although honestly, I couldn't complain because I'd lived at Beth's house for nearly a year since my marriage broke down with Lisa. Beth was my closest friend, right back to high school, and had taken me in when I was destitute.

Lisa had taken the house and left me with a suitcase of clothes and a few household items. Strangely, for some reason, the biggest custody fight was over the steam-iron. There was a screaming match between us on the phone after I'd removed the iron from the marital home, as I apparently had no right to do so. This was frankly ridiculous, as I was the chief ironer, plus we had at least three other irons stuffed somewhere in the loft. A few days later, after pathetically losing the custody battle, I ended up handing over the precious iron late at night in the local supermarket car park. From a distance, it probably looked like a drug deal going down as I handed the iron through the car window. And that was that – a failed thirteen-year childless marriage.

We were the last of a large group of friends to get married. Over the summers of the middle years of the noughties, every Saturday there seemed to be another wedding until it was just us two who hadn't tied the knot. I don't think I even proposed. It just seemed to get booked in for June 2006, and there we were, Mr and Mrs Apsley, but not remotely in love.

Mike, as always, was outside the front of his house as I left for work, stretching and bending, preparing for his running session. Dressed in skin-tight leggings, with running shorts over the top to cover his modesty, he looked like a right tosser – well, he was, so it suited him, I guess.

"You off to work, Jake?" Mike called out.

Every morning, he shouted the same tossy question over the perfectly trimmed box-hedge that separated the two large properties in this desirable suburb of Fairfield.

"Yup," I called back.

Well, yes, of course I was, as I did every weekday, but what I wanted to shout back was, *"No, I'm off to my hundred-foot yacht to sail around the Med with twenty scantily clad gorgeous women."* However, I didn't have a yacht, and it was unlikely that twenty gorgeous women would be queuing up to be with me anytime soon. I was forty-two-years old, just over six feet tall – half an inch to be precise – still thin, with no bulging belly and all my hair still in place, but no, there were no women falling over themselves wanting me. Probably because I was a miserable tosser.

There were two infuriating and irritating things about Mike. No, there were millions, but two of them were: firstly, at weekends, he would shout, *"Not working today, Jake?"* Well, fucking hell no, I'd never worked weekends; as I stood in my shorts and t-shirt, unshaven and hair seriously out of control shaped and moulded by my pillow, aided and abetted by the remnants of yesterday's hair gel. But always the same dumb question. Secondly, calling me Jake. He knew my name was Jason, but I'd given up correcting him. Trigger in Only Fools and Horses calls Rodney, Dave, but it was in an innocent, almost affectionate way. I was convinced that Tosser did it deliberately, just to keep his tosser skills active and razor-sharp.

Mike jogged towards me, stopped and kept jogging on the spot. *Tosser.*

"Hey, Jake. Amanda and I are having cocktails in the spa tonight. You and Beth can come over, just the four of us; it'll be super nice and intimate," he stated, with a wink of his right eye. My eyes instantly swivelled to the large eight-foot-high Pampas grass that sat squarely in the middle of his front garden. Surely not? I'd heard all the rumours and links of pampas grass and erotic suburban adventures, but surely that was the stuff of '70s folklore – wasn't it?

"Err, yeah, okay, err maybe, not sure what we have planned, and I think I might be late home." This was all I could come up with in response to the invitation – *pathetic.*

"No worries, Jake. I'll let Beth know, and you can join us when you get back. Gotta take advantage of the weather whilst we've got it."

Still jogging up and down, Mike swivelled around and peeled away to start his morning jog. I stood there rooted to the pavement with my hand still holding the car door handle. I wasn't sure I wanted to sit in a bubbling bath of steaming water with Mike, whilst slowly being poached in a marinade of the remnants of his dead skin that had deposited and taken up residence in the spa over the past few months. However, a hot spa with Amanda conjured up all sorts of other thoughts.

I will admit that Amanda was seriously hot, fit, sexy, or whatever the term is, but you get my drift. She was at least ten years younger than Mike, and I wasn't sure what her attraction to him was, definitely not his jogging attire. Although I'm embarrassed to admit it to anyone, I had craned my neck against the bedroom window and ogled at her in their garden on too many occasions that was healthy or acceptable for a forty-two-year-old divorcee.

Think of the perfect hourglass figure, more Jayne Mansfield than Marilyn Monroe, but hair more Marilyn. Stuck in my mind was the vision of my last ogling session. Amanda was in the spa, not one of those plastic blow-up jobs that seemed to be all the craze now, but a proper large, square, permanent one that must have cost a fortune. I'd positioned myself in my preferred ogling spot that I'd perfected, which afforded me at least three and a half minutes before severe neck cramps took hold.

Amanda stood up, water cascading off her perfect sun-tanned skin, her tiny post-box-red bikini stretched tight on her amazing body – she was a perfect ten. Yes, definitely a ten. Bo Derek was a very poor second. She stepped out of the spa, but disappointingly disappeared from view. Only a few seconds later, I was rewarded as she reappeared wearing the flimsiest white strapped dress. Instantly her wet body transformed it to see-through, as it clung to her every gorgeous curve, leaving very little to the imagination. Cigarette in one hand, the other on her hip which slightly shifted her stance, delivering an erotic, sexy pose. With her head held high, it reminded me of Madonna's nude hitch-hiking poster that adorned many a teenage boys' bedroom wall. There she stood, a goddess of beauty, and she knew it.

Daydream over, no, I couldn't get in the spa with Amanda. "Get a grip," I muttered. "Jeeeesus," how low could I go? Now a peeping-tom – a right wanker – literally.

4

Seagull

I absolutely had to get my life sorted, find a house and move on before staying at Beth's put a strain on our friendship, and my obsession with Beth's tossy neighbour's wife got out of hand.

My adult life was okay-ish, bordering on crap I guess, but mostly like playing a real-life game of snakes and ladders – a brief moment of getting somewhere, whizzing up a ladder only to land on a snake and shoot straight back down – this I repeated constantly. I felt like a mole in the Whac-A-Mole arcade game. Every time I dared to poke my head up and move forward, life was there, holding a large mallet to smack me back down.

This all led to a cocktail of mental health issues, not so catastrophic the men in white coats turned up and bundled me off to a padded cell, but enough to halt daily life and give me a bumpy ride. This was coupled with a strong sense of yin-yang. If something good happened to me, I couldn't feel happy about it. None of this *'enjoy the moment'*. All I could do was hold, wait in anticipation, and look over my shoulder to await the conversely bad event that was surely on full steam ahead to ruin everything. Often, it didn't. However, it was enough to ruin the enjoyment of the good stuff that occasionally did happen.

The four-year-old three-series BMW fired into life. A great car, the best I'd ever had. When Graham, the Finance Director, had stated I was now at a grade that made me eligible to have a company car, I couldn't wait to zip around the car showrooms. Although, as a 'junior' executive, I wasn't entitled to a top-of-therange model, but hey, at least I was one of those rare drivers who used the indicator stick.

I started my laborious journey to work, thinking about Beth and our friendship. For sure, I had to get my arse in gear and move on. I couldn't afford anything like Beth's house, no, but I could buy a decent place in a cheaper end of town. We'd never been romantically involved, as Beth was like the sister I never had. Although attractive and had maintained her slim physique, she struggled to find romance and was often distant. The term *'ice maiden'* had been thrown at her so many times by a long line of scarred men. Over the last few years, the main thing we had in common was that we were both unhappy with life, a feeling of being unfulfilled and not whole.

Beth was a successful Marketing Executive with balls bigger than a rhino. I knew that rhino's balls were on the hefty side because I'd sat through one of those tea-time documentaries about vets working with large animals. That particular episode showed a graphic account of an operation to correct a strangulated testicle on a large white rhino. There was no warning by the presenter the horrific scene was coming, and that any male member of the human race may find this distressing to watch. Too late, with a meatball in tomato sauce stuck in my throat, I wasn't sure whether to swallow or throw up.

The fifty-minute journey to work was always my opportunity to catch up on the news. It provided just enough time to get a grip on what was happening in the world. Any longer, and you had to suffer the repeat newsfeed. When this happened, I'd find myself tutting and moaning at the radio, *"Yes, yes, I know you have already told me, for fuck sake."*

Today's main news story centred around five murdered women and a possible serial killer connection. All victims were blonde and in their late thirties or early forties, a really grim story. Memories flooded back of the Yorkshire Ripper that had dominated the news in the early '80s when he was eventually caught. Although I was very young then, I remember thinking it was scary. The newsreader revealed that partial DNA evidence had linked two of the murders before switching to Detective Chief Inspector Nigel Miller, who made a statement:

"This morning, we have made a significant breakthrough regarding the brutal murders of five women. We are very keen to speak to David Albert Colney, aged fifty-nine, to help with our enquiries. I must stress the need for continued vigilance by the general public, and all women to take care in the Greater London and Home Counties areas. Under no circumstances, if seen, should David Colney be approached, but call 999 if you have any information regarding his whereabouts."

David Albert Colney – that name seemed familiar. Although I couldn't place it, I'd heard it before, I was sure.

When switching from the news to a music station, my phone rang; that sonar sound filled the car. I could see from the in-car display it was Debbie, Gary Oxney's personal assistant. Debbie always stated that as she supported the CEO, she was not a personal assistant, but an executive assistant. She was very clear about this, correcting me on several occasions when I'd slipped up. Although I now found it fun to do, she'd failed to see that I was intentionally making this mistake. I was fully aware this made me just as big a tosser as Beth's neighbour, Mike.

Job title banter aside, I liked Debbie. We enjoyed a good working relationship, and she would always cover my back by giving me the heads-up if Gary was on the warpath. Gary had successfully mastered the art of 'seagull' management – sitting high in his nest reviewing what was going on, then gliding down and shitting on everyone before swooping back up to his nest – it was his way of ensuring that we all knew who was in charge.

"Morning, Debbie, PA extraordinaire," I chirped, trying to sound engaged and enthused.

"Hi, Jason, yes, very funny. Err … look, just a quickie. I've cleared your diary this morning because Gary would like to see you as soon as you get in."

"Oh, what for?" I replied, in a slightly concerned shaky voice.

"Err … oh err … not sure, nothing I guess, but he's in a good mood."

"Oh, right, okay. I'll be about another twenty minutes."

"Okay, I'll let Gary know. Gotta go, loads to do," she babbled before the line disconnected.

"Oh, bollocks."

I'd just remembered I needed to pick up Martin Bretton on the way in today. He lived on my route to work and had asked for a lift as his wife needed to take their car for an MOT. Martin was on my team, good at his job, and I thought we got on well. He and his wife had been around for drinks at Christmas and attended a couple of summer barbecues. Lisa and his wife were friends now, although I couldn't remember her bloody name.

I hated giving lifts to people. It was such an invasion of my car space, and then I would have to talk to them, which is not what I wanted to do – small talk in the morning was the pits. Martin had caught me off guard last week, so I was unprepared with a reasonable excuse why I couldn't pick him up. As I practically had to pass by his front door, I'd reluctantly agreed. Turning off the main drag down into Enfield, I pulled up outside his house. Fortunately, he was waiting on the pavement. Although a pity he couldn't have walked up the road to the main junction, then I wouldn't have had to make the detour. Oh well.

"Morning, Jason, I really appreciate this. Lovely day again," Martin happily chirped. Although it might be lovely, I didn't know what he found so positive about any morning.

"Morning," I responded flatly, hoping my short, monotone response was enough for him to realise that I had no intention of holding a conversation.

Martin fortunately understood the non-verbal request and immediately pulled out his phone and appeared to be scrolling through Facebook. He sat there chuckling to himself at some inane post from one of his friends – probably a picture of their breakfast – tagged with a *'Hey, look at my breakfast'* comment. I just didn't get Facebook and really couldn't be bothered to look at shit pictures or comments from other people about mundane crap – but then I had very few friends – Martin probably had millions. He was ten years younger than me and a hugely popular guy. I suspected I was a wee bit jealous of him.

To ensure Martin didn't start talking after he'd scrolled through his phone, I turned the radio up, so allowing time to think about the call from Debbie. I realised that the call was odd as Debbie usually chatted, but today she couldn't wait to get off the phone, and if it was *'nothing'*, why did Gary want to see me?

The realisation hit me of the impending doom that my life, if it were at all possible, was about to sink to a new, previously undiscovered low. I'd probably face a brown envelope as Gary unsympathetically slid it across the desk before surrendering my phone and laptop and being forcibly removed from the office by Vinny, the gate security operative. I actually didn't know if he was called Vinny, but his striking resemblance to Vinny Jones made the name stick. No, Debbie said Gary was in a good mood – perhaps a promotion, yes, or a pay rise? Sales had been excellent this year, so maybe I could get excited about this morning's meeting? Yes, that was it, a whacking great pay rise. Fuck you, yin-yang, I was going to stay positive.

I allowed myself the luxury of contemplating that perhaps today was to be a turning point and, at last, I could shove the previous six months behind me.

Lost in my thoughts, I can only assume I didn't see the red traffic light. Martin wouldn't have either because he still had his head buried in his phone. There was a strange sensation as everything seemed to happen in slow motion. My movements were reminiscent of Steve Austin, the Bionic Man, but nothing about this was bionic.

For some unexplained reason, a white van had crossed right in front of me. I yanked the steering wheel to the right whilst my foot attempted to push the brake pedal through the car's subframe. Severed vehicle parts floated past my windscreen.

Concerningly, I thought I spotted my wing mirror gracefully glide past. Then, like the flick of a switch, everything increased pace, no longer in slow motion but at tremendous speed, with ear-piercing sounds and a vast, wondrous kaleidoscope of vibrant colours.

Then, there was nothing – just nothing.

5

Gentlemen Prefer Blondes

"Ravi, let me be totally clear, totally clear. The presentation for this Christmas campaign has got to be ready by Friday. All you need to do is get Ben and Mel to complete the graphics and we're done. I was quite clear last week and my expectation is by Friday, it's complete." Beth stabbed the red button to end the call before lobbing the phone to the end of her bed where it sunk and rested in the duvet.

"For God's sake, aaaaagggghhh," she screamed. Just a few days off, that's all she wanted, but already they needed her. Why couldn't any of them make a decision without her?

No, that was a bit unfair, Ravi was excellent and had made a significant difference since joining her team. Although he was wet behind the ears and straight out of university, she was so impressed within seconds at his interview, his real passion and drive, which was so rare. She found that so many graduates she met assumed it was their bloody birthright to get a magical corporate position just because they had studied sociology for three years, and now they believed they had the full understanding of the human mind.

However, she just wished sometimes Ravi would grow some balls and be a man. Although every man she had ever met seemed unable to locate their balls. *They're hanging between your legs,'* she wanted to scream.

Beth was fully aware that she intimidated men. Well, not Jason, as they had been friends since the age of eleven. On the first day of high school, everyone piled into their form class and instantly paired up and sat next to their best buddies. That left the two loners, misfits, that no one was particularly interested in or even noticed. She was one, and Jason the other, so from day one, he was the kid who sat next to her.

Whilst staring up at the ceiling, she thought about her life. Rarely did she get a moment to think, which was good because her childhood had been horrendous. Sink-or-swim was the phrase that came to mind, and she'd made up her mind from a very young age that it was swim – fuck 'em all. But now she had so much to be thankful for, a brilliant job, although she'd worked hard for it. She'd achieved this with no university degree, straight out of school after pissing up her A-levels, mainly due to her love of partying and working to grab every penny to do more partying, which left very little time for study.

She'd worked as a part-time supervisor at the local supermarket, running the checkout line. So, the first taste of telling others what to do and not always being told what to do – to have a voice and be heard – it was a good feeling.

"Mavis you're scanning too slowly, pick your speed up," she could hear herself shouting across the line of checkouts to the downtrodden checkout operators who flung the goods down the checkout belt in an attempt to hit the unachievable scanning-speed targets.

Beth's house could only be described as breathtaking, delivering heady excitement when she bought it four years ago. Sporting five double bedrooms, three reception rooms, a galleried landing, and a hallway in which you could absolutely swing a cat, it oozed opulence. If a domestic feline had unfortunately been used as a space measuring tool, as it swung around, the poor creature could be quietly confident that its head would at no point collide with any wall or door frame – the hallway was that big.

However, the excitement of owning this vast house soon wore off because she had no one to share it with. Yes, okay, Jason was billeted here short-term, but he would soon move on.

She loved him like the brother she'd never had; well, there was her half-brother, but she had only met him a couple of times many years ago, and God knows where he was now – probably banged up in jail.

Over the last few years, she'd realised that this life wasn't what she wanted. Yes, for sure, the money and luxury were good, but it wasn't making her happy. She'd wanted children, but now at forty-two, with a string of very short and unsuccessful relationships behind her – mainly due to all of them struggling to find their balls and not helped by her constantly reminding them of their location – the chance of having children was fading. Also, there was no sign of anyone coming over the horizon any time soon. No, she was alone and doomed to stay that way, and now the clock had probably ticked around too far for her. If she had her time again, it would be children and a home, not a house and loneliness.

Beth grabbed her coffee. She liked the coffee treat brought to her in bed that Jason supplied every morning, although rarely did she get to drink it before it was cold. "Blaaaaaarh," she exclaimed, after spitting the stone-cold mouthful back into the cup before placing it next to the three other full cups of cold coffee that adorned the windowsill.

Following a week of sunshine, Beth suspected that today would continue that trend – a rare treat for a British summer, she thought, whilst reviewing the stunning tram-lined lawn and the cacophony of colourful shrubs and flowers that adorned the perfectly maintained borders. Her garden could easily feature in any beautiful homes and gardens magazine.

Of course, none of this vision of beauty was any of her doing because there was absolutely nothing green about her fingers. No, this was all Tom's work, who, for three days a week, tended and nurtured her garden. Although he was slow and, at twenty quid an hour, she suspected this was some of his motivation for his methodical plodding. But he impressively knew his stuff and could give Monty Don a run for his money. So, she had a fantastic garden but no swings and no climbing frame, football net or paddling pool. She would swap Tom's masterpiece for that any day.

Her bedroom afforded Beth a clear view of Mike and Amanda's garden. Oh, there she was again, all tits and hair wallowing in the spa. Jason would have loved this. She often spotted him straining his neck against the window in his bedroom, ogling 'Tits-out-Amanda'. Jason didn't know she'd seen him, and although great friends they were, there was a line that needed to be maintained. Interrupting his pleasure or mentioning it later was not somewhere she was going to go.

'Hey Jason, come and look out my bedroom window. Amanda has her tits out again.'

No, that wasn't going to happen.

The doorbell rang, *'We Wish you a Merry Christmas,'* peeled out. Jason had changed the tune a few weeks ago, but she hadn't got around to changing it back. God knows what people thought because it was the middle of August. However, somewhere, someone would be preparing to put their Christmas decorations up. Thankfully, none of the residents of Winchmore Drive lowered themselves to do this deed until at least December. She hated Christmas and always had. Beth couldn't think of any Christmas that had been anything better than totally, totally shit.

Bouncing downstairs, Beth expected a parcel of clothes or shoes to be delivered. Unfortunately, because of the vast amount of online orders she regularly placed, Beth could never be sure of the specific content of each delivery. However, she always enjoyed the surprise.

Disappointingly, ninety-nine per cent always had to be returned because the items never quite fitted as they appeared to on the models or looked like they do on the websites. She'd been removed – 'banned' was the word used – from two online retailers due to her returning all purchases over a six-year period that apparently amounted to over eighteen grand's worth of clothes. Warning emails had been sent, and then she was blocked and banned. Well, if their products had looked like the photos online, she might have been inclined to keep some of them. She spent a fortune on clothes, so their loss not hers. To quote Julia Roberts in Pretty Woman, *'Big mistake! Big, Huge!'* Fortunately, many other online retailers were still happy to deliver and didn't employ an algorithm that tracked her percentage purchase rate.

As Beth traversed across her vast hallway, it became clear this wasn't a delivery of soon-to-be-returned online purchases. Instead, through the leaded glass front door stood two police officers. Odd, she thought, had 'Tits-out-Amanda' made a complaint about her lodger's peeping-tom antics? Beth opened the door; the female officer gave a tight smile.

"Hello, sorry to disturb you. Are you Amy Hall, Amy Elizabeth Hall?"

Beth had dumped her first name and now preferred to use her shortened middle name. The name Amy just pulled her back to a part of her life that she definitely didn't want to be reminded of – basically the whole of her childhood. She'd never changed her name, so officially, she was still Amy.

"Yes, I'm Beth Hall. Can I help you?"

"Can we come in, Miss Hall?" The female officer asked.

"Can I ask what this is about? I'm rather busy with work at the moment."

"Err … sorry, it's rather sensitive and would prefer it if we could come in, just for a moment."

At this point, both officers allowed their eyes to drift downwards. With eye contact lost, the dynamics of the conversation shifted, that small act leaving Beth with a feeling of dark doom cloaking down upon her.

"Okay, come through." Beth stepped aside and ushered them into the hallway and through to the kitchen. She sat at the breakfast bar, the two officers deciding to stand about six feet away after the female officer declined a hot beverage or a glass of squash. Beth wondered if the male officer was a mute, as he'd managed to say absolutely zip so far.

Since entering the house, their eyes were not looking at the floor anymore, but not at Beth either, which was rather odd when you're trying to hold a conversation with someone. Instead, both had their eyes wandering around the space behind her – yes, it was a kitchen of luxury, but not that exciting.

When she was a student, Rachel, the checkout manager at the supermarket, always looked at your forehead when talking to you. Beth often found herself nipping off to the locker rooms to see if she'd developed a new spot or grown a third eye in the centre of her forehead like Cyclops. Back then, she found herself moving her head around to place it in Rachel's line of sight. Now this was the same, trying to make eye contact with either police officer.

"Miss Hall, can you confirm that this is the temporary address of Jason Apsley? We've visited his registered home address of twenty-two Homebrook Avenue, but a neighbour advised us that his ex-wife, Lisa Apsley, is out of the country, and we've been unable to contact her."

Oh, fuck, that's it, 'Tits-out-Amanda' must have made a complaint. This was indeed truly embarrassing!

"Yes, Jason does live here, but he is at work today. If you like, I can give you his mobile number, but can you please tell me what this is all about?"

"Can you tell me what your relationship with Mr Apsley is?" Still nothing from the mute. The female officer was doing all the work.

"Friends, yeah, close friends. He's lived here since he split up with Lisa. His ex-wife, Lisa, that is."

At this point, full eye contact was made, Beth's and the policewoman's eyes coming together like two parts of a space station slowly lining up to join.

"I'm afraid you will need to prepare yourself for a shock. Jason Apsley was involved in a road traffic accident this morning."

"Fuck! Sorry, but fuck, is he alright? Where is he? What the fuck happened? Is he okay?" blurted Beth.

The policewoman's eyes still locked on, she'd closed the six-foot gap between them and now stood stroking the top of Beth's arm. Beth hadn't noticed this happen, but there she was.

"I'm so sorry, but I need to inform you that Jason was pronounced dead at the scene."

Beth was aware that the policewoman was still talking and her hand was gently resting on her shoulder. She could hear the conversation but couldn't make out any of the words, as they became muffled and distant, like the mumblings from a different room. Jason was the only positive part of her life; he was the only one who knew her true past, what happened to her as a little girl, and the trauma she'd suffered. They had grown up together, laughed at each other's jokes, and cried together when things went tits up, which they often had for both of them.

David Albert Colney had taken her innocence at the age of four, now Jason had been taken from her – both could never be returned.

6

Novus Ordo Seclorum

Nothing, just nothing …

Then, the kaleidoscope of colour re-emerged in the centre of the darkness. Distant sounds, a U-boat submarine surfacing, perhaps. Some distant voices, shouting, yes shouting, but no identifiable words.

A metallic taste filled my mouth, burning my throat, but no other physical sensation. Panic rose quickly, I couldn't see or feel anything, but in my mind flashes of red lights and white metal reoccurred. But slowly the taste, light, and then sounds faded.

"Geezer driving the Beemer is fucked, mate. Forget him. You need to tend to the bloke in the passenger seat – he's cut up real bad."

That was the last thing I remember hearing. They say your life flashes in front of you at the point of death. I'm not sure how the hell anyone can know that unless they're dead, and then you're dead, so there's no chance to tell your tale. So how can I tell you mine? All will become clear – well, clear-ish.

Memories of my life spun around inside my head. Pictures were floating into my mind like the screensaver on my Apple-Mac, which bounced images in from the sides of the screen. Mum and Dad, a cherished memory of the four of us sitting on a wall in Ostend in Belgium. All my mates went to Spain's hot sunny beaches with their parents on holiday. Returning with their dads wearing sombrero hats and mums holding their Flamenco dolls in opulent red layered dresses. But not us. For our one

38

excursion abroad we visited Belgium, which was cold, wet and boring. But that moment in time, sitting on that wall, cuddled by my mother, was so precious.

The Belgium image faded, and in came Stephen at his graduation from Durham University, all decked out in his mortarboard and gown with dark grey trim. Stephen graduated in Veterinary Science before emigrating to New Zealand to run a successful practice, probably with his arm permanently stuck up a sheep's arse.

Lisa and the squat toilet – a momentary flicker across the memory screen, best forgotten. I wished her well.

'Tits-out-Amanda' as Beth called her – that pose in the white dress.

My father helping me strap on my Timex watch when I was six years old – I'd loved that watch.

My grandparents, a picnic in the park, both laughing whilst lying on a red and white checkered blanket. Grandad's shock of thick white hair, in a shirt and tie – he always wore a tie. Nanna with horned-rim glasses, and of course, that Rothmans poking out the side of her mouth.

Beth, oh Beth, the real shining light of my life. Both of us with troubled lives, a line of ticker tape continuously punched with holes of sadness. The image of Beth at the age of fourteen and her obsession with Madonna, as I had too. However, I preferred the nude version, as discussed. Beth modelled herself as Susan from the film *Desperately Seeking Susan*. Bright red lipstick, mesh top, ankle boots, lace gloves, rough-dried hair, and that mole thing going on above her lip. Oh, and that jacket, you remember the jacket, gold with the pyramid detailing on the back, *'Novus Ordo Seclorum'* or translated *'new order of the ages'*. Beth was undoubtedly that.

This was it – I was going. The Apple-Mac in my mind had run its sequence of pictures, screensaver time over, darkness and standby mode about to arrive. My affliction and slavery to my OCD was now at an end, which meant no new beginnings that

I'd promised myself last night. My brave decision to stop at least ten compulsive acts this morning had proven unquestionably that I was not a fruit-loop. I'd paid the ultimate price of breaking the OCD rules – death.

Where would I end up? Was failing to go to Sunday school or church a missed opportunity? Would the gates of heaven and eternal happiness be closed to me?

"Sorry, Mr Apsley, heaven works strictly on a points-earned based system, and you have fallen short … your gates are on the lower level."

Could have done better, my life mantra …

7

12th August 1976

Regan and Carter

Nothing, just nothing – everything seemed eerily still. I must have been in the waiting room whilst God and the Devil decided on the appropriate door for me. There was a balance of some good, some bad, and a lot of miserable tosser. They may have played *'rock, paper, scissors'* to decide.

But I was aware there was nothing, which, by the very nature that I was aware, meant there must be something. Drifting into my senses were sounds of car engines, buses with air brakes, and a strange two-tone siren, that seemed vaguely familiar but – old, yes, that was it, old. It was like I was hearing a re-run of The Sweeney, Regan and Carter burning up rubber in their brown Ford Consul with a single blue light slapped on the roof.

Voices again, but different.

"You okay, mate? Didn't you see the traffic lights? I know they're new, but it's been a few weeks since they went up. You're lucky I missed you ... hey, mate, wake up. You okay? Wake up."

Who was he talking to? Who was he? My eyes opened. A bald man, or should be bald, who sported the most ridiculous comb-over job – you know, the Bobby Charlton look – had his head stuck through my open passenger side window. He wore a brown smock overcoat thing over a shirt and tie, with two pens protruding from the top pocket.

"There you go, mate, no harm done. Good job you had your seat belt on, don't see that very often. Reckon that saved you."

I just stared at him – mouth open like a gormless pillock.

"The Old Bill are 'ere, just seen a panda pull up. Sorry, mate, gonna have to say you jumped the lights."

I spotted a police car parked about a hundred yards up the road. It looked old – pale-blue with white doors. A Ford Cortina Mk2 similar to one my grandfather used to own, although his was red with a black roof. It was like something out of Z-Cars, not that I could remember the TV show, but it was what I imagined it would have looked like. Struggling to understand why they were driving that old thing, I briefly considered this might be a film set for a new TV show set in the '70s. But, hell, no, that was insane. Jesus, I really was losing it. Anyway, I thought I was dead, and this wasn't what I imagined heaven or hell to look like.

The officer in the passenger side of the police car hopped out and, after a quick glance left and right, jogged across the road towards me.

"Hello, sir. Can I check that you're alright?"

"No, I'm dead," I replied with some degree of confidence.

Understandably now, and looking back, that wasn't the greatest start to this conversation I could have come up with. However, at that point, as far as I was concerned, I was dead.

"Sir, have you been drinking? Can you step out of the car, please?"

"What? At eight-thirty in the morning, you're 'aving a laugh," I retorted.

The officer turned and waved to the other officer, putting his hand to his mouth, making an O shape with his thumb and forefinger as if blowing through a hole. Then, he turned back to me and opened my car door.

"Please step out of the car, sir."

Gingerly, I stepped out, not quite sure how I was able to move due to being convinced I was dead. But I was moving, and every sensation, noise, touch and smell appeared real. Whilst glancing down to ensure my safe footing on the road, I noticed my somewhat strange attire – Cuban-heeled, grey slip-on shoes – where the bejesus had I got those from? And flares, green and brown pinstriped, flared trousers. What the fuck was going on?

If I wasn't dead, the only reasonable explanation had to be I was pissed or high. No, I hadn't smoked anything apart from Marlboro cigarettes for twenty years. I didn't drink in the morning, and I didn't drink last night, not on a 'school night'. I must have smacked my head hard in the crash. Yeah, that was it. I was concussed. Normal shit world would surely return in a minute. Whilst waiting for normality to return, the officer instructed me to blow into a tube, filling a small plastic bag with my breath. I'd been breathalysed a few years ago, although that was a small black box with a tube on top, not a bag.

"Keep blowing, keep blowing, keep blowing. Good, stop, thank you. Sir, take a seat in your car for a moment, please."

The first officer I'd met was now walking around my car inspecting it, and then he stuck his head through the open passenger window. I didn't know what had happened to the Bobby Charlton look-alike, as he seemed to have vanished.

"No damage to your car, sir. The front nearside tyre is close to the limit, so I suggest you get it replaced soon."

"No trace, he's clear," the second officer shouted over the car roof, then wandered back over the road to the police car. A panda, that was it, that was what it was called, and Bobby Charlton said panda a few minutes ago. They were driving a bloody panda-car.

The officer who'd replaced Bobby Charlton with his head through the passenger window pulled out a small black notebook and flipped it open. "Now, let's take a few details, sir, and we can get you on your way – name?"

"Jason Apsley, no middle name."

"Date of birth."

"30th of March, '77."

43

"Sorry, can you repeat that, please? What's your date of birth?"

"30th of March, '77," I replied again.

The officer, leaning through the window, pen and notebook in his hand, sighed, looked up and stared at me. "Look, sir, this can go one of two ways; you cooperate and stop messing about, or we continue this down at the station. But, quite frankly, it's ten to six, we're off duty in a minute, and I don't fancy the paperwork. So, let's go again. Date of birth, please?"

Ten to six, am or pm? No, it was about half-eight in the morning. Where had I lost a whole day? And also, where the fuck was Martin? This was nuts; I was going insane.

"30th March, '77," I replied, now for the third time.

The officer waved again to his colleague over the road, beckoning him back before, once again, sticking his head through the passenger window.

"Have it your way, sir, but this is not a joking matter. As it's the 12th of August 1976, you are slightly older than minus six months, you will agree. So, you can accompany us to the station; my colleague will bring your car back."

8

Officer Dibble

After over an hour inside what I could only describe as a movie-set police station, my head was in a complete spin. I'd fully expected at any moment to see Regan and Carter return with their latest collar. Or perhaps Officer Dibble pounding up the corridor, truncheon in hand, shouting *"Top Cat,"* – it was that surreal.

The only path I could follow to avoid a night in the cells or committal to a secure institution was to say I'd banged my head in the crash and I was actually born on the 30th of March 1934. Details of my marital home address were given, and I was very sorry to have caused all the fuss – this seemed to do the trick. The desk sergeant handed over my wallet and car keys, along with a document stating that I had to present a copy of my driving licence and car insurance at the station within fourteen days.

"I have a plastic licence here in my wallet and a copy of insurance on my phone. You can have them now. Save me coming back later," I offered.

"Your documents, sir, that's what we require. I'm not sure what you're on about, plastic what, and what's your telephone got to do with it? I suggest you get on your way, have a good evening and remember, back within fourteen days."

Standing on the pavement outside the police station, I rummaged through my pockets, searching for my phone while trying to take stock and work out what was occurring. Where was my phone? It must still be in the car. Yes, it was in the centre console when I had the crash. It would have shot forward into the passenger seat footwell – it would be there. I needed to ring Beth and tell her about the crash. But what crash? The officer had said my car was fine. No, that wasn't right, I remembered the collision with the white van, my wing mirror gracefully somersaulting through the air in front of my windscreen – there was a crash.

Oh yeah, and I'm dead. I pinched the skin on my forearm as hard as I could, expecting it would wake me up, or confirm that I had no feeling, and I was actually dead. However, all I managed to achieve was a red mark on my arm, which hurt, and I was still standing there – and where the hell was that? Christ almighty, where the fuck had Martin gone?

Across the street, the buildings looked familiar. Well, I passed them daily on my way to work, so they should have. I guess they were purpose-built shops and flats, built in the '50s, from one end of the High Street to the other. The shops, mostly bespoke boutiques, intermingled with independent coffee shops and wine bars, and directly opposite should be the restaurant Steak Ta Ta. Lisa and I'd enjoyed their fare on a few occasions – a crap name, although they served fabulous steaks. However, it wasn't there where it should be. Instead, stood Chelsea Girl – when had that changed?

Glancing further up the street at the stores and restaurant fronts, I realised there was another problem with my mental wellbeing. Woolworths, Wimpy, Bejam, Fine Fare, Etam, International Stores and Midland Bank. Oh, but thank God some sense, there was a Sainsbury's, although that didn't help much because none of those were supposed to be there, well, not in my world anyway.

The desk sergeant had said my car was at the side of the station. I scooted around the side of the building to discover two vehicles, neither of which was my BMW. Firstly, another panda-car, not mine, and secondly, a bright-yellow Mk3 Ford Cortina. Still bemused, I plucked the key fob from my trouser pocket, inspecting it to assess what it was – not a key fob, but an old-fashioned car key with the Ford logo. Stepping up to the retro yellow car, there was nothing else to do but stab the key in the lock and see if this was the car that the sergeant had said was mine. I hadn't remembered the car I was sitting in an hour or so ago after the crash, or non-crash, as I was starting to realise. The lock turned, and I opened the car door.

A rummage under the car seats and passenger side footwell yielded no mobile phone. For a brief moment, I considered nipping back into the station to use their landline, but I decided no, I'd had enough of the Keystone Kops today. I knew finding a public payphone would be a miracle because I couldn't remember seeing one for years. However, and somewhat bizarrely, there on the pavement straight ahead of me was a bank of two red telephone boxes. Yes, a miracle, or it will be if they worked and hadn't had the guts ripped out of them, then spray-painted by some Banksy wannabee.

A handful of oversized-looking coins and a letter sat in the console in front of a large gear stick. After flicking away the envelope and grabbing the coins, I hot-footed to the two red telephone boxes. As I expected, the first one appeared to have been trashed, but the second one looked hopeful – all good, a dialling tone.

I dialled Beth's number. I hadn't seen a dial style telephone since I was a kid and it seemed to take forever for the dial to spin back after every turn. However, my call failed to connect, only receiving a long-drawn-out tone. I tried again. I tried Beth's landline before dialling my mobile – all attempts delivered that same long, drawn-out tone.

Frustrated, I slammed the handset down. "Fuck Sake!" I screamed, much to the consternation of an elderly lady waiting patiently to use the phone, presumably hoping I wasn't some vandal about to trash it.

Right, that was it. I would just have to drive that classic car back to Beth's, then surely I would achieve some sanity in this mad world. God, I needed a cigarette.

Lying on the passenger seat where I had flicked it was the unopened letter and, hallelujah, a packet of Marlboro Red. Not in the familiar green drab-coloured packet with a picture of a black lung, but the actual red and white packet of yesteryear.

I lit the cigarette with the heavily used car cigarette lighter and coughed. Christ, it was strong enough to rip your lungs out.

When fumbling for the cigarettes, the letter had flipped over, landing face up. Now it consumed my field of vision, address:

Jason Apsley

Flat 121

Belfast House

Broxworth Estate

Fairfield

Herts

No postcode, and this was not where I lived. I stared at the envelope, struggling to understand how my name could possibly be associated with a flat on that God-awful Broxworth Estate.

'Yesteryear' I'd just said to myself a moment ago; the ten and five pence pieces in my hand that were too big; some day in August 1976 that officer had said it was; the wrong shops in the High Street; the weirdest hour of my life with 'Officer Dibble' debating my actual date of birth. I pulled the document the desk sergeant had given me from my back pocket; my hands shook uncontrollably as I fumbled whilst attempting to unfold it. In the top right-hand corner was a date stamp – 12th August 1976.

I'd not cried, like an uncontrollable breakdown, since my grandmother passed away twenty years ago and, even then, that was in private. I have the good old British stiff-upper-lip, and I don't show much emotion – ever.

Lisa had often called me a reptile because she was convinced my blood was cold. *"You have no heart,"* she would often say. Now huge cascading waterfalls of tears poured down my face. I'd morphed into the real-life Loudly Crying Face Emoji as I sobbed out my cold heart.

This couldn't be right, but it was — it was as real as pinching my skin, to the red telephone boxes, to the car I was sitting in. Unfortunately, although it appeared I wasn't dead, I seemed to have been catapulted into some alternative world six months before I was born where I wasn't me anymore. But I was me, somehow.

9

Multi-Coloured Swap Shop

I'm an intelligent man, well, sort of, yes, I am. I have a bloody degree, for Christ sake – a minor miracle. Alright, not in the 'water into wine' magnitude, but nevertheless, a bloody miracle.

I'd achieved a 2:1 degree from the University of East Anglia in some totally useless subject. Three years of studying seventeenth-century Central American culture of the calamitous decline of the Indigenous population of Mexico. Gripping stuff that I never put to good use, but it was hard to see what use it actually had. I remembered those questions regarding my degree subject at many a job interview—

"Mr Apsley, talk me through your degree subject and the correlation to your interest in a banking career."

That was a super-tough question. All I could think of as a response was to tell the truth. Yes, that was always the right approach. Tell the truth—

'Well, you only needed three 'C's at A-level to get on to the course, and I just scraped in. My brother, Stephen, had loved uni and said it was a great piss-up, so I grabbed the place offered,' I had confidently replied. At the second job interview, I changed tack, realising that the truth wasn't always the correct path to success.

But university had been a positive time in my life, and I might even stretch to – if pushed on it – say I was reasonably happy. Norwich sported a pub for every day of the year, and I'd spent many hours in most of them. Also, twenty-seven clubs, my favourite one being Samantha's, which I frequented many times at the expense of doing my dissertation. There were fifty-two churches, one for every week of the year – but I didn't visit any of them.

I'm a sceptic. I do question everything, often deciding I am right and they are wrong, and invariably finding out the reverse. Still, it doesn't stop the continued scepticism about everything, which could be quite exhausting. Sitting in that classic yellow car, I knew I had every right to be sceptical. I was awake, not dead, but nothing was right. As my tears had dried on my cheeks, I started to accept the possibility that I appeared to be present in the early evening of the 12th of August 1976. And, yes, that did, as expected, raise my scepticism to new heights.

Rather than sitting here blubbing outside Cockfosters' police station, I decided my only option was to drive back to Fairfield – hoping Beth's house was still where it was when I'd left it earlier. Unfortunately, the car appeared to lack powered steering, also sporting a manual gearbox, which meant I needed arms like Popeye to manoeuvre it. However, I was confident I would be able to cope with the four-speed transmission.

The heat was still stifling, even at this time of day. Winding the window crank handle, I lowered the window, allowing heat and fumes from the heavy traffic to engulf me. It seemed it didn't matter where or what year it was, when in the Greater London area, traffic was always bumper to bumper.

Initially, the road layouts were as I expected. The Cock Inn was where it should be, with swathes of punters sitting outside enjoying a cold beer in the early evening heat. The problem was nothing else seemed to be as it should, as the people were all wrong. The women wore flared, high-waisted jeans, tie-dyed blouses or very short A-line checkered skirts and ruffled tops, some in flared jumpsuits. The blokes were worse, wearing bell-bottom flares and brightly coloured shirts with Harry Hill style collars – many of them sporting shoulder-length hair and Noddy Holder styled sideburns – well, the men, that is.

A quick glance in the rear-view mirror delivered a further head-screwing shock. Staring back at me, was me, definitely me, the same face in every detail – slate-blue eyes and slightly sticky-out oversized ears. However, my mouse-coloured hair had morphed into a thick mop with a centre parting, plus I had a goatee beard thing going on. All I could think was I had modelled myself on Noel Edmonds from the Multi-Coloured Swap Shop. How the fuck had my hair changed or grown? A few hours ago, I didn't have a goatee beard – it should have taken me weeks to grow that.

The next few miles of my journey returned to a blur again. Fortunately, I managed to stop at the red traffic light that early today – or was it two hours ago – I'd ploughed through, oblivious to its existence? The catalyst to the crazy situation. A bloody good job I stopped this time, as otherwise a young woman in red hot-pants, pushing a blue Silver Cross pram across a pelican crossing, would be in the air after bouncing off the bonnet of this car.

I planned my usual route home: head north out of London, pick up the M25, around to St Albans, then up to my home town of Fairfield. However, I faced another issue to contend with when discovering the slip road to the M25 was not where it should be; the roundabout was missing, and so was the bloody M25. This rather odd omission to my usual route home left me with the only other option of ploughing through the back routes. A decision I'd taken at least once a week to avoid the M25 backlog of traffic, which often resembled a field that your car gets shoved into when using airport parking – miles and miles of stationary vehicles as far as the eye can see. However, not today – today, it was farmland.

Just after eight-thirty, I drove along North Street in Fairfield, expecting to turn into Winchmore Drive and back to Beth's house. However, this provided further confirmation that I'd become mentally unstable. Perhaps I was secured in a straitjacket bouncing off the walls of a padded cell, or the surreal previous four hours were actually real, therefore now stuck in some alternative world of a time gone by. Alas, there was no turning, no road, no houses, just fields of late summer corn gently swaying in the warm evening breeze. I lit up another tar-coating, lung-killing cigarette. Whilst leaning against the Ford Cortina, it wasn't amiss to me – although not at the same scale as earlier – that I was crying again. I was utterly sure that before today, I'd never cried twice in one day.

Options, I had to think of options. Friends, ah friends, now there was another problem with my life, or was that my previous life? Christ, I couldn't work that out at the moment. Friends. "Stick with the task in hand, Jason," I muttered.

You see, friends would or could maybe help, but I can honestly say I had only one friend, and I had no idea where she was. I knew so many people, but they were acquaintances, not friends. Those people I knew from work or through Beth and Lisa, but were not what I could class as friends. Friends, you go for drinks with, on holiday together, you text, phone and tell each other secrets. No, I didn't have any of them. Well, I had one, but she was missing.

To have friends requires a certain amount of effort on both sides so that the relationship can hit an acceptable level of equality of trust and love, but Jason '*twat*' Apsley was a dip-shit island. Twat could be the middle name I never had – yes, it suited me and had an inevitable ring about it. I could imagine the call in the doctor's surgery when eventually after waiting a lifetime to see a doctor, and what you originally booked the appointment for had naturally cleared up, or you had just plain forgotten what the problem was—

"*Jason Twat Apsley to room five, please.*" Yes, it sounded about right, a good fit for me.

I had about seven contacts on LinkedIn. The average member, I believe, was closer to three hundred. I had almost double my extensive LinkedIn network on Facebook – pathetic. All because I couldn't be bothered to make an effort, so why should anyone else? Most of my uni friends had, over the years, drifted away. They made contact – I never replied.

'Hey, Jason, how you doing? Loads of us getting together this weekend, Joe, Sam, Jay, Lucy and Jess, all the old crew. See you at Browns at eight and go on from there.' A recent call I had from Mark, a great friend from uni, but no, I didn't turn up because Twat Apsley couldn't be bothered.

Darkness was descending, literally and metaphorically. So, with my current state of mind, the decision was made – tonight, I had one depressing option – flat 121 Belfast House.

10

Genghis Khan

The Broxworth Estate is not somewhere that I would usually visit. Although it was only a few miles from where I had lived, either with my grandparents or with Lisa, I'd only had the pleasure of visiting once before. That excursion into this unpleasant place was to collect a wooden wine rack that I'd purchased from eBay. Entering the estate and parking up the Beemer, I'd instantly seen the potential error I had made.

From the labyrinth of '60s concrete that covered the whole estate – which looked as though it could have easily been a maze in an adventure theme park – twenty or so male youths appeared on pushbikes that were way too small for them. It looked like the bikes were borrowed from their younger brothers. No, they probably nicked them from other younger kids, which seemed more likely.

The majority dismounted and hoisted themselves up onto a concrete wall which sported an impressive covering of graffiti, or what these days is called modern street art, but, in my view, it was graffiti. It had acquired a *'full sleeve'* tattoo, whether it wanted it or not. Four youths positioned themselves at each corner of the car, standing with the bike frames between their legs as if on sentry duty. The two youths near the front of my car held my stare – I blinked first.

At that point, I considered driving off, but that option was no longer available. So, there was nothing for it but to get on with it, and I exited the car. The youth at the front-right, the side directly in front of me, raised his head as if sniffing the air like in the Oxo adverts. Although I didn't believe he would have fitted into the '80s Oxo family and Lynda Bellingham would not be making gravy for him. From behind me, another youth on sentry duty called out.

"Hey, twat, what's in your wallet?"

Thinking back now, or was it forward, it was clever how they knew my middle name. The upshot was I parted with twenty quid or the Beemer got trashed, and I left with a very expensive, shit wine rack.

Now back on the estate again and uncertain which concrete Lego block Belfast House was, I opted for parking somewhere in the middle of the estate near the community centre, which looked very different from my previous visit. Instead of boarded-up windows and black smoke-damaged brickwork, the windows were wide open with music pulsing out – *'You Should Be Dancing.'* I couldn't remember who sang it, but I could remember it was often played at discos – very retro.

I parked between a blue Morris 1100 and a dark-brown Ford Zodiac, noticing only four other cars in the car park and, unbelievably, my Cortina looked to be the newest car there. I crossed the car park in front of the community centre. The gravel had turned multi-coloured from the lights, bouncing off the large disco ball spinning above the dance floor and, streaming out of the windows. The dance floor appeared packed with people, and I silently prayed the whole estate would be there. I didn't want to meet anyone tonight after the previous encounter, thirty-four years or so in the future.

Belfast House was the second block of brutal grey concrete, with each floor accessed by a series of concrete steps attached to the ends of each block. There seemed to be no sense to the numbering system, but I managed to locate the flat after vaulting up and down a couple of flights of dimly lit stairs. The number 121 was in two pieces of white plastic screwed into the red door. The two 1's were in place but the 2 was missing. However, the faded paint signified where the 2 once was.

With three keys in my hand, the car key being one, I chose the obvious-looking other one of the remaining two and rammed it into the lock. The door opened, and I peered into the semi-darkness of what I assumed must be where I lived – I stepped inside.

After snapping on the hallway lights, I could see through to the kitchen. The plain white-painted door stood ajar, and the kitchen light was on. I froze. What I hadn't considered, I potentially didn't live here alone. It didn't occur to me that I might live with someone who I didn't know. Oh, God, I might even have a wife. Rooted to the floor, I stood utterly still, listening. Fortunately, no sounds were coming from inside the flat.

"Err … hello, it's me," I called out.

I was still unsure who I was, but I was me, now with a Noel Edmonds styled makeover. Although I knew I was me, no one had confirmed that I was me, and perhaps I was no longer Jason Apsley – oh, apart from that letter left on the car seat. Although I'd had no confirmation from a human being, it was a reasonable assumption to make I was still Jason, albeit a *different* Jason.

Confirming that no reply had come, and based on the fact that the whole flat was no bigger than Beth's kitchen, I, at last, exhaled and moved forward into the flat – Jesus, what a shithole. The lounge sported a filthy shit-brown sofa and fifties-style sideboard with splayed-out round legs. Positioned underneath the window, dressed in orange and brown striped curtains, stood a vintage folded gate-leg table. A TV, albeit tiny, perched on the top of what I can only describe as an old wooden drinks trolley, the bottom hosting an array of bottles of spirits. I could have forgiven myself if I was an alcoholic for having to live in this dump.

The interior design didn't improve when assessing the first bedroom. Although with no headboard, a double bed with a cream blanket neatly made over the top filled the majority of the space. Next to which stood an old dark-wood chest of drawers with two missing handles, and above that hung a small, chipped mirror. To the left was a wooden rail resembling a long broom handle wedged between two walls, serving as a makeshift wardrobe. This supported a collection of clothes, beneath which lay an additional heap on the floor. A quick rummage confirmed they were all men's clothing, so probably no wife existed. The thought of a wife I didn't know returning from the disco and wanting some fun in the bedroom was horrifying.

The second bedroom appeared half full of boxes. Well, they were more of the wooden tea chest variety – was I moving in? The Sunday Express newspaper on the red Formica table in the kitchen caught my eye, specifically the date stamp in the top right-hand corner – Sunday 8th August 1976.

The paper appeared to have been read, its broadsheet pages folded and refolded to its original state, although now crumpled. The pages were white – surely they would have yellowed over time if it were an old paper. No, this paper was only four days old. Moving a box of Swan Vesta matches and a large glass ashtray full to the brim of spent and crumpled cigarette ends, I unfolded the newspaper. The headlines splashed across the front with a small picture to the right were—

Viking 2 enters Martian orbit.

Space race for the Red Planet is on.

Flipping to the back page, the principal picture was of Niki Lauda in a hospital bed. Below a small picture of his racing car in flames, the headline read—

Lauda claims miracle to survive German Grand Prix.

Being a petrolhead and obsessed with motor racing, I knew all about this. He'd crashed in the German Grand Prix at Nürburgring on the 1st of August 1976; his car had burst into flames, trapping him inside. I read the whole article about his memories of the crash and his long road to recovery. Then, dropping the paper on the table, I slumped down into the seat of the wooden chair. The realisation hit me – I wasn't in an alternative world – I was in the same world, but now in 1976. It appeared the same events had happened on the same day as they had in my world.

Theoretically, I'd only been awake for about six hours since repeatedly stabbing my iPhone's snooze button as I'd lain in bed this morning in one of Beth's spare rooms, but I was absolutely knackered. An overload of thoughts pummelled my brain. Was what happened tomorrow, 13th August 1976, going to happen again, so every minute detail of history repeating itself? Niki Lauda was in this world, so were all the people exactly the same? Was time repeating itself, apart from the introduction of me, or the new me? Will I be born next year, as I was already here? Were Mum, Dad, and Stephen at home right now? This was brain overload, but I had to accept this was real, and I had somehow been pushed back to this year – but why? I definitely died in the crash this morning – I could just feel it – I just did.

Did everyone on the planet, when they die, get catapulted back to yesteryear to have another go? I pondered that thought for a few moments whilst sitting in the strange place that didn't look much different from how I remembered my parents' kitchen. There was no microwave – Mum had loved her microwave – but the white cooker with an overhead grill looked very familiar. No, absolutely not. If everyone could return after dying, the world would be in chaos. Everyone would be talking about their past life. Adolf Hitler or Genghis Khan would have returned for a second go. No, they didn't come back, but I had, and the burning question now, was why me?

Oh, and what the fuck had happened to Martin?

11

13th August 1976

Evita

I rarely dream. I guess I'm one of those lucky ones. My head hits the pillow, and I'm out. Last night was no different. However, as I awoke, it was like I'd stepped into a nightmare. I wasn't in my room at Beth's, but in that bedroom with the broom handle wardrobe. And it hadn't escaped my attention that today was Friday the thirteenth. Oh, lucky me.

The bathroom, which I hadn't ventured into last night, continued the themed décor that the rest of the flat offered – a shithole. A pink rubber hose with suction cups connected to each tap that led to a mouldy shower head lying in the yellow-coloured bath could, I guess, be loosely described as a shower. Only one toothbrush lay on the windowsill above the matching pale-yellow sink, providing further confirmation that I lived here alone.

I completed the necessary deeds, although it was a strip wash, as I couldn't be bothered with a bath and wasn't going near that hose contraption. Venturing back to the broom-handle wardrobe to see what was on offer, I rummaged through the array of odd-looking clothes.

Dressed in flared jeans, a Rolling Stones '73 tour t-shirt, and Adidas trainers that didn't look too dissimilar to a pair that I already owned, I hunted for the kettle, discovering a cream-coloured contraption splattered with prints of orange and green leaves on the side – an old gas-hob job with a whistle. Only tea was available, no coffee.

I grabbed the newspaper and started making some notes down the side of a full-page advert, *'A Few drinks, and you're a real lady killer',* which displayed a picture of a man looking at a dead woman in a car. It must have been one of the first hard-hitting anti-drink-drive campaign adverts. I had to make some plans and work out what was going on. Making a to-do list for the day may help me start to make some sense of this madness.

The long sleep had helped clear the fuzz out of my head. It had occurred to me that after the crash, all I wanted was to be dead and not in this strange world. I was doing my usual glass-half-empty, miserable-bastard-Jason-twat self. Now, thinking differently, I perhaps had a chance to start again, or *'go again',* that annoying term Gary Oxney loved to use. *"Team, let's go again with this and really push the envelope hard,"* I recalled him saying – Christ, I think he said it every day.

Another option that had floated around my mind was to go back and re-jump those traffic lights, have another crash, and maybe go back to 2019. But no, this was a chance for a brand-new life; my only loss was Beth, nothing else. This was my metaphorical kick in the bollocks to my OCD – it didn't matter anymore. No more repeatedly trying door handles or closing my eyes when switching off lights, that was gone. New beginnings, although I'd said that before and look what happened.

I set about my list for today. If I was now living in 1976 as some other Jason, I needed to search the flat and work out who I was, and then venture out and see if my parents were here in this world with me. Of course, whether I had a job and my financial situation were also immediate considerations.

I certainly couldn't approach Mum and Dad, but I wanted to see them. Even if I parked near their home and watched until they left the house, I knew a conversation wasn't possible.

"Hi Mum, hi Dad, hello little Stephen," ruffling his hair, *"Great to see you again … I've missed you. Oh yes, I'm Jason, your son, and I will be born next March."*

No, that wasn't going to work.

However, if I could see them, I would know what I had to do and why I was here. Somehow, could I stop them from boarding that train in 1984? Mum and Dad had tickets for a show in the West End – *Evita,* I think it was – one in a long line of successes for Andrew Lloyd-Webber. Sixteen minutes after catching the train, it derailed due to a points fault. All three hundred and twenty-two passengers in second class were fine – no one even went to the hospital. The thirteen passengers in first class all died. Mum and Dad were two of those thirteen.

Starting with the large heap of paperwork piled up at the end of the shit-brown coloured sofa, I sifted through the letters, magazines and scraps of paper. On the top lay a grocery shopping list penned in my handwriting. A somewhat bizarre feeling seeing something I'd written, although I'd never written it. The innocuous list briefly grabbed my attention before I moved on to the more important stuff. Namely, letters that might indicate who I was.

I plucked up two unopened letters and six opened ones stuffed back into their original envelopes. This was something I would have always done – a quick read, shove it back in, then chuck them on a pile and hope they all disappeared. Only when I had two or three stacks of paperwork would I ever get around to properly dealing with the 'heaps', as Lisa called them, and then I'd realise I'd missed some critical letters that needed attention weeks ago. Oh yes, this heaped filing system was very me – new me and old me seemed to have a similar filing system.

Reopening one of the envelopes revealed a solicitor's letter from Brockett and Co., reference twenty-two Homebrook Avenue. The letter confirmed the exchange of contracts and the completion date set for Friday the 27th of August 1976. It appeared that I was moving out of this shithole and into the marital home that Lisa and I bought in 2005, nearly thirty years in the future. But this time, no Lisa, I'd purchased the house myself. Somehow, new me had managed to buy an up-market three-bed detached house in a desirable part of Fairfield.

I guessed this information presumably meant I was gainfully employed but not at Waddington's Steel because that company only started in 1982. Old man Waddington was now retired, well, retired in my old life. He hadn't started his company in 1976. I could now hunt him down and inform him that in a few years, his new successful company would make him a millionaire.

The rest of the heap revealed very little other than to confirm I paid utility bills at this address and a new cheque book from Midland Bank. I didn't think I'd written a cheque for over ten years.

Rummaging through the sideboard, I discovered a Post Office savings book. As of 28th July 1976, the balance stood at a little over seven thousand seven hundred pounds. Okay, not a fortune, but I was in 1976, not 2019, so that amount could be huge. A large, tatty manila envelope yielded a bundle of share certificates for several mining companies I'd never heard of. However, quickly totting up the amounts, suggested new me owned somewhere north of forty thousand shares, and God knows what they were worth.

I rummaged back through the heap of paperwork and grabbed two old newspapers, searching for the financial pages that should detail the prices of those stocks and shares. The Express revealed nothing; yes, a shares page, although the mining companies weren't listed. The other paper was pink, The Financial Times, which I had never bought in my life – well, old me hadn't, but a good job new me had. Running my thumb down the page and squinting at the tiny print, I found the share prices and, although maths wasn't my strong point, those shares were worth over twenty-five grand. Whatever year I was in, that was a lot of money. So, maybe I was loaded – that was a big tick for one of the points on my list.

Buoyed by this new financial situation, I postponed rummaging through the rest of the flat, favouring a trip out to see if my parents were in this strange world. Although excited at the prospect of seeing them again, in reality, I was terrified of what I might discover. However, it would confirm, without a doubt, that I was now in 1976.

Opening the front door, I could hear shouting in the corridor. There stood a young woman with long, mouse-coloured hair. Without being too uncharitable, you could say she was a bit rough-looking, heavily pregnant, wearing dirty flared jeans and a striped tank-top over a cream blouse stretched tightly over her belly. To complete her ensemble, the scraggy woman sported a pair of platform boots that elevated her a few inches higher than her short stature. The odious woman directed a torrent of obscenities at a small boy who held his hands over his head, cowering as if preparing himself for the smack that was soon to land.

"You fucking shit, I ain't putting up with this today. I've had enough of your fucking antics. Now get your fucking shoes on."

Oh, nice, really nice. I stood and stared, mouth open, something I seemed to be doing a lot over the past twenty or so hours. Instead of landing the slap, she turned around as she noticed me stepping out of the flat.

"Or-right Jason, 'ow you doing? This fucking heat is doing me head in, can't wait to get this bastard out of me," she said, patting her protruding tummy.

An elderly gentleman poked his head out of the door from the next flat along. All I could see were his grey hair, heavy black-rimmed glasses, and tartan slippers sticking out the bottom of the door. It was as if the rest of his body didn't exist.

"You okay, Carol? Oh, hello, Jason, you moving soon … up to that new house?" he asked in a gravelly cockney accent.

"Yeah, I'm okay, Don. This little prick is getting on my tits. He needs a strong hand, but that useless wanker father of his never comes around anymore. Well, only when he fancies a bit, and that ain't going to happen in my state. Jase, you can take me wiv you to that new house. Get me out of this fucking shithole," she said with a grin. "You need to get yourself a bird, Jase. I'm always happy to oblige," she added with a smirk and a flick of her greasy hair.

Although this was the first encounter with people who seemed to know the new me, it wasn't the most engaging conversation I've ever experienced. I was keen to move on … at pace.

"Sorry, gotta shoot, lots to do, I'm afraid," I replied.

"Go on, Jase. He's on a promise, dirty fucker! Fill your boots," she cackled, as I hot-footed along the concrete landing towards the stairs.

12

Match of the Day

Number fifty-eight Campbell Crescent was my home for the first seven years of my life, with my parents and my older brother, Stephen. A super happy home. I often visited over the years, just parking up along the street and looking at the house and the family who now occupied it. I think it changed hands three times from 1984 to 2019; three families, all seemingly as happy as my family had been.

The house, a '30s classic Arts and Crafts-styled three-bed dwelling, appeared pretty much how I remembered it. Although this visit was forty-odd years before the last time I sat in my car looking at the house. I suspected this time I wouldn't be parked up for just a few minutes; it was potentially going to be for much longer.

I'd purchased the Daily Express from the newsagents at the end of the road. The shopkeeper was the same man I remember back in 2019 when I occasionally popped in for a packet of cigarettes. However, now his appearance was as I remembered it in the early '80s when Stephen and I would buy a bag of Fruit Salads and Black Jacks with our pocket money. Spookily, he'd become younger by nearly forty years, although I'd stayed the same age – weird.

Parked up about twenty yards down the road from my old home, I opened the paper to give the appearance of a man innocently sitting in his car reading, just in case any curtain-twitching neighbours wondered what was going on.

As I expected, Dad's car wasn't parked on the driveway, presuming he would be at work. I tried to think what car he would have had, but as this was a year before I was born, it would be the best guess I could come up with. From pulling hard on my memory banks that either Dad or my grandfather had told me over the years, I thought it was probably a Ford Cortina Mk3, but a white one, not yellow like mine – well, I assumed this was my car.

The street remained relatively quiet for over an hour, and yes, the curtain-twitching had started. I wasn't sure how long I could stay in this position before someone reported a strange bloke in the neighbourhood. I considered knocking on the front door, but I struggled to conjure up a plausible excuse for doing so. As luck would have it, my patience was duly rewarded.

An elegant thirty-year-old lady with shoulder-length blonde hair, dressed in green trousers and blouse, and a multi-coloured tasselled belt to complete the look, stepped out of my parent's driveway whilst holding the hand of a four-year-old boy – I was looking at my dead mother and older brother, Stephen. They stopped at the top of the drive as if deciding which way to walk, then turned left in the direction of my car.

This was an emotional moment and further confirmation that this was, unbelievably, 1976. All I wanted to do was run and hug my mother. I hadn't seen her for thirty-five years, and I missed her. However, knowing that course of action could probably lead to an arrest, I plumped for the less risky option and followed them on foot at a safe distance.

Stephen skipped along whilst bouncing and continually dropping a small ball, which my mother kept grabbing and handing back to him. Although trying to avoid appearing like some weirdo stalker, I increased my pace to close the distance between us. Curiosity had got the better of me, now wanting to hear their conversation.

Stephen continued to bounce and drop the tiny rubber ball – he'd always been crap at sports. I guess he got the brains, and I got the athleticism, of sorts. Once again, in true Stephen style, he fumbled his catch, resulting in the ball bounding off into the road. Like so many children do, he had one focus – save his ball. However, he failed to notice the ice-cream van as it careered down the street, its tune blaring out.

I think it was the tune to Match of the Day or M.O.T.D as it was rebranded a few years ago – what the hell was wrong with just calling it Match of the Day, for Christ's sake? The driver appeared oblivious to Stephen as he gazed around, presumably to see who'd come out of their house to buy an ice cream. Now, the impact of the van and Stephen was only seconds away. Leaping into the road, I managed to grab the neck of Stephen's t-shirt and attempted to haul him back from danger. I succeeded, which resulted in a squeal of brakes, the smell of rubber, Stephen crying, and a dead leg for me as the van banged into my thigh and stopped.

My mother shrieked, "Steeephen," whilst grabbing hold of my tearful brother. "Oh God, Stephen, come here, come here. It's okay, you're fine, don't cry, you're fine, shush, shush. You can't run into the road like that."

Hobbling back to the kerb whilst clutching my right thigh, I plonked down on the grass verge and rubbed my leg as if rubbing would do any good, but I presumed I wasn't going to get a cuddle from my mother. The sweating ice cream man scooted around the van's bonnet, looking as if he was about to throw up. With hands slapped to his cheeks and his mouth wide open, he'd taken on the appearance of the 'Scream' mask.

"Oh hell, is the boy okay? He appeared from nowhere! I just didn't see him!" he exclaimed.

Whilst tightly hugging Stephen and with a tear in her eye, my mother seemed unable to answer. So, I assumed, based on the fact that I'd been in the thick of the action and my leg bore witness to that, I should respond.

"Stephen is fine, mate. But you need to look where you're bloody going! You could have bloody well killed him."

"Look, mate, I'm so sorry. He just appeared. Christ, I'm glad he's okay. What about you? Are you alright?"

"Dead leg, but yeah, I'm okay. It'll be bruised in the morning, I guess."

"Shit, sorry, mate … you sure you're alright? Tell you what, ice creams on me, for all of you." With that, he disappeared back inside his van.

Looking at my mother cuddling my brother, I became somewhat lost for words. In my time, this would be police, ambulance, crime scene investigators, compensation, and a court case. Then, following on for the next five years would be a plethora of cold calls from claims handlers pestering your mobile —

"Hello, you have recently been involved in an accident, is that right?" a sugar-coated, smooth, sweet voice would say, and it didn't matter what my response was, like, *"No, I haven't."* through to *"Oh fuck off,"* the calls would keep coming.

My Mother continued her silence, appearing not to want to get embroiled in an argument or prepare to sue for compensation. I accepted my double-cone ninety-nine with a flake before the flustered ice-cream man sped off, presumably keen to distance himself from the situation.

Stephen and my mother's tears appeared to have dried and they now stood clasping their ice creams. However, Stephen's iced treat seemed to have consumed his head as the first lick deposited lumps of ice cream across his nose, cheeks, and even his ear. It never ceased to amaze me how children manage to do this. Mum stuck out her hand, straightforward, similar to a quick-fire gunslinger from one of those Spaghetti Westerns, very forthright. I rubbed my hand across my t-shirt to remove the sweat.

"Joan Apsley, pleased to meet you, sir. I can't thank you enough for what you just did, can we, Stephen?" she said, bending down to look at her son, my brother, who now appeared covered entirely in ice cream and loosely resembled a baked Alaska.

"You're welcome. I'm just so relieved he's okay. You are okay?" I asked the ever-growing blob of ice cream that seemed to have replaced what previously was his head.

"Oh, shit, sorry, how rude of me. I'm Jason Ap ... Ap ... Apple ... your, your ... s ... servant ... err, at your service."

Christ, dick-head. Apple, servant, what the hell was I saying? And now she probably thought I had an uncontrollable stutter. What a knob. I had to think and pull myself together before I completely blew it.

"Oh, how lovely. Lovely name, Mr Apple, how unusual, and at my service, so gallant!" my mother replied with a generous smile.

"Ha, that's okay, really it is. It feels great to be able to do something good," I responded, amazingly, without a hint of a stutter this time.

"Well, you did, Mr Apple, that's for sure. Stephen and I are truly in your debt."

"Please call me Jason."

Notwithstanding our handshake continuing longer than could be considered normal, like two world leaders posing for the cameras, being able to touch my mother after thirty-five years was a dramatic moment that engulfed my emotions. My heart raced, whilst the sweat forming on my back had nothing to do with the weather. It was a somewhat surreal moment – two supposedly dead people having a conversation – one of them knew the other so well, well, seven years' worth – the other had no idea who they were apart from an unusual name and a stutter.

Sadly, whilst still clinging to my mother's hand, I knew I must let go of her again. It hurt, oh, it hurt, but the feeling of doing good was immense. Yes, I had done something right, and my mother had said so. When did I last do something good? I really couldn't remember.

"Goodbye, Jason, and again, thank you."

Now firmly rooted to the grass verge, I watched Stephen and my once-dead mother as they walked off hand in hand. Stephen turned around to look, but my mother didn't.

I hadn't had the chance to know my parents properly because that train crash had stolen them from me at such a young age. For many years, I'd not made any effort to keep in touch with Stephen, losing a closeness that brothers should have; yet another example of how I'd isolated myself. Tears came again. Of course, they did. It was so emotional I just couldn't help it. In the space of two days, I'd morphed from *cold heart* to *blubber boy*.

This time, although I was now thirty-eight years older than him, I had to get to know Stephen better. Was this the reason I ended up here to save Stephen, and was I supposed to be here on this day? Would he still attend veterinary college and end up in New Zealand with his arm firmly embedded in the backside of a sheep or whatever vets do over there? And was I here for anything else?

I stumbled back to the Cortina, my right leg stiffening due to the altercation with the ice cream van's nearside wing. The road was tranquil again, and the twitching curtains were now still after the nosey neighbours had had their excitement for the day.

Just a solitary man walking his dog, who crouched down and deposited his doo on the verge – the dog, not the man, for clarity – and then trotted off, followed by the man who had no intention of collecting his dog's offerings in a poop bag. How times had changed; that would be a hanging offence in my day.

13

Ghost Kid

Nursing my leg, I considered staying in position until my mother and Stephen returned so I could see them again. However, the curtain twitchers would be back, so time to move on – also, I was starving. I hadn't eaten since yesterday as I'd been consumed by the events of the last twenty-four hours, but now I was so hungry I started to feel ill. Although I quite fancied a Frappuccino, a Panini, and a slice of lemon cake, I knew that wasn't going to happen, so settled on the greasy-spoon-type cafe in town.

Whilst perched at a table next to the window, pondering the scene of a summer's day in 1976, I struggled with the surroundings. The High Street was, as with my experience yesterday, all wrong. The physical buildings were correct, but nothing was as it should be. Fairfield was a large town with built-up suburbs around an existing small market town. The High Street consisted of a mixture of late-nineteenth and early-twentieth-century buildings, all with their collection of different facades and angled roofs. Without the shop fronts, it had a chocolate-box-cover appearance or even a thousand-piece jigsaw puzzle. However, as I peered up and down the road, none of the shops were in the right place, and I couldn't see one that existed in my old world. In my time there were many shops closed and boarded up, the majority of the rest were charity shops. At least this version of the High Street had different stores, and they were all open, which was a strange kind of reverse progress.

The gum-chewing waitress appeared through the somewhat off-putting haze that hung heavy in the air. Although I'm a smoker, I'd grown used to the pleasant smoke-free cafes and restaurants of my time. Unfortunately, everyone in this place was smoking or eating with a lit cigarette in their ashtrays. Well, the baby in the high chair had abstained but was seriously passive smoking.

After swapping the location of the tomato-shaped sauce bottle with the stinking half-full ashtray, I plucked up the menu, a red plastic card with pictures of their not-so-delightful offerings. After a perfunctory glance at the menu and an impatient tut from the waitress, I settled on ham, egg and chips with a coffee and planned to have a knickerbocker glory to finish off; the whole meal was only sixty-nine pence.

"Is that everything? Sorry, prices have gone up again today, like they do every week," stated the young waitress, although weirdly, she was probably twenty years older than me.

I offered a tight smile, whilst she finished scribbling down my order, before taking a moment to think things through. It appeared my finances were in good order. Maybe I'd won the lottery? Err, probably not, as that didn't start until the '90s. So, perhaps the Football Pools? My grandfather used to do the Pools every week, trying to predict those score-draws. However, I didn't think the odds were better than the lottery. Presumably, I must have a job, and if so, I wondered if I should be there today. I needed to find out more about myself. However, there was no internet, and wouldn't be for many years, so I was just going to have to talk to strangers – Christ, what a thought. Tonight, the community centre would be my first outing. As I lived on that estate, there was a chance someone would know me in there.

I'd seen Mum and Stephen, and I was sure Dad was okay at work, so next on my list was to check on my grandparents, but that was it. I had no one else to check up on – as with 2019, in 1976, I had no friends and was pretty much alone. Although I was sure I'd prevented my brother's death this morning, what the butterfly effect would be, I couldn't fathom. Perhaps I'd kept every future event on track, and nothing had changed. Was this it and, if so, what now?

Presumably, I wasn't meant to leap from one event to the next, like Sam Beckett in *Quantum Leap*. No, that wasn't me, and there was no hologram called Al by my side helping me through this; that was even more ridiculous than this situation. Would I have to kick around for seven and a half years before conjuring up a plan to stop my parents from boarding that train? What then? Will I have to co-exist with my other self at the same time?

"Holy shit," I pronounced to the whole cafe. I stuck my hand in the air and nodded an offer of apology for my outburst. I just realised my mother would have been about eight weeks pregnant when we met today – or was she?

Although the meal was just about edible, the coffee was shite – I mean really shite. I was going to miss proper coffee if this was the standard to go by. Fortunately, my newly acquired wallet contained a wad of one and five pound paper notes, displaying a very youthful-looking Queen staring back at me. I placed a one-pound note next to my empty coffee cup. A thirty-one-pence tip was probably excessive, but I didn't want to wait for the change, as I was now itching to make my next discovery.

Squeezing the car into a small space, I parked on Milton Road about forty yards from my grandparents' house. Parallel parking without power steering was a real physical workout. The line of terraced houses rose steeply up the hill, plateauing off at the top where my grandparents' house was situated. The postage-stamp-sized front gardens afforded just enough space for a couple of wheelie bins, although there were no such bins in this era, and I thought the street looked better for it.

My grandmother would have been retired in 1976, and I considered the possibility she could be at home. However, I calculated that my grandfather still had another year to work, so I expected to see him walking home anytime soon unless he'd gone to the pub after work, as I recall he would often do.

Whilst waiting for something to happen, I glanced at the letter on the passenger seat that was still there – I'd forgotten it. Plucking it from the seat, I spotted the envelope had previously been opened, and then the content shoved back in – typical me. I peeled it back open and read through the single folded sheet of paper. It provided an answer to what I'd pondered about in the café. But no, oh no, this was getting nuttier by the minute. How the hell was I going to do that? No way – absolutely no way.

Although my school days were okay-ish, they were slightly better than my adulthood, so somewhere hovering above crap is the right marker. I had few friends at school – a familiar theme running through my life – due to a combination of shyness and becoming withdrawn after the shock of losing my parents. So, I drifted through school as one of those invisible kids – you know the ones – the *ghost* kids that no one can remember.

'Do you remember Jason Apsley at school? He was in our class – nope don't remember him. I can remember everyone. You sure he was in our class? Yes, skinny kid, friends with that scrawny blonde girl who lived in the children's home – oh, I remember her but not him, no, don't remember him.'

I suspected that conversation happened a lot over the years with the members of the class of '89 from Eaton City of Fairfield School. John Hales, the school bully, stuck in my mind's eye for a brief moment. He'd noticed me and decided that I, Jason Apsley, had reached the time for a good pasting, which he duly dished out to me at the age of thirteen in the school locker room, whilst his disciples kept watch for any potential interfering Masters that might be floating by. It was the only physical fight I've had the pleasure of and, of course, I lost.

I reread the letter.

Dear Jason,

I am so delighted you have accepted the position back at our school. So many years have gone by, and it's truly wonderful to have you back. It seems a long time ago since we enjoyed lessons here together in 1948. You will be delighted to know that little has changed. The school is still an extraordinary institution, and having you on my team will further enhance this.

As stated in your offer letter, your start date is 31st August in preparation for the new term. However, I will be holding a staff meeting on the morning of the 26th at 10 am, so you can meet the rest of the team and the four teachers in the Maths and Science department, who will report to you.

It will be wonderful to see you again,

Yours Sincerely

Roy Clark

Headmaster

Eaton, City of Fairfield School.

Oh, Christ, I'm a bloody teacher. No, I didn't know how to teach. I had no idea about Maths or Science either, plus another slight problem – I hated kids. Also, who the hell was Roy Clark? Whoever he was, he seemed to know me.

Striding up the road came a tall man with a shock of thick, white hair, wearing a shirt and tie, light grey zip-up jacket – my grandfather. Unfortunately, he died in 1997, aged eighty-five. His death was devastating, being the only dark cloud of my three years at uni, which, as stated, I loved, except for the lectures, of course.

Overwhelmed with loneliness, I so desperately wanted to talk to him, but what was I going to say? *'Hi, I'm Mr Apple, your servant.'* – the same crap I stuttered to my mother a few hours ago. No, not that, or the impossible, *'Hi Grandad'*. Even if he thought I could be a long-lost grandson that he didn't know about – which would be difficult as my mother was an only child – it wouldn't work as I was forty-two and he was sixty-four; the maths didn't stack up either. Even though I was totally crap at maths, I could work that one out. Racking my brain to come up with what to say, I exited the car and approached him.

"Excuse me, sorry to bother you, but can you tell me where Meyrick Avenue is, please?"

Although I knew it was the next road, it was the only thing I could come up with in the thirty seconds I had before he entered his house, the same house where I'd lived for eleven years. My grandfather halted his stride and, with a broad grin, assessed his grandson, who wasn't yet born – although he wasn't to know that.

"You're not far, lad. It's the next road."

Lad, that's what he called me all those years ago, never Jason or Stephen. We both had the same name – *Lad.*

"Oh, great, thanks … err, thank you," I replied, now lost for words and sporting a stupid grin.

Presumably concerned I was some nutter on the loose, he shot past me to enter my childhood home, leaving me wondering why all I could conjure up was to ask for bloody directions.

Now I had established that my dead family were alive, and presumably, I was too – as the red mark was still evident on my arm where I had pinched myself yesterday – I decided my next move was to return to the flat. I would see what else I could discover about myself, then brave that God-awful community centre. I detoured on the way to look at my new home in Homebrook Avenue, not that I needed to, as Lisa and I had lived there for over ten years – I knew that house like the back of my hand.

With a mug of tea in hand, I settled into the spare room and attacked the tea chests full of someone else's possessions, hoping to find some maths and science books packed in those moving crates as I may need to do some swotting up. I was fearful that *other* Jason had similar crap paperwork organising skills as I had. If so, I would be in for the long haul.

14

Crafty Cockney

As I suspected, *other* Jason appeared to use the same filing system as me. Which involved a complex process of random paperwork stuffed into an array of cardboard boxes with absolutely no order whatsoever. All letters were shoved back into their original envelopes – Christ sake – new me needed to sort this out. From the content of the boxes of paperwork, I yielded very little information. However, why I seem to have so few possessions became very clear.

I completed my teacher training, ah-ha, and then changed career choices. After graduating from St Andrew's University with a Bachelor of Arts in Applied Science, I spent nearly fifteen years as a mining engineer in South Africa as Principal Director of Engineering for a diamond mining company. That explained why my financial situation seemed pretty healthy.

It appeared I returned to the UK six months ago and purchased my new house for cash, renting this shithole of a flat as a stop-gap. Why *other* Jason chose this place was anyone's guess.

Notwithstanding the information gleaned regarding *other* Jason's education and career choices, there appeared to be no further information about his family. New me could have parents, siblings, or a brood of children potentially dotted around the world. It was as if I had just landed on Earth with almost no history, which was ironic based on the current situation. As far as I was concerned, Joan and Neil Apsley were my parents, but they weren't, so who was, and where were they? Who were my other relatives, and had I just teleported into some random family tree, all of them suddenly knowing who I was?

I had fourteen days until I moved house, and then I was starting my new job. That provided me with a couple of weeks to get some information together and work out my next steps. However, what was abundantly clear, I needed some help. I desperately wanted to be able to talk to someone about what had happened, but I knew that was a ridiculous thought. If I opened my mouth about any of this, I would be branded a loony and then carted off to that padded cell.

Whilst rummaging around in a tea chest full of what looked like junk you'd see at a scouts' jumble sale, I poked my hand down the side and discovered a small framed photo. The beach scene with Table Mountain in the background depicted me – well, *other* me – dressed in a dangerously small pair of budgie smugglers, with ten friends posing in a line looking like they were about to perform the Riverdance. The bikini-clad, auburn-haired beauty I had my arm around didn't appear to be a stranger based on the positions of our hands and the smiles on our faces. This new, happy me clearly enjoyed the company of many friends, which was a marked difference between *other* Jason and me.

I made a decision; it was risky, super risky, but I had to have a go. I grabbed a reporter's notebook and flicked over the pages full of random stuff that made no sense. On the first blank page, I scribbled down a list of information pulled from Jason's old brain.

After twenty minutes of penning near illegible scribbles, I headed off to the community centre. I wasn't looking forward to the evening, but every minute of the last twenty-four hours had been a discovery, and I needed more information. But more to the point, I fancied a pint.

The bar positioned to the left side of the main room in the community centre was nothing short of hideous. However, on a positive note, there was no disco tonight. It reminded me of the Winchester Club in Minder – any minute now, I expected Arthur would barrel through the door and order a large VAT, moaning about 'er indoors. The décor wasn't so much retro, just awful. With its worn-out patterned carpet, containing a multitude of colours arranged in some psychedelic pattern, and the red-flocked wallpaper, it afforded a look similar to my favourite curry house.

The bar offered an array of familiar optics, covering shelves containing bottles that didn't, like Babycham and CherryB – not sure any bar in my day would still stock those. The three beer taps were equally unfamiliar to me. No Guinness or anything that looked remotely drinkable. With this depressing choice of Watney's Red Barrel, Double Diamond Pale Ale, or Skol Lager with 'You're a Skolar' blazoned on top of the tap, I plumped for the latter based on my newly instantly achieved Bachelor of Arts Degree.

"Hello Jason, the usual?" asked a heavily made-up bar lady. Wearing a leopard-skin headscarf and matching top, she could have easily been mistaken for Bet Lynch from Coronation Street.

"Err … yes, please." I was a bit taken aback that I had a usual. Not Skol Lager, not even a pint; she placed a double scotch and a red soda syphon in front of me. My drink explained the bottom of the drink's trolley in the flat – *other* Jason was a spirits man.

"I'll have a pint of Skol as well, please." I needed a pint.

"Blimey on the chasers already tonight. You had a crap day?" Bet Lynch replied.

"Ha, yeah, something like that." When the pint was deposited next to the scotch, she handed me a set of darts.

"There you go – fifty-six pence, please, love."

I stared at the darts, open-mouthed. The new usual look I had developed. What the hell had I got these for?

"Alright, Jason," I heard from the side of me. Two guys were playing darts, and the younger one had turned around and called over to me – the second person in the last few minutes who seemed to know me.

"Hi." That's all I could come up with – Christ, I was no good at this social communication stuff – and I was sure I had never played darts in my life.

"Jim, look, 'dead-eyed-dick' is in. We should easily win the match tonight," the same younger guy called to his mate. Concerningly, he was pointing at me.

Oh, bloody hell, it would be a miracle if I hit the board, let alone be dead-eyed-dick. I would just have to apologise and say I had an off night, but what the hell, some social interaction could be what I needed. As I lit a cigarette, I considered I'd endured a somewhat lonely existence over the past few days, so perhaps it was time to relax. Certainly, being able to smoke in a bar was a luxury, none of that standing outside the front of the pub when winter arrived. I would appreciate this. The downside being the air was already thick with smoke; a blue haze was forming at eye level throughout the bar.

To my amazement, I played well, and it seemed I was at my usual standard. I had no problem pummelling the twenties, and the double-out was a piece of cake. We trashed the other team with my teammates all patting me on the back, and they seemed pleased that dead-eyed-dick was on the team tonight. Loosened up with beer and whisky, I somewhat surprisingly enjoyed chatting and laughing with my newly discovered mates. For sure, the hangover would be stunning in the morning. Although I had no idea who the new me was, I found it easy to make stuff up about myself.

Unfortunately, as my drunken chat reached full flow, I blurted out a few verbal cock ups. Firstly, calling myself Eric Bristow the Crafty Cockney – I was a little ahead of my time on that one. Not much, but enough. Luckily, no one knew who I was talking about, and I successfully fobbed it off by saying it was a South African thing. Secondly, which was slightly trickier, was my reference to England thrashing Germany five-one in 2001. Fortunately, we were all half pissed by then and, after a couple of blank stares, it was forgotten.

After enjoying the evening, probably more than any night I could remember for years, I staggered back to the flat with a grin on my face. I realised that it was surprising how you could enjoy yourself when you made an effort to talk to strangers in the process of making friends.

I crawled into bed with my hangover for company. However, fortunately, sleep came quickly – tomorrow could be one of the most important days of my life.

15

14th August 1976

George the Talking Rabbit

In history, August 14th has had some memorable events: in 1945, Harry Truman announced that Imperial Japan had surrendered, ending World War Two; in 1947, Indian Independence from British rule was established; and in 1969, British troops entered Northern Ireland to return law and order, a planned limited operation – little did they know at that time.

Today could be another momentous day in history or a calamity for Jason Apsley. In a few hours, I would know success or failure. After a sluggish start, my hangover was receding, but all too slowly as there seemed to be an invisible force holding it in place. I headed out mid-morning with my reporter's notebook in hand and a feeling that this could be the stupidest thing I had ever done, and I had done many stupid things. Christ, I prayed I was wrong.

For as long as I could remember, my grandfather frequented the pub on a Saturday lunchtime. He would take the paper, enjoy a pre-lunch pint, and chat with friends before going home to potter about in his garden shed, listening to Saturday afternoon sports on the radio. Today, I hoped his routine was the same as before, as I planned to have a chat, armed with facts in my reporter's notebook and one risky prediction.

The Three Horseshoes was, as I remembered, an olde-worlde sort of pub, with low ceilings, brass horseshoes mounted around a large stone fireplace – a cosy, intimate pub. I'd been there many times with my grandparents, usually given a bottle of Coke with a straw, a bag of Smiths Salt & Vinegar crisps and a tennis ball. Stephen and I would play 'catch' to keep ourselves amused in the pub garden whilst my grandparents enjoyed the company of their friends in the lounge bar. Children and public bars didn't mix in the early '80s.

Based on consuming a month's worth the previous evening, I avoided alcohol. Instead, I plumped for what I usually had in this establishment, a Coke, but this time, no straw – and no tennis ball. A smattering of punters entered the bar over the next forty-five minutes, all men, but not my grandfather. I feared that my plan was doomed.

George Sutton, my grandfather, was an unusually open-minded sort of chap who held an unwavering belief that the vast majority of people harboured good intentions, coupled with an ability to defuse situations – my grandmother was the opposite. The ridiculous story I was hoping to tell George would understandably raise her scepticism, and that would be that. I'd inherited her traits, not my grandfather's. If my plan was to work, I needed to talk to George alone.

I repeatedly checked my watch, willing time to slow down. If I'd managed to jump back forty-three years, slowing time down by a few minutes should have been a piece of cake. However, now the minutes whizzed past, time evaporating in front of me. Unaware I'd been holding my breath, I sighed with relief when the lounge-bar door opened and in stepped a tall, well-dressed man with a shock of white hair carrying a newspaper. Before he'd even closed the door, the elderly barman who had served me about an hour ago called out. "Morning George … usual?"

Notwithstanding the relief that George had followed his usual routine, I was acutely aware that the real challenge lay ahead. I patiently waited a few minutes whilst George chatted to a few locals before plonking himself in the window alcove seat. He took a generous gulp of brown ale from the beer mug before unfolding his newspaper. This was it – time to make my move.

The next few minutes would be critical to my new life. I needed to share the last thirty-six hours with someone, and who better than the person I knew best – well, second-best, but Beth wasn't born.

"Oh, hi, do you remember me? I asked you for directions yesterday." My opening gambit. I was sweating, and my heart rate had risen. I could hear it banging in my chest.

"Yes, lad, I remember. Did you find it alright?"

"Yes, I did, thank you. Can I join you? I wanted to ask you something."

"Well, okay, lad, but I had come to read my paper."

"I only want a few minutes of your time, then I'll buy you a pint. I know you always enjoy two pints on a Saturday lunchtime before spending the afternoon listening to the radio in your shed."

George raised his left eyebrow, Sean Connery style, clearly surprised that I knew his Saturday routine. I grabbed the vacant seat and plonked my reporter's notebook in front of me. I'd never been so nervous in all my life; that gormless, open-mouthed new look I had developed was back. Reviewing my notes – a random collection of facts I could remember about my grandfather – and in no particular order just how they came into my head sitting on a tea chest in the spare bedroom – and that one hopeful prediction, I prepared myself to speak.

"Well, lad, apart from reminding me that I like two pints on a Saturday lunchtime, what is it that you want to chat about?"

"I'd like to tell you some information that I know to be true, totally true, and then I'll tell you how I know. I'm not a nutter, and I don't want anything from you, just ten minutes of your time for you to hear me out," I blurted out like some nutter that I claimed not to be and then sat there with a stupid grin on my face.

The eyebrow went up again and stayed there; no verbal response, just a small nod of his head.

"Okay, your name is George Cecil Sutton. You were born on the 10th of July 1912, and you married Ivy Jane Williams in 1938. You have one daughter, Joan Monica Apsley, born in 1946, who married Neil Apsley in 1969, and one grandson called Stephen, aged four."

I continued with my list of factual dates, including deaths and marriages, all mundane stuff, but I felt the need to run through the family tree and then move on to stories he'd told me over the years.

"You served in the RAF during the war, stationed in North Africa. Your wartime buddies painted on their kit bags all the exotic names of where you were stationed, like Timbuktu, but you thought this was ridiculous. So, for a laugh, you painted Aylesbury and Woburn Sands on yours. The table in your backroom has a deep scratch on it. Caused by you when returning home after a drinking session with Neil, your son-in-law, just before your daughter's wedding. Ivy, your wife, never fails to remind you of it."

I threw in a few more before progressing to my pièce de résistance.

"You read a book to Stephen and me at bedtime; it's a book you wrote, although never published. You never read it to anyone except us boys. It's called 'George the Talking Rabbit'. The book is twenty-two pages long, bound with orange-striped wallpaper and the pages are held together with brown shoelaces. You keep that book on the bottom shelf of your bureau in the front room."

I continued with a few more facts that were at the bottom of the page in my notebook, not looking up until I'd blurted them all out. The speed of my speech increased with every line I read, like the terms and conditions at the end of TV adverts. Looking up, I was concerned what his expression would be. I was still sweating, and it had nothing to do with the searing heat of the summer of 1976. My grandfather's expression hadn't changed, and the eyebrow was now permanently raised as if fixed with a whole can of hairspray.

"What's going on here, lad? Do we know each other? How on earth do you know all this?"

I sighed heavily. Phase one completed. Phase two was going to be a whole new level and, although I'd repeatedly rehearsed it this morning, I was struggling to know where to start.

"I err … I err … um, well it's um, err … really odd, but the truth is I'm your gra … gra … oh shit." The new stutter that I developed yesterday when talking to my mother returned and took hold, gripping my tongue and vocal cords. I took a large gulp of Coke and focused.

"What?" George spat in a very uncharacteristic, almost aggressive manner. I guess he could have been forgiven as he listened to some weirdo dressed in a Bowie Diamond Dogs t-shirt, stuttering and sweating, and spouting random information.

"Oh crap, well, look, I'll just say it. I'm your second grandson. I was born in March next year, and I've travelled back in time from 2019. Look, I don't know why this has happened, but I need your help. You're the only one who can help me." That definitely didn't come out as rehearsed in the mirror that morning, but there, it was done – I'd said it.

George pursed his lips, then roared with laughter, causing the vast majority of fellow drinkers to spin around to assess the commotion. I was left to sit, stare, and contemplate this may have been a foolish mistake. Finally, after what seemed a lifetime, all heads slowly rotated back around, and the usual pub chatter continued.

"Well, you're funny, lad, I will give you that," he chuckled. "Right, I'll have that second pint you offered, and then you can leave me to read my paper."

Defeated, I purchased his pint and placed it on the table. I was about to make a hasty retreat and slide out of the pub to regroup, then work out what the hell I was going to do, when my grandfather called after me.

"Lad, take a seat. I need to talk to you."

I stared at him like I would have when I was about eight or nine years old. Perhaps my grandmother had just told me off for being naughty, and then he would perform the smoothing out process, calming the whole situation down. He had a fantastic ability to defuse situations, a rare and wonderful skill.

"Some of that information you could have got from many places, but some you couldn't. I need to know where you got it from, and more to the point, why?"

This was ridiculous – I couldn't look him in the eye – what was I thinking? I would have told me to bugger off if I were in his shoes. Now firmly boxed into a corner, with the truth as my only option – although I'd learnt before the truth wasn't always the best policy – I considered honesty was all I had left.

"Look, I'm your grandson. That's how I know this stuff. I know how this sounds, but it's the truth … it is."

George frowned and shook his head. "That book 'George the Talking Rabbit,' how do you know about it? Only three people know – Ivy, Stephen, and myself, that's it."

"I've told you how."

I loved that book. My grandfather had read it to me a million times, sometimes twice, back-to-back at bedtime, and I knew it word for word. I think Stephen had the book now – old Stephen, that is, the sheep fiddler. I recited the book almost word for word. As I recounted the story, his expression changed from mild curiosity to total disbelief. He was now sporting that gormless staring look that I'd recently developed.

"Okay, who's the Prime Minister in 2019?"

Oh, shit, I recalled the *'Back to the Future'* moment and the Ronald Reagan reply from Marty McFly to Doc Brown's question. Actually, George's stare wasn't too dissimilar to Doc's bulging eyes. Why did this question have to be asked when questioning a time-traveller? Was it some kind of subconscious part of everyone's brain?

If you meet a time-traveller, the first question you must ask is who is the UK Prime Minister or President of the USA.

"Boris Johnson, he's just succeeded Teresa May."

"Boris, a Russian? No, ha, and a woman?" More laughter ensued. "No, lad, that can't have happened! No woman will be Prime Minister, especially not that 'Thatcher, the milk snatcher'."

"Well, Thatcher was Prime Minister for eleven years, and Teresa May was the second female Prime Minister."

My grandfather wasn't a sexist by any stretch of the imagination, but those comments brought home the vast gulf of acceptable language between now and my time – well, my old time.

"Right, lad, just suppose you're telling the truth … just in some silly, imaginative way. What do you want?"

I recalled the story from leaving Beth's home to now and, to be fair, he listened, although interspersed with tuts and shakes of his head. "I'm all alone in a strange place … yes, everything is kind of familiar, but all in the wrong time. Look, I'm not born and have no idea how the world works here in 1976. I need to be able to talk this through with someone, work out why this has happened, and what I'm here for."

"Look, lad, you seem like a nice bloke but, come on, this is a bit fantastic, don't you think?"

"Okay, when you went to school, in Woburn Sands by the way, if someone would have told you that in ten days after your fifty-seventh birthday the Americans will land on the moon, you would've had the same reaction."

George leant back and picked up his pint, taking a large gulp. I took a moment to light up a cigarette; I'd earned this one. Twenty minutes had passed since we started this conversation, and we were still talking – that had to be a positive sign.

"They're not good for you, lad. If we were supposed to smoke, we'd all be born with a chimney on our head."

For the second time in as many days, I laughed, realising that at the age of forty-two, laughing felt good, really good.

"You say that to Nanna every day. I remember it's Rothmans she smokes … twenty a day, every day. Her ashtray sits on the small bookcase by her chair in the front room, and the ceiling has a small brownish, yellowish-coloured stain above her head."

"Look, lad, what's your name again?"

"Jason Apsley."

"When do you reckon you were born?"

"30th March 1977."

This was starting to sound like the conversation with *'Officer Dibble'* on Thursday. Hopefully, I wouldn't end up at the police station this time.

"Okay, Jason, you've got me intrigued, really intrigued. For the life of me, I have no way of understanding how you know some of this stuff. How much money have I got? What am I worth?"

"Nothing, well, not much, I don't think."

"Correct, lad. So, you're not after money, then?"

"No, certainly not, but to add to what I have said today, I can give you a fact for the future, which only I could know if I have actually come from the future."

"Go on."

Being a petrolhead and with my obsession with Formula One, hopefully, if my memory served me correctly, this would help. "I know you have no interest in motorsport, but it's my passion. Tomorrow, it's the Austrian Grand Prix, the first race since Niki Lauda had his accident in Germany on August 1st. John Watson, the British driver in the Ford car, will win the race. If my memory is correct, he'll lead the race from the tenth lap, and you'll get huge odds at the bookies on this because the chance of John Watson winning are very slim … but he does."

George smiled and mockingly shook his head. Then, with his eyebrow still raised, he leant back and swallowed another mouthful of beer. "Right, lad, I'm going home now, and if you want to carry on this conversation, I can't do that with Ivy around as she'll think I've taken pity on some nutter I've met in the pub and taken leave of my senses. I'll see you here at half-five on Monday, and let's see if your racing driver does his stuff … is that a deal?"

"Deal, and thank you."

George excused himself, leaving a quarter-inch of brown ale sitting in his pint mug, something he had always done, and I never quite knew why.

All things considered, I thought my attempt at convincing a rational human being that I was a time-traveller had panned out pretty well – hopefully, I'd secured a second audience. But, bloody hell, I hoped I was right about John Watson. Had I got the right bloody race or even the correct bloody year?

16

Good Night Jim-Bob

I had two days to wait until I could see my grandfather again, which seemed like a lifetime. Opting for the safe option of a cheese sandwich and a second Coke, I spent some time thinking about what I would encounter and discover over the next two days. I had to think about Monday's meeting with George – there would be no third chance, that's for sure. If I had my facts right about the Grand Prix, it could be the clincher. With a planned trip to a supermarket, I left The Three Horseshoes and headed off to get some provisions, then back to the flat to complete some planning.

Lying on the grim brown carpet, as I stepped into the equally hideous flat, was a large manila envelope. The single word, *Jason*, was written neatly on the front, but no address – hand-delivered then. I ripped it open. Inside was a thick pack of papers and a small slip of paper attached to the front via a paper clip – no Post-it notes in this era.

Hello Jason. This pack contains this year's 'O' level syllabus for chemistry and mathematics. I know you are concerned about your knowledge to be able to teach, but hopefully, this will put your mind at rest. You will see that the content is elementary for someone with your background.

Yours Sincerely

Roy

Well, it might be basic, but I could only remember being shite at Maths and Chemistry at school. I was more English, the Classics, and was damn sure this would lose me on the first page.

I settled on the sofa with a cup of coffee. The choice at the Wavy Line store was horrific for a coffee freak like me: Maxwell House or Mellow Birds. I considered Maxwell House may be the lesser of two evils – however, the coffee still tasted shite.

Reviewing the syllabus pack dragged my mind back to school. I was in the top band for all subjects – a bright kid – except for Maths. For that particular subject, I had to join the lowest band, just above the group of kids that spent most of the day gardening because the school deemed this a better option for them. Most of my maths homework scored *'Ds'*, the *'D'* denoting dunce or dumb arse probably, and invariably written in a red pen was *'See Me'*. That was an instruction from Mr Ronson for me to stand at the front whilst he humiliated me in front of the class, scribbling on the blackboard what he considered my ridiculous calculations. Of course, that put the rest of the class in a fit of hysterics. It's fair to say Mr Ronson wasn't my favourite teacher. *Tosser.*

I flipped over the front cover, Mathematics and Statistics 'O' level syllabus 1976. Oh, God.

As I read the pack, I was amazed that I could fully understand and pre-empt the following pages of the theorems for that syllabus year. I was bemused about how I could do this, as I couldn't do this stuff thirty years ago, so why was it so clear to me now? It was like the darts match on Friday night; I'd never thrown a dart in forty-two years, although I was the best player, definitely the *'Crafty Cockney'*. I seemed to have both minds fused into one. I could easily understand this pack, and I still could confidently talk about Central American seventeenth-century culture. I recited my knowledge in my mind just to make sure.

New me seemed to make friends easily; the photo frame with the picture of *other* Jason in South Africa attested to that fact. Apart from uni, I could think of very few photos of old me with friends, and it had been years since I enjoyed a good night out with mates. Friday night was great fun, and that was with a group of people I didn't even know.

New me had forgotten old Jason's OCD problem. Whilst consumed with the last two crazy days, I'd not checked any car doors, God knows how many times, and I seemed quite comfortable switching off a light without tightly squinting my eyes shut.

So, had I finally given my OCD the Spanish Archer? God, I hoped so.

Saturday drifted into Sunday, with a drive around Fairfield Town in the morning and a fill-up of four-star leaded petrol. Exhaust emissions were clearly of no concern in 1976; no wonder so many people suffered from asthma. At less than a pound a gallon, it seemed very cheap, although that might have been due to my lack of understanding of the year I was now apparently living in. Christ, I needed my grandfather's support.

I'd read the Sunday papers back-to-back and planned to watch the Austrian Grand Prix on the nineteen-inch black-and-white TV. If I were to be successful in my quest to convince George, my prediction of the race winner had to be correct.

Unfortunately, there appeared to be only three TV channels available – no dedicated sports channel, no Grand Prix live – only highlights of the race due to be aired at seven that evening.

Bloody hell, it was awful, squinting at the tiny screen. All I had to watch was The Waltons. After they'd all said goodnight to each other at the end of the show, I gave up and spent time planning Monday's meeting whilst increasingly becoming more anxious in anticipation of the Grand Prix highlights at seven.

BBC2 highlights were crap. With limited camera positions on the track and no cock-pit cameras, the highlights were centred around the finish line. Well, I wasn't watching it for the entertainment value – all that mattered was the result.

John Watson took the lead from the tenth lap, and I was now convinced he would go on to win. The only positive regarding just having the highlights to watch, as opposed to the whole race, I didn't have to wait long for the result.

With only a thirty-minute program to sit through, I had my answer – John Watson cruised to victory.

17

16th August 1976
Jessica Rabbit

Monday was all planned out, starting with a trip into town to get my 'School Teacher Uniform' which I believed should consist of a few pairs of slacks, shirts, ties and a tweed sports-jacket type thing – similar to my Ted Baker one stuck forty-three years in the future. I envisaged it would have to have leather patches on the elbows because I remember that was the standard issue for all teachers ten years in the future, so ten years back, I assumed it would be the same. Unfortunately, there was no Ted Baker shop available. However, during my Sunday drive, I'd spotted C&A and Dunn and Co. Menswear outfitters in the High Street.

Fully ready to go into town, there was a banging on the door. I hoped it wouldn't be that awful woman from next door or Roy. Jesus, I couldn't face Roy at that moment. I didn't know who he was as I'd never met him, but we were great friends, apparently.

Two young women stood there as I pulled open the door. I guess both in their early thirties – funny how as you got older, it seemed to get harder and harder to judge age. The dumpy-looking one of the two wore a police uniform, the tunic buttons straining as they fought to contain her ample chest that appeared to be trying to wriggle free. I considered there was a real possibility that, at any moment, her tunic buttons would ping off at the speed of light and embed themselves in my eye socket. I guessed her small black handbag, slung over her shoulder, could be handy to whack you with if in a difficult situation. However, no stab vest, handcuffs or utility belt that they wear today – no, not today, in the future.

The other lady – a civilian, slim, about five feet seven inches tall, dressed in a bright-blue trouser suit – did the talking.

"Good morning, sir. Sorry to bother you."

She carried on talking for a minute or so, although I heard nothing – I was consumed and mesmerised. I'd been sucked into a whirlpool of her gorgeousness which oozed from her. My brain struggled to take in her true beauty as her soft voice gently wafted around me. Every feature perfect: slim with an hourglass figure, bright emerald-green eyes, and long auburn hair – she was stunning. She smiled twice in that minute, a small slight smile, followed by a fuller one – both of which lit up her stunningly beautiful face. In front of me was the most gorgeous woman I'd ever seen, and it wasn't the one on the right with the body fighting to get out of the black tunic.

Gorgeous paused and delivered a huge smile whilst I subconsciously pulled myself to my full height, shoulders back, and stomach sucked in.

"Oh, I'm so sorry. Are you okay? Did you hear me? You look a little distracted." These were the first words I'd actually heard, delivered by this mesmerising soft voice, finished off with the cutest giggle. I stood still and said nothing. If I could have spun around and looked at myself, I think I'd have been sporting that new, gormless, open-mouthed look that I'd recently developed and now seemed to be at the mastering stage. She was Jessica Rabbit, and as in the cartoon film, my eyes must have been on stalks.

"Oh hi … no, I'm okay … sorry. So sorry, I did miss what you said … so sorry," I nervously babbled. *Pathetic.*

"Oh, okay, let me start again," she smiled – that smile.

If Gorgeous wanted me to listen, then the smile was going to have to go. I really couldn't take my eyes off her.

"As I was saying, I'm from Fairfield District Council. WPC French and I are trying to locate your neighbour, Carol Hall. Unfortunately, despite repeated visits, we've been unable to contact Miss Hall. However, it's a matter of some urgency that we are able to locate her. So, as I was saying, could you tell us if you've seen her in the past week?" Delivered with beauty, grace, a slight sideways turn of her head, and that smile.

Composing myself and feeling an urgent need to keep this conversation going for as long as possible – also wishing Frenchie would naff off – I took a moment to think.

"I'm sorry, but I don't know my neighbours very well. I did see her on Friday morning when I was going out. She was leaving her flat with a young boy ... I guess her son ... but other than that, no, I've not seen her. However, I'm out a lot ... not here much. I go out a lot, you see ... I don't stay in much, and I'm moving to a new house soon ... well, in two weeks, soon ... and I start a new job soon."

I shut my mouth abruptly. My God, I was babbling as if asking a girl out at school, which I had once, only once, and that was a painful, embarrassing memory.

'Get a grip, Tosser.'

Ignoring my mind talk, I bashed on. "Sorry," I added with a slight bow and shake of my head as if to convey that I knew I was a tosser, as I guessed she was thinking it. "Look, sorry that wasn't helpful, but I can get her to call you if I see her. Will that help?"

"Oh, that will be great, but could you call me when Miss Hall returns rather than asking her to call? I'm aware that is a little strange, but as you can see, I have a WPC with me today, so the matter is quite urgent."

Gorgeous outstretched her hand, which I presumed was an offer of a handshake. However, an embarrassing moment ensued because the handshake wasn't on offer. She was handing me her business card and not the offer of physical contact. The ensuing fumble of fingers resulted in the business card floating down to the shit-brown carpet, leaving both of us a little embarrassed. Gorgeous took the lead to resolve the embarrassment and offered the handshake, which I took. The physical feeling of her skin sent tingles up to my head, each hair follicle alert and goosebumps engulfed my body. I was sure every hair on my body would now be standing to attention as if Frenchie had just Tasered me. That said, I didn't think she was carrying one in her handbag, which I presumed was purely for clubbing bank robbers into submission. Frenchie hadn't moved a muscle during the whole encounter, which, for my eye health, I was grateful for.

"Jenny Lawrence, Child Services, Fairfield District Council," she said, with that smile.

"Apsley, Jason Apsley. I will be in touch … definitely."

Jenny and Frenchie walked off towards the stairs on the left side of the block. Jenny taking the lead, Frenchie blocking my view. I studied the business card and held it tight, as tight as you would if it were the winning lottery ticket and you were about to collect a life-changing sum. Jenny Lawrence could be life-changing. Could love at first sight happen? Well, certainly not for me, never, but those few minutes with Jenny may have changed my belief. Disappointment flooded me, realising she was probably married. No, I hadn't spotted a wedding ring. A long-term boyfriend, then? Maybe, well, of course, she was amazing. Jenny could surely take her pick. Of course, that's assuming she wanted her pick – very presumptuous of me.

Anyway, I must have come across as a right knob. I looked at my attire – Queen Night at the Opera tour t-shirt and what were now fast becoming dirty jeans – could have been better, a lot better. I was sure she didn't look twice at me, but I planned to contact her again whether that scraggy woman next door showed up or not.

As I now had to get through life without a smartphone – something I was surprised I didn't miss as much as I thought I would – I couldn't add Jenny's number to my contact list. So, I made a note of her number in my reporter's notebook and underlined it a few times, then carefully placed the precious card in my wallet. Time to go shopping and get that teacher's school uniform sorted.

Bounding down the concrete stairs, two at a time – the same ones Jenny had used a few minutes ago – I was determined to feel optimistic about Jenny, not letting negative old Jason take hold. Yes, okay, she was a few years younger than me, or maybe ten, but I could ask her out for dinner. The worst that could happen was she'd say no, or laugh; oh poo, she might laugh, but I had to ask. There would never be another Jenny in this world or any world for me, which I was clear on from only a few minutes of meeting her.

I stopped at the bottom and paused as the name Carol Hall popped into my head. Beth's surname was Hall, her mother lived on the Broxworth Estate, and Beth had those four horrific years here before going to that bloody children's home. 1976 – Beth was born September 12th 1976, and that Carol woman was heavily pregnant – could it be, could it? Beth never mentioned a brother, not that I could recall, and that Carol woman had a young boy with her, so not sure how that fitted in, but this was really spooky.

I needed to nudge my grandfather into believing my ridiculous story because these rather annoying discussions with myself were starting to drive me nuts.

18

Abracadabra

Sitting in the Three Horseshoes waiting for George, nursing a Coke, no straw, I hoped that John Watson's victory would be enough to nudge him closer to believing my somewhat ridiculous claim of being a time-traveller. However, I knew it was a massive step for anyone. It was for me – and I was living it.

The morning had been successful, and I was surprised that C&A far exceeded my expectations because the last venture to that shop was with my grandmother to buy my school uniform. So, purchasing wearable clothes was a pleasant surprise. I managed to pick up some shirts, although with way too big collars, and some plain t-shirts. *Other* Jason seemed to have only band tour t-shirts, and I needed something more me – well, old me – clothes-wise that is. There was very little else of old me that I'd any desire to hang on to.

Dunn and Co. had also been a success, and I'd acquired three jackets for school, all with leather elbow patches. Overall, I'd spent a fortune, well, a fortune for 1976 – nearly one hundred and fifty quid – but I'd now established I was reasonably loaded, so what the hell. I enjoyed the retail therapy. However, nothing I'd purchased today, I would have bought last week. This '70s fashion was not for me, but I had no choice in the matter.

I'd spent some time wandering around, looking in the shops and marvelling at how cheap everything appeared to be. Lisa and I had holidayed in Florida in 2006. The dollar rate was almost two dollars to the pound, and we'd gone mad in the outlet stores, literally buying everything we could lay our hands on. Fortunately, we had travelled light on the way out, but we had four new massive suitcases full of clothes coming home. I'm not sure I wore many of them, but the buying was fun.

Situated next to Midland Bank, which I could remember regularly visiting with my grandparents on shopping trips, there was a small shop with a 'New Opening' banner across the top of the front window. A group of young teenage boys had crowded around the shop front, so I ambled up to see what the attraction was. Oh, yes, I remembered this, it was Athena. I used to go there and casually flick through all the posters on the big hanging racks. In reality, I was longingly looking at the nude women posters and trying to pluck up the courage to buy one. Of course, I never did because my grandmother would never have allowed that. So, as a pubescent teenager, I settled for just looking.

The group of lads moved on, all smiling and nudging each other. As the view of the shop front became clear, there in the window was a new poster just released. A poster which took pride of place on my bedroom wall at uni twenty years from now. A blonde woman on a tennis court with her white tennis dress slightly lifted to reveal one cheek of her bare bottom. I stood and stared, then stepped aside to let an elderly couple walk past arm in arm.

"That's disgusting! Don't you dare look at that, Stan," the elderly lady belligerently instructed. I presumed the obedient Stan to be her husband. However, I continued to gawp, the poster reminding me of the good times at uni.

Daydream over – it was time for my second meeting with my grandfather, as he was on time and punctual.

"Evening, George," the barman shouted, pulling his pint as if telepathic and knowing he was about to come through the door.

"Just a half tonight, Brian, not stopping for long," George replied, a real purpose in his voice. I couldn't decide if that was a good or bad omen for our meeting. I nodded in his direction and patiently waited for him to join me.

"Thanks for seeing me again. I know this all sounds completely nuts, but I do appreciate it, Mr Sutton."

"Ah, what's happened to all this Grandad nonsense then? Now it's Mr Sutton, eh?" George fired back at me.

I sighed. "You are my grandfather, but this is awkward, so I plumped for Mr Sutton … to be respectful, I guess."

"You guess, or you know, lad? What is it? What are we guessing then?"

Language had changed over forty years – *Hello* had moved to *Hi* or *Hey*, and *I believe so* became *I guess so* – I needed to remember this otherwise I would stick out like a sore thumb; another reason I needed my grandfather to keep me on track in 1976.

"No, it's 'I know', not 'guess'," I responded, now concerned this was a poor start to our meeting.

George didn't seem to be in the greatest of moods, which was unusual because he spent the vast majority of his life in a happy state. I don't mean high on magic mushrooms; I mean happy and contented, but I guess we could class this as an unusual situation. There I go again with, *'guess'*. Not really knowing now how to address him, Grandad, George, Mr Sutton, or even Mr Grumpy, I pushed on regardless. "Look, there's part of my account of the past few days that I didn't go through with you on Saturday. It happened last Friday morning, and it's about Stephen, but—"

"Yes, lad, I'm aware," George interrupted. "My Joan told me all about it yesterday and how a gallant Mr Apple had saved the day. I agreed with her; it was a very odd name. So, out of curiosity, I asked her to describe this Mr Apple." he stated, waving an accusing finger in my direction. "The way my Joan described him, I'm thinking that it must have been you, lad?" His raised eyebrow suggested this was a question rather than a statement.

"Yes, that was me. I just wanted to see them. I wanted to know they were okay as there's stuff in my past about Mum …

err, Joan and Neil that I need to talk to you about, and I know I'm going to need your help."

"Well, well, lad, I have to say that I'm truly grateful for your actions on Friday. My Joan was convinced you saved Stephen's life, and apparently, you were injured in the whole affair?" George seemed to be softening now, returning to his usual congenial self.

"Yes, a bang on the leg, bruised, but nothing serious."

Taking a gulp of brown ale, George leaned back in his chair and fell silent for a moment. I also seemed to have lost my train of thought.

"Evening, George," a middle-aged lady called across from the bar. She was perched on a wooden barstool beside a middle-aged man who waved.

"Is that your son with you? He's a good-looking chap and looks like you, George … spitting image, I'd say. Nice to meet you. I'm Dawn, and this is my husband, Dennis." All I could think was they looked like June Whitfield and Eric Sykes.

"No, just a … just someone I know," George offered back.

"Hi, I'm Jason," I waved.

Eric Sykes look-alike held up his glass of beer in what I assumed was a cheers gesture. "DD, Double Diamond, DD, Dawn and Dennis," he chuckled.

More silence, the air thickening between us, thick enough it felt as if I could reach out and grab handfuls of the stuff. I opened my mouth to speak, but George raised his right index finger, which I instantly knew meant I had to be quiet. He just stared at me, picked up his glass and took another gulp, finishing his ale, his eyes still firmly fixed on me – I was wondering if it had become a blinking game.

I risked opening my mouth. Well, hell, I wasn't ten years old, I was a grown man, for Christ sake. That finger-in-the-air stuff was to keep dogs in check.

"Another," I offered and reached for his glass. He nodded.

After being treated to a short life-run-through by the June and Eric lookalikes at the bar, I returned with his half-pint of mild ale and a pint of Skol for me. It was strange, but I enjoyed the chat for a few minutes with them both. Of course, old Jason would have turned away or pulled out his phone to feign a call just to avoid talking. God, old me was a proper, miserable tosser.

George leaned forward and raised his head, staring again. "Well, lad, your man Watson won the Grand Prix race then, and I did check the odds. They were huge. I should have put a bet on. I'd considered you'd rigged the race, but that was even more ridiculous than your story."

"Yes, he did. I absolutely knew he would, and he led from the tenth lap," I replied with an air of triumphant achievement.

"Right, lad, I have some questions for you. I've made a list, so let's see how you get on with these. By my reckoning, you should know all the answers if you are who you claim to be."

"Okay, but Christ, I hope they're not too detailed; it's thirty years ago for me," I replied, a little concerned about facing a test – *focus, Apsley, focus.*

George applied his spectacles pulled from his inside jacket pocket. Thick black-rimmed glasses, they were the height of fashion again – you know what I mean, in the future, not now, well yes, now. Oh, this time-travel stuff was so exhausting.

The questions came thick and fast, as if I had two minutes in the black Mastermind chair with Magnus Magnusson machine-gunning the questions at me.

'Name? — Jason Apsley.'

'Occupation? — Mining engineer and sheet metal Brand Executive, oh, and yes, a teacher.'

'Chosen specialist subject? — The life and times of George Sutton 1912 to 1976-ish.'

'Your time starts — now.'

"Ivy smokes what brand of cigarettes?"

"Rothmans Blue." Yes – an easy one. I almost wanted a bell to ding for the correct answer. What I couldn't afford was too many 'uh urrs' for incorrect ones – I had to perform well.

"I planted a tree in the garden in '69. What type of tree is it?"

"Crab apple." Two out of two, come on.

"I played semi-professional football from 1932 to 1935. For what team?"

"Bedford Town." Three out of three, I was on a roll here.

George had prepared thirty questions, and I was sure I had confidently hit twenty-nine correct answers. If this were Bullseye, I would have won a speedboat – there would be no *'This is what you could have won,'* moment from Jim Bowen. I would be a winner – especially with my newly acquired *'Crafty Cockney'* darts skills.

"How did you get on, lad?" George asked, removing his glasses.

'Jason Apsley, you have scored twenty-nine points with no passes.'

"Only one wrong. I just can't remember the name of your cousin who lives in Brighton, but the rest was spot on," I said, with an equal measure of relief and confidence.

"Oh, okay, well, I don't know how you did it, but yes, you scored twenty-nine out of thirty."

"Look, George, I'm your grandson … that's how I know this stuff." I could sense my eyes had started to water. Jesus, I was about to blub again. But I guess I was so desperate for him to believe me and could now almost feel the scepticism that appeared to ooze from him.

"I don't know, lad, I just don't know. You're asking a lot here, you know, but your knowledge of my life is as good as my own. For the life of me, I can't work out how you would know unless … well, you know … unless."

"I know," I responded in a whisper, so quietly I could hardly hear my own voice.

"I know that my Joan told me when Stephen was born that they couldn't decide what to call him. It was a toss-up between Stephen or Jason."

I nodded but had nothing left in my armoury to convince him. I knew significant events that were coming up, but nothing over the next few weeks. I could tell him that James Hunt will win the next Grand Prix in Holland, but that was two weeks away. Too long, I needed my grandfather to believe me now.

George sat up, grinned, and folded his arms across his chest, looking pleased with himself. "Tell me what happens tomorrow."

"Hell, I don't know, it's before I was born! There's nothing that stands out in history that I can remember."

"It's Stephen's birthday. He'll be having a party, but you should know that, shouldn't you?" He responded, raising his eyebrow and pointing his finger at me as if he were Lord Kitchener in the '*We-Want-You*' posters.

"Oh, hell, it's the 17th of August. Yes, that's Stephen's birthday. I always forget his bloody birthday."

Well, the truth was I always forgot everyone's birthday, as twat me usually couldn't be bothered to make an effort. I'd always remembered Lisa's because the fall-out of not was potentially horrific. I'd placed a reminder in my phone one month out, and then every week leading up to it, which ensured I remembered and maintained a quiet life. Lisa was already convinced I was the coldest human being ever born, so I made an effort once a year. Everyone else just had to put up with my lack of interest that I didn't bother with birthdays. Beth was okay about it, although Stephen had sent a text last year, a week after his, and it said—

Thanks, tosser, for my birthday card … not! Guess your phone is restricted to domestic calls only. Yes, I had a lovely birthday last week, thanks. Hope you're still alive.'

I read it and deleted it. I always receive three cards on my birthday: Lisa, Stephen and Beth. No presents. This year, it was only two cards. I guessed next year, in my new world, I would hit zero.

"Ah-ha, yes! I can tell you exactly what's going to happen tomorrow. It's Stephen's fifth birthday, and although it's a few months before I was born, an event happens that is retold and retold over the years. Mum hires a magician, and the party is going well. Ten or so kids are all sitting on the carpet in the lounge when the magician performs the old 'rabbit in a hat' trick, and he requires an assistant to help him wave the wand to say abracadabra. The problem occurs when he accidentally chooses the wrong kid to assist, as it should have been Stephen. That all led to Stephen having a complete fit and storming off to his bedroom. Unfortunately, Mum and Dad couldn't persuade him to come out again until the party was over. It was a disaster. It was quite normal for Stephen to have tantrums and fits, and from a young age your nickname for him was – '*Fits*'."

I leaned back in my chair and lit up a cigarette. Yes, I had the evidence, the irrefutable proof that I was who I said I was. George also leaned back in his chair, drained his glass except for the last quarter-inch of ale, and shook his head before offering a wry smile. He placed the glass carefully on the heavily ringed Watney's Red Barrel beer mat and chuckled.

"Well, lad. Yes, I do call him Fits. However, I'm amazed you could know that. And if you're right about tomorrow, I may well have to start believing you … then we have a lot to talk about."

"Yes, yes, that's fantastic!" My bum had risen out of my seat as I stretched up to hug him.

"Steady on, lad. No need for that silly business."

"Christ, sorry," I replied, now feeling somewhat embarrassed.

"I often grab a pint on the way home from work, so let's meet Wednesday at the same time. Now, I must get home before Ivy sends out a search party. Also, Mr Sutton won't do, and I'm not sure of the Grandad thing at the moment, so it's George, okay?"

"Yes, that's very okay," I replied with a massive sigh of relief. "Thank you, George, thank you," I added, perhaps a little too enthusiastically.

We shook hands, and then he was gone. I had secured a third audience, which was a real result – Christ, I hoped Stephen threw a fit at his party.

Finishing my beer and feeling enthusiastic, I thought of Jessica Rabbit. I thought of Jenny.

19

17th August 1976

Frank Bruno

"Oh hi, err hello, good morning. Can I speak to Jenny Lawrence, please?"

"Hold please, caller," the voice at the other end responded.

The line went quiet, no music, just crackles whilst I waited to be connected – hopefully. I stood in the hallway holding the retro cream handset tightly to my ear, my left-hand fingers crossed, and through my socks, I tried to cross my toes for extra luck.

The noise from the flat next door had been deafening that morning. The shouting from Carol and a booming male voice had been going on for at least half an hour. Occasionally, I heard the boy crying, usually after a volley of obscenities were thrown his way by either adult. The gist of the shouting appeared to be regarding money, or lack of, as I believe most arguments were in every home, whatever the year, money was always top of any league table of causes of domestic disputes.

I'd slept late that morning. In fact, I'd slept soundly after what I hoped had been a successful meeting with George. Then, at a little after nine, next door's front door took a fist hammering. It was that loud I was convinced it was my door; it certainly wasn't like the gentle knocking delivered by Jenny yesterday.

I'd leapt out of bed and spotted through the net curtains a large man hammering on Carol's front door, his arm swinging back and forth as he pummelled it to death. Without question, if he used that force on Carol, she would need a trip to A&E, and if it were aimed at the little boy, I dreaded to think. So, a perfect excuse had presented itself to ring Jenny about my neighbour, for selfish reasons, of course.

However, as the altercation seemed to become more violent, I considered I might need to ring the police – although, in my current situation, I just fancied keeping a low profile from that lot at the moment.

"Good morning, Jenny Lawrence speaking. Can I ask who is calling?"

Wow, that voice! So smooth, silky and sexy. I imagined her voice would work well on a sex chatline, not that I'd ever used those services. However, just a few words from Jenny and you'd be swallowed up, hooked in and, whilst being charged by the minute, I reckoned you'd rack up a bill the size of the national debt in no time.

I squeezed my eyes shut, toes and fingers tightly crossed, *don't fuck it up, Apsley.* My thoughts were demanding a good performance.

"Oh … err, hey … err, hello Jenny … hello … hi." *Fucking useless, absolutely, fucking useless, don't fuck it up, I said, and what do you do Apsley … you fuck it up. Tosser.*

"Sorry, hello again, Jenny," *Better Apsley, better … keep going.*

"It's Jason here, Jason Apsley. We spoke yesterday regarding Carol Hall and to call you if she returned to her flat."

"Oh yes, Mr Apsley, how can I help?"

"Well, she is in the flat now, Carol Hall that is, and having a blazing row with a man who turned up about half an hour ago. To be honest, I think the police should attend. Shall I call 999 as well?"

"Oh, right, thank you, Mr Apsley. We will take it from here."

"Jenny, I was wondering—" but Jenny had interrupted me just when I'd got to the real reason for calling, well, the important reason for me.

"Goodbye, and thank you," she sang.

The line went dead; she'd hung up. All was quiet apart from the shouting, thumping through Carol's flat as if the walls were a pulsating Marshall speaker banging out the noise at over a hundred decibels.

I stood and listened for what seemed an age – at least five minutes – whilst I still held the phone receiver in my hand. Now I was seriously considering that calling the police was the right option, even though Jenny had said they would take it from here, whatever that meant. I certainly wasn't going to let Jenny turn up and intervene on her own, although she may turn up with Frenchie, or she might not turn up at all. Perhaps someone else from that department would attend instead of her. Then, I'd have no real excuse to call her again.

After another few minutes, the noise moved to a new level, with a step up from swearing and insults to flying objects. I could tell the other side of my bedroom wall was the recipient of what was being lobbed at some considerable force. Christ, oh fuck, she was heavily pregnant, and it was just possible that bloody awful woman next door was Beth's mother. At that very point, Beth could be in the firing line of an object thrown by that madman. I had to act and call the police now.

In a split second, I changed my mind and let go of the receiver like 'Dropping the Mic.' Then, I yanked open my front door and hammered on Carol's door. I wasn't sure it was as loud as the madman's hammering, but the side of my hand started to hurt.

What I hadn't considered was what the hell I intended to do if the door opened and he confronted me. From what I'd seen, he was a lot younger, had a good two stone of muscle, and six inches reach advantage on me. It would be like putting Barry McGuigan up against Frank Bruno – although, in reality, Barry McGuigan could have flattened me with one punch.

The door wrenched open, swinging back, hitting the wall, causing the plaster to flake down to the floor. The giant of a man filled the door space. At about six feet three inches tall, with long shoulder-length black hair, a missing front tooth – the third on the left – black leather bikers' jacket, and a blue swallow tattoo next to his right eye, I guess he didn't appear the friendliest of chaps.

I froze.

"What the fok do you want?" he barked in a heavy Irish accent.

From behind him, I couldn't see Carol, but I could hear her. "Just fuck off, Fin! Fuck off. Fucking leave me alone!"

He turned, grabbed Carol's hair, and punched her full in the face. Now, as he had moved sideways, I could see past him and the full horror of his actions. Carol sank to the floor with no hands out to break the fall. The poor girl literally went straight down like a felled tree, hitting the carpet, her head bouncing up and down. I thought he'd probably killed her. Also, Beth, if that unborn baby was who I thought it might be.

The only physical confrontation I'd ever been involved in was that fight at school, and the result was a foregone conclusion, even before John Hales had decided he fancied punching my lights out. So, the odds of me surviving the impending altercation with this massive bloke without severe or life-threatening injuries were very low.

The thought that the unborn child could be Beth, and she'd now been potentially fatally injured inside Carol's womb, brought something to the surface that I wasn't aware was within me. Raising my right leg, I brought the full force of my heel down on the top side of his right knee. The giant screamed before he crumpled to the floor, his leg now at an odd angle, giving it the appearance of an incorrectly assembled mannequin – he wasn't going to move.

Don, the man with no body, peered around his front doorframe. "Nice one, Jason, nice one. Well done, son."

Barrelling along the concrete corridor came Frenchie. She could move at a pace, arms swinging side to side, her upper body fighting hard for freedom from her tunic – eight ferrets in a bag came to mind. I suspected at the pace she was moving, she would need a reasonable length of the corridor to slow to a stop – an oil tanker scenario – but with some graceful agility, she swiftly nudged me out of the way and grabbed hold of Fin by his jacket.

"Fin Booth, I might have guessed. You're coming down the station; there's a couple of outstanding warrants for you, sunshine."

It looked almost comical. Short, rotund Frenchie appeared to have put the fear of God into him – she clearly knew how to handle herself. Peering through the hallway, I could see Carol had sat up. Blood was pouring down her face, and she'd likely acquired a broken nose as well as a fat lip. However, I was more concerned about any potential internal injuries.

"She's pregnant. She needs medical assistance," I shouted.

Frenchie, now regaining her breath, had Fin pinned to the floor. "Yes, sir, they're on their way. I saw it all as I arrived and called it in."

No-body-man Don had ventured out and was standing next to me. He did actually have a body, which was clad in blue-striped brushed-cotton pyjamas. "He's a bloody hero, you know, a bloody hero! Took that swine down nice and easy like, needs a bloody medal."

"You okay, Carol?" I shouted down the hall. Dumb question, I know. I wasn't sure if I expected Carol to reply with *"Oh yes, just dandy, mate,"* but it was all that came to mind. However, I was more concerned about the unborn child.

"Bloody hero," Don repeated.

"Who's a hero?"

A new player had arrived at the scene, and I knew that voice. I spun around, and there she was, right next to me, wearing an above-the-knee blue A-line dress, those sparkling green eyes, and that smile.

114

"This lad is. He's a bloody hero," Don repeated whilst pointing in my direction.

"Well, Mr Apsley, well, well," Jenny commented, as she stepped past me and approached Carol. Two ambulance crew followed Jenny in, and Frenchie had a whimpering Fin pinned to the floor on the landing outside Don's flat, where she'd miraculously managed to drag him.

"When you've attended to the woman, you'd better look at this lump. No hurry, though. I'm enjoying the moans coming out of his mouth," Frenchie called after the ambulance crew.

"Is she going to be okay? She's pregnant, you know?" I shouted, stating the obvious, but I was ignored as the ambulance crew continued their work.

Jenny knelt near the kitchen, talking to the young boy. Everything looked in control, but I was seriously concerned about Carol – well, to be honest, about the potential Beth inside her. I stepped back out of the way to let everyone get on with what they needed to do.

Frenchie shot me a look whilst her knee was firmly in place, crushing Fin's spine. "Don't you go far, sir. I need a word when I've got rid of this lump."

"Okay." That's all I could manage to respond – my mind was consumed with concern about Beth.

The ambulance crew took Carol balanced on a stretcher. Two more officers arrived and relieved Frenchie's knee from Fin's lower back as I watched Jenny walk off with the young boy hand in hand.

"Gonna need a statement, sir."

"Yes, of course, of course. Do we do that now, or shall I come to the station?" I asked, still gazing at Jenny, who disappeared down the corridor, whilst keeping my eyes away from the direct firing line of Frenchie's tunic buttons, which looked even more likely, after her exertions, to fire off like a couple of button-shaped synchronised Exocet ballistic missiles.

"No, a run through now, so I can make some notes in my book will do, and then if we need to, you can make a full statement later at the station."

I delivered a blow by blow account. Frenchie repeatedly nodded and scribbled in her book. She didn't look up until I'd fully recounted my version of the events.

"Okay, that'll do for now." As she turned and walked off, she glanced back. "Be careful, Mr Apsley. Fin Booth is not someone you should be on the wrong side of. Just be careful."

Whilst mulling over the morning's events, I considered visiting the hospital to establish what was happening with Carol and Beth, assuming she was the unborn child.

In the space of four days, I'd intervened in two events that involved Stephen and Beth, the two people I cared about, and I had put myself in danger for both. Old Jason just wouldn't have done that. He would have stayed on the sidelines, like never helping a stranger if they fell over or avoiding the homeless guy asking for food. No, he would have walked on to avoid getting involved – that would be his mindset.

I, the new Jason – still old Jason but living *other* Jason's life – had got involved, and what effect had I had? Was this another kind of reverse 'butterfly effect', and would both Stephen and Beth have been dead in the space of four days if I hadn't intervened?

Was this why I was here? And who or what put me here? Again, those same unanswered questions.

20

Nazis

"No, I have told you already, you are not related, so no, you can't see Miss Hall, and I can't give you any information regarding her condition. I have been quite clear on this matter … three times now."

I knew the hospital's admission receptionist was only doing her job. Still, I was sure they must undergo years of training to be so officious. She refused to give any information and delivered it like a Nazi prison guard with half the humour.

Defeated and concerned about Carol, I slumped into a chair whilst pondering my next move. I mused that the waiting room at Fairfield General hadn't changed much in forty years. In the future, the new front desk was fully screened off – unlike the current one, which I could have reached over and strangled the Nazi receptionist if I was so inclined. The chairs were new in the future, but comfort hadn't improved in those forty years. These chairs I could pick up and throw – something I felt like doing – not like the ones screwed to the floor in 2019. As I sat there despondent, I noticed a woman in that blue A-line dress strolling down the corridor towards the exit. She stopped, turned, and smiled at me.

"Mr Apsley, hello. Why are you here? Did you get hurt this morning?"

"No, no, I'm fine. I just wanted to find out if Carol is okay. As you know, she's pregnant, but as I'm not next of kin, they won't allow me to see her or give out any information."

"Oh, I see. I didn't realise you were close, you and Miss Hall."

"Oh, no … no … not at all, but as she's my neighbour … well, until I move in a couple of weeks, that is … I just thought I'd do the right thing and check that she's alright after all that happened this morning."

"Yes, it's dreadful. That man! Well, he is no man hitting a woman like that."

"No, I agree, a real monster. A huge bloke like that hitting a woman was shocking … he was as big as Frank Bruno."

"I hear you were quite the hero this morning as well." She moved her hips from side to side, the dress swishing around, smiling with her head slightly on the side.

Was she flirting with me? I had no idea because I was pretty useless at reading signs from women. Even if they wrote in big letters, *I LOVE YOU*, I would probably miss it or analyse it to see if there was a different meaning.

When I'd been seeing Lisa for about six months, she'd saved up and bought a crash helmet signed by Michael Schumacher – the helmet he'd worn on the final race of the 1996 season. She'd attended an auction house in London and bid for it, paying a bloody fortune. I loved it, but all I could say was, *'Why did you buy me this?'* Lisa had replied, *'Christ, man, you're so stupid, because I love you, idiot.'* And yes, I guess that was obvious to any normal person but not short-sighted, cold-hearted Jason – I missed the signs as usual. Of course, that also worked the other way around. When nearing the end of our marriage, Lisa found someone without a cold heart – I didn't see those signs either.

"Oh, and who is Frank Bruno?" Jenny asked.

"Bruno, he's a big bloke I know … well, know-ish … kind of." That's about the best I could come up with to cover my time-travel mistake.

"Look, I don't suppose you could find out how Carol is and the baby? You know, from a professional point of view." My total focus was Beth.

Jenny chewed her lip, staring up at me with her hands on her hips. "Yes, of course, but I need to be able to trust you. The information didn't come from me, okay?"

"Sure, thank you."

Jenny swished off to the desk and swished a bit more in front of the Nazi receptionist. No, she wasn't flirting earlier. This was her usual walk, gorgeous walk. Unless she was flirting with the Nazi as well – no, probably not.

It took quite a while because the Nazi had several calls to make to obtain the information which Jenny had requested. Eventually, Jenny seemed to have acquired it, and then she swished her way over to me as I sat in the waiting area.

"Let's take a walk outside, Jason. It is Jason, isn't it?"

"Yes, it is. Is she okay?" I asked, as I sprung out of my seat.

"Let's walk outside first. Too many other people in here. Walls have ears, as they say."

I expected Jenny would deliver bad news. Otherwise, she would have just stated that Carol and the baby were fine. I thought earlier I'd saved Beth by intervening. However, by hammering on the door, I considered I may have caused her death. Would that animal of a bloke not have hit Carol if I hadn't been standing there? Christ, I thought, what have I done?

As we exited the front door, I held it open for an elderly couple shuffling in whilst Jenny marched on ahead. The elderly man plodded along, one foot in front of the other as if walking a tightrope. *Come on, come on, come on for Christ sake*, I screamed in my head, whilst trying to relax and smile. Trotting up to Jenny, I grabbed her arm and yanked her around to face me.

"What's going on? What's with all the cloak and dagger?" I blurted.

"Excuse me, what do you think you're doing?" Jenny exclaimed, glaring at my hand on her arm.

I pulled my hand away and performed a kind of one-handed surrender. "I'm sorry, I'm sorry, but what's happened? What did they tell you?"

"I should think so! Look, I shouldn't be saying anything. But as you seem obsessed with Miss Hall, I'll tell you. She's okay, just a bit battered and bruised. However, there's some concern regarding the baby, so they're keeping her in."

"What does concern mean? Is the baby going to be okay?"

"I don't know any more, and I shouldn't be telling you this. I must say, you're acting as if you're the damn father! I think this chat is over." With that, she spun around and marched off, still swishing but in an assertive way rather than a flirty manner, although still very sexy.

"Jenny, Jenny, I'm sorry," I shouted, but she'd walked off. "I'm not the father, I'm not, just concerned," I added, but she was too far away to hear me.

Oh, bloody brilliant, Apsley, you total prick. What's the matter with me? This morning I planned to ask her to go on a date, and now I'd pissed her off. Also, I'd probably convinced her that I was the father of Carol Hall's unborn child – brilliant, just fucking brilliant.

Although worried, there was nothing I could do at this point and, standing here, I wasn't going to find anything out. Today was turning to shit. All I needed now was for Stephen to behave himself at his party this afternoon and I was screwed.

A blue Ford Granada careered into the car park and parked about twenty feet away – well, more abandoned than parked. A big bloke and two women jumped out and marched towards the entrance. As they passed me, I caught part of their conversation.

"Mark, you better get that foking wanker who done Fin's leg in."

Oh, great, the day just got better.

21

The Good - The Evil - The Happy - The Sad.

Retreating to the flat to lick my wounds, I felt the need to hide away for the rest of the day. For the best part of five days I'd been in this new world, and with so much that had happened, I needed to take stock, shut the front door and hide for a few hours. After wandering from room to room, which in this temporary shithole didn't take long, I focused on more practical tasks to take my mind off this morning's events.

My planned house move was, thank God, in just over a week, so thumbing through the Yellow Pages, I searched for a removal firm. I guessed I'd need to take all the crap from the flat, although most of it needed to go to the recycling centre if such a thing existed.

Back in my old world, one particular operative at the recycling centre used to check everything I took up there, shouting across the bins, *"That doesn't go in there. That goes in the wood bin."* Officious tosser. He caught me every time I tried to dump everything in the non-recycling bins. He must have been trained at the same Nazi school as the hospital receptionist, or he could well have been her son, trained by mummy on how to be a right wanker.

Old me would have just googled removal firms or asked Alexa, although most things I asked her, I got the *"Sorry, I don't know that one,"* – fucking useless thing. When frustrated with her answers, I asked her, *"Alexa, why are you so fucking shit?"* she replied, *"I am learning all the time."* At least, it was a different answer.

Now I was starting to sound like old Jason again. I didn't like old Jason, and the guy at the recycling centre wasn't the wanker – I was the wanker. He was just trying to ensure wankers like me recycled, so we reduced the requirement for landfill sites, and together we saved the planet for future generations. Lisa had moaned at me daily about recycling, *"That empty milk carton goes in the white recycling bin, not the silver bin. Why can't you just do it? You really piss me off,"* I recall her saying.

Gary, at work, had imposed a plastic ban about two years ago following the Blue Planet TV series. No plastic water bottles were allowed in the workplace, a water dispenser was installed, and he bought every employee a metal flask. Everyone at Waddington's Steel wanted to get on board and play their part, apart from one – yes, it was me. For the first few months, every day, I'd taken in my plastic Evian bottle and prominently placed it on my desk for all to see. I wasn't going to be part of that recycling shit, and who cared? I had no kids, so I couldn't give a flying fuck if the oceans were full of plastic and a turtle had a straw suck up its nose. Even when challenged and it started to feel awkward, I stopped bringing the plastic bottle in but filled my flask with Evian before going into the office. Yes, I'd been a right selfish wanker.

No one liked me much. Yes, Beth forgave me, but no one actually liked me. I wasn't a particularly nice person, and now someone, or something, had given me a second chance, a chance to be different, a chance to be liked, a chance to have friends, and maybe a chance to find love.

Jenny popped into my mind. I'd only met her three times, and we'd only spoken a handful of words to each other, but I had never met anyone like her. After today, she probably thought I was like any other typical bloke from the Broxworth Estate, smashing a bloke's knee – although for good reason – and then forcefully grabbing her arm because everything had to be my way. I would have to ring and apologise. I couldn't let Jenny drift from me and had to show her I was worth getting to know. If I did that and she wasn't interested, well, so be it, but I had to try. I had to stop the negative *'fuck off world'* attitude and grasp this opportunity before I just settled in to being old me, living in a different time.

There were about seven removal firms in the local area. I was aware it was short notice, but the contents of the flat would fit into a small lorry, so I hoped that one of these firms could accommodate my move. So, I plumped for Sharps Removals. They had a small advertisement, not one of the half-page ones, and not a tiny entry that you'd need a magnifying glass in order to read it. Also, a previous tenant had circled the advert with a red pen.

I dialled the number.

"Yes, Mr Apsley, we are due at your flat on Friday the twenty-seventh, as agreed two weeks ago. We've sent you written confirmation, and we spoke on the telephone as well. Don't you remember? Also, one of our chaps dropped the tea chests around for you to start packing about ten days ago," the chap at Sharps Removals stated.

So, *I* had circled the advert – well, *other* me had circled it. I guessed this would be the problem I would have for some time. I had forty-two years of history that I knew absolutely nothing about, and it would probably catch me out – constantly. With that desire to learn more about the new me, I settled down to sift through the rest of the paperwork and stuff in the flat.

My grandparents would have been at Stephen's party by now, and hopefully, Stephen would have thrown a fit and retired to his bedroom. If so, my grandfather would now be in a state of realisation that I was who I said I was. Well, I hoped so.

"Stay positive, Apsley. Why not try glass half full for a change?" I muttered.

Apart from a few banging front doors and the occasional burst of foul language, the landing outside my flat stayed reasonably quiet throughout the afternoon. I remembered that woman's comment at the hospital to the big bloke called Mark, *'You better get that foker who done Fin's leg.'*

I was now concerned that I might have to face this Mark bloke very soon, although Fin may not have noticed where I'd come from. I also hoped he couldn't remember my face. Even so, I did jump a bit when I heard a few loud bangs from slamming doors up and down the outside landing.

The bottom drawer of the sideboard yielded my passport: a thick black book. Mr Jason Apsley had been written in the white window at the top. The visa stamp pages were nearly full of mostly South African entry stamps, and it appeared I had regularly returned to the UK. The picture inside was me, well, Noel Edmonds lookalike me, and I was born in Hackney on the 30th of March 1934. The back page stated my next of kin was Mary Apsley, my mother. Of course, I didn't know who Mary Apsley was. As far as I was concerned, Joan Apsley was my mother, but perhaps I had another mother in London. The super tough question was who would be born next March to Joan Apsley? Or was there no baby due, and that birth in my old world had moved to Mary Apsley in 1934?

"Christ, Christ almighty," I exclaimed. I would have lived through the Second World War. I was probably even evacuated to a farm in Dorset. I smiled, perhaps living with Angela Lansbury, the trainee witch in my very own version of Bedknobs and Broomsticks, with that cat, Cosmic Creepers and that spell *'Treguna mekoides trecorum satis dee'*. Maybe it was Miss Eglantine Price who had delivered a spell that had put me in 1976. Stephen and I had loved that film, running around the house casting spells and pretending to be floating through the deep blue sea on Mum and Dad's bed. Stephen must have been ten or eleven then; kids seemed to have had a greater innocence thirty-odd years ago compared to today – well, future today.

Further rummaging revealed some American Express charge card bills and bank statements. My bank balance as of last month was a little over six-thousand pounds – I was seriously okay for money. At the back of the drawer, I discovered a brown, crumpled envelope that had been folded and creased so many times it had taken on a soft, velvety texture.

When poking inside, the revealed content was a bundle of mostly black and white photos, and they kept me transfixed for some time. Laying out each picture on the carpet, it was a story of perhaps the last ten years of my other life – there were over a hundred photos. Separating the ones which I appeared in, I tried to lay them out in some kind of chronological order, guessing my age. I had to keep spreading further over the carpet as I thumbed through each picture.

It was strange looking at a picture story of my life that I knew nothing about. Was I like one of those people who had had a traumatic experience and then had no idea who they were? Like Jason Bourne, perhaps? No, I was pretty sure I wasn't an assassin, although my knee-crushing skills were well versed this morning. No, I was a mining engineer, soon to be a schoolteacher, not a highly trained weapon for the CIA.

The auburn-haired beauty in the framed photo featured in many of the snaps, and some of the colour photos were close to risqué. In all the images, she appeared to look happy – I wondered what happened to her and *other* Jason. Turning a picture over, on the back in my handwriting was '*Annie 1968*'. I flipped over a risqué one of Annie to find a message from the woman I didn't know. '*For you, my darling J. You are everything. My love, my life*'. *Other* Jason was a lucky man – no one had loved me like that, but I guess I hadn't earned it.

"I'm sorry, Jason, for taking your life," I muttered, as if he was standing there listening to me. I kept reminding myself how I needed to be more like *other* Jason – I wanted to be loved like he was.

Although now dusk, the early evening heat was oppressive. However, I kept my windows closed because I just felt safer that way. My thoughts drifted to Beth and whether Carol was okay, but I had no idea how I could find out, unless Don, Carol's other neighbour, had some information. I decided to venture out and ask.

"Ah, the hero of the hour," Don announced, as he opened his front door.

"Hello, Don, sorry to knock late. I went up to the hospital earlier but, unfortunately, they wouldn't give me any news about Carol. Do you know any of her relatives, as they might have some information and know if she's okay?"

"No, son, no idea. She only moved into that flat about two years ago, her and that little boy … well, she's only a young girl herself. Some bloke knocked 'er up when she was still at school. She moved in next door with the lad when she turned eighteen; right proper rum affair if you ask me." Don took a breath and continued, appearing pleased to have an opportunity to talk. "No one visits her apart from young blokes, and they're all the wrong sort. God knows who the father is of this latest one she's going to have, but different blokes turn up all the time. Reckon she might be paying the bills that way, if you know what I mean. Rumour has it her family disowned her when she got pregnant with the lad."

My shoulders dropped, and I stuffed my hands in my pockets, slouching like a stroppy teenager. The conversation appeared to be going nowhere. "Oh, right, I see. So, do you know anyone else who would know any more information?"

"Feel sorry for the lad, poor little nipper, always hear him crying. I hope after today's shenanigans they've given him somewhere nice to live, even that Lexton House over on Coldhams Lane would be better than with Carol, in my opinion."

"Do you know anyone else who I could ask for information about how she is?" I repeated, as he seemed to have missed my question.

"What, … oh, err … no, Jason, no idea. Hey, you want to keep an eye out, son, that bloke you took down this morning … he's a wrong 'un, you know? But you look like you can handle yourself. You coming in for a cuppa, or something stronger? I've got a bottle of whisky under the sink. We could have a nip together."

I presumed Don didn't get many visitors and took my appearance at his door as an opportunity to have some company, but I didn't fancy going in. Old Jason would be off like a shot, running down the landing as if being chased by Freddie Krueger. But I was new Jason and, anyway, what the fuck else had I got to do.

"Go on then, Don, but I'll have a coffee if you have any."

I was fast learning this week that it was amazing what you can find out if you invest the time in other people and show an interest. I had about an hour of looking at photos of his wife, Peggy, who passed away six years ago, and his two daughters. One lived in Scotland and the other in Cornwall, so about as far away as you could get from Don. I wondered if that was by design.

Don picked up a large photo of Peggy. It had been taken just after the First World War when she was twenty-one years old, a natural shot rather than the formal ones like most of the photos of that era. It was unframed. He said he had dropped it a couple of years ago, and the frame broke, but it was his favourite.

Don had fought in the First World War, and I listened to tales of his exploits in the trenches. Each chapter of his story started with *'During the war'*, which made me smile, thinking about Uncle Albert in Only Fools and Horses; albeit a different war, but it sounded the same coming out of Don's mouth.

"Well, son, I firmly believe that everyone falls into one of four categories … the good, the evil, the sad and the happy. None of those German soldiers were in that evil bracket, as with us Tommies. We were all caught up in a war that none of us wanted. We all fitted into the sad category – the war-makers were the evil ones."

"I've never thought of it like that," I said, now nursing a glass of whisky from the bottle under the sink.

"The good and the evil, they make things happen, the sad and the happy just float through life, their lives guided by the good or the evil. Mark my words that Carol lass falls into the sad category. So young, but the evil ones have already mapped out her life."

"Like Fin Booth?"

"Yes, he falls into the evil category, along with many others on this estate."

It made me think, what category was I in? Well, I guessed my life firmly had me in the sad category, no question, that was an easy answer. However, was this now an opportunity to move it to happy, or even good?

Now I had him in full flow, I used the fact that I had apparently been in South Africa for so long that I was out of touch with the UK and Fairfield. Don filled in many gaps, and together we demolished the bottle from under the sink. As I said goodnight and prepared to stagger the twenty feet back to my flat, Don called out to me.

"As I said, son, don't know anyone who would know how Carol is, but you could try that lass from the Council. You know, the one with the red hair? She comes around all the time. Also, you might want to step out with her. She's a right good-looker. Rather easy on the eye, I'd say."

Yes, she is, I thought, and I was going to try.

22

18th August 1976

Carry On Doctor

For the second time in less than a week, I woke with a hangover. I wasn't used to handling alcohol, and this hangover was a thumper – half a bottle of Don's whisky was going to take its toll on me today.

Lying in bed, I reviewed my plan for today. Firstly, somehow, I had to find out how Carol was and, more importantly, Beth. Secondly, I must ring and apologise to Jenny. And thirdly, the big one, a meeting with my grandfather later this afternoon. If Stephen had had that fit yesterday, then unquestionably, he would now believe me.

The potential butterfly effect and the changes to history I'd already caused slammed back into my mind and heightened the hangover to a higher level. When I was young, I'd not heard of stories about Stephen, an ice cream van incident, or a certain Mr Apple who came to the rescue. If it had happened the first time around, then I was sure the story would have been told by my mother many times over. Every time we were near an ice cream van, the story would be retold again and again, but no, I didn't recall that story. So, had my actions changed the future?

One significant change was that Stephen had stayed alive and existed in the old future world. However, had my actions caused more minor changes? What if that incident had changed Stephen's mindset, and he was okay that the magician chose another kid to hold the wand? If he didn't have a fit, I was screwed with convincing George that I was his grandson.

My new positive self decided to bury this thought and wait until five-thirty this afternoon because there was nothing I could do about it now – what was done, was done. Old me would be now spending the day performing a variety of ridiculous rituals to ensure the right outcome, like tapping my coffee cup four times before drinking, amongst many others. Old Jason would be convinced these would guarantee success. However, the last few days' events had taught me that such obsessive actions were just a mental condition that didn't affect anything. All they served to do was to debilitate me and make me a miserable tosser.

Today, I planned to rock up at the hospital and claim to be one of Carol's relatives bringing in some clothes for her. If the Nazi wasn't on the desk, I reckoned I could get through. All I needed was a few minutes with Carol, and I would have completed my first task of the day. Then, I'd ring Jenny and see if I could repair yesterday's damage. I would be new charming Jason, and that would be that whatever the outcome. I decided the only shit thing that was going to happen today was my hangover, which would recede in time. This glass-half-full attitude felt quite liberating. Being optimistic about future events seemed to make me feel happier, and I wouldn't allow yin-yang thoughts to attack my brain – no, not again.

~

Glancing around the hospital car park, I searched for the blue Granada that pulled up yesterday, just in case that Mark bloke decided to revisit Fin. Although, I expect by now, Frenchie and her crew had Fin secured in a holding cell to answer for his outstanding warrants. Fortunately, the blue Granada was nowhere to be seen. Parked directly behind my car was a red Vauxhall Viva, and it looked just like the red car I'd seen Jenny drive off in yesterday. I guessed there were quite a few red Viva cars in this era, so I considered it was probably just a coincidence. For sure, if I bumped into Jenny here, she would be convinced I was the father of Carol's unborn child. Which was kind of amusing because I believed the child would be my best friend Beth, not my daughter.

The first test was to see if *'Helga'* was at the desk. In my mind, I had changed her from a Nazi to the wife of *'Hagar the horrible'*. I thought it suited her better. That said, I didn't want to see her again. My plan, if she was there, was just to hang around until she went on a break and then make my move. Positive half-glass-full had worked, a much older lady was at the reception desk. She reminded me of my grandmother from years ago, but fortunately this lady had no Rothmans poking out the side of her mouth. But no, it was not years ago, I think it was how my grandmother would look now. I had to get a handle on time; this was 1976, and it looked like this was now my time, not 2019.

I calmly delivered my lies with a big smile, and I was through. I'd successfully passed the sentry post and headed up to the ward. However, unfortunately I hadn't considered visiting times, and the morning session ended in ten minutes, but that was all I needed.

The ward appeared dated. Well, I guess it was. There was no security in and out, and no hand sanitising dispensers. The rows of tubular steel-framed beds, devoid of bleeping and buzzing electronic equipment next to them, were archaic. In fact, the whole place looked like a set from one of the Carry On Doctor films. I half expected Hattie Jacques, the bustling matron, to be in charge whilst marching up and down the ward, barking at the nurses and swooning over the doctors. Although there was no Hattie Jacques, three nurses, all wearing starched-stiff pink uniforms with white hats and aprons, buzzed around the blue linoleum floor-covered ward.

All but a few patients had visitors, all chatting with their loved ones. Many were smoking, including some of the patients. I spotted Carol propped up in bed smoking, blowing plumes of smoke through her purple, bulging, fat lips. Her nose sported a type of cone-shaped bandage, and her eyes were puffed up in shades of blue, yellow, and green.

"Hello Carol, just coming to see if you're okay."

"Bloody hell, Jase, didn't expect to see you 'ere."

"Well, after yesterday, I just thought I'd pop in and check you're okay." Not that I was that bothered about Carol, but I was concerned about the bump. So, I was somewhat relieved to see that was still there, pushing up the bed covers.

"Yeah, I'm alright. That bastard, Fin, has smashed my fucking nose up. Not sure how I'm going to pull any blokes with a crooked conk. You took 'im down nicely, though. Reckon he's got a busted knee," she chuckled, before taking another drag on her cigarette. "That bastard won't be climbing up to my flat any time soon, that's for sure."

"How's the baby? I heard they kept you in for observation. Is everything alright?" I asked, whilst taking a second glance to see if the bump was still there and hadn't disappeared in the last few seconds.

"Yeah, the little bastard's fine, kicking the shit out of me all night long. Got no bloody sleep, I can tell you."

"Oh, that's great. So, everything is okay, then?"

Tears welled up in her eyes, although it wasn't cigarette smoke causing it.

"Hey, you okay? What's up?"

"Stub this out for us, Jase," she said, handing me a half-smoked cigarette, which I squeezed into the already full ashtray, suggesting she'd spent all night smoking.

"That ginger bitch has taken my Christopher from me. They reckon they've warned me about my ability to raise 'im proper. They've put the little sod in Lexton House, and that bitch reckons it's for his protection."

"Oh right, I'm really sorry, Carol, really I am. Look, best you rest up here, that's the best thing for now."

I struggled to think of anything else to say, but I could see why Jenny had removed the little boy. Her flat, with all the comings and goings, was no place for him, as sad as it was, and for sure Beth would be going the same way in a few years after that bastard bloke has abused her.

"Look, Carol … I have to go. I'll drop in on you when you get back to the flat, get you some shopping and stuff."

"Yeah, alright. Shouldn't you have brought a bag of grapes for me? That's what people do when you visit someone in the hospital."

"Oh yes, sorry. I've been in a bit of a rush today. Sorry, I should have."

"Ah, don't worry, you've done enough wiv stopping that prick in his tracks yesterday. Reckon he would have killed the baby and me if you weren't there, thanks, Jase. And you don't need to worry, I ain't telling no one who you are. They've already been to see me yesterday to ask about you, but I'm saying nuffin'. They can all go fuck 'emselves."

A large lady dressed in a dark blue uniform appeared in the centre of the ward, then clapped her hands together to get everyone's attention. "All visitors, visiting time is now over. Say goodbye to your loved ones and leave by the exit at the far end of the ward." Bloody hell, it was Hattie Jacques, well, it looked like her. I now half expected to see Kenneth Williams in a white doctor's coat.

With a spring in my step, I traversed my way back to the car park, relieved Beth was alive and well. Okay, as alive as an unborn could be, but you get my drift. Perhaps my intervention yesterday had saved Beth and kept time on track, as I had with Stephen.

I was somewhat shocked that Carol was allowed to smoke. Beth would probably be born with nicotine addiction. Beth didn't smoke, well, apart from trying Consulate Menthol cigarettes when she was about thirteen. We'd purchased a packet together from the local newsagents. No one gave a shit about the legal age to buy, and I remember that shop selling single No.6 cigarettes to kids for ten pence each. There was no *'Think 21'* then or whatever it was called in 2019. We'd smoked most of the packet together, both feeling cool and grown-up. However, Beth had been violently sick, and consequently that was the last time she'd smoked. However, from that day, I became a slave to nicotine and, by now, I expected my lungs sported a life-threatening coating of tar. Although, on a positive note, now back in 1976, I wasn't the social leper that I was in 2019.

Leaning against the red Vauxhall Viva – which was still parked near my car – stood an elegant, gorgeous woman with bright auburn hair dressed in a tight-fitting, green-halter-neck, flared jumpsuit. She appeared to be in a trance as she stood there, smoking a cigarette. I stopped and looked for a moment, burning that vision into my memory – *this is it, Apsley* – things are going my way today, so seize the moment.

"Hello, Jenny."

She spun around, exhaled a plume of smoke, and glared at me. Her eyes appeared a little watery and, as was with Carol a few minutes ago, I didn't think the cigarette smoke was causing it.

"Oh, Jenny, are you okay?"

"Yes, I'm fine, Mr Apsley." A clipped answer in reply.

"Oh, okay, just you looked a little upset. Sorry, none of my business, but just wondering."

Jenny maintained her angry glare that suggested I should piss off. "Quite right, none of your business." Dropping the cigarette to the asphalt, she stubbed it out under her white high-heeled sandal before wiping her eyes with the back of her hand. "Yes, I'm fine, really, I'm fine," she said, before bursting into tears. I closed the gap and laid my hand gently on her bare shoulder. She flinched a little, but not enough that suggested I should remove my hand.

"Hey, Jenny, what's up? What's happened?"

Jenny blurted out that she'd been visiting her grandmother, who was in the geriatric ward and was quite unwell – a heart condition, and the prognosis wasn't good.

"I'm so sorry. I'm so sorry, Jenny, I didn't realise. I assumed you were here yesterday getting that lad checked out, not here visiting your own family. I'm sorry to hear that."

Jenny composed herself, and I removed my hand from her shoulder. I didn't want to, but it was the right time to do it.

"What are you doing here again?" she asked.

"I just wanted to check on my neighbour, Carol. I'm not a friend in any way, but I was passing by, so it seemed the gentlemanly thing to do." Not knowing what to do with my hands, I rammed them into my pockets, then continued whilst awkwardly shuffling my feet. "Look, I know I was rude yesterday, and I shouldn't have grabbed your arm." I glanced up, transferring my attention from my twitching feet to Jenny. "I'm sorry, Jenny. Please forgive me. Honestly, I'm not the kind of bloke that grabs women, if you know what I mean."

That kind of came out wrong, although it made us laugh and broke the slightly thick atmosphere between us. Jenny wiped her eyes with her hand again. Presumably, she was expecting me to offer a handkerchief that all men carried, but those times had moved on. I never carried a handkerchief and, unless you were of a certain age, I didn't think many men did.

"How was Miss Hall?"

"Yes, apparently, she and the baby are fine. Although I have to admit, I did lie to the receptionist, telling her I was a relative so that I could get in, which was a bit naughty."

"Yes, that's very naughty of you, Mr Apsley," she smirked.

"Jason, please call me Jason. Well, it worked, and I think Carol was pleased to have a visitor. I don't think she gets many … well, not the ones she wants. She said yesterday, one of Fin Booth's mates rocked up to get information on who I was. I can certainly see why you had to re-house that little boy ... it's not a good living situation for him."

"Rocked up," Jenny said in a questioning tone, her head to one side. "You're intriguing, Jason. You use funny words, you care enough to visit a neighbour in the hospital twice in as many days, and you clearly know how to deal with the wrong sort. You put that thug in his place yesterday, and you take it all in your stride. You're very intriguing indeed." Her tears had all gone, the radiance of pure beauty beamed from her.

This is it, Apsley, it's now, Jason, it's now.

"You intrigue me too, Jenny Lawrence. So, if we are both intrigued, can I buy you lunch? I promise I don't bite, and I promise not to grab your arm, scout's honour."

Jenny smiled and looked at me but said nothing for what seemed an age. It was as if the world had stopped rotating; everyone on the planet was suddenly behind me, watching her as I was, all holding our breath whilst awaiting her to answer.

"Okay. I drive, you pay," she delivered with that smile.

There are not many moments in my life that were genuinely euphoric, unbelievable moments that are imprinted in your memory in permanent marker pen that can never be erased. Of the very few I did have, this moment had entered the Jason Apsley's greatest moments chart – straight in at number one.

Jenny suggested the Five Bells Pub. I knew the pub as I'd visited it once, I think, but I didn't care where we went as long as I had time with her. The conversation flowed smoothly, the only tricky issue being that Jenny wanted to know about my life in South Africa, so I just made stuff up and rambled on, trying hard to avoid time-travel cock-ups. Surprisingly, considering we were from entirely different generations, we shared the same humour.

We didn't arrive back at the hospital car park until mid-afternoon. Jenny parked next to my car, and we stood chatting whilst leaning against her car in the warm afternoon sunshine.

"Jenny, I've had a fabulous afternoon. Thank you."

"Me too. It was lovely. You've cheered me up no end after this morning."

"Yes, it was lovely. Look … err … can I take you out for dinner?" I asked, almost desperately begging.

"Oh, err …" Jenny replied, and then fell silent.

Holy crap, this can't end now, it can't – *do something, Apsley, for Christ sake, do something,* my mind screamed, demanding action.

So, to comply with my inner voice, I slowly leant towards her, stopping my mouth three inches from hers, checking and waiting to see if it was okay. She moved her mouth in line with mine, her head tilted up slightly. I kissed her, my arm encircled her back, and I gently, ever so gently, guided her closer to me.

Jenny pulled out of the kiss first, her arms now around my neck, and gazed at me with those sparkling emerald eyes.

"Yes, you can. Saturday night. I will meet you at the Five Bells at seven, and you can surprise me where we are going … nice and expensive, though. I'm not a cheap date!" she smirked before kissing me again.

"They sell sandwiches in the hospital shop if you two are hungry," some bloke shouted whilst walking across the car park. Fair enough, we did look like a couple of loved-up teenagers.

"Saturday is a long time away … that's three days and four hours. How will I cope with waiting?" I mocked, as we broke our embrace following the sandwich comment.

Jenny placed her hand gently on my cheek. "Well, Mr Apsley, I'm worth waiting for."

I had to be the luckiest man alive. Pretty much forty-two years of nothing great, but it was all worth it for the past few hours. They made up for all those crappy years – and then some.

After parking the old yellow Cortina in the pub car park, I flipped down the sun-visor to block out the late afternoon August sun as it streamed through the windscreen.

"Yaaaaarh," I yelped, still a little shocked at my reflection. Although I'd looked at new me many times now, it still wasn't easy to get used to.

With less than half an hour until the meeting with George, Jenny consumed my thoughts. Well, I'd thought of nothing else. Quite frankly, the whole world could have been sucked into a black hole, and I wouldn't have noticed. What was Jenny's future life planned as? If I hadn't been teleported back to 1976, what would have happened to her? Would she have gone to lunch today with *other* Jason, the poor sod whose life I'd taken? But no, she wouldn't because he wouldn't have visited Carol at the hospital today. Would they have gone to lunch another day? Well, the pictures of Annie were not too dissimilar from Jenny, so it appeared we were both attracted to similar-looking women; God, that was so weird.

During lunch, I discovered Jenny was twelve years my junior. She would be seventy-three years old in 2019 – a lady who had a history. I was getting good at this maths stuff. Had she had a happy and contented life? Had I changed that today with the one small act of kissing her, and should I be messing in other people's lives? I was certain that I would alter the course of history if I could, whatever the consequences and the butterfly effect that caused. I had to have Jenny in my new life – I wasn't letting her go.

Hyped-up with the anticipation of what my grandfather would say, I found myself pacing the car park, having decided not to venture into the pub where I expected Dawn and Dennis – the Double Diamond couple – to be perched on their personalised barstools. From a hundred yards away, I spotted him with his formidable stride and wavy white hair.

Part three of my day was coming up. So far, following my hangover and a rare foray into maintaining a positive attitude, I'd established that my best mate, Beth, seemed to be okay, and I'd taken to lunch and snogged Jessica Rabbit. So, with my only task left, convincing George that I was a time-traveller, I hoped it wouldn't be two out of three today. So far, it was a perfect day, and although Meatloaf was quite satisfied with that number, I wasn't. I was with Queen on this one – I wanted three out of three – I want it all.

23

Seize the Moment

"Hello, lad. You're always punctual. I'll give you that."

"Evening, George," I said, not knowing what else to say as I scanned his face for any signs of how this conversation would proceed.

"Ivy has gone to see her sister, Eva, for a couple of days over in Aylesbury. She's in poor health and needs a bit of a helping hand. So, rather than the pub, let's go back home and have a cuppa. I think we have a lot to talk about."

"Yup, sounds good."

I seemed to have lost the power of conversation as we walked side by side up Milton Road to my grandfather's house. Neither of us spoke, which felt very strange considering the events of Stephen's party and what that could mean. It reminded me of our trips together when I was a little boy going down to the newsagent's shop. That seemed a lifetime ago, although, in chronological order, this was the first time I'd ever walked up this road. Of course, the big difference to my memories is that my grandfather wasn't holding my hand this time.

The front room looked so familiar; every piece of furniture was the same in 1984 when this became my permanent home. The Ercol style chairs with the neat white lace overlays, marked and greasy – George should have purchased shares in Brylcreem as he smothered it on daily. The light-brown sofa with heavy, splayed, wide arms; the material less worn than I remembered. Behind me, the fifties-style bureau, which had the hand-written book 'George the Talking Rabbit' stowed on the bottom shelf. I couldn't see it, as the desk flap was up, but I knew it was there. On the ceiling was the circular brown-yellow stain above my grandmother's chair.

"There you go, lad, nice cuppa. Sit yourself down." George slid over an empty smoked-glass ashtray next to my teacup and then sat in my grandmother's chair, something I didn't recall he'd ever done before. However, I couldn't remember my grandmother going away for a few days, so perhaps this was his way of keeping her close.

"You can smoke, lad. Ivy has always got one on the go, so it seems odd to have clean air," he chuckled.

"No, no, George, I'm fine. I never smoke indoors." It was funny how things had changed. Back in my uni days, I would wake up with my head under the duvet, my hand would snake out, grab my cigarettes and light up. The smoke would waft out of the top of the quilt, similar to an old Hamlet cigar advert. Now, I found the smell of stale smoke in a house repulsive. That very smell lingered in my grandparent's front room, but it was familiar and seemed okay – even right. George watched as I looked around the room, both of us quiet for a moment.

Eventually, George broke the silence. "Well, lad, does it look the same? It's a long time since you've been here."

My eyes swivelled around at lightning speed, with the rest of my head catching up a second later. I seemed hardly able to speak, struck dumb. I opened my mouth and tried to make a noise that resembled a word, but my mind seemed detached from my vocal cords, and all that came out was air, with a slight grunt that sounded like I'd given my last breath on my death bed. I swallowed and focused.

"Stephen had a fit?" I asked, looking for confirmation.

George wiped away a tear and smiled, "Yes, lad, he did, precisely as you described."

"So, does that mean you might believe me and my ridiculous story?" My hopes were high now, with both eyes covered in a film of tears that started to distort my vision.

"Ha, well, lad, what can I say? You have proven it, I think, though it's bloody ridiculous, and it just can't happen, but it seems that it has. I believe I'm talking to my time-travelling grandson that I've never met."

That was it. My new ability to sob took hold, caused by an overwhelming sense of relief. I was exhausted as every bit of energy had left my body. My head sunk into my hands whilst I sobbed everything out. When I looked up, my grandfather had left the room, and I sat quietly as my skin tightened up with dried tears.

"Alright, lad, here, get this down you. I think we both need this." George handed me a large brandy, swirling around in a brandy snifter.

"Cheers. I'm sorry about that, but it's this week. It's been exhausting," I babbled, taking the glass with a shaking hand that now gave the appearance that I was suffering from full-blown Parkinson's disease.

"Lad, I think we have a lot to talk about. I've had a full day to get my head around this, and there is one very clear rule before we start. I don't want to know what happens to Ivy or me. Clearly, we are both dead when you travelled back, unless one of us turns out to be one of the longest living human beings. I don't want to know when Ivy or I die because that would be terrible to know … whether it's tomorrow or in thirty years. So you're going to have to keep that information to yourself. Agreed?"

"Agreed, but—"

"No, lad, no buts. You must agree."

"Yes, okay … okay."

"Also, I am worried about knowing too much, so we are going to have some further agreements on what you tell me. For example, the Cup Final last year was a fantastic day. The anticipation and the build-up to the game with the delight when the Hammers won. If I knew the result before the day, the excitement would have been taken away, spoilt, if you see. So, I'm worried about knowing things that will change my life."

"Yes, I see. Okay."

"But also, lad, there are things I could know that I think would be okay for you to tell me. Hypothetically, let's say that you know I will break my arm falling off the shed roof in 1980. I think that's okay to tell me, so I'll know not to go up on the roof and get someone else to repair the felt. I haven't got my head around it all yet."

George carried on whilst I sipped my brandy. "We have to be extremely careful because the knowledge you have is so powerful. That power must be used wisely and not for personal gain."

I thought of my actions so far this week. I believed I had made the right choices, but could my desire for Jenny be classed as personal gain? As always throughout my life, George's wise counsel should have helped me, but so many times I didn't take that advice and look what a shit life I'd had.

"I understand, George, but anything I do now changes everything. Just sitting and talking to you, I've already changed your history. Everyone I meet, I change history. Just by breathing, existing, I'm potentially changing the course of so many events that domino together."

I talked through the events since last Thursday, leaving out anything about Jenny as I really couldn't listen to him telling me that I shouldn't get involved with her. So, selfishly, I removed her existence from my story. In my mind was the future event of Mum and Dad's death, and I would need to talk to him about this as I had to change that course of history. However, I had plenty of time, so I felt that could wait for the moment.

"So, the two big impacts I've had so far are saving Stephen and Beth, but what does that mean for their futures? Without my intervention, their lives could have gone off track. So, I now wonder if my actions have put them back on track, do you think?"

George had been leaning forward and listening intently the whole time I'd been talking. He now leaned back and slumped in the chair, looking up at the smoke-stained ceiling.

"Bloody hell, I can change things for the better. Beth was abused as a child by one of Carol's boyfriends … surely I need to stop that? I know a child is going to be abused, so I have a duty … a duty to do something, don't you think?"

George pondered this, pursing his lips, still staring up at the stain as if analysing it, deep in thought.

"I can't remember the bastard's name, but Beth was taken away from Carol at the age of four, so it's between now and 1980, that's for sure. Although I guess Carol will have a few blokes coming and going over the next few years based on her history," I added to this now one-sided conversation.

"Who wins the next Grand Prix?"

"What? I thought that was off-limits? You said we couldn't discuss that sort of thing," I threw back at him.

George kept looking at the ceiling, and he repeated the question, "Who wins the next Grand Prix?"

"James Hunt, in Holland, but why do you want to know that?"

"Ivy has had her eye on a new watch, and I know the one she wants, but it's too expensive, so she will never ask for it. I could place a bet on that race and buy the watch for her birthday."

"George, what about all that stuff about not acting for personal gain? The responsibility of power and all that," I reminded him. It was as if the tables had turned, and I was now the one offering wise counsel. George smiled and pondered more, still fascinated by the stained ceiling.

"Lad, you're right. However, I also believe, as you know, about taking your chances when they come. Seize the moment, I always say to my Joan, don't let an opportunity pass."

Yes, my grandfather had always said that, but unfortunately, I'd rarely taken that advice. However, Stephen had, and was successful as he grabbed every opportunity that came his way. Forty-two years had passed – perhaps now might be a good time to start learning from George's wisdom.

"Lad, you're absolutely right. You have to change history and stop that bloke who abused your friend. I think you said she's hugely successful, so the only concern I have is that your actions could change that."

"Yes, Beth has an amazing job and is well-off, I guess."

"You guess, or you know?" he chuckled.

"Oh, yes … I know. We've done that one, haven't we?"

"So, she's hugely successful and rich, and what about being happy? Is your Beth happy?" George asked. He'd now lowered his head and was looking at me again.

"Well, no, not happy. She's about as miserable as I was, I guess. Still, it's a bit easier to be miserable and rich than miserable and poor, don't you think?"

"Depends on how you define success. In my book, success is happiness whether you have a pound in the bank or a million. Money is no good if you're not happy, lad. Happy in life equals success, and it has nothing to do with how big your bank balance is."

Another example of his wisdom that hit me square between the eyes. Yes, all I wanted was to be happy, nothing else. If I'd died last Thursday, that would have been it. Now I had a second chance, so perhaps it might be a bloody good idea to get it right this time.

"You should stop that chap, and maybe young Beth will be a happy person in life, don't you think?"

"Yeah, I think you're right."

George grinned, "Also, I would like to know when the Hammers win the league?"

"Well, the first bit of bad news is they haven't yet and, although they are in the Premier League, it's unlikely they ever will."

"Oh, that's disappointing, lad, and what's the Premier League?"

"George, I believe if you look in the back of the pantry there is a large blue china coffee pot. Ivy has had it donkey's years. Let's have a big pot of coffee – it's going to be a long night."

24

19th August 1976

Snakes and Ladders

The morning sun flooded my bedroom with light. The somewhat dishevelled, outdated, thin yellow curtains weren't going to hold it back from lighting up the room.

A week had now passed since my arrival in 1976, and this morning I'd woken with an odd feeling. Whilst planting my hands behind my head and staring at the ceiling, I tried to put my finger on what that peculiar feeling was. Certainly strange and unusual, not my typical mindset when I woke each day. Positivity, that was it, I was feeling optimistic, and that definitely wasn't a state of mind that I was used to when waking.

Not that I was disappointed – no, this was, although different, a good feeling.

Notwithstanding my apparent time leap, I considered I'd had a packed week. I'd saved two lives and made a new friend called George – although I previously knew him as my grandfather. I felt that our evening together had bonded us close, closer than before.

Then, the cherry on top of the cake was I'd fallen for Jessica Rabbit. I didn't think I could call her that until the film *'Who Framed Roger Rabbit'* was released in the late '80s, but I had every intention of being with Jenny when it was. Perhaps I should be worried about the teaching job I had acquired, but no, that didn't seem to flatten my mood.

Launching myself out of bed, I bounced into this new, glorious day, ready to continue climbing ladders on my snakes and ladders board of life. This time, I wasn't going to slide back down a snake – no, not this time.

Nothing was going to spoil it – nothing.

Part 2

25

1984 (first time around)

Autobot

"Joan, your mum and dad have just pulled up. Are you going to take much longer? We need to get a move on, or we'll be late. The train goes at five-twenty-two, and we can't miss it," Neil Apsley called up the stairs.

"I'm just going to the loo. I won't be long. We will have plenty of time," Joan called back down.

"Hello Ivy, George, thank you again for looking after the boys. Come in, come in." Neil stood aside and let his in-laws into the hallway, wishing that Joan would hurry up. He hated being late. Because of his wife's tardiness, they'd been late for the last show, catching a later train and thus missing the first act. Consequently, they were forced to stand in the theatre lobby until the interval before taking their seats. It always frustrated him, and he really couldn't fathom why his wife didn't start getting ready earlier.

"Boys, Nanna and Grandad are here," he bellowed out to the whole house, unsure where Stephen and Jason were.

Jason came bounding down the stairs all excited, as he loved Nanna and Grandad coming around, it was such fun. Grandad often fell asleep, but Nanna would always play games – Mum and Dad never had time.

"Grandad, look, look at my Sunstreaker car. It's an Autobot car! An Autobot car!" Jason exclaimed with super enthusiasm.

Jason proceeded to jump up and down whilst waving around his yellow toy car, assuming Grandad would be just as excited as he was – well, it transformed into a robot, so surely everyone would be excited, he thought. "Look, Grandad, it can turn into a robot. It's a car and a robot … it's a robot, look … look."

"Hang on, lad, hang on. Let's get my shoes off, and I will have a gander."

"Come on, Jason. Let your grandfather get in the house. Calm down a bit."

"Christ, Joan, are you ready yet?" boomed Neil. With Jason's antics and Joan's faffing, his patience was wearing thin.

"Stephen, where are you? Come and say hello, and get your head out of that thing," he added, but not quite so loud.

Stephen failed to reply due to having his head buried in his ZX Sinclair Spectrum that he'd become slightly obsessed with. Neil didn't think it was fitting that his son stared at the tiny screen all day long, and he failed to see what the attraction was. Surely it would be a fad or a phase. He couldn't see the point of a home computer – ridiculous, he thought.

"Hello, Mum, are you alright?" Joan greeted Ivy, as she swished down the stairs.

"Oh, you're ready at last. Well, I must say you look stunning, my dear, quite stunning. Now let's get going, please." Neil had his hand on the front door handle, poised and ready to go, but he still had the forethought to compliment his wife – well, she'd taken long enough.

"Mum, the kids have had their tea. There's some mashed potato and ham in the fridge for you both. In fact, let me show you—"

"Oh Joan, come on, come on!" spat Neil.

"Sweetheart, off you go. I have plenty of experience making your father his tea. Now, go and enjoy yourself."

Joan and Neil left for their train and the West-End show. A show they never got to see and, as the front door closed, a door they would never walk back through.

George and Ivy stayed the night, although they hadn't intended to. Neither slept. George spent all night holding his wife, both crushed by the loss of their beloved Joan. Their only child, a beautiful daughter, a loving wife, and a wonderful mother to their adorable grandchildren.

Stephen and Jason had lost both their parents – a strong father who provided for them in what was relative luxury and a mother who showered them with love. The news those two boys would hear on Sunday morning could destroy them. If they weren't strong enough, it would affect their lives forever.

George was a caring man with great wisdom. However, the job of sitting both boys down on Sunday morning to deliver the devastating news was going to fall to Ivy, as she was simply stronger. Ivy would be able to tell them clearly and then comfort them. It was the worst thing she would ever have to do.

26

21st August 1976

Malibu Goggles

With my newly discovered optimism and *'feel good'* feeling that I had woken up with on Thursday morning, I'd had a productive two days. My flat was pretty much all packed up, ready for the removal team on Friday. I'd visited my new home, well, my old home – you know what I mean – and met the vendors. They seemed to know me, well, presumably from when *other* me had viewed the property – whenever that was.

It intrigued me that Jason, that's *other* Jason who no longer existed, had liked the house and wanted to buy it, and I – yes, old Jason, now with *other* Jason attitude – had bought it with Lisa thirty years ago – no, thirty years in the future. So, I'd deduced that we had many similarities. Well, I guess we would because we were both the same person, or were we? Except for one key difference: our attitude to life, and old Jason – that's me – was now learning very quickly that *other* Jason – that's him who had disappeared – had a much better outlook than old Jason – that's me. This new invigorated Jason – that's me again – had now adopted this positive attitude. Still with me? Yes, I know, it was a head fuck, and I was living it!

I was sitting in the kitchen with the vendors – which was soon to be my kitchen with the same sixties-style units that I ripped out in the future – having a cup of tea and a chat. I was disappointed it was tea, but coffee was not on offer. I guess *other* Jason had visited and had had tea, so they assumed me – being

154

the same person – liked tea and not coffee. Maybe he was offered coffee and said, *"Oh, no, I don't like coffee. Can I have tea?"* So, I guessed that was one of the differences between us, but I had to remember we were the same person.

Anyway, sitting there on Friday, I had this weird feeling that Lisa could be sitting in precisely the same spot forty-three years in the future – bizarre. I could have left her a note on the wall behind the wallpaper or in an envelope taped under the kitchen sink.

Not to be opened until 12th August 2019

Hi Lisa, it's Jason here. As you are aware, this morning, I am now dead. I've been teleported back to 1976 and repurchased this house. See, I told you I liked it as well – and that much I have bought it twice. However, it was a bit cheaper this time. (I could attach a grinning Emoji at this point). Anyway, I know I was an absolute tosser during our marriage, and I really don't blame you for running off with that bloke, whatever his name is. When it's 2019 again, I will be eighty-five, so not sure if we can catch up then for old time's sake, but let's see. Have fun, Jason.

Lisa and Steve, that's the vendors – yes, she was Lisa as well as my ex-wife – had said that the house was a happy house and the Cannington family – that's Lisa and Steve – were sad to leave but needed four bedrooms now, so time to move on. I think they were trying to say it was a happy house for them, so assumed it would be a happy house for me, and I hoped they were right. With my newly discovered positivity, I was confident that they were.

On Saturday lunchtime, George and I had our second planning meeting at The Three Horseshoes. We enjoyed a ploughman's lunch in the beer garden, free to talk as Double Diamond – Dawn and Dennis – didn't venture off their barstools. At this planning meeting, as we now called them, I decided that I needed to tell him about Mum and Dad and the train crash in 1984.

I was concerned about the shock it would give him. However, I need not have worried because George appeared confident regarding our ability to prevent that crash from happening or ensure my parents never boarded that train. Apparently, although I had no memory of this, Mum and Dad regularly went up West to see the shows. Tonight, planning to see a play called *A Chorus Line* whilst George and Ivy babysat Stephen.

Lisa enjoyed the theatre, often going with various different girlfriends, but on one occasion, she was let down at the last minute and persuaded me to go with her. West End shows were not my thing. I most definitely hadn't inherited my parents' love of the theatre. The music was dreadful, and everyone in the theatre was up on their feet clapping, swaying and singing along – except me. I just sat there stony-faced and miserable, begging the thing to end. I never went to another show – I enjoyed it that much.

George and I invested a good hour trying to work out how we could stop the train from leaving Fairfield station to save Mum and Dad along with the other eleven passengers. We came up with some crazy ideas, one of which was to sneak into Fairfield station late at night and remove a piece of track, then place a large cone in the gap to highlight it was missing. This plan we felt would ensure that the train couldn't leave the station. However, we both soon realised this wasn't the greatest idea, and we had a good seven years to improve on it, which wouldn't be difficult.

We decided to form a plan for the Beth situation after she was born, so again, we had plenty of time. Also, I needed to remember this bloke's name who was with Carol at the time of Beth's abuse. Beth had told me about it on a few occasions, and I remember the day when he was released from prison when she was a young teenager. I'd racked my brain but couldn't remember the bastard's name. However, we had time.

"You definitely know this Carol lass is Beth's mother, you're sure?"

"Yes, definitely, the timing is right, and her surname is Hall. Beth took her name from her mother, as her mother had no idea who the father was. It's her. It will be Beth born on the 12th of September."

"Okay, but how will you know it's Beth when the baby is born, assuming that Carol calls her the same name?"

"Well, hell, I don't know. I mean babies all look the same. I guess there will be a problem if it's a baby boy, but I can tell the difference in that respect."

"Yes, lad, I'm sure you can," George replied with a chuckle.

"I know it will be a girl, and I know she'll be called Amy Elizabeth … I just know it."

There was a period of silence as we finished off our ploughman's lunch, and my thoughts had drifted to tonight. It had been a long few days since seeing Jenny, but it was such a great feeling to be able to look forward to something without worrying that it would turn to shit – a new feeling for me.

"George?"

"Yes, lad."

"You know I want to see Nanna as well, don't you?"

"Yes, I know, lad, but you know your grandmother is going to be a tougher nut to crack than me … impossible, I'd say. You could tell her what she's thinking and she still wouldn't believe you."

"Yes, I know, but I want to see her."

"I've had some thoughts on that, and I reckon I could introduce you as a friend from here at the pub and see how we get on. Best I can come up with, lad."

Lunch over, we shook hands and departed on our separate ways after we had set our next planning meeting for the following Saturday.

I was a tad nervous as this was my first proper date with Jenny, and it had been a long time since I had one of those. In the spring of 2004, I asked Lisa out after a drunken night at the Ritz nightclub in Fairfield – a grand name, although a shithole inside.

Lisa was dancing with a group of girls who all benefited from a certain natural rhythm, as most girls did. After eight pints, I thought I could dance just as well, so I joined her on the dance floor and performed my demented baboon dance style – this had nothing to do with the amount of alcohol consumed, as it was my typical dance performance. Lisa had had a skin full of Malibu and Coke, so I guess my dancing didn't look too bad to her at the time.

After drunkenly exchanging numbers, we agreed to meet up a few days later. We were both in an advanced state of inebriation that night at the club, so when we met at the restaurant, we hardly recognised each other – that broke the ice, and we got on well. However, I was definitely punching above my weight, and I think Lisa was disappointed with what she saw – you could say her Malibu goggles had been firmly in place that night in the club. We were both in our late-twenties, Lisa being a couple of years my senior, and felt we were running out of time for young love, so we hooked up, although I don't think either of us knew what real love was.

~

The red Viva swished into the car park at five minutes after seven. Her car seemed to move with the same grace as Jenny. Sashaying out of her car, she flashed a gorgeous smile. "Hello, you. I didn't know if you would stand me up or not, but you're here, looking all tall and dashing."

Clearly, Jenny had no concept of the way I already felt about her in this short space of time – nothing would have stopped me from seeing her this evening. Trying to get the right look to impress my dinner date, I'd tried on about ten different shirts and trouser combinations. This dilemma isn't reserved for the ladies, as us men are just as bad – only we make out we're not. However, I did have the additional difficulty of not understanding the era I was living in, so nothing I put on looked particularly suitable. Jenny had yet again turned up looking stunning in a long red dress which complimented her hair. I half expected her to say;

"I'm not bad, I'm just drawn that way."

Well, she was my Jessica Rabbit, and a devilish part of me hoped she had that *'bad'* side that I dreamed of seeing soon.

The Yellow Pages had come to my rescue again, and I'd booked the *'Terrazzo'* Italian restaurant. George had confirmed it was a posh place – too posh for him and Ivy to frequent – and it lived up to its one Michelin star in fine cuisine. The bill was eighty-eight quid. Jenny was shocked at the cost, but she loved it.

"Jason, eighty-eight pounds. That's a fortune, an absolute fortune."

"Well, you said expensive, didn't you," I said, smirking. Pleased with myself that I had plumped for a quality restaurant – sod the cost.

"Oh yes, but I thought it would be just a nice restaurant, not this place. I don't think I know anyone who could afford these prices. Sorry, I didn't mean for you to spend that amount." Jenny looked concerned, small tiny crinkles across her forehead. I'd seen her angry, concerned and happy, and all those looks were gorgeous.

"Well, I enjoyed it. I hope you did too, because you're worth it."

"Of course, I did. It was wonderful, thank you … oh … and am I worth it?" That beaming smile again.

"Yes, Jenny Lawrence, you definitely are."

After leaving the restaurant, we took a stroll down to the river then up to the main bridge in the centre of Fairfield, arm in arm, and often her head nestled against my shoulder. We talked, laughed and kissed, the warm breeze adding to the blissful feeling of a perfect evening. Jenny said she was a massive football fan – for a woman in this era, I thought that was somewhat unusual. She loved seeing the Hammers play – George would have approved – and she had an enormous crush on Frank Lampard –

not the one I knew, but his father. So, we agreed to go to the next game together at Upton Park on Saturday. Although I was football mad, I didn't have a clue what the score had been, knowing that was too much of a stretch, so that meant I could enjoy the game as well.

During our date, I hadn't mentioned Lisa. Well, I couldn't, as that was in the future. I mentioned a girl called Annie in South Africa, but that was over now, which was a fair assumption to make.

Jenny had said she had a boyfriend a year ago, but that relationship didn't end well, and she'd started seeing a bloke called Tom. I instantly hated him, but she said it wasn't serious, and they had only been on one date that hadn't gone particularly well.

One thing was for sure, even though her recent date with a certain Tom had not been a roaring success, I had to ensure there was never a second date.

27

22nd August 1976

Time

Life is cruel, and you have to be resilient, which can be tough. Old me had known that every day of his life.

Yesterday was simply the best day of my life, and the evening with Jenny had left a permanent grin on my face. Nothing could wipe it away, nothing – or so I thought.

Mid-morning on that Sunday, the telephone rang. The conversation that ensued ripped my heart clean out of my chest as if some giant hand had reached in and yanked hard, leaving an empty hole inside my rib cage.

"Hello, Jason here," I'd said when picking up the receiver, standing in the hallway dressed in just my underwear. That bit had been okay – the rest wasn't.

"Jason … Jason, it's George. It's George. Are you there?" He sounded panicked and breathless as if he had just finished running the London Marathon. His voice was frail, that voice I had remembered in the last few years of his life as his body had started to break down and the strong, tall man withered.

"George, are you okay? What's going on?"

"Lad, Joan and Neil died last night. The five-thirty-three train from Fairfield derailed, and all thirteen passengers in first-class were killed. How can this be … how can it be?"

"What … what are you talking about? No, they can't have. This happened in 1984, not now. No, they can't be."

"Lad, it did. My Joan has gone." His voice had broken, and I listened to his sobbing down the phone. I couldn't understand it. How could this have happened? Every other event seemed to be taking place as it had previously, but this event had moved seven years, and before I was born.

Sliding my back down the wall, I crouched on the floor and buried my head in my knees. This was the second time I'd had to hear this news, not that it made it any easier for me. The first time at the age of seven, I hadn't immediately fully understood, but I then had a further thirty-five years to try and deal with it. For George, there was no first time, and he'd had only about twelve hours.

"Lad, you there?"

"I'm here, George … I'm here."

"Lad, Joan told Ivy yesterday that she was pregnant again … the baby was due in March."

Fortunately, I had nothing planned for the day because I found it challenging to focus on anything. All that kept coming back into my mind was the memory of that Sunday morning when I was seven.

My grandparents had stayed, although they hadn't gone to bed. Mum and Dad weren't home; that never happened. Usually, when my grandfather had eventually got me off to sleep after at least two full run-throughs of his book 'George the Talking Rabbit', I would awake in the morning to find Nanna and Grandad had gone home – that Sunday was very different.

When my grandmother delivered the news that Mum and Dad were dead, I didn't cry because, in my mind, it wasn't real. I remember not understanding why Stephen was blubbering because he was thirteen and didn't cry anymore. It was sometime later that morning that my young brain processed this new information and delivered it to my senses – it destroyed me.

Last Wednesday evening, sitting in the front room with George, discussing my time-travel escapade, we had dwelled on what would happen in March next year when I was born. Would I be born, or would another unknown sibling be born, or was no one born at all? If I was born and a new little Jason was on the scene, could we co-exist simultaneously, or would I be catapulted off to death or another time? It was a mind-spinning conversation that produced no answers, just lots of questions.

This morning's news had answered those questions. Both Jasons could not co-exist. One had to die, and that tiny baby forming in my mother's womb was the loser, along with my parents. They were not in the future, so had some higher power decided to take them now to ensure two Jasons didn't exist? Had my time-travel escapade killed my parents early and killed me as well?

I certainly felt dead today. Perhaps I couldn't affect the future but only keep it on track to what was supposed to happen – maybe time was too powerful to be messed with. Although I was no longer born in 1977, and my parents had died seven years too early, I was sure I'd caused that change just by being here.

28

25th August 1976

Skeleton

I experienced a numb, cold feeling all week, a sense of detachment from what had happened, and I wasn't comfortable with myself feeling that way. It wasn't right because I should have been totally devastated. It was as if my mind and the feelings it produced were old Jason. Wrestling with that emotion, yes, I had the correct feelings when I was seven, so now, should it feel different the second time around? I'd only seen my mother in thirty-five years for those few moments last week, and regrettably, I'd not seen my father since 1984. Time heals, they say. No, it hadn't healed for me, and never would, but perhaps the wound had scabbed over a little.

I potentially had another mother called Mary Apsley and perhaps a father as well, but I didn't know them, although presumably they would know me. I would need to find out if they were still alive. Maybe I should be ringing them every Sunday to say hello as any caring son would, although that felt like a betrayal to my parents, who I'd just lost again.

Performing some functional tasks kept me busy that week. Although I didn't know what I was heading into, I'd planned out the meeting for school on Thursday as I needed to be clear in my mind about the conversation I was going to have with Roy. George and I agreed to postpone our planning meeting on Saturday morning, as there seemed little point now, and he needed to be there for his family – it was his family, not mine.

The heaps of paperwork had yielded my car insurance and driving licence, a tatty-pink piece of paper that I presented at the local police station – that job was complete. I hadn't replaced the front tyre as 'Officer Dibble' had suggested – that job could wait.

Jenny called and agreed to come around Friday evening after work to help me unpack. Although I wanted to see her, I found staying positive in the conversation difficult. After all, I couldn't talk about my parents' death because in this world – to everyone but George and me – my parents were strangers to me.

Carol had left the hospital on Tuesday. I'd popped around and then completed some grocery shopping as promised, and the bump was still firmly in place.

It was clear that over the next few weeks, I needed to keep close to Carol to ensure Beth was safely born on the 12th of September. Although, after that, I hadn't quite worked out how to protect Beth from what was coming her way. I'd run through the alphabet, writing down every boy's name I could think of, trying to jog my memory of that bastard's name. I wanted to prepare myself for when he arrived on the scene as Carol's live-in boyfriend, but not one name I wrote seemed familiar. Certainly, keeping tabs on her new blokes was going to be difficult.

Up until the mid-morning on Sunday, I'd been reasonably clear I was here for two reasons. Firstly, to prevent my parents' death on that train, and secondly, to change the course of events of the first four years of Beth's life. The first I'd failed at – time had cheated me – the second one I had to get right and be aware there might be another time shift.

It was reasonable to assume that there was a vast amount I didn't know about myself. A few documents and pictures hadn't told me the whole story. I still didn't know what the third key on my keyring was for or why I'd left South Africa, where I assumed I held down a well-paid job. Also, what had happened to Annie, the girl in the picture? There were a million, trillion questions that I couldn't answer and potentially many skeletons in many cupboards.

There are two certainties in life after you are born. Firstly, there is your death, and I had already completed that task nearly two weeks ago and would have to repeat that at some point in the future. Secondly, you have no idea what will happen in your life before death occurs. I had a slight advantage on task two because I knew the following forty years of history. However, I didn't know specifics regarding what would happen to me and when.

During the late afternoon, there was a loud banging on my front door. My immediate thought was maybe it was Fin's mate. However, taking a sneak peek through the net curtains revealed it definitely wasn't that Mark bloke, as a tall, slim, red-haired lady in her mid-thirties stood at my door.

"Err … hello," I nervously greeted her as I opened the door, already fearing that I knew the identity of this stranger.

"Jason, at last, you are a hard man to track down, and I never expected to find you living in this dump. Look, I know you probably don't want to see me, but I want to see you … I need to see you," she rambled quickly in a strong Afrikaans accent.

I just stared, open-mouthed – you know the look. Standing in front of me was the woman from the photos I'd found – and from recalling them, I knew what was under her short yellow dress – Annie.

"Oh, err … yes … hello … um, yes … oh." Just the usual dithering response I'd developed.

I stepped aside, allowing Annie to enter the dump as she had described it. She was more stunning than in the photos, the ones with clothes on, that is. She hovered in the hallway before I invited her into the lounge.

"Take a seat."

Annie looked at the old sofa with disdain, as if I'd offered her a seat in a cowpat, but to be fair, the sofa wasn't much better. With no other options, she smoothed the back of her dress with her hands and perched on the very end of the seat.

"Well, I don't really know what to say." And I didn't. Annie was part of *other* Jason's life. She knew me very well, but I didn't have a clue about her, only some pictures – and a few racy ones at that.

"You don't have to say anything, Jason. I just want an opportunity to explain because the years we had together ended so abruptly. I know this was my fault, but you left South Africa, and we never really got a chance to talk."

Feeling this could be a long conversation and would probably be somewhat one-sided, as I tried to piece together what she was talking about, I thought coffee was in order.

"Annie, can I get you a drink, coffee, tea, or something stronger?" I gestured to the array of spirits on the wooden trolley.

"Tea, please, Jason. I like English tea."

Annie followed me out to the kitchen. Whilst I made the drinks, we exchanged small talk about the weather before I handed her a cup of tea. We sat at the kitchen table, as I assumed she had no intention of re-sitting on my cowpat-sofa.

"Jason, I know that we ended because I left you for him, and I was awful to you. You didn't deserve what I did, but I loved you, and I still do … I'm so sorry." We lost eye contact as she looked down at her tea as if inspecting it, checking to see if it was drinkable.

"I don't know what to say. I know I've just said that but why are you here, in England, and here at my flat?"

"I've come over for a seminar, a two-day event with a gala charity dinner on Saturday. I'm staying at the Ritz for a few days before flying home on Tuesday morning."

I guessed she meant the Ritz in Piccadilly, not the shit nightclub in Fairfield town centre, which didn't exist anymore, either now in 1976 or 2019. Although it must have been a work-related seminar, I had no idea what she did for a living.

"I so desperately wanted to see you. Frank and I have split up. Well, the truth is I left him. I wasn't in love … it was just lust,

167

and I realise I've ruined everything. Jason, I do regret what I did, and I do love you."

Jesus, both Jasons couldn't hang on to their women. Lisa had left me for another, and I didn't blame her. I wasn't anything worth having – not particularly handsome and, as I said, my ears were too big and stuck out too far. Also, I was just plain miserable and not pleasant to live with. Now it seemed that *other* Jason couldn't hang on to Annie; she had run off with this Frank bloke for a bit of lust and fun under the sheets. So, the combination of both Jasons was a miserable wanker and shit in bed – incredible.

"Annie, what do you want? I'm not the same person that you knew." And that was absolutely true.

Annie looked up from her tea. She hadn't drunk any, so I guessed she'd decided it was undrinkable.

"Can we try again? I know I don't deserve it, but I love you, and I'll always be faithful … I promise."

Silence had fallen between us, both just staring at our drinks.

"I'll leave South Africa, give up my work and come to England if you'll take me back … I love you."

Oh boy, this was a dilemma. I'd met Jenny, the woman who consumed my thoughts and desperately wanted that relationship to grow. Now, I had another beautiful woman here in front of me begging to get back into a relationship; how things had changed. I'd been reasonably useless with women all my life, probably an average amount of relationships, mostly two-week affairs at uni, which involved bed-hopping after drunken nights out. But serious relationships had not been easy. Yes, okay, Lisa and I got together and married, although I think Lisa was just desperate at the time. Yes, desperate covers it, and I thought she would be much happier now she'd moved on.

"Annie, I don't know. You hurt me." Well, I guessed it was a reasonable assumption to make.

Annie looked up from her tea for the first time, searching my eyes for the truth. "Have you met someone else?"

"Maybe, I don't know." Well, that was the truth. I knew what I wanted from Jenny. However, at this early stage, I had no idea what Jenny wanted, so maybe that was about right.

"Oh," Annie replied, then bowed her head, staring down at her undrunk tea. "Jason, have dinner with me over the weekend so we can talk? Maybe we can work it out?"

"I can't. I have plans … I just can't."

"With her, this someone else?"

"Look, Annie, you turning up here today has come as a bit of a shock. I need to think about it. You understand, don't you?" A shock was an understatement.

"Yes, of course. Have dinner with me Monday night then, for old times' sake, please? Before I catch my flight on Tuesday. But what I want is not to catch it at all."

"Oh, alright, Monday night. Where shall we meet?"

Annie raised her head and smirked. "I'll book a table at the Ritz for seven-thirty. Can you get into London for that time?"

"Your hotel?"

"Just dinner, Jason, and a time to talk properly."

"Alright, yes, okay."

"Thanks. I know I don't deserve it, but I will make it up to you."

"Annie, I'm not promising anything."

"I know, I know."

"Look, I'm not being rude. But I have an important first day at work tomorrow, and I still need to finish some prep work, so let's leave this until Monday, yes?"

"Oh, yes, of course." Annie put down her untouched tea. There was a theme about my hot-drink-making and women not drinking it. To my surprise, she stood, swung her arms around my neck, and kissed me. I resisted but then relented. Annie moved her hand to my trouser zip.

"No, Annie, no."

"Oh, really? You never minded before."

"Annie, it's complicated. It just is."

Removing her arms from around my neck, we held hands, just looking at each other for a brief moment.

Annie stared at me, leaning forward to kiss me again. "I will make this up to you."

Not trusting myself, I leaned back. "As I said, it's complicated. So, let's leave this until Monday."

"Hmmm, Monday. Don't be late."

I managed to shovel this gorgeous woman out of the flat before giving her any more encouragement to take things further. Nipping through to the lounge, I watched Annie walk away down the landing. Bloody hell, what was going on, and why did I kiss her? I suddenly felt a pang of guilt about Jenny. However, I'd stopped Annie going any further, and for any man, that was a real achievement.

29

26th August 1976

Concorde

Eaton City of Fairfield school – as it's now called – sits between Eaton and the Broxworth Estate. The dividing line is Coldhams Lane, which acts almost like the *Berlin Wall* between them and, although so close, the two areas were totally divided. Whichever side of the road you lived on, that's where you stayed. There was no cross over, apart from the school, which sat at the north end of Coldhams Lane on the Eaton side. Eaton was a typical post-war suburb of semi-detached houses. Back in the '50s, they were at first considered a step up from the old town terraced houses, but over the years the estate had lost its appeal.

In 1964, Fairfield applied for City status through the Royal Charter Act. The local Council at the time put forward the proposal, and there was a significant movement that involved many community leaders and businesses in achieving the award. Everyone was confident of success. That perceived certainty led to many organisations jumping ahead, resulting in some changing their names in anticipation. Fairfield Town Football Club changed their name to Fairfield City FC, which was ridiculous as they were a non-league team and a poor one at that – and still were in 2019. After the failed bid for city status, the football league forced the club to re-name back to Fairfield Town, which caused massive embarrassment.

Eaton Grammar School also jumped the gun and, in 1964, was renamed Eaton City of Fairfield School. After the failed bid, the local authority allowed the school to keep its new name, so I went to the 'City' school in 1988, the only city school in town. The whole council resigned after the failed bid due to the scandal of wasted public funds.

However, as you enter Fairfield from the south side, the sign was still in place in 2019—

'Welcome to Fairfield, a Fine City.'

~

I wasn't as nervous when arriving at the school for the meeting as I thought I would be. I was much more anxious in 1988 when attending high school for the first time. My grandmother had instructed Stephen to take me in and ensure I was okay, which he was not happy about as he was a school senior in the sixth form and didn't want to be associated with his younger brother. However, my grandmother had been very clear, and when she was clear with us boys, we knew we had reached a line that must be obeyed.

Stephen dumped me in the central courtyard as soon as we were out of sight of my grandmother, who had walked with us to ensure Stephen complied with the given directive. I stood completely still in my new stiff clothes, the sewn-in name tag in my purple blazer had already rubbed my neck sore – a blazer that was way too big, but my grandmother was insistent that I would grow into it. I knew many of the other first-year students who were all standing around because they had attended Houseford Park, my primary school, but I had few friends. The four years since the death of my parents had transformed me from a happy, enthusiastic little boy to a sultry, quiet lad who found mixing with others difficult, so I stood on my own on that chilly September morning.

I was the last to walk into my new class, and all but one seat had been taken at that point, as it appeared all the kids had pre-planned their seating arrangements – certain mates with certain mates. The one seat left was next to a scrawny little blonde-haired girl who I didn't want to sit next to.

"You boy, what's your name? What are you doing?" the form teacher boomed. He was a short elderly man with John Lennon style glasses and looked like he should have long since retired. I recall thinking how terrifying he appeared as he held me with a skull-piercing stare.

Whilst trying hard not to shake and concerned that I now had the urgent need to pee, I mustered up the courage to reply. "Um … I don't know," I mumbled.

"Um, I don't know, Sir! It's Sir, boy, Sir! And you don't know your name or what you're doing or both?" he bellowed again. No one laughed as all students stared down at their desk lids, thankful, I guess, that they were not in my position.

"Now, boy, sit there." He pointed to the place next to the scrawny blonde girl.

One thing was for sure, Mr Bumstead – nicknamed Bummer out of his earshot – had given me a precious gift that day by forcing me to sit next to Beth, a friend who would become the closest person to me for the rest of my life; well, until two weeks ago.

~

I parked up outside the main entrance and composed myself. I wanted to check LinkedIn or google Roy Clark, so at least I knew what my friend and new boss looked like. I just hoped he had a nameplate on his desk so I could confidently assume who he was. Unfortunately, all I had to go on was that he was a forty-two-year-old male. Roy Clark must have moved on by the time I attended school, as the Head was a quiet man called Elkinson.

The school was an impressive building purpose-built in 1910 as a prestigious Boys' Grammar school – an imposing Edwardian building that oozed luxury and elegance with a hint of aristocracy. Etched in the stonework between two white stone pillars was 'Excellence In All', the school motto, that I recall the headteacher would remind us all of at the morning assembly. The new science and sixth-form block that I remembered protruding out of the front of the building wasn't there, as it was added in 1985.

Time to meet my old buddy, Roy, which did feel strange as I didn't know him, although walking to the school's main entrance was very familiar. Bounding up the two steps and into the main lobby, I was greeted by a short man about my age with round Lennon-style glasses. Of course, I instantly knew who he was, which was so weird.

"Good morning, you must be Jason. I've been placed on sentry duty as a lookout for your arrival. Neil Bumstead, woodwork. Good to meet you." With that, he thrust out his hand, and we enjoyed a firm handshake.

I knew what he meant by woodwork as he taught it, but I thought it an odd greeting. That moment was a tad different to the welcome he gave me on that first day in 1988. Old Bummer himself, although he was not as old as I had remembered, and when I attended school, he would only be fifty-ish, but I remembered him as ancient.

"Thank you, Neil. Yes, correct, I'm Jason Apsley. Good to meet you, too." I was close to calling him Bummer, but I was on high alert today – no fuck-ups allowed.

"I guess the old place has changed a bit since your school days. Boys' Grammar then, I presume it was all mortarboards, the cane, and being buggered by the older boys," he chuckled. "However, you'll be pleased to know the Eaton Fives courts are still in place."

I had no idea what he meant by Eaton Fives, but I guessed I would find out. As for chuckling about being buggered by the older boys, I found that a somewhat strange reaction. We marched off together, presumably to meet the rest of the team. I'd arrived early for the meeting, so hoped I wasn't last.

"You're early, and not everyone is here yet. I'll take you along to catch up with Roy; I believe he's in his study," Old Bummer called over his shoulder.

The headmaster's study was as I remembered it, with the original dark-oak wood panelling. Rows of books adorned a large bookcase on the back wall, and in front of that was Roy's desk, which was awash with paperwork and books – it appeared to be utter chaos.

I'd only had the pleasure of visiting the headmaster's study on one previous occasion. During my school days, it was very unusual for any student to enter that inner sanctum. When I was in my final year before the sixth form, Beth and I were marched in by Jones, the Deputy Head, who resembled and afforded the grace and humility of Hermann Göring. Being handed over to Mr Elkinson was akin to the Gestapo handing over prisoners to the Red Cross for interrogation.

In the years after joining the school, Beth had grown from a small, scrawny kid to a confident teenager with strong views on everything; she took no shit from anyone. She was heavily influenced by Madonna – dressed and chewed gum, just like her – which was in direct odds with Sharon and Joanna, aka Cindy and Barbie. They hated Beth, and as the perceived leaders of the girls in the school, they would do everything to undermine her.

Once Hermann Göring had handed his prisoners over to Mr Elkinson, we stood awaiting the Head to address us. That was when I had an opportunity to look around at the previously never-seen inner sanctum.

"Mr Apsley, Miss Hall, can you explain why two female students, Sharon Cook and Joanna Bush, had to run naked across to the female locker room because their clothes and towels had been removed from the girls' shower block?"

It was a wonderful moment in my school memory, and to be fair, there weren't many. Beth had planned the attack with military precision. Cindy and Barbie were always the last to shower after PE as they liked the showers to themselves. Beth had ensured that she took all clothing and towels whilst they showered, forcing them to run naked fifty feet to the locker rooms to grab their coats. She'd organised a large posse of boys to be lined up to watch, telling them that a great show was about to happen and they would not want to miss it. Although I was one of those boys, I wasn't aware of her plan and then ended up with Beth in the Head's office by association – by the sheer fact that we were always seen together at school.

~

"Jason, come in, come in, wonderful to see you. It's an exciting day to have your brain at the school. You're going to be such a great addition. Sit down, old chap." Roy greeted me whilst shaking my hand like a rag doll. He appeared older than me, his hair still in the style of the '50s: a neat parting, short, held in place by some kind of oil, and a lot of grey. I couldn't stop focusing on the large boil that adorned the end of his nose. I could only imagine the names he got called by the students out of his earshot.

"Thank you, Roy. It's really exciting to be back. A new chapter in my life. I'm hoping I can support you and, of course, deliver excellence in all my work." I had rehearsed my opening gambit and thought getting the school motto in would be a good start.

"You will, without a doubt. Look, sorry I missed you when I dropped by last week. Was the information I left you helpful? I suspect you found it all rather basic."

"Yes, it was beneficial, and all seems relatively straightforward."

"Fantastic! I knew it would be."

"Would it be possible to have some time with my team today to discuss how the term will look?"

"Yes, absolutely. I've set aside time for department heads to chat with their teams later. We're on the same wavelength already, as I knew we would be."

Leaning across the desk and looking sideways as if checking no one was in earshot, he beckoned me closer as if about to tell me a secret, which was odd as we were the only two people in the room.

"Do you remember Old Hoskins in our class? Would you believe the old bugger got arrested last year for kerb-crawling?" he whispered with a boyish grin.

"Oh, yes, I remember him. Kerb crawling, really, that's unbelievable," I replied. Good to play along, but I had no fucking idea who the fuck old Hoskins was.

"So, Jason, tell me all about your South African adventure. Got to say it sounds wild, and I'm a bit jealous of you if the truth be known."

I had a planned script in my head, so what I told everyone was the same, as I was aware this would come up. The trouble with lying is if you steer too far from the truth, it's easy to make mistakes. I had no idea what the truth was with this story, so a carefully choreographed speech was already in my mind.

By mid-afternoon, I was feeling more comfortable. I'd met the team; some I remembered, like Jon Waite – or Concorde Waite, as I knew him because of the size of his hooked nose – and others who were new to me. My team were all younger than me; the eldest was Colin, at the age of thirty-three. He had a few years of teaching under his belt, but joined our school this year. So, like me, we were both new boys – I felt we would get on well together.

After the horrific start to the week, I left the meeting with an increased feeling of positivity. At last, I was now involved in work that meant something because being a brand executive for a sheet metal fabrication company was simply bollocks and helped no bugger except the shareholders. Teaching was very different, and there was a slight possibility I might enjoy doing this. However, I hadn't met any of the pupils yet, and I was well aware that could change everything.

George was going to call that evening as he hoped to have details of the funeral. As that rolled around my head, I struggled to hang on to any positivity from the day. Plus, I had the Annie and Jenny thing buzzing about, which needed resolving.

30

27th August 1976

The Clash

The move from my shit flat went relatively smoothly; Sharps Removals were sharp, on time, and efficient. The two removal men took only an hour to move the packed-up tea chests and collection of dilapidated furniture. Handing the flat keys back to the landlord was a pleasure. I reminded him that the '2' was missing from the flat number 121, but I don't think he gave a shit.

Whilst the activities were coming to a close, with the last few items being hauled down the concrete steps, I nipped around to see Don as I needed a big favour from him.

"Morning, Don."

"Alright, son, you're off then. Don't suppose you know if anyone new is moving into your old flat yet, do you?"

"No, sorry, Don, the landlord didn't say, but I guess it won't be empty for long. Can I come in for a moment? Do you mind?"

"Yes, of course, son, in you come. I'll stick that kettle on unless you want something stronger?"

"Err, no, Don, thank you. It's only ten in the morning, so coffee will be fine."

"Not seen Carol for a couple of days, have you, son? I was going to knock on her door and see if she was okay." Don threw over his shoulder, as he shuffled towards the kitchen in the tartan slippers I now believed were permanently welded to his feet.

"Yes, I spoke to her yesterday. She's just resting up. With all the attention the police have given that flat, I think a lot of the usual comings and goings have stopped."

"Yes, you're right, son. The lot that who visit her aren't keen on the Old Bill. Here you go, strong black coffee."

"Thanks, Don."

"Cheers, Jason, good luck to you, son." He raised his coffee and clinked my cup.

"Cheers, Don. Look, can you do me a favour? Can you keep an eye on Carol for me just so that she's okay? What blokes come around, that sort of thing?"

"Can do, but why are you interested? You're moving on, and she's not the sort I thought you'd want to be mixed up with, if you know what I mean?"

"Well, after last week, it would just be good to know she's okay. I don't like to see any woman treated the way she was, so just a good Samaritan kind of interest."

"Yes, okay. If there's any trouble, are you going to come around and sort it out as you did with that Fin Booth?"

"Well, let's see, but I'll pop around later this week when I have the phone connected so you have my number. The couple leaving the house are taking their number with them. BT are going to have to assign me a new number, but when I have it, I will let you know."

"Okay, what's BT then, son?"

"Oh, sorry, I mean the GPO." I'd seen the Buzby billboard posters all over town – the yellow cartoon bird with the slogan *'Make someone happy with a phone call'* – a new era of the telephone with cheap direct calls. Christ, I just needed my mobile. Also, I thought that slogan was required in 2019 because no one called anyone anymore, it was all WhatsApp, Instagram and TikTok.

"Right, will do. It's all going to be a bit cloak and dagger. I'll keep a record of what's happening and report back." He performed a kind of salute as if I were his commanding officer.

180

"Ha, thanks. I will pop round and see you next week."

I completed some essential shopping, which included a tall stainless steel coffee percolator with a teak handle. It was seriously retro, but I had to have some decent coffee. After another trip to Dunn and Co. and British Home Stores to add to my clothing collection, I nipped into Fine Fare for some essential groceries. In my new home – the second time around – I started the process of unpacking, just enough to get some order in the kitchen. However, one discovery in a crate of assorted kitchenware did answer another unanswered question.

A black folder contained general household paperwork: some insurance policies, some instructions and two death certificates, one for Mary Apsley, who died 1974, and one for Arthur Apsley, who died 1968. These were sad documents, but *other* Jason's documents – not mine. By late afternoon, I'd achieved some sense of order, with only a few tea chests left to sort through.

When the doorbell rang, I ripped open the door, nearly tearing it from its hinges with the anticipation of seeing Jenny again. There she stood in a trouser suit. It was the same one she wore the first day I met her, although it didn't matter what she wore as she'd look fabulous in a potato sack.

"Welcome to Chez Apsley, M'Lady."

"I've brought wine to celebrate your new home." She swished in with a quick kiss and then zipped through to the kitchen, waving the wine. "I didn't know which one you preferred, so I got these two. Mum and Dad drink these, so they must be nice," she continued, still waving the wine – a bottle of Blue Nun in one hand and Mateus Rosé in the other. Christ, I thought, who the hell buys those?

"Mum and Dad have these as table lamps for the caravan. It's really clever of Dad to make them," she stated, whilst waving the bottle of rosé before placing it on the kitchen table.

"Thanks, Jen, that's nice. Shall we have a glass of the rosé whilst we sort through the rest of the kitchen tea chests? Then I will make us some supper."

Jenny moved over and reached up and kissed me gently, placing her now free hand on my chest. "Yes, that's nice, but a house tour first, please, darling."

The house tour didn't take long, and it was clear I had some extensive furniture shopping to do as most rooms had bugger all in them.

"Jen, will you help me choose some new furniture for the house? I've pretty much got to start from scratch because anything that came from the flat will have to be thrown away."

"Ooo, yes, lovely. Nothing better than shopping! It beats sex, you know," she replied, blushing bright red, nearly as red as her hair.

"Well, I have to disagree with you there. You must have had some pretty horrendous sex in your life to think that."

"Excuse me, Mr Apsley, now that's not the way to talk to a lady," she jibed back.

"Sorry, quite right. Shall we go shopping tomorrow morning before we go to football? Are you free?"

"Oh yes, I love spending money, especially someone else's," she sniggered. "We can go to that new Habitat store … their stuff is really modern, although a bit pricey."

"Okay, sounds good." Habitat – well, at least that's one retailer I had heard of, although I'd only seen them inside a Sainsbury's store. I wasn't fussed about where we went, but I needed some stuff and if it meant I got to spend all day with Jenny, that was good.

Since my marriage breakdown with Lisa and because Beth was an appalling cook, I'd learned to get proficient in the kitchen. Either that, or starve to death, or visit the Spice Lounge Curry house every night – apart from the cost, I didn't think that was a particularly good idea.

I'd cooked once for Lisa, and that occasion was for her birthday, although I'm not able to remember which one. I thought it would make a pleasant surprise – oh, it was indeed a surprise. Not knowing what I was doing, I decided on chicken curry, which seemed the easiest to do. How hard can it be? I thought. However, I underestimated the power of the curry powder, so the upshot was Lisa spent half the night with her head down the toilet and was subsequently too unwell to attend the birthday bash her parents had planned the next day. After that, Lisa didn't let me cook again.

This time, I cooked a mild Thai curry that went down a treat, and Jenny seemed suitably impressed with my culinary skills. I'd discovered a full box of white candles, not table candles, but the sort of old-fashioned household candles that the Canningtons must have left by mistake.

"Here we go, candles to make it more romantic." I lit one and stuck it in an egg cup in the middle of the table. "Lord knows why they had all these. There must be five boxes of them."

"Leftover from a couple of years ago, I should think. Those power cuts were nearly every day. Helen and I had just got the flat, and we had to light candles every night."

"Oh, really?" I responded, not sure what she was talking about.

Jenny shot me a confused look. "Blimey, Jason, you can't have forgotten that. It was only a couple of years ago."

"I was in South Africa, so I must have missed it." This South African thing was proving to be a bit of a life-saver when needed.

"Oh, well, you were lucky. It was awful here. I must say I've never seen a man able to cook before. My dad can't even use the grill to make toast. You're full of surprises. I think I'm going to have to sharpen up my cooking skills when I cook for you."

"So, you will be cooking for me, then? I like the sound of that."

"If you're a good boy," she delivered with a cheeky smile; sexy, yes, sexy. But being a good boy was not in my plans for the rest of the evening.

We relaxed on the old sofa and cuddled up with our wine. We'd progressed to the Blue Nun after lobbing the empty Mateus Rosé bottle in the bin because I had no desire for a new table lamp.

"Sorry, I don't have a record player or any records. I travelled light, back from South Africa." Another reasonable assumption, as I had very few possessions.

"I remember you had a Queen t-shirt on the day we met. Is that your kind of music? Fortunately, my flatmate Helen and I love the same music, and we play The Beatles all the time. Mum and I got to see them live in '66. It was wonderful."

"Yes, I like Queen, but I'm more into that old punk stuff like The Clash. London Calling was epic, a fantastic album, but that's not very romantic so it's probably a good job I don't have a record player," I chuckled, as I leant down and gently kissed her nose.

Jenny pulled back and made a face at me. "Punk? You're too old. My little brother, Alan, is into all that crap, and that band you said, The Clash, he's going to see them in Islington on Sunday; it's their first gig. Mum and Dad are not happy about Alan going, and there was a right old argument about it this week. They asked me to have a word with him, but I think he'll go anyway as he's a bit out of control. So how do you know The Clash?"

Bollocks.

After necking nearly a whole bottle of wine, I'd dropped my guard, producing my first time-travel balls-up with Jenny – well, discounting my Frank Bruno comment that I got away with. But wow, The Clash live in Islington on Sunday. Now, that would be amazing. I wondered if I could suggest that I chaperone Alan to ensure he didn't get into any trouble.

"Oh, yeah … um, I heard about them on the radio. I think they played some of their songs. They were really good," I lied, wincing, whilst hoping Jenny wouldn't push the subject.

"You said it was old stuff, though?"

"Well, you know what I mean. Hey, I love that Elton John and Kiki Dee song, *'Don't Go Breaking My Heart'*. And make sure you don't, Miss Lawrence, because I have fallen for you."

The deflection from The Clash to Elton John had worked, and I'd escaped the fuck up. However, I'd just told Jenny I was in love with her, which was ridiculous because I'd only known her for a couple of weeks.

"Oh, have you now … have you?" she giggled, although I could see my declaration of undying love had been well received.

I might have gone mad, but yes, I think I had fallen in love. My heart that was unceremoniously ripped out of my chest last Sunday had now been gently placed back in.

"Yes, Jenny Lawrence, I have."

"Say it again, please."

"I have fallen in love with you, Miss Lawrence."

The next two hours were spent finishing the wine, talking and laughing whilst entwined in each other as we lay on the sofa. Dusk had turned to night, and I thought about walking Jenny back to her flat. No way could she drive, and I wasn't going to let her walk alone.

"Can I have another tour of the house, please?" she asked, breaking the silence that had fallen a few moments ago.

"It's not that big, can't you remember it?" I was too tired to get off the sofa at that point.

"I can't quite remember what the bedroom looks like." She turned and looked at me. "Can you show me again?"

31

Frank or Mervyn

We moved upstairs, Jenny taking the lead, holding my hand. The excitement was intoxicating, and my heart was thumping. I wanted to move slowly and not rush the moment. The anticipation was so erotic everything else cleared from my mind, ready to soak up this moment, preparing to experience this pure new arousal.

I slowed her down, stopping her from ripping off my jeans. Taking her hand to her trouser zip, we lowered it together, hand in hand, our hot breath mingling in the inch between our open mouths. We kissed whilst stumbling around the room as we ripped each other's clothes off, fumbling with clasps and tearing buttons before collapsing on the bed. The foreplay was brief because we both were desperate to get to that moment – so close.

"Jen, I don't have a you-know-what."

"What's a you-know-what?"

"You know a thingy."

"Oh, a thingy," she chuckled.

"Yes, a thingy, as you call it."

"Jason, it doesn't matter, really, it doesn't matter." A tear ran down her face. She wiped it away with the bedsheet and sniffed a little – a sadness had engulfed her.

"Hey Jen, what's up? We don't have to do this." Although, I was abundantly aware that a particular part of my body was somewhat unhappy with that statement.

"Jason, it doesn't matter because I can't have children. A few years ago, I had to have an operation which left me unable to conceive."

She buried her head in my chest. I just held her tight, kissing her hair – and after a while, we slept.

"Morning, gorgeous, coffee for you." I plonked it on the bedside table and sat on the edge of the bed, gently moving a stray hair from her face as I stroked my thumb down her cheek. The sadness I'd seen in her last night was still oozing from her.

"I'm so sorry. I ruined our night."

"No, you didn't. It doesn't matter. Hey, remember what I said – I love you."

"I'm in love with you too, Jason, but what about … you know what I said?"

"It's okay. As I said, I want to be with you. Now, come on, drink that coffee. I've made too many cups of coffee in my time that have gone cold."

I kissed her, handed her the coffee, and then headed for the bathroom. It had an electric shower above the bath – bloody luxury. "We're off shopping soon, and as you pointed out, that's better than sex, apparently," I threw back over my shoulder.

The shopping was reasonably successful. We'd detoured to Jenny's flat so she could freshen-up and, I expect, give the low-down to Helen, so I stayed in the car whilst she got ready.

Habitat furniture looked trendy and not much different to 2019: all bright-coloured chairs, teak tables with chrome steel legs and storage units with space to place a TV in the centre – as long as it was no bigger than a twenty-two inch. I murdered the American Express card and flashed my newly received cheque book around, acquiring a fair few items. A trip to Moore's department store was apparently also necessary to purchase soft furnishings. Once again, Jenny expertly spent a fortune of my money while I marvelled at the glass cases and bespoke wooden counters showing off their wares. I felt like I was in Grace

Brothers and fully expected young Mr Grace to appear from the lift with a dolly bird on each arm spouting, '*You've all done very well.*'

We arrived at Upton Park in good time for the match because Jenny wanted to be early so we could get a spot by the barriers that gave us something to lean against. However, as the stadium filled up, I became concerned about how many people were in the stands. There were still fifteen minutes until kick-off, but we were already crushed against the barrier with even more people piling in.

It was impossible not to be close and personal with everyone around us, so I stepped behind Jenny and placed my arms around her to protect her from pushing and shoving. Next to us was a little lad standing on an upturned milk-bottle crate, with whom I presumed was his father holding on to him. It was surely only going to be a matter of time before he was flung forward off that crate.

The teams were on the pitch, and with five minutes until kick-off, a garbled message from the public address system advised fans to move from the North Stand to the West and East Stands, as that stand was now overcrowded. He wasn't joking – this was ridiculous. I could see why all-seater stadiums were put in place. I knew the future, but any idiot could see that it was only a matter of time before a disaster happened at a football stadium.

The match kick-off was then delayed when fans spilt over the advertising hoardings onto the pitch. A couple of yobs ripped off a Texas Homecare advertising hoarding, with one of them proceeding to dance around the pitch, swirling it as if he was the leader of a group of cheerleaders. Police were everywhere – literally hundreds of them – physically shoving fans back into the stands. I guess they were trying to clear the pitch, but they were just making it worse – this really was a nutty situation. Unbelievably, I seemed to be the only concerned fan, as everyone else was pointing and laughing at the scene in front of our eyes.

A large section of supporters in the opposite stand started chanting and pointing their arms in unison at the travelling supporters.

"You're just a bunch of northern wankers,"
"You're just a bunch of northern wankers,"
"You're just a bunch of northern wankers."

I'm not easily intimidated, but I felt very uneasy about the whole situation. Then Jenny turned around and kissed me.

"This is exciting, isn't it?" she giggled.

Fucking hell, everyone was nuts, including Jenny. What's the matter with them all? This wasn't exciting. This was bloody dangerous. Eventually, the police prevailed when successfully shoving all supporters over the hoardings and back into the overflowing stands. One officer wrestled the Texas Homecare hoarding twirler to the ground, losing his helmet in the process when another fan snatched said helmet before disappearing into the crowd.

Kick-off at last, and Jenny burst into excitement as Frank Lampard came to our side of the pitch. Jenny turned and shouted in my ear. "Oh, he's so lovely. I like Mervyn Day as well. He's so cute."

The match was goalless and could only be described as drab. On the rare occasion when the Hammers came close to scoring, the whole crowd shunted forward, resulting in anyone not against a barrier being shoved down about eight steps of concrete terracing and then back up. This movement was similar to a shoal of fish moving in unison through the ocean, avoiding a predator. Fortunately, we benefited from the protection of the barrier, thus avoiding being shunted down the terracing. However, we were squashed flat by the crowd behind us. It was utterly crazy, but I seemed to be the only one thinking it. Jenny loved the game even though it was goalless. For me, it was amazing to watch those football legends play live, like Trevor Brooking, previously only ever seen on old re-runs of Match of the Day.

Although low in the sky, the relentless summer sun still shone, holding back dusk before presumably reappearing the following day. The TV weather presenters, with their fuzzy-felt-type weather maps, predicted this could be the hottest summer on record – even the Government had appointed a Minister for Drought.

Now back at my place, I was a little anxious about what would happen because I didn't want Jenny to return to her flat. I wanted her to stay again – well, clearly I did – but I was so rubbish at saying the right thing and making the right move at the right time. As it transpired, I didn't need to make any moves or think about what to say because Jenny sorted that out on her own. With no consultation with me, she took my keys and opened the door, throwing them on the floor whilst grabbing my hand.

"Bedtime, darling. Is that okay?"

Oh yes, that was more than okay.

Sunday was another steaming hot day in more ways than one.

32

30th August 1976

Perrier Water

Jenny spent the Bank Holiday visiting her grandmother in hospital, who'd made a significant turn for the better over the weekend. I amused myself in the house, emptying crates and attempting to get the house in some sense of order.

I just managed to catch the six o'clock train from Fairfield Station, the timetable stating it would make it into St Pancras Station by ten-to-seven, so plenty of time to tube it across to the Ritz for my dinner date with Annie.

I'd agonised over telling Jenny that I was going to meet Annie, and I'd nearly rang the Ritz to tell Annie I wasn't coming, but I feared that would mean she would just return to Fairfield again. I had taken *her Jason's* place – *sorry mate* – so she just needed to move on with her life and return to South Africa. I knew I would have to tell her face to face to ensure it ended tonight.

The return ticket cost a little over two quid. Vaulting up the steps from the ticket office to the platform dead on six o'clock, the station guard, dressed in a smart dark-blue uniform and cap, greeted me as I rushed to board the train.

"Good evening, sir, the 6:02 will be leaving any moment. Enjoy your evening." This was a slower pace of life: no mobile phones, people spoke to each other, greeted each other with a hello and good evening. Progress through the millennium had lost the art of strangers enjoying social interaction.

The old diesel train fired up its engines, ready to start the journey; the blue velour seats with the British rail logo blazoned across the overhead luggage storage, it seemed from a bygone era – well, it was. An era I was starting to fit into, and maybe I could begin to enjoy my life.

I have only been to the Ritz Hotel once before. Lisa and I'd booked afternoon tea to round off an Oxford Street shopping trip. We'd had a lovely time, which, from my memory, was a rare occurrence. Lisa had loved the sandwiches and cakes, all beautifully presented on ornate cake stands, delivered by smart, attentive waitresses, who all made us feel special.

A short man dressed in a waistcoat and top hat greeted me as I entered the foyer, doffing his hat and enquiring how he might be of assistance. After explaining I was meeting a guest for dinner, he ushered me through to the lounge bar, clicked his fingers for a waiter to attend to me for drinks, and then explained he would do his best to locate and advise my dinner date of my arrival. He had a tough job because I'd replied, Annie, when he'd asked who I was meeting. When then asked for said Annie's surname, I didn't know, which was a touch embarrassing, but he took it in his stride and assured me he would inform my date.

Nursing a Perrier water with ice and lemon, wondering if Mr Efficient had managed to locate Annie – assuming her name was Ann, or Anne – with whatever surname, I waited patiently, determined to end this with Annie before we even got to dinner. I could then be on the return train to Fairfield and grab a British Rail sandwich, which would suffice as my evening meal. However, recalling the jokes about said sandwiches from my childhood, that could have been a culinary mistake.

Annie entered the bar in a silver, full-length dress that clung to every curve of her slim, shapely body. The dangerously low neckline barely holding onto her chest. She wore her long auburn hair scooped up in ringlets. She was stunning, and there was me in that jacket with leather-patched elbows.

Mr Efficient guided Annie to my table and clicked his fingers for the waitress to attend to her immediately.

"You look stunning."

"Thank you. Just something I threw on." She flashed a huge smile, a beautiful smile, but not anywhere near as beautiful as my Jenny. *My Jenny,* that sounded good. I liked that. Feeling somewhat guilty about my plan and not looking forward to the British Rail sandwich, I decided to have dinner and try to enjoy the evening but let Annie know it was over, and that would be that.

My steak demolished, and pleased that I had chosen that option over the sandwich on the train, I glanced up as the waiter attended our table.

"As requested, Miss Declève, coffee will be served in your room," he nodded gently and peeled away.

"Is that okay, Jason? I thought it would be more comfortable."

God, I was tempted, I really was. Well, I'm a man, and she was stunning. We'd had a terrific meal and got on well together – who wouldn't? Any red-blooded male would be scooting towards the lifts before hot-footing to Annie's room.

"Annie, no, it's not. I've moved on, and I think it's time you move on as well. We had a great life together, but that life has ended." Well, I assumed Annie and *other* Jason had.

Annie looked down as she rubbed her fingers along the fold of the tablecloth. She flicked some invisible dirt with her red fingernail; silence descended.

"Annie?"

She didn't look up as she'd located another crumb that needed flicking.

"Annie?" I repeated.

"Have I lost you?"

"Yes." I couldn't think of anything else to say.

The journey back to Fairfield was a sad one. I don't know why, but maybe because I'd just finished with a beautiful woman who I didn't even know, so I wasn't sure why it was sad – but it was.

33

1st September 1976

Yes Sir

Tuesday was a good day. Well, clearly not as good as Sunday. No, I was reasonably convinced that no day could ever be as good as last Sunday – ever.

The Science and Maths teaching team, led by yours truly, had enjoyed a productive day planning for the start of term, and for some reason I felt in control. Although I was starting to enjoy my new life, I fully expected Thursday would be horrific. My parents' funeral was to be held at All Saints Church, the church they got married in, and the very same place as their other funeral in 1984. However, that funeral in seven years' time was now cancelled due to this funeral preceding it.

At that now-cancelled funeral, I'd sat in the front row with my grandparents and Stephen. However, tomorrow, I'd be the stranger at the back of the church – you know, that person that couples nudge each other and say, *"Who's that bloke? Do you know him?"* Another trip to Dunn and Co. last Friday afternoon added a black suit and tie to my wardrobe, so I was ready for it – well, with the required attire at least, but not in my mind.

The school's atmosphere had changed – there were pupils and hundreds of them – it made me feel uncomfortable and somewhat nervous. Although I'd completed teacher training, well, the *other* Jason had, I was concerned about what my performance would be like when actually teaching. So, on day one, I planned to attend Colin Poole's class to learn some pointers. When I suggested to my team that I would be attending their classes on the first day, just to observe and not taking a class myself, all three looked quite nervous and presumed I was assessing their teaching skills. How wrong could they have been because, in reality, I was using that opportunity to learn how to teach.

The classrooms were all set around the main assembly hall. The second floor was galleried, affording you the ability to peer over the landing bannisters right down to the ornate marble floor below. During my student years, an initiation for first-year students was to be dangled over those bannisters by the senior boys who held your ankles as you chanted that you would obey them before being hauled back to safety. It was a miracle that no one was ever dropped to their death. I was one of the first to go through this ritual with Stephen as one of the ankle-holders; I never forgave him for that.

The first class of the day that Colin was taking was mathematics and statistics. It followed an assembly that included what could only be described as a dreary speech from Roy, followed by all teachers and pupils banging out the hymn, *Jerusalem*. It was a hymn I had always favoured, but the collective eight hundred that morning destroyed it – and I don't mean in a good way.

With all the students in the class, I grabbed some chalk and scribbled my name on the blackboard, realising it's harder to do than I'd imagined. Trying to keep my writing in a straight line was quite tricky. It reminded me of Frank Abagnale in the school class scene from the film *'Catch Me If You Can'*. He was an imposter, and so was I. Now, I had to be as confident as he was.

"Right, good morning, all. Quiet … quiet!" I boomed. Good start, I thought. With all eyes now fixed on me and the room silent, I had their full attention.

"My name is Mr Apsley, that's Apsley, not Aplee or Aspley, or Apple, but Apsley. I am your Head of Year for Maths and Science. I will be observing class today, but can I remind you all

196

that this is your final year culminating with your 'O' level exams. So, we are at the business end of your school lives, and I'm expecting you all to knuckle down and deliver excellence this year. Mr Poole will be taking the class today, so I will hand you over to him."

Colin took over whilst I retreated to the back of the class, relieved that I seemed to have successfully negotiated the first five minutes. Although, why I had said Apple, I had no idea, and I was now pretty clear that I had just formulated my nickname – that said, it was slightly better than Bummer. Colin opened the register, a large book with the names of each student on the left preceding a column to tick attendance for each day – bloody hell, it was antiquated. He fired through their names, receiving a strong 'SIR' response from each pupil when confirming their presence.

"Neil Batt."

"Sir."

"Joseph Broom."

"Sir."

"Peter Cockshott."

"Sir."

"David Colney."

"Sir."

"Adele Cooper."

"Sir."

"John Dawson."

"Sir."

"Sarah Moore."

"Sir."

Hang on, what the fuck! He said David Colney. That's the bloody name I couldn't remember, the name of that bloke who abused Beth. It couldn't be, could it? I completed some calculations, which I had recently discovered I was remarkably more capable of than I used to be.

Beth was abused when she was about four years old, so around 1980. This kid was about sixteen, so he would be twenty, and Carol would be nearly twenty-four. So yes, the maths worked, and I remembered he was released from prison when he was still a relatively young man in his late twenties. Also, how many David Colneys could there be?

Scanning the room, I tried to remember which boy had said *'Sir'* when Colin had called out the name David Colney. However, unfortunately, I hadn't been paying enough attention when the register was being completed. I'd narrowed it down to three students, not that I knew what he looked like, but I focused on scrutinising them intently.

Colin was somewhat nervous, with me observing at the back of the room. I did have a pang of guilt, but needs must, I feared. But hell, I needed some visual guidance if I was going to pull this charade off. Throughout the lesson, Colin addressed many of the students and, nearing the end of the class, he asked David a question, I guess to involve him as this kid had not taken part in any of the discussion. He was one of my three.

David Colney appeared to be older than sixteen. His tatty blazer, presumably a hand-me-down, was clearly too small for him, and his tie was ridiculously short. It seemed a theme that the boys tied the largest possible knot to make the tie only a few inches in length. I was surprised Roy accepted this poor compliance to uniform standards. David responded to Colin's question with a blank *"idunow"* that clearly showed his lack of interest. The bell signalled the end of the lesson – tea-break had arrived – and the students filed out of the class. I made a point of talking to a couple of the students on the way out and ensured I caught up with David.

"Dave, can I have a quick word?" I asked, nudging him away from the door with my arm.

"It's DaVID," he replied, emphasising the VID. "My name is David, not Dave, only Dave to my mates, and I don't think you're a mate, Mr Apple, or whatever your name is."

That was a shit start, and I wasn't capable of dealing with stroppy teenagers – well, I had no experience. Yes, Beth could be stroppy, but I was a teenager myself then, so it was completely different.

"Right, okay, DaVID," I emphasised the VID to make a point. "And, as I made it quite clear, my name is Mr Apsley. You didn't participate in today's lesson. Can you tell me why that is?"

Not that I gave a toss whether this bastard did take part or not, but I felt the need – almost compelled – to talk to him. Was he the man who abused Beth? I had to find out, but asking him about mathematics and applied statistics obviously wouldn't offer me any information.

"Look, Apple, I don't like maths much. Anyway, it's my break time, and you're stopping me from 'aving a fag behind the sports gym," he delivered with a grin before side-stepping around me and disappearing into the melee of students leaving class.

"Jason, how did I do today? Was that okay?"

Spinning around, I spotted Colin nervously hopping from one foot to the other like a four-year-old about to pee themselves.

"Great, really good. I made loads of notes, so yes, well done," I replied with a grin I seemed to have copied from DaVID.

"Loads of notes … oh, did I do anything wrong?"

I flung my arm around his shoulder as we walked out of class together.

"Not at all. Excellent lesson, Colin. Perfect." Well, I could hardly tell him the truth that the notes were to help me deliver my first lesson because I didn't have a bloody clue what I was doing.

Before attending the next lesson, Chemistry, that Jayne would deliver, I nipped down to the school office, urgently needing to complete some investigations. Trish, the school secretary, a lady who would be well into her sixties, with grey hair styled in a bun, wearing brown horn-rimmed glasses, sat typing, looking efficient even if she wasn't. I'd met her a couple of times now and we seemed to be getting on well. I hoped my request was not too unusual.

"Morning, Trish. How are you today?"

"Oh, good morning, Mr Apsley, nice to see you. How did your first lesson go? You were with Mr Poole, I believe? Nice that you're supporting him on his first lesson here, although it's yours too!" she nervously chuckled.

"Please call me Jason, and yes, Colin was excellent. He delivered a wonderful lesson. I couldn't have done better myself."

"Ah, that's lovely. Sorry, but Mr Clark likes to keep things formal during school hours, so Mr Apsley, it is." Well, I guess it was better than being called Apple, but that was my fault.

"Trish … err, sorry, Miss Colman, would it be possible for you to look up a student's records for me?"

"Yes, Mr Apsley, I can. Who's the student, and what's the reason for the enquiry? You see, I'll need to record that on their file?"

Bollocks.

I didn't have a reason, apart from believing in the future that this student would abuse my best friend who wasn't born yet. Whilst trying to conjure up a plausible explanation, I ploughed on.

"Yes, of course Miss Colman, the student is David Colney, senior year," I said with real confidence, still trying to magic up that reason.

"Yes, I know him. Not our finest student at all, a right troublemaker." Trish's face flushed bright red as she shot her fingers to her mouth.

"Mr Apsley, please forgive me. That was very wrong of me. I shouldn't have said that … that's not my place to say. Whatever must you think?"

I leaned across the desk, glanced each way and lowered my voice, Roy Clark style. "Miss Colman, don't worry. I won't say anything, and anyway, you're probably right. So, let's keep this between us. Allow me to have a sneak look at his file, and then we can call it quits, okay?"

"Yes, thank you, Mr Apsley, thank you. Let me grab the keys to the filing cabinets," Miss Colman replied, clearly shocked at what she'd blurted and presumably searching for an escape route.

The file held little information: absence and detention records that were both quite extensive. However, the information I wanted was straightforward – his full name and address.

David Albert Colney

Yes, this was him. I now remember when Beth had talked about him and how she would always use his full name as if it was a kind of therapy to say all the names out loud, banishing everything about him from her and not leaving the middle name lingering inside. There could only be one David Albert Colney in this era, in this town, who lived on the Broxworth Estate and was destined to hook up with Carol Hall in a few years.

I hoped I had time on my side and that there wasn't going to be another time-shift that had happened with my parents' deaths. However, I was reasonably safe because Beth was tucked up inside Carol at the moment, so I put this information to the back of my mind and focused on teaching for the rest of the day.

After lessons were completed, all the teachers congregated in the staff room to discuss the day, a real decompression time. One thing for sure, teaching was hard work and much more demanding than working at Waddington's Steel. Old Jason used to moan about teachers, saying they were always on holiday with short working days. I would become animated at the TV when teachers complained about workload, with the teacher unions calling on the Government for increased pay and improved working conditions.

Yes, I can hear my old self saying—

"Lazy fucking wankers, six weeks' summer holidays. What do they do all fucking day? Fucking pay rise, they don't know they're born."

How wrong was I? But I was establishing that old Jason was a right tosser – and good riddance to him.

34

2nd September 1976

Timex

Although I'd told him the funeral was not for a family member but close friends, Roy had been very understanding. Of course, this cut deep because they were my parents, but I needed to avoid complications. Take the whole day off, he'd said, which was a relief as I suspected I might struggle to function after the funeral.

In 1984, I hadn't cried at the service. Stephen was a mess, as were most of the mourners, but by then I had cried all my tears out. The tears-tank was empty, nothing left. I was just a shell of bones and skin with nothing inside.

My grandparents and Stephen had to wait whilst I insisted on staying by the graveside. I just couldn't leave it. I felt that if I left, it was over and my parents were never coming back. As I stood there, I promised to be better – make my bed every day, do the dishes with Stephen without moaning, and clean my teeth at night, which I never saw the point of doing – I would have done all these things if Mum and Dad became undead.

My mental illness had started, gripping my brain and those tentacles burrowing deep. Standing at the graves, I convinced myself if I stayed for half an hour longer than anyone else, Mum and Dad would spring to life and crawl out and hug me. I know this sounds like something from the *Evil Dead*. However, at the time, my innocent mind believed they could just spring back to life, give me a hug, and all would be well again.

As I stood there, praying they would somehow spring to life, I continually checked my Timex watch, a birthday present I'd received that year from my parents, willing the thirty minutes to pass. I'd treasured that watch, and my father had shown me how to do the strap up without dropping it, which was a fiddly operation at that age.

During that half an hour, which seemed to pass excruciatingly slowly, my grandmother approached me twice to take me away from the grave, but I kept saying I wanted a few more minutes. I thought if I could hang on for half an hour, Mum and Dad would return. Twenty minutes into my thirty-minute target, my grandfather came to me and took my hand – we had to go now, he said. I refused and snatched my hand away. He tugged my arm, but I pulled back. Then he grabbed both arms, and I pushed him away. "No!" I screamed. I fought with every muscle to stay for just ten more minutes because I firmly believed Mum and Dad would return.

My grandfather was a well-built man, strong and with big hands, so he easily scooped me up and carried me away from the grave. I screamed again, but my energy was ebbing away, and the tear-tank had refilled, so I sobbed. Before being forcibly bundled into my grandmother's arms, I ripped off my Timex watch, throwing it towards the grave. I thought if I couldn't stay, my watch could – and Mum and Dad would return.

As with all OCD problems, even a child could establish that these actions were futile. Whatever you do, those actions would not change what had happened or prevent certain future events. The act of throwing my watch was hopeless. I knew it wouldn't work, but I had to do it anyway. One of the things I've regretted all my life is not having that Timex watch. It was my memory of my father and, as a seven-year-old boy, I'd thrown it away.

All Saints Church is your average run-of-the-mill church if such a thing exists. However, I only visit these places when forced to – weddings and funerals – so I'm not totally sure what average is. But if you asked anyone to describe a church, it would be grey stone, with a square tower, an arched doorway inset with a heavy wooden door, surrounded by graves from throughout the ages, and a scattering of headstones now unreadable through the passage of time. Well, yes, that was All Saints Church. However, there was nothing run-of-the-mill about this particular church because it was where I had attended my parents' funeral – twice.

I arrived later than most to ensure I was at the back, away from the crowd of mourners. I wasn't the centre of attention today as I was last time when everyone was worried about the little seven-year-old boy who had lost his parents. Stephen was only five years old this time, so he was the centre of attention today. I was the stranger, the one at the back, and that was where I firmly stayed.

As with the first time, during the ceremony, I had no tears, not because the tear-tank was empty, I just think it was different this time. However, they did come later, as they had last time, in the arms of my grandfather.

The function room above the Three Horseshoes Pub served as the location for the wake. The attendance at the church, as per the first time, was enormous, so there were too many mourners to fit into my grandparents' house. As with all wakes, the mood improved as the alcohol flowed, turning it from sadness to some level of a celebration of their lost lives.

George and I had the opportunity to chat for a few moments. I hugged him before taking my leave and sobbed, just as I had thirty-five years ago.

35

3rd September 1976

FA Cup

My first week of teaching could be described as successful. Well, no one rumbled that I had no teacher training. I'd completed lessons all on my own and surprised myself as to how much I enjoyed teaching. Moreover, I found it somewhat mind-blowing that most students were interested and genuinely grateful when I offered to help them if they struggled with a particular subject.

Somehow, I'd obtained *other* Jason's knowledge, not having to think to understand the syllabus, and miraculously had acquired three years of his university knowledge in an instant. I taught David Colney for two classes, although his involvement was the same as the first lesson I observed – zero.

David was, as Miss Colman, the school secretary, had described, not one of our finest students. I suspected he had the real prospect of leaving school with limited qualifications. That said, I struggled to see how this boy would end up doing what he did. It would be at least three or nearly four years before I needed to concern myself about him and what he would do to Beth. However, in under five years, he would start an eight-year sentence in Brixton prison unless I could change time by preventing him from committing the crime.

I was pleased I'd dealt with the Annie situation earlier that week and was now coming to terms with my parents' deaths for a second time. I was ready to move on with life, and the most significant part of that was Jenny. Since Sunday, we had talked every day, me sitting on the bottom stair in my hallway with the yellow phone handset to my ear whilst twiddling the curly cord wire around my fingers. Odd that phones were always in hallways, which provided nowhere to sit, so there was no option but to sit on the stairs. I used to talk to my school friends sitting on the stairs, with my grandparents continually asking me to move each time they wanted to traverse up and down. I remember my grandmother saying on many occasions—

"Jason, come off the phone. You have been on there for half an hour. You will see them at school tomorrow, and I need to telephone your great aunt Eva, so come off the phone please, and mind out, I need to take the laundry up – be off it when I come down."

Tonight, Jenny was cooking for me at her place, as she wanted me to meet her flatmate, Helen, which I found a bit nerve-racking. God, I hoped Helen approved of me. I didn't want her nagging in Jenny's ear, saying derogatory things—

"Jenny, I just didn't like him. How old is he? He looks ancient. You could get any man ten years younger. He must be over forty, and his ears are far too big. Haven't you noticed them? He looks like the FA Cup!"

Christ, I was getting worked up, and then I would have the nightmare of meeting her parents. Meeting girlfriends' parents in my history hadn't panned out particularly well.

After I'd been seeing her for about a month, Lisa had persuaded her parents that we should have a dinner party with me as the principal guest. It got off to a poor start as I didn't understand the dress code. So, when Lisa answered the door, looking all sexy in a short black cocktail dress and me in jeans, trainers and a shirt, we'd had a bit of an argument on the doorstep. Lisa had pulled the door half-closed behind her so no one could hear—

"What the fuck are you wearing, Jason? It's a fucking dinner party. Mum and I have got all dressed up, in case you haven't noticed, and Dad has his best suit on. Fucking hell, you'll have to go and change, you dickhead!"

But there was no time for that; Lisa's father had pulled open the door—

"Are you trying to hide your young man from us, Lisa? Oh, hello, you can't be him, are you? Well, if you are, you better iron that shirt. The ironing board is in the utility room ... Lisa, I expect you can sort that out."

After the wardrobe issues were sorted, and even with Lisa's mum walking into the utility room, me half-naked, and Lisa ironing, I thought the evening improved. Great food and loads of wine, which I helped myself to at regular intervals, becoming pissed with a significantly loosened tongue, much to Lisa's dismay judging by the number of kicks to my shins. However, it ended somewhat disastrously when Lisa's mum asked how I'd plucked up the courage to ask their beautiful daughter out on a date – unfortunately, my reply was alcohol-induced—

"Well, to be honest, I don't remember much about it. I'd had a skin full of beer, saw Lisa on the dance floor, and thought fucking great tits on that."

I realised immediately that the response to her question was not good, although strictly, I was being honest. I left the dinner party a few minutes later. Needless to say, it was a long time before I was invited back.

With a straw-covered bottle of Chianti in my hand, I knocked on Jenny's front door. On this occasion, I had ensured my shirt was pristine and perfectly ironed – lesson learned. Jenny ripped open the door, grinned and bounced like Tigger. She leapt forward, flinging her arms around me and knocking me back a few feet.

"Bring him in, Jen. Don't eat him whole in the hallway," said a voice coming from inside the flat, which I assumed must have been Helen.

Grabbing my hand and pulling me inside, Jenny presented me to Helen like a prize bull at a county show.

"Here he is," she stated, all pleased with herself. God, I was a super lucky bloke.

"Pleased to meet you," said Helen, with an air kiss to each cheek. Irrespective of what generation I was now living alongside, Helen, at slightly north of six feet, could only be described as a tall woman. Not unattractive with a slim face, but it had a fish-like look to it and big sticky-out ears ... so I was safe from any FA Cup comments.

"Hi, good to meet you too. Jenny has told me all about you." That old opening line. I was so awkward in social settings and a little disappointed that I couldn't come up with anything better to say.

With her hands placed on her hips, Helen studied me, inspecting Jenny's prize bull. "I bet she has, but don't believe any of it, especially the good stuff," she chuckled.

"Right, I'll open this wine. Jason, sit yourself down ... the TV is on. Helen, I need you in the kitchen with me," instructed Jenny, giving me a kiss and a wink before they both disappeared, whilst I settled down in front of the TV.

Richard Baker was presenting the BBC evening news. With just his head and shoulders in camera shot and the BBC News logo behind him, it looked like a sketch from The Two Ronnies. The first item on the news was about the aftermath of the riots on Monday in Notting Hill. Like football matches, this was another example of how things had improved since the '70s.

The news moved to a report that the police had made a connection between the two murdered women in the Leeds area in January and last October, and were now merging enquiries, thus creating a single task force. My mouth dropped open as two massive realisations hit me; I didn't even notice that Jenny was next to me, holding out a glass of wine.

"Jason ... Jason ... hello, anyone there? Your wine, darling."

I took the wine and smiled back, but the news occupied my thoughts. Those murders were the Yorkshire Ripper. He would go on to kill God knows how many women. I knew this, no one else did, probably not even the Ripper. I would have to tell someone, but before I could even process that information, I recalled the Radio Five-Live news from the 12th of August 2019. That news item I'd heard whilst driving to work the morning of my crash—

'This morning, we have made a significant breakthrough regarding the brutal murders of five women. We are very keen to talk to David Albert Colney, aged fifty-nine, to help with our enquiries.'

David Colney was sixteen, born in 1960, and was fifty-nine years old in 2019. I'd remembered the name when it was announced on the radio, but I hadn't made the connection at the time. I hadn't connected him with the future news reports when his name was called out during registration on Wednesday, but it was him. He progresses from child abuse to become a serial killer.

Stunned by this revelation, I downed the wine in one. I needed to think and work out what I had to do. I had four years to protect Beth and probably forty years to stop him from becoming a serial killer. Jesus, and then there was the issue of the Yorkshire Ripper, which was immediate. So, there was no time to plan what to do about him because it was already happening. Tomorrow, I'd planned to meet up with George. However, I suspected that could be a somewhat tricky meeting based on the fact my parents' deaths were still so raw for both of us. Therefore, I would have to tread carefully, but I needed to talk this through with him.

I put my thoughts to one side to avoid Helen thinking I was a quiet recluse, no-hoper, and remembering my concern that I wanted her approval as Jenny's new boyfriend. There was nothing I could do that night, but I knew George would help me tomorrow.

We started with a fondue, which I struggled to get my head around. Fortunately, although the cheese sauce was probably not my thing, that was followed up with a steak. Jenny said her man must have a nice steak and his girl should know how to cook it properly for him, which was a very '70s style statement. When I offered to do the washing up, both looked at me very strangely.

The record player had undulated its way through two Beatles albums, which I had suffered. I didn't dislike them, but there were about a million artists I preferred. Taste in music was about the only thing that Jenny and I differed on, oh yes, and fondue. When Helen changed the record to the David Cassidy album *Cherish*, I prayed for The Beatles to return.

I found Helen easy to get on with, and it was obvious to see why they shared a flat so well and for so long. The girls had planned the evening perfectly – after dinner, Helen left, saying she was staying at her mother's. Jenny and I enjoyed the rest of the evening, but tonight's discoveries were never far from my thoughts.

36

4th September 1976

Luger

The balmy, oven-like August heatwave extended into early September. George and I opted for the beer garden to catch the sun, but mainly to ensure we had some privacy. At first, the conversation was somewhat of a struggle, with both of us unable to find the right words. Nearly two weeks had passed since the train crash, and exactly two weeks ago we'd discussed at length how we could stop the '84 crash that had cruelly become the '76 crash.

"How are Stephen and Ivy?"

"Not very good, lad. Ivy cries every day, and Stephen is just quiet all the time; he stays up in the spare room, well, his room now." George took a deep breath, sighed, and stared at the wooden table. I couldn't recall ever seeing him like that. "How are you doing, lad?"

"It's hard, George, but I went through this thirty-five years ago, so I've had all that time to get my head around it, although I never did. Time does move on. You and Ivy brought Stephen and me up brilliantly; now you will only have Stephen to worry about because I'm already here."

"We did a good job with you both, then?"

"Yes, George, you did. Although we'd lost Mum and Dad, you were both brilliant, and I have the greatest memories of you both."

George nodded a few times, styled on a nodding toy dog on the parcel shelf of a car. "That's good, lad, that's good."

"George?"

"Yes, lad."

"I need your help, but with what's happened, I feel it's wrong to ask—"

"Lad, you're my grandson," he interrupted. "I'm here to look after you as well. I want to help you just as much as Stephen, so don't hold back."

"Okay, thanks, George."

"Look, I can assure you, lad, any distraction from the past two weeks will be more than welcome. So, what's on your mind? What can I help you with?"

"It's a long story, but let me bring you up to speed, and then you'll see my problem."

I talked through the events. Some of it he'd heard before, although this time I included Jenny. George listened with the hair-sprayed eyebrow making a comeback as I recalled the news stories from yesterday and 2019.

"Bloody hell, lad, that's a lot to take in."

"Hell, yes, you're telling me. So firstly, I'm going to have to deal with David Colney, although I've no idea what that will be. I mean, I can't just walk up and shoot dead a sixteen-year-old kid, not that I have a gun."

"I have a gun."

"What do you mean, you have a gun?" I exclaimed rather too loudly. A young couple seated at a table near the rear of the garden both looked around at my outburst.

"Lad, calm down. You'll have us both arrested! Look, I have a German Luger, just a war souvenir. Trouble is, I don't have any bullets."

"George, I can't go around killing people. I'm not a murderer, he is. Well, he's not yet, but he will be in forty years from now. Actually, as we stand today, he's not even a child abuser."

"Sick bloke. I would wring his neck if I got hold of him."

"I don't think I can even do that. I imagine there are laws against teachers wringing the necks of their students."

"Maybe, lad, you could have a quiet word with him, put him straight on a few things."

"Oh, come on, George, what will I say?" I asked, now a bit miffed that this was going nowhere. "David, come here a minute. I need to tell you I'm a time-traveller and you don't turn out too well in the future. In a few years, you will go to prison for child abuse, and then, as you get older, you will become a serial killer, so be a good chap and tone it down a bit." I blurted out, somewhat frustrated by the lack of feasible ideas. "Not sure that's going to work, do you?"

"Sorry, lad, just trying to help."

"No, George, I'm sorry. It's just I don't know what to do. And then there's the immediate problem of these murders in Leeds. He goes on to kill loads of women. I can't remember how many, but if my memory serves me correctly, he became the biggest serial killer of all time. They failed to arrest him until the early '80s."

I leaned in closer to George, both of us now bent over the bench, talking in low voices like two boys sharing secrets. "And I know who he is. No one else does!"

"You could go to the police, lad. Tell them that this bloke has committed the two murders. Stop him in his tracks, so to speak."

"I could. I've thought about that. But they're going to want to know how the hell I know, and at that point, I'm going to struggle to tell them, don't you think?"

"Yes, you are. That's no good. You're right, lad. That won't work either. How about you send an anonymous letter to the police? That will save you having to explain. Then they can follow up and catch him."

"Yes, I thought of that as well. The problem is, I can't remember all the facts, but I think it was a bit of a botched investigation. They arrested him several times throughout the years but could never get anything to stick, so they let him go again. If I send a letter, that will probably have the same outcome, even if they do follow it up."

"Oh, Christ, I don't know then. When does he kill again?"

"George, I don't know if I'm honest. All I know is he went on a wild killing spree in the late '70s … so it could be next week or even next year."

George pursed his lips, presumably contemplating this information. With neither of us capable of producing any sensible ideas, I changed the subject.

"I was also thinking that I have a lot of knowledge that no one else has, stuff I could tell you that will blow your mind."

"What, more so than you are my time-travelling grandson?"

"Well, no, but big stuff that happens over the next forty years. For example, just about everyone on the planet, and I mean everyone, will have a small device that will fit into your pocket. It is a telephone and a computer. It's more powerful than any computer on the planet, probably better than what NASA has right now."

"What, no way? Did I have one of these things in the future?"

"No, George, you die—"

"Lad, stop! Remember the rule I made."

"Oh, fuck, sorry, George, a slip of the tongue."

"Mind your language, lad. You're too big to put across my knee, but I can still remind you of your Ps and Qs."

"Sorry, George. Anyway, I know all the big disasters that will happen over the next forty years. Well, not all, but there's a fair few of which I know the exact date. Don't I have a duty to warn the world?"

"What, like Nostradamus?"

"Well, yes, kind of, but these are facts about the future, not predictions."

"Also, I know pretty much all the F1 results, so I could bet on every race and be mega-rich."

"What's F1, lad?"

"Oh yeah, Grand Prix, it's short for Formula-One, but I could do that. Also, I could invest in companies that grow over the next forty years and make a fortune."

"What, like oil companies?"

"Well, no, more like the pocket computer companies, really."

"Oh yes, of course, they would be worth a fortune if everyone on the planet has one of those things."

"But is that right? Is it morally right that I do that? Will I have an unfair advantage that I shouldn't have?"

"Lad, I think you should use that knowledge. As long as the future hasn't changed, otherwise you could lose a fortune."

"Well, James Hunt won the Grand Prix last Sunday as I said he would, and Ronnie Peterson will win the next one at Monza in Italy, I know he will. You could put a bet on that and buy Ivy that watch."

"Lad, with what's happened, the watch doesn't seem important anymore."

"Yeah, I know, you're right."

"I need another pint, lad ... you want the same again?"

"Yeah, go on then."

George trotted off to refill our glasses whilst I lit a cigarette. Although George wasn't coming up with any ideas, being able to talk through the issues with someone was such a relief. George returned to the beer garden, skilfully negotiating two young children running around, generally being annoying. They reminded me of Stephen and me from all those years ago.

"Lad, time has changed. Joan died eight years before you said she would," he said, taking his seat and plopping my pint down. A quarter of an inch of beer bounced over the top and onto the table.

"Yes, I think that's my fault. Well, the fact that I've arrived here now, and I can't be born again, if you get my meaning. I'm so sorry, George."

"No, lad, it's not your fault, it's not. It was going to happen, but we just couldn't stop it."

"So, what if I can't stop other things, like the Ripper, like David Colney? It would be hell knowing what's going to happen and not being able to do anything … as if time just won't let me."

"Look, you can't change the whole world, you just can't. I think you've got to think about your life. Concentrate on this lass, Jenny, who you're fond of, and just the one change, stopping that Colney fellow."

"I don't know, but you're probably right. Christ, this is driving me nuts."

"Are there any wars in the future? Or have we all learned at last that wars solve nothing?"

"No, lessons not learnt. There are loads of wars. In fact, would you believe, we go to war with Argentina over the Falkland Islands in a few years. It didn't last long; we won it, but more men on both sides died, as they do in all wars."

"Bloody hell, none of this nuclear stuff, though?"

"No, thank God. That's one weapon too far. That would be the end of it all."

"Right, lad, let's focus on this Colney chap and what we are going to do about him. So, what do you know so far?"

"Well, he's not good at schoolwork and will probably leave with no qualifications. He lives on the Broxworth Estate. I'm afraid that's about it."

"Look, lad, I think we need to know everything about him. I'll discreetly ask around at work. Lots of the chaps live on that estate, so they'll know the family. If you could spend some time with him and try to improve his schoolwork, he might get a qualification, and that could change what happens to him. We have plenty of time. What do you think?"

"Okay, but knowing what he becomes, I don't really want anything to do with him. You're right, though. It's a starting point, I guess."

"Right, lad, that's the plan. Now, look, I need to get going," he said, checking his watch. "Let's catch up next Saturday. I'd also like to meet that lass of yours. Ivy isn't one for having folks around, and certainly not at the moment, so perhaps I could bring Ivy down one evening and casually chat at the bar. What do you think?"

"That would be great, George, and I will try with David Colney. Although, as you said, I just want to wring his neck."

37

5th September 1976
Pink Panther

On Sunday, Jenny and I enjoyed the morning at my house. It was reminiscent of the first week when Lisa and I had moved in – thirty years in the future – a point at which I think Lisa and I were happy. Jenny had now notched up my contentment to a higher level.

Don had called Sunday morning to report that all was quiet at Carol's flat. He'd checked in on her on Saturday, and she was fine, although she'd ranted about Fin Booth, using language he thought was too colourful for a young lass. Don was lonely, so the new surveillance job I'd given him kept him busy. I kept the conversation going as we chatted for half an hour while he gave me the low-down on events.

Jenny popped around early, bringing the Sunday papers and the ingredients to knock up a full English breakfast. She insisted I sat and read the papers whilst she cooked breakfast for her man, as she put it – a comment that sounded like it belonged in a different era to where I'd come from. That comment certainly wouldn't have been uttered from Lisa's mouth. The woman looking-after-the-man thing was alien to me, and two things concerned me with this. Firstly, I was not used to it, and secondly, I wanted our relationship to be equal, more modern. Although Lisa and I had failed, we had an equal partnership, and I would have to steer Jenny that way. Reading the paper, I looked up at Jenny across the breakfast table.

"Jen?"

"Uh-huh," she responded, whilst munching her way through a piece of toast.

"If you were able to time-travel, and you went back, I don't know, let's say twenty years or so, and you knew a terrible thing was going to happen in the future, what would you do?"

"Oh, what a strange question. I do remember seeing that *Time Machine* film at the ABC Cinema when I was a teenager. I think I went with a boy called Charles. Dad wasn't happy, collecting me straight after the film ended, which I don't think Charles was very pleased about, especially as I kept removing his hand from my knee throughout the film. I thought the film was terrifying at the time. I can't remember how old I was, probably about sixteen. Did you see that film as well?"

"Yes, I know the one. I think I saw it on TV, but what would you do?"

"Oh yes, something terrible is going to happen, you say, and what would I do?"

"Yes, you know, silly idea, but just wondered," I added with a nervous laugh. I now regretted going down this route. However, I couldn't get the Yorkshire Ripper out of my mind.

"What sort of terrible thing?" Jenny asked, her head on the heels of her hands, propped up by her elbows on the table.

"Well, let's say you remember that bloke, Christie, from the '50s, and you time-travel back before then, knowing he will murder people. What would you do?"

"Oh, that was horrible. I was only a little girl, but it was all over the news when he was caught and hanged." Jenny gave a slight shudder as if to remove the memory. "So, I go back, and I know he will kill, so what would I do, you say?"

"Yes, just hypothetically."

"Hmmm, well, I would tell a policeman, of course, or my mum. Although I don't think they would believe a little girl."

"No, sorry, I meant if you went back in time and you were the same age as you are now."

"Oh, okay, well, I would still tell the police."

"Hmmm, you're a time-traveller, and you know John Christie will murder people soon, so you tell the police this and expect them to arrest him? Not sure that will work." The conversation was starting to go down the same route as the one with George.

"Hmmm, good point," Jenny pondered, moving her mouth side to side, weighing up the options. "Well, I could call the police anonymously as the murder is about to occur, so he got caught."

"What if you didn't know the exact time? Do you know the exact day Christie murdered someone?"

"Hmmm, no … good point. I know," she exclaimed, sitting up with her hands in the air, appearing all excited. "I would just kill him first. There you go, it's easy."

"Oh yes, that would do it," I chuckled, realising that neither Jenny nor George could help with this dilemma, and both had the idea that I could kill the Ripper or David, or both. Well, killing the Yorkshire Ripper was not an option. No, definitely not, but David Colney, well, it was possible. However, I'm not a murderer, and I just didn't think I had it in me to kill another human being. So, that left me with George's plan to try to improve David's chances at school, then maybe, just maybe, that would change his life, thus stopping him from travelling down that dark route, which only I knew he did.

"Anyway, silly notion. Why ever did you come up with that thought?" Jenny asked, as she started to clear the table of empty plates.

"Oh, nothing really, just an article in the paper made me think about it." I quickly folded the paper, plopping it on the table. "Let's go out somewhere," I suggested, urgently wanting to change the subject.

"Good idea, and talking about the cinema, there's a re-run of *The Return of the Pink Panther* showing. I didn't get to see that last year. Shall we go and see that one?"

"Yeah, let's do that." Anything to take my mind off David Colney for a few hours was welcome because this dilemma was starting to consume me.

~

After being handed two red paper tickets peeled off a roll from the usher at the kiosk, we purchased a large packet of Revels and a Kia-Ora orange drink each, then moseyed our way into the auditorium. As it was the matinée show, it was only half full, so we opted for seats near the back row where there was plenty of space around us. To my right, a young couple were clearly ravenous. I could only surmise that they'd missed lunch as they appeared to be devouring each other. *"Get a room,"* I muttered. It was going to be like having two movies in one: The Pink Panther in front of me and a soft porn show on my right as the lad's hands explored the girl's breasts under her top – the rubbing, I expected, would leave her sore.

The seats were ancient and uncomfortable, with dirty ashtrays in the armrest full of cigarette butts where they'd failed to clean them after yesterday's showing. We settled down with our goodies – if you can call a Kia-Ora drink a goody – and watched some crude coloured light show playing on the heavy red curtains that covered the screen.

At last, the curtains swished back – however, not the start of the film but a volley of outdated, cringeworthy adverts. The Marlboro cowboy was up first, somewhat ironic that the actor died at a young age with pulmonary heart disease caused by smoking. I made a mental note – I must give up. The next three reinforced the era I was now living in, depicting women in the kitchen cooking for their husbands: Cookeen, Yeoman tinned meat and Rose's Marmalade. No wonder Jenny had that mindset. The curtains started to slowly close as the screen displayed an

222

opportunity to visit the toilet facilities. Bloody hell, everyone must have had a bladder issue because we'd only been in the auditorium for twenty minutes.

The curtains reopened with yet more adverts – I groaned – before glancing to my right to check out the live porn show that appeared to be in full swing. I considered this might pan out to be a better entertainment option if the film didn't start soon.

An advert for Solvite wallpaper paste with a bloke stuck to a board hanging from a helicopter was next up on the silver screen. Personally, I thought soya milk would perform better. That was followed by a competition to win a Chrysler Sunbeam car if you bought some Head & Shoulders shampoo. However, looking at the car on offer suggested a good reason to avoid that particular shampoo purchase.

To my great relief, the adverts ended. Although I'd seen all the Pink Panther films, they were so old I couldn't remember the storyline, so I thought I'd still enjoy the movie. Jenny linked her arm through mine and leaned her head on my shoulder. To my right, the porn stars were all hands, exploring each other's body parts in more detail than before. It appeared her chest was now getting some light relief as the boy had moved his hands lower.

The interval came an hour into the film, just as Sir Charles Litton attempted to escape the clutches of the Fat Man's henchmen. A cliffhanger moment and, unsurprisingly, a loud groan reverberated around the auditorium as the curtains swished across the screen. A lady appeared with an usherette tray, presumably selling ice creams. In anticipation, many of the audience had already started to form a long line.

"Ice cream, darling?" chirped Jenny, as she jumped up to join the queue.

"Yeah, go on then. Get those two some as well. They look like they've nearly eaten each other," I said, pointing to the young porn stars.

"You're only jealous, darling," she chuckled, as she bounded down the steps.

The film restarted, and the basic plot – which had come back to me as the film got going – was the hilarious, bumbling efforts of Inspector Clouseau to recover the stolen Pink Panther diamond, whilst Dreyfus attempts to kill Clouseau, resulting in him ending up in a padded cell. It was not far from my situation with David Colney, although I wasn't sure a bomb was an option to sort my problem out.

On the left, about halfway down the auditorium, it was clear that a group of lads were mucking about, talking and annoying some girls sitting in front of them. Although somewhat irritating, I ignored them as best I could. A gent positioned near the fracas loudly shushed them, resulting in him receiving some verbal response from one of the lads.

"Piss off, grandad."

At that point, the girls stood up, moving to the right to exit the aisle, but one of the boys reached out, grabbing the hand of the girl who was last in the row. She turned around, pushing him away, but he didn't let go.

The commotion alerted the usher, who moved up the aisle, waving his torch before nervously asking them to sit down and be quiet. He was only a young lad himself, and it didn't look like he would have any impact. The man who they'd called grandad stood up and moved towards the group of youths; the boy who still had hold of the girl's arm pointed at him.

"Piss off, grandad, nothing to do with you."

The film stopped, and the lights came up as chatter broke out in the auditorium. The usher received backup support in the form of a colleague and a young man dressed in a shirt and tie, presumably the manager. Not surprisingly, the porn stars to my right were oblivious to the whole event. I released Jenny's arm from mine and stood up, ready to move down towards the man who'd been told to piss off. It had now reached the point where I just couldn't stand by because this lad was out of control. Then the situation escalated, with the boy yanking the girl's ponytail

224

with his other hand. She screamed and swung her free arm, slapping him hard across the face.

"Jason, don't," pleaded Jenny, presumably sensing the situation was about to turn ugly.

"Hang on, sweetheart," I replied, as I steamed down the steps.

"You bitch, you'll do what I bloody want," the boy shouted.

"That's it," said the grandad bloke, who was actually only about my age. Both of us waded in, grabbing the boy and pulling him away. As I pinned his arms behind him, the other guy took hold of his collar. Out of the corner of my eye, I could see Jenny had hopped down the steps to comfort the girl. The manager now joined in and helped us restrain the lad, who continued to hurl verbal abuse.

"You fucking frigid bitch. I'll teach you a fucking lesson, just you wait."

The three of us frog-marched him out of the auditorium, receiving a cheer from the rest of the audience. All his mates had vanished, probably realising this was not the place to be. The manager chap informed us of the imminent arrival of a police officer, who'd been alerted and should arrive at any moment. The young ruffian calmed down, realising he couldn't overpower the three of us as we pinned him to the wall. As he lifted his head and looked at me, I instantly recognised him – David Colney.

"Oh, fuck, it's that bloke, Apple. Fucking hell!"

The manager shot me a look. "Do you know this ruffian?"

"I'm a teacher, and he is a pupil at our school." Keeping my eyes firmly on David's, I applied pressure to his throat with my arm, furious at what I'd just witnessed. "What the hell do you think you were doing with that girl?" I challenged him.

Colney grinned, "She asked for it, frigid bitch. Just a fucking prick tease."

"That's enough, that's enough." The police officer had joined us, thank God, as I was close to wringing his neck.

"Right then, Colney, you're going the same way as your old man at this rate," said the police officer, as he applied handcuffs to David's wrists, then almost dragged him out of the cinema.

The flustered manager sighed with relief as David disappeared through the front doors. He appeared quite shaken by the whole episode. I guess dealing with this kind of incident wasn't in his workplace training manual. "Gentleman, thank you. We don't usually have this sort of trouble," he stated, still trying to compose himself.

We moved back into the auditorium where I spotted Jenny comforting the girl, who understandably appeared extremely distressed. The rest of her friends were all about to leave, a couple of them thanking Jenny and then cuddling their friend as they made their way to the exit.

"You okay, darling?"

"Yes, the police have taken him away. It was a boy from my school, and I can't believe he was treating a girl like that. What a monster. Are you alright?"

"Yes, darling, I'm fine. The young girl was okay, just shaken up, I think."

We returned to our seats and settled down to watch the rest of the film. The manager nervously addressed the auditorium. "Really sorry, folks, the film will now restart," he babbled before sprinting in the direction of the exit.

The film resumed, normality in the auditorium was restored with fewer people and the porn stars still heavily engrossed in each other. Despite the events, I enjoyed the rest of the film, but nagging in my brain was David Colney. He'd already developed a horrendous attitude towards women, and I could see why his future panned out as it did.

Following his arrest today, I expected he would be expelled from school. Therefore, George's plan for me to help David improve his schoolwork would go sideways. Time seemed to have taken control to keep David's path fully on track.

38

6th September 1976

The Spoon

Monday morning came with a break in the weather. The steaming hot summer was now coming to an end as the rain fell steadily from the dark black clouds that cloaked the sky. The end to the hose-pipe ban and dried-up river beds looked to be not too far away. Perhaps the removal of those water-rationing standpipes in the road would also be soon if the rain continued.

Conversely, my mood was as bright as the sunshine which had flooded the country for some months. My relationship with Jenny was past the blossoming stage, and we were both very much feeling we'd found the right person, even though we had only known each other a short while.

Of course, my two problems were not resolved. However, I now had a clear plan of what to do about David Colney. The first job was to ensure he wasn't expelled from school when yesterday's events came to light. This would allow me to teach and help this boy, but I also had a clear backup plan to ensure he never got near Beth. The slightly trickier issue that he would become a serial killer, I couldn't resolve at this point. However, I had time and plenty of it.

I felt guilty about my plan to get Beth removed from her home and the effect that would have on Carol. That said, I knew this had to happen and would be my backup fail-safe plan to ensure Beth was protected. In my previous life, Beth was taken from Carol, albeit in a few years, so I tried not to feel too guilty.

With the support of my surveillance man, Don, I would build a compelling account that proved to the Child Protection team at Fairfield Council – or whatever they were called – that Beth was in danger if she stayed with her mother.

If successful, I could then get Beth removed as soon as possible and placed into care. Maybe a loving family would adopt her, which would ensure, if I failed to change David's path, Beth would be protected. It seemed like a solid plan, with the ace up my sleeve being Jenny due to her working in the department that I needed to influence.

Regarding the other issue of the Yorkshire Ripper, I still had no idea of what action to take. The conversations with George and Jenny were going around in my head. However, no solutions were forthcoming, so I prayed my procrastination didn't endanger another young life.

A few years ago, one of my Christmas presents from Lisa was a book called *Hideous Crimes*. This large hardback book detailed the crimes of serial killers throughout the twentieth century. At the time, when tearing off the wrapping paper sitting in my in-laws' front room, I thought it was a very odd present to receive. I'd expected it to be another F1 book, as that was Lisa's default position for stocking fillers when she ran out of ideas about what to buy me. But no, it was a book on murder, the most hideous kind of murder, as the book title suggested.

I invested a few hours reading the book that Christmas afternoon. Not that I was particularly interested, but it afforded me the excuse to avoid conversing with my in-laws whilst they watched the Queen's speech and The Sound of Music that seemed to be re-run every Christmas Day. One large chapter detailed the disturbing story of Peter Sutcliffe, the Yorkshire Ripper, listing his crimes, including the dates committed. Now, living back in the 1970s, it was nothing short of criminal that I couldn't remember anything I'd read.

The first part of my plan was simple – catch up with Roy first thing this morning and talk through the events of Sunday. I would promise to take responsibility for ensuring David's behaviour and schoolwork improved, thus stopping the expulsion that was surely on the cards. When nipping into the main office as I arrived at school, the efficient Miss Colman was already behind her desk, looking efficient.

"Good morning, Miss Colman. The weather has turned. I nearly got drowned crossing the car park this morning."

"Good morning, Mr Apsley. Yes, it has, and it's about time, too, I say. It's been far too hot, and my garden is in desperate need of rain. I'm not sure my lawn will ever recover. It's been yellow for months, and not being able to use the hosepipe hasn't helped."

"Is he in?" I ask, nodding towards Roy's office.

Miss Colman stood up from her chair and performed that furtive sideways look, although we were the only ones in the office. She then moved closer and whispered, "I don't like to gossip, as you know, and I shouldn't tell you this. However, he's in a meeting with Mr and Mrs Skeet. Apparently, on Sunday, that dreadful boy you enquired about last week, attacked their daughter at the pictures and subsequently got himself arrested. I think Mr Skeet is getting quite angry, as I've heard him raise his voice on several occasions."

"Oh, shit."

Miss Colman abruptly shot her head back, sporting a deep frown. "Sorry, Mr Apsley, what did you say?"

"Oh … err … oh shoot," I replied, louder this time. "How long have they been in there?"

Appearing comfortable that I hadn't sworn, she leant forward again, taking up her preferred gossiping position. "Well, it's eight-twenty-five, and they came in at eight, so it's been going on a while."

"Hmmm, what do you think will happen to David Colney?"

"Mr Clark will expel him, without a doubt, and bloody good riddance, I say." She blushed as her hand once again shot up to

229

her mouth. "Oh, excuse me, Mr Apsley, that wasn't the language becoming of a lady."

"Fully excused, Trish," I grinned, amused by her prim and proper persona. "Right, well, I need to speak to Roy, so I'll just make sure my team are set up for the day, and I will be back in a moment. If Roy becomes free before I return, can you let him know I would like to see him, please?"

"Yes, of course, Mr Apsley. And remember, during school hours, it's formal address … surnames only please, Mr Apsley."

I zipped off without replying to get Colin and Jayne set up for the day. Barrelling down the corridor on the lower level, I observed a group of senior boys shouting and shoving – general laddish banter – which appeared to be causing a disturbance near the main school entrance. I spotted some junior pupils stuck outside in the rain who seemed nervous about walking past them. Clearly, I would have to intervene.

"Boys, separate and move on … clear the doorway," I bellowed.

The boys all turned to face me. In the centre of the group stood David Colney. With his head held high and chest puffed out, a broad grin crept across his smug face.

"What you gonna do, Apple, 'ave me arrested?"

Laughter ensued, and the boys slapped Colney on the back, all of them in awe of their ringleader.

"Move! All of you! Except you, Colney, you stay exactly where you are," I ordered. "Now!"

The boys held their positions for a few seconds, presumably weighing up their options. Finally, one boy came to a decision and walked off, quickly followed by the rest. Colney stood there, grinning, generally looking pleased with himself. I moved up close to within an inch of his face. Being a large-framed lad and nearly as tall as me, he clearly wasn't remotely intimidated by my presence.

"Watch yourself, Apple … I know people who can turn you into pulp."

Ignoring his literary attempt at a metaphor, I resisted the urgent need to punch him. Although my last fight at the school – as I remember – hadn't gone well, I grabbed his forearm.

"Colney, don't threaten me. Now get to Mr Poole's class. I will deal with you later."

Colney smirked, sidestepped and moved around me, then called back over his shoulder, "Be careful, Apple, be very careful."

After ferrying the juniors in from the rain, some soaked to the skin, I resumed my quest to find Colin and Jayne. Once they were sorted, I scooted back to see Roy. My plan to help David Colney appeared to be faltering – that boy really was a piece of shit. I struggled to see how I could change his behaviour and improve his chances of achieving an education. Potentially, I'd just have to rely on the second part of the plan and get Beth's timeline changed, ensuring she never encountered that monster.

Back at the office, Mr and Mrs Skeet were just leaving. As they brushed past me, Mr Skeet's expression suggested he wasn't best pleased. With a ruddy complexion, Roy stood by his office door, wringing his hands.

"Morning, Jason. Have you got a minute?"

"Yes, Roy, I need to speak to you, anyway."

We moved into his damp-smelling, chaotic office. Roy's raincoat hung from the coat stand, the bottom hem still dripping, causing a puddle to form on the polished wooden floor.

"Jason, that was Mr and Mrs Skeet. Their daughter is Sarah Skeet. There's been an unfortunate incident, not on school grounds, but at the ABC Cinema yesterday, where one of your students assaulted Sarah and subsequently got himself arrested. It's a serious matter."

I decided to keep quiet and let Roy push on with his story. Clearly still ruffled, following what I can only assume must have been a somewhat tricky meeting with Mr and Mrs Skeet, Roy appeared highly concerned. I guess that came with the territory of his position as the Head Master. Of course, I was aware that yesterday's events were not good for the school's reputation.

"The boy in question is David Colney, and he is in your form group. You are aware of whom I am referring to?"

"Yes, I know him." Far better than Roy could possibly know.

"Well, he's been a problem all his school career. He comes from a particularly difficult family who live on the Broxworth Estate. The father is in prison, and his two older brothers, who also attended this school, are nasty pieces of work. Present company excepted, but nothing good comes from that estate, I can tell you."

I knew he wasn't correct on that part because Beth had come from that estate. Roy's comment was a typical statement from a middle-class man who tar-brushed everyone just because they lived in a particular area. After a few drinks with Don, my surveillance man, Roy would realise that his blanket slur included brave war heroes. However, based on his flustered demeanour, I felt this wasn't the time to correct him.

"I'm going to expel him indefinitely! I'll arrange to get him admitted into the Howlett School to complete his final year because he can't continue his education at this school, not with Sarah Skeet here."

"Yes, I understand, but I need to tell you some information about yesterday's incident."

I relayed the story from the cinema and included today's events whilst Roy rocked back in his chair, placing his hands behind his head.

"Jason, I think you should have told me this information first thing."

"Well, I tried, but you were in with Sarah's parents at the time."

"Right, okay. Can you get him down here to the office? I'll also need to get hold of his mother to advise her we're expelling him. It's not a conversation I'm relishing as I've had dealings with her before and fully expect a barrage of foul language."

"Yes, Roy, I'll get him now," I replied, hopping up from my chair.

As I feared, the first part of my plan was indeed dead in the water. There wasn't going to be a chance to support David to achieve better results and thus change his fortunes.

Heading off to get David, the corridors were now quiet as all classes had started. Pushing open the heavy oak door of room twenty-two, I entered to find the whole class standing and facing the back wall. At the front of the room, Colin appeared to be brandishing a large wooden spoon-shaped object, almost like a pizza paddle drilled with penny-sized holes. A boy, who I believed to be James Baxter, lay bent over the desk whilst Colin administered swift corporal punishment.

At school in my day, we had the *slipper* and the *spoon*. At the time, they were the modern-day cane. However, the vision of this sort of punishment being meted out was somewhat of a shock. Physical violence being dealt out publicly to a child – action in my old world that would have made headline news, plus a criminal charge of assault for the teacher – was unacceptable, whatever misdemeanour James had performed.

"Mr Poole, can I have a moment, please?" I said with calm authority.

Colin, who appeared ready to land a blow on James's posterior, halted mid-flow and glanced in my direction. I wasn't sure if this was his first swing or working his way through dishing out the punishment. I guess that depended on how many *'lashes'* James had been sentenced to. "Stay there, James," he ordered, before joining me in the corridor.

I chose to ignore the pizza-paddle incident and just deal with David Colney. "Colin, can you ask David Colney to come out of class? I need to take him to the school office."

"He didn't come in today, so I've marked him absent on the register."

"Oh, right. Not seen him at all?"

"No."

"Oh, okay, thanks, Colin. I'll let you get back to class."

Walking away and wondering where David Colney had disappeared to, I halted and swivelled around to ask Colin another question. "What's James Baxter done?"

"He exposed himself to a group of girls."

Teaching was a difficult job. Yes, I had to pull into line the occasional unacceptable banter at Waddington's Steel, and I had dismissed one of my sales team for inappropriate behaviour. Paul Bass, a *Jack-the-lad*' type, like a sketch from a Benny Hill show, had pinched the bottom of a young lady standing at the coffee machine. Amazingly, he couldn't see what he'd done wrong. However, these kids were a nightmare compared to my previous bunch of misfits.

39

Wagon Wheel

The school day had finished. David Colney did not attend any classes, and Roy had received a barrage of verbal abuse from Mrs Colney when she'd arrived at the school at lunchtime. Miss Colman had been shocked and said she had never heard language like it.

I took a trip into town because I had a couple of purchases I wanted to make before the shops closed. On my list was to buy every Beatles album I could lay my hands on, plus a record player. Andy's Record Shop had recently opened up in town. Sadly, I could remember it closing about the time of the Millennium, which was a real shame. It would have been good to see the store survive for just a few more years and reap the rewards of the vinyl resurgence. The new store looked as I remembered it. I purchased an extensive collection of Beatles albums and headed off to acquire the required record player.

Rumbelows was next on my list, and I picked up a Hitachi Hifi, which sported a double tape-deck and, of course, a record turntable on top. It came in a particularly fetching retro smoked-glass cabinet. It felt good to have proper kit to play music on and not my iPhone, although I would have to wait for another thirty years to see one of those again.

With only six days until Beth was due to be born, I took a trip up to the Broxworth Estate to see Don. After yesterday, I didn't want to bump into the Colney clan. However, I needed to check that Carol was okay and that her last few days of pregnancy were going to be smooth.

Walking past my old flat, I noticed that the landlord had listened to me and applied a '2' in between the two '1s' on my old front door. However, due to the '2' being significantly larger than the other two numbers, it now appeared worse than before.

Don yanked open his door and saluted, his back ramrod straight.

"At ease, soldier," I chuckled.

"Good evening, sir," he replied, as if addressing his senior officer. Although he'd finished fighting in the First World War over fifty years ago, those four years of trench warfare had left its mark on Don's life, as I suspected it had with all war veterans. I couldn't imagine the horror he'd witnessed, and strangely, I thought a part of him yearned for those times again. I guess the camaraderie with his fellow soldiers, though facing death every day, was probably better than the sad, lonely existence he had in that depressing concrete block he now called home.

"Come in, son, come in."

"Thanks, Don. How you keeping?"

"Good, son. Cuppa or something stronger?"

"Coffee, please, Don. I'll be here all night if I start drinking with you." I chuckled. "Look, I've bought this to replace the one we drank last week, but maybe we can tackle it another night," I suggested, placing a bottle of Johnnie Walker Black Label on the dark wooden table. Although Don's kitchen appeared dated, sporting a collection of painted white freestanding units, it was immaculate – the old soldier used to keeping his kit in good order.

"Ah, lovely, son, but there was no need for that. It was just nice to have some company."

"Well, I'll help you with this one as well, but not tonight because I need to keep a clear head."

"Actually, son, I was going to call you because Carol had a few visitors last night and also today."

"Oh, who?"

"Looked like a lass from the Council. Not the redhead that usually comes around. This one came this afternoon and stayed about an hour."

"How did you know she was from the Council?"

"They have a look, similar to the Old-Bill, if you know what I mean. Talking of that redhead, have you done anything about that yet? If I were a few years younger, I would be chasing her myself."

"Well, hands-off, old man. I *have* done something about it … and very glad I have too."

Don swivelled around with a broad grin and handed me my coffee. "Good man … well done, Jason. I'm eighty this year, and I've been about a bit in my time. I'm a good judge of character, and she's a good'un, son, as well as being rather easy on the eye. Hang on to her, or you'll be a fool."

"Don, never a truer word said."

"Well, make sure you do. Finding a good woman ain't easy. You know I was a lucky lad to find my Peggy."

"So, who else has been around to see Carol?"

"Well, that's the one that concerned me. Paul Colney, a right nasty piece of work. Do you know the Colney family? If you don't, I advise you to steer well clear, my boy."

"Yes, one of the Colney boys is at my school, so I know him. Tell me about this Paul."

"The Colney's are in cahoots with the Gowers. Now, you have heard of them?"

"Yes, unfortunately."

"Exactly. They are untouchable. They're definitely all in the evil category. Whatever you do, you have nothing to do with them. Old man Gower had links to Ronnie and Reggie."

"Christ, what do you reckon Paul Colney was doing at Carol's last night?"

"Paul Colney is the main supplier of street drugs, controlling the drug scene and pays the Gowers for the pleasure. The

Gowers control the top-end stuff like cocaine and heroin. Only one reason Paul visits someone, that's to peddle his stuff or give someone a good pasting."

"Oh, bloody hell, I'm not very knowledgeable about drugs, so what's he selling, do you think?"

"It will be Angel Dust or LSD … that's what's on the streets these days."

"Christ, Don, how do you know all this stuff?"

"I live on my own, son. I don't hear from the girls, so not much else to do but snoop." I noted a sadness in Don's voice. He was firmly in the sad category.

"So, you think Carol is on this stuff? She's pregnant, for Christ sake, and about to give birth on Sunday. Bloody hell!"

"Sunday, son, that's a bit accurate. I think Carol said she was due early October?"

"Oh, I don't know, just a guess."

I needed to be more careful, as now it was going to look odd when she gave birth on Sunday. Although it now appeared at least a few weeks early, probably due to the lifestyle she was leading.

"Has that Paul bloke been coming around a lot?"

"I have to say, I've never seen Paul Colney there before, but it wouldn't surprise me if he has. As I said, Carol's a rum one, you know. She'll have this kid taken from her as well, which will probably be the right thing to happen. I just don't know what's happened to the world. It's the bloody Government's fault. That idiot Callaghan and his lot haven't got a bloody clue. Ha, that said, son, I certainly don't want the other lot in. Can you imagine a woman Prime Minister? That really would be the end."

"Well … hmm, don't know." I wasn't sure what to say to that comment. It would have been good to let Don know that a woman would be Prime Minister, right through until he was ninety-four years old. Christ, he'd have a fit, and it would probably kill him.

"How long did he stay at Carol's?"

"Oh, not long, about fifteen minutes at the most. You want a Wagon Wheel or a bit of Battenberg? Actually, I've got a packet of Fondant Fancies somewhere, if you prefer?"

"Go on then. I'll have a Wagon Wheel. I've not had one of those since I was a kid."

Don arched his eyebrow, shot me a surprised look and chuckled, "Don't think you had those during the war, son, or have you forgotten rationing already?"

"Oh yeah, I meant not for a while. Anyway, tell me about the Colney family."

"Old man is doing time for sticking a pool cue through a bloke's eye in a pub brawl. He'd only been out a month after doing a stretch for something similar. There are four boys ... your boy at school is the second youngest, and the older two, Paul and Patrick, are twins. They're a right couple of thugs, I can tell you. The little lad ... can't remember his name, but he must be about ten years old. Colney's missus is a frightening woman, and she keeps all the women on the estate in line, I can tell you. None of them work ... well, pay taxes as such ... it's all drugs and protection, that sort of stuff."

"What part of the estate do they live on?"

"Left-hand side of Dublin House, don't know the flat numbers, but they have two flats together. I think some of their relatives live on that landing as well. Anyway, you keep well clear. They're a lot more dangerous than that Fin Booth bloke you sorted out."

"Oh, don't worry, I'm not going near them. I just wanted to know what company Carol was keeping."

"It's good of you, son, to be concerned about your old neighbour, but there is no helping lasses like Carol. You're well shot of this place; just focus on keeping that redhead happy."

"Jenny—"

"There you go, son ... she has a lovely name, too."

"Well, it's just after living here for a short while. I feel like Carol needs a chance. If I can help, then I'd like to."

"Very noble indeed, but I wouldn't bother. Although I'm enjoying being your chief intelligence officer."

"And a good one you are, too."

"You going to have a nip?" asked Don, as he snatched up the bottle of Johnnie Walker.

"No, not tonight, but thanks for the offer. Look, I better be off. I'll pop around next week at some point."

"Good, don't want to drink this on my own. That's the slippery slope."

Leaving the half-eaten Wagon Wheel, now remembering why I hadn't eaten one for years, I left Don's flat and banged on Carol's door. Finally, after a few thumping sessions, she opened up but kept the door ajar. From what I could see through the crack, she appeared to be in a right old state. Her bloodshot eyes and sallow complexion suggested she may be taking the drugs the Colney brothers were probably supplying. Her mop of greasy hair that poked out at all angles framed her sweat-covered face.

"Hello Carol, is everything alright?"

"Hi, Jase … yeah, alright … you know."

"Right, okay. Do you need anything? I can nip to the shops for you."

"Nah, you're alright, just tired. Gotta go, I need a shit." And with that, she closed the door.

"Oh, okay," I said to the door.

After Sunday, and as soon as possible, I had to get Beth out of that flat. Carol was on the way down, and if she was doing drugs, then God knows what would happen. The resolution to my short-term problem was going to have to be to remove Beth from danger. I had to forget David Colney for now, and my focus after Sunday was getting Beth to a safe place as soon as I could. The problem of David as the future serial killer would have to wait.

I'd parked my car off the estate due to not wanting to be spotted returning to it, especially as I was clearly not on the Colney family's Christmas card list. So, I had a bit of a hike through the estate's labyrinth back to Coldhams Lane. The rain had stopped, and the narrow concrete-walled alleyways were filled with kids on bikes – Choppers and Tomahawks. I remember owning a second-hand Chopper in the eighties and hated it because all my mates had the new Grifter bikes.

As I neared the edge of the estate, four teenagers were messing about on skateboards, using a set of concrete steps to perform various stunts. As I started to shimmy my way through them, they flipped up their boards and surrounded me.

"Err, excuse me," I confidently asked, not intimidated by four teenagers. Plus, I had no Beemer this time, so there was no opportunity for this group to demand protection money. No one moved, so with a degree of confidence, I started to push through them. However, they changed their formation, and all moved to form a line to block my path. Two men, dressed in black leather jackets, I guess in their early twenties, strolled out from the shadows of the steps and took up position behind the teenagers. They walked towards me as the boys parted like the Red Sea. Apart from their beards, the men looked nothing like Moses, nor did I believe they harboured any intent on a Christian act.

The following moves happened at lightning speed. Within a few seconds, my nose was pouring with blood, and the air in my stomach had been punched out, leaving me lying on the steps, gasping for air. Then, one bearded man leant in close to my face.

"You're not welcome here, Apple, you got it? Come back and visit the old man again, and he might have a fall … now, that would be a shame. The Hall girl might just be persuaded to kill herself; you clear?"

I nodded.

He grabbed my hair and banged my skull on the concrete step whilst, for good measure, the other thug booted my kneecap. Then they disappeared into that concrete labyrinth, leaving me to hobble back to my car – one set of school attire now ruined. They'd called me Apple, so I knew this was an attack administered by the Colney clan.

As I arrived home, I was faced with yet another problem. Parked on the driveway was a red Viva. Jenny leant against her car, smoking and waving enthusiastically. I couldn't drive off, so I had to think quickly to explain my current state. As I gingerly stepped out of my car, Jenny bounced towards me but stopped two feet short and shrieked, her hands flying up to her mouth.

"Oh, Jason, what has happened … where have you been … are you hurt?" she blurted out.

"I'm fine, I'm fine," I said, putting my hands in a surrender position.

Jenny laid her hand on my cheek. "No, you're not! What happened?" she asked again whilst wiping a dribble of blood from my top lip. "Oh darling, you're bleeding. We need to get you inside and cleaned up, and we may need to get you up to the hospital." Jenny took my keys from my hand and led me to the front door.

"I was mugged."

"What, in Fairfield? And in broad daylight? Come into the kitchen so I can see to your poor nose. I think we need to call the police."

"No police, Jenny … no police."

I couldn't risk the police involvement, even if they arrested the Colney family, because Carol and Don would suffer. Even though, as the weeks went by, Jenny was becoming the most important part of my life, protecting Beth was still at the forefront of my mind. We would never know each other in this life, but I loved Beth and wanted to ensure her life was safe. Police involvement would put that in danger.

"What do you mean, no police? You've been mugged!" she shrieked, becoming slightly hysterical.

"Jen, I will explain, but can you get me some Nurofen? My head is pounding. I think I'm slightly concussed."

Jenny shot a confused look at me. "Get you some what?"

"Oh, aspirin."

"Sit yourself down while I clean you up."

Jenny supplied the aspirin, then fussed with a wet tea-cloth around my nose. It hurt like hell, and Jenny's gentle prodding caused me to yelp. I think it was safe to presume those thugs had broken it.

"Jason, what's happened? I don't understand. Where were you mugged, and why are we not calling the police?" Jenny continued to poke the wet cloth around my bloodstained face, her green eyes searching into my eyes for answers.

"I see you still have your watch. Did the muggers take your wallet?"

I involuntary patted my jacket pocket, but I knew my wallet was still there before completing that action. Then I instinctively checked my trouser pockets.

"Oh, shit! Where's my mobile?"

Jenny pulled the cloth away from my face and narrowed her eyes. "Your what?"

"My phone."

"It's in the hall. It's not going to be in your pocket, is it? I think you're concussed … you're saying some very strange things."

I'd been without my mobile for weeks but, automatically in that moment of panic, I'd checked where my mobile was. For most people in my old life, those were the concerned, panic-filled few seconds when unable to locate your phone. I think in my old world, mobiles had become more precious than a limb.

"No, I'm okay, Jen, just a bit shook up. I'm absolutely fine, honestly."

"Where were you attacked?" Jenny had relented from her hysterical shrieks about the state of my face and thankfully stopped prodding my nose. Now, slightly calmer, she sat beside me, holding my hands.

"On the Broxworth Estate. I went to see Don, you know, just to check up on him."

"Your old neighbour?"

"Yes, he's lonely, so I just popped in for a coffee."

"What about your old next-door neighbour, Carol? Did you go and see her as well?"

"I knocked on the door just to see if she was okay."

"Why are we not calling the police, Jason?"

"Jenny, just leave it."

Jenny narrowed her eyes whilst slowly releasing her hands from mine, leaning back in her chair. Her expression had now morphed from concern and panic to a troubled, questioning look. She folded her arms and huffed. "How's your head now?" she asked abruptly. Her tone had changed – all sympathy had evaporated.

"Yes, it's okay."

"Jason, I need to know what's going on? You are so different from anyone I have ever met, and I've got this niggling thought in my mind that there's a part of you that I don't know. I believe it has something to do with Carol Hall."

"I—" Not sure of my next word, I closed my mouth.

"Jason, I have a right to know. I'm in love with you, and we can't have secrets; what's going on?"

"Nothing," I replied, dropping my eyes to lose eye contact. She knew I was lying.

"Nothing! So, I can call the police and report this mugging then?"

"No … leave it, Jen."

Jenny stood; her eyes had developed a watery glaze. I reached out my hand to her, but she snatched it away.

"Jason, there is something, and when you are ready to tell me, you can let me know."

With that, she disappeared down the hallway, and the front door slammed behind her.

"Oh, bollocks," I muttered.

40

10th September 1976

Coco Chanel

It wasn't the first time a woman had stormed out of my house and slammed the front door. Well, it was the first, but the second time happened first.

Lisa had performed the same act a few years after we'd moved in together, treading the same path and slamming the same front door after an argument. She'd delivered an ultimatum that I change my ways, or the marriage was over, and she could be contacted at her parents' house when I'd reached a decision. At the time, our view of life was very different. Lisa was nesting, thinking about children and settling into married life in suburbia. On the other hand, at the age of thirty-two, I was still in party and drinking mode and thus still too immature to move to the next stage, where Lisa was firmly rooted.

There were bound to be problems with our different outlooks on life. The final straw came one evening when I crawled in pissed again after another bender at the pub that involved a lock-in until the early hours. It didn't help that I broke the hall lamp when I stumbled in, which had been a wedding present from one of her best friends. This was then further exacerbated when I puked all over a pair of her favourite suede boots. However, the clincher for her was I stank of a woman's perfume, Coco Chanel, apparently. Although I had no idea why I smelt of that perfume and pleaded ignorance and innocence, it was too much for her to put up with, and she was off.

The next day, her father turned up to rip my head off. It didn't help that I had a head-splitting hangover, and I winced through his verbal tirade at what a total prick I was and that he had never thought I was good enough for his daughter. It took a whole week of grovelling and promises of improvements in my behaviour to coax her back. I hoped this time I could repair the damage quickly.

I phoned Jenny later that evening, but her flatmate, Helen, answered and was quite clear that Jenny would not talk to me. Also, if I messed her about, I would have her to deal with. It seemed the only option now open to me was to tell Jenny the truth. However, I'd discovered on far too many occasions that honesty didn't always work out. Persuading Jenny I was a time-traveller would be a step too far, and I expected would spell the end of our relationship. So, I had to sew together a lie and make it as plausible as possible so it couldn't be unpicked.

I dropped into The Three Horseshoes on Tuesday evening to discuss my latest dilemma with George. As was panning out with all these conversations, George didn't offer any solutions. Still, he provided the sounding board I needed in my new life. We both firmly agreed that telling the truth to Jenny was a complete no-no. George had no further information on the Colneys than Don had supplied. For now, I planned to distance myself from that evil family, mainly for Don and Carol's protection.

Jenny proved challenging to get hold of, but after multiple failed attempts to contact her, we had a short, curt conversation on Wednesday. She hadn't thawed but, after some grovelling on my part, we did agree to meet up on Friday when she expected a full explanation. I just hoped that I'd covered all the angles because if my lie had holes in it, I would need to be able to fill them convincingly. What I had realised, although saving Beth was my priority, I could not under any circumstances lose Jenny.

School had been okay. I'd added another lie about the state of my nose, saying I'd tripped up and fallen down a set of stairs. I was sure Roy believed my lie and showed great concern, but suspected many others didn't. You can just tell, can't you?

When I updated Don regarding my altercation with the Colney twins, he wasn't surprised. He duly promised to keep very close to Carol and asked me not to come to the estate. In fact, he instructed me to stay away, an instruction I would adhere to for now. He assured me he would supply me with daily updates of his observations from his surveillance duties. I talked through my latest dilemma with Jenny because I needed his help. However, I left out the time-travel bit because that was, as it would be with Jenny, not a feasible conversation to embark upon. I'd taken a real risk involving Don with my lie, but I needed to keep it simple.

Driving to Jenny's flat, I fully expected Helen to be there in the role as her pet Rottweiler, going by her tone on the phone on Monday evening. However, I was reasonably confident I could convince Jenny and Helen of my story. Nevertheless, the bad feeling in my stomach wouldn't disappear because the lying issue bothered me. That said, the truth would mean the destruction of our relationship.

Clutching an offensively large bunch of flowers I'd purchased at the florist on the High Street, I made my way up to her flat. The flowers were a difficult decision because blokes often get this wrong. If you bring flowers, they can get thrown in your face accompanied with a − *'Don't think a bunch of flowers is going to sort this out.'* comment. And conversely, if you don't turn up with flowers, you get − *'Well, you don't care that much; you couldn't even be bothered to bring me some flowers.'* That decision had always been a dilemma for me, and history suggested I'd achieved a fifty per cent success rate at getting it right.

Trying to convince Lisa that I had changed my drunken ways and wasn't seeing another woman who wore Chanel perfume was difficult. I'd turned up at her parents' home with flowers, but the school-boy error I'd made was I'd picked them up from a petrol station forecourt on the way. They were a cheap, drab-looking bunch, and as they were thrust into my face by a pissed-off Lisa, I received the waft of their lovely bouquet of car exhaust fumes. I was learning; this time, I don't think I would have bought flowers from a petrol station even if they sold them, and they didn't. I realised if I was taking flowers, they had to be from a florist.

The Rottweiler opened the door.

"Hello, Helen," I said, ready for the verbal mauling that was sure to come whilst pathetically hiding behind the bunch of flowers.

Helen stared with her hands on her hips, a sneer across her face, baring those Rottweiler teeth. "Don't think those are going to sort this out," she barked, glaring at the flowers.

"Can I come in?" I lowered the flowers and smiled, but she had already turned sideways, looking into the flat with her nose pushed in the air.

"Yes, but don't upset her, or you will have me to deal with."

"I promise I won't."

Helen turned and scowled. "You better come in then."

Jenny sat embedded in the corner of the sofa, legs folded underneath her as if about to perform yoga. Dressed in jeans and a t-shirt, she looked stunning. However, her expression was ice cold, and her green eyes like kryptonite.

"Jen, these are for you."

"I'll take them and let you two talk." Helen snatched the flowers and marched off. "Jenny, I'll be in the kitchen if you need me."

"Can I sit?"

"If you must." Jenny shifted to the end of the sofa, still in the yoga position, and I gingerly sat myself down at the other end. It was a small sofa, so we were still only a foot apart. Jenny tucked her legs in tighter as if I were a spider she didn't want to touch.

"Jen, I'm sorry about Monday. I really am, but nothing funny is going on."

"Well, what is going on?" she stabbed out, looking away from me.

"Look, Don, my old neighbour, is an extremely lonely man. He's lost his wife, and his two grown-up daughters have nothing to do with him. They have their own lives and rarely make contact. Since Carol moved in two years ago, he's taken her under his wing, so to speak, treating her like a daughter and becoming quite protective of her."

"What's that got to do with you?" she asked, still avoiding eye contact.

"Well, I said I would keep in touch after I moved, and if he were concerned about Carol, I would help if I could. He phoned me to say that he thought she had the wrong sort going into her flat over the last week and was concerned, so I said I would pop around on Monday."

"I don't see why you wouldn't call the police when you were mugged, or were you mugged? Was it more of a street brawl?" She shot me a look and glowered. Those Kryptonite eyes x-raying my brain and scanning for lies.

"No, I wasn't mugged. You're right. A couple of drug dealers who supply Carol didn't think I should be interfering, so they gave me a message with their fists. They said if I called the police, that could be very bad for Don and Carol. I'm sorry, Jenny, I was wrong not to tell you the truth."

"Well, I'm inclined to agree with the drug dealers. You shouldn't be involved because it has nothing to do with you."

"I know. I was just trying to do the right thing, and I like Don. He's a nice old gent, so I just wanted to help."

"Okay, I understand that, but why couldn't you tell me this?"

"Jen, I've just returned after many years in South Africa. It's a violent country where you have to be very aware of your surroundings at all times. I'm used to just keeping these things to myself. You don't always involve the authorities over there, as they can be just as bad as the gangs. I know, I should have told you the truth in the first place. I'm sorry."

The newspaper reports I had in my old flat about the June uprisings in Soweto had come to my aid, but I felt a real shit spinning this story out.

"Also, Jen, you asked me when we met why I'd left South Africa. I said I wanted to change my career, and it was time to come home. That is true, but also, the lifestyle there is difficult as it's an extremely unfair society … I just wanted out. My life out there was making me someone I didn't want to be, and I needed to start again. I should have told you all this. I know I should have, but maybe that's why I'm different from other people. Please forgive me … I do love you."

Well, I'd delivered the lie, and I prayed it was enough. Although I couldn't see her, I was aware Helen was listening behind the kitchen door, and I hoped it was enough for her to lose the Rottweiler persona.

"Jason, I love you too, but I can't be hurt. As I told you before, I've been in a relationship where I got let down. I didn't love him, I don't think, but it hurt. I love you, so if you let me down, it wouldn't just hurt, it would kill me." After releasing her legs from the yoga position, she continued. "I was wondering if maybe we've gone too fast, and should we perhaps slow it down a bit? We don't really know each other well enough, do we?"

"If that's what you want, of course, we can slow things, but it's not what I want. I won't hurt you, I promise."

"No, it's not what I want either because I do love you, but you can't hurt me … you can't." The kryptonite was losing its power, her eyes were softening.

"I won't, I promise you."

Jenny poked my chest. "No more lies. I want the truth every time from now on, mister. Do—you—understand?" she said, repeatedly stabbing my chest. It wasn't a question but a demand. Although I harboured the feeling that the reconciliation meeting had probably panned out better than I had expected, it was clear I needed to be very careful over the next week with Beth's birth due.

"Helen, you can come out from behind the door now," Jenny shouted, whilst shifting closer to me.

Helen appeared and pointed at me. "You hurt her, and you're dead, mister, and your nose will look a lot worse than it does now! Okay?"

"Agreed," I sheepishly replied, pleased to see that her Rottweiler's teeth had retreated into her head.

Jenny took hold of my right hand. That shitty feeling which had consumed me all week started to lift. Helen disappeared into her bedroom and left Jenny and me on the sofa. I reached in to kiss her and held her tight.

"Jen, what I said about Carol and Don is concerning. What will happen to the baby when it's born? If Carol is on drugs, will your department get involved as you did with her son?"

"Yes, she is one of my cases, and I will have to talk to Barry, my boss, on Monday about it."

She couldn't see my huge smile as her head was on my chest, but what a right-royal result. Although feeling guilty about using Jenny to help Beth, it was the right thing to do. If I could only tell Jenny what happened in the future, she would understand, but I couldn't. I would just focus on loving this woman, which was so easy to do.

"Jason, if we're serious, I would like you to meet my parents. Is that okay?"

"Yes, Jen, I'd like that." Although I had history when meeting girlfriends' parents, I felt sure I'd matured since the last disaster.

Mental note to self – iron a shirt this time and, at the very least, avoid referring to Jenny's great tits.

41

11th September 1976

The Key

The beer garden appeared deserted apart from three children sitting together, each nursing their Coke bottles with straws in their mouths and an obedient Border-Collie crouching under their bench seat. With the lunchtime trade in full swing and the recent turn in the weather, all punters were inside, swelling the lounge bar to capacity.

Pushing my way through to the bar whilst waving a pound note in the air, I squeezed in near Dawn and Dennis, who, of course, perched on their usual bar stools. "Hello, you two. How are you both?"

"Hello, Jason, you're George's friend, aren't you? Nice to see you again. I expect George will be in soon," stated Dawn, swivelling on her stool.

"Yes, he'll be here in a minute," I replied, pleased that one of the bar staff had nodded in my direction as they started pouring my pint.

"How do you know George?" asked Dennis A.K.A Eric Sykes.

"Oh, just a friend. I've known him for quite a long time, you might say." I was unprepared for these questions, but I had known him for a long time, that was for sure.

Dawn stopped swivelling and faced me. "Such sad news about his daughter and son-in-law, so sad. I just couldn't believe it, and now George and Ivy have got to bring up that little lad on their own, and at their time of life. Well, I just don't think I could do it."

"I know they will do a brilliant job bringing Stephen up." And I was right, they did.

Dennis pointed to my car key that I plopped on the bar. "You have that yellow Cortina, lovely motor. I have a Zephyr, it's a bit older than yours but a lovely car. Is yours the 1.6-litre engine? Bet it goes like a rocket."

"Yes, that's mine … yes, it's quite fast," I chuckled. The truth be known, it was heavy and slow – a quick whiz up the road in Beth's Porsche would blow his mind.

"I'm in line for the Mk4 Cortina when it's launched next month, and looking forward to getting my hands on it, I can tell you."

Dennis plucked up my keys and leaned forward, lowering his voice – just like Roy Clark and Trish Colman had – performing that sideways glance, ensuring no one overheard what he was about to say.

"None of my business, but that's one of our box keys. I wouldn't carry that around with you, as it's a bugger of a problem if you lose it. Unfortunately, it's happened to a few of our customers, and getting a new one cut can be bloody difficult."

"I'm sorry, I'm not quite with you." Now wondering what the hell Dennis was talking about.

"Your safety deposit box key on your key ring. I'm the manager of Midland Bank in town. That's a key to one of our safety deposit boxes. I'd store it in a safe place at home if I were you."

"Oh, right, yes. Good idea, thanks."

I'd looked at that key a few times and wondered what it was for because it obviously wasn't a front door key. So I'd ignored it, just swapping it onto the new keyring when I'd changed over house keys. Now, this was a bit of a revelation. I had a safety deposit box. What the hell I'd got in there, God only knows. I hoped it wasn't a dozen passports with various names and a gun. Again, the Bourne Identity film came to mind. I'd never known anyone to have a safety deposit box before, assuming those were reserved for the super-rich or criminals. I hoped I slotted into the first group and not the second.

I fished out some change from my pocket, which I was only just getting used to as it had been at least a year since I carried coins. I'd always opted for contactless payment and had forgotten how heavy they were. Slotting sixty pence into the cigarette machine, I selected a packet of Embassy; Marlboro seemed tricky to find. Returning to the bar, George and Ivy had arrived. Although I'd seen Ivy at the funeral, seeing her close up, I could see the recent events appeared to have sucked the life out of her. She would hopefully still live for another twenty-five years, but I guessed the past few weeks had aged her. Now, her appearance was closely aligned with childhood memories of my grandmother.

Whilst George and Ivy joined Dawn and Dennis at the bar, a long line of well-wishers offered condolences, which, as usual, my grandmother didn't handle particularly well. She was – or is – a private person. George and I exchanged a glance, both presumably not quite knowing what to say, but he took the lead. "Ivy, this is Jason. He's become a regular here and a friend."

"Hello, Jason, nice to meet you. You look very familiar, I must say," said Ivy, shaking my hand.

"Jason came to the funeral with a few other regulars from the pub, so you may have seen him at the church," George interjected.

"It's wonderful to meet you too, Ivy," I said with some confidence, now I'd got the hang of meeting my dead family.

"Thank you for coming. That was very good of you. No mother should have to bury their daughter … it's a truly terrible thing. George and I will be strong for our grandson, Stephen. That's what's important now. You do look very familiar, though. I'd say you look a bit like George from twenty years ago. George, what do you say? You think he looks like you from twenty years ago?"

Keen to deflect the family resemblance, I quickly threw in my reply with a nervous grin, "Ha, I think George is far more handsome!" Ivy could see the family resemblance that Dawn had spotted a few weeks ago.

Although I'd wanted to see my grandmother and had pushed George to arrange this meeting, I found it difficult and somewhat upsetting. Now feeling as comfortable as if suffering from a collection of haemorrhoids, I made my excuses to leave after agreeing to meet George later in the week. As I said my goodbyes to the group at the bar, George said he would walk with me as he needed the toilet.

Clear of prying eyes, he grasped hold of my arms and faced me. "Jason, look after yourself, please. I've lost my daughter; I can't lose a grandson. You will please be careful?"

"I will, George, I will."

~

Jenny had swiftly organised this evening's event, calling this morning and saying her parents had invited us for tea tonight. So, I was going to be paraded on show – again.

I had a few hours before tonight's 'tea party' and, relieved it wasn't a dinner party when recalling the disaster at Lisa's parents, I settled in to enjoy listening to the football on Radio Two. West Ham were losing again, this time to Arsenal, although I loved the commentary with Alan Parry and Peter Jones. The football match round-ups were equally as entertaining, with Stuart Hall and his description of the '*beautiful game*', hmmm … enough said. It was another example of knowledge I had which I could use to stop events in the future but, as George had said, I couldn't change everything. The radio trip down memory lane was nicely rounded off with the start of Sports Report and James Alexander-Gordon reading the football results – no one did it better.

42

Tequila Sunrise

Although in my early forties, and shouldn't have felt nervous about meeting Jenny's parents – I was. I'd now rejoined the dating merry-go-round after my failed marriage and a time-travel leap. Although I'd *'swiped-right'* on a few occasions back in 2019, none of those led to anything more than the act of *'swiping-right'*. I guessed my heart wasn't in it, contented and comfortable with being miserable. Also, I imagined many, when faced with my profile, quickly *'swiped left'*.

Jenny was ready for our evening when I arrived at her flat, so there was no need to go in, which was a relief. Although the Rottweiler was muzzled, I had this nagging concern that Helen was not fully on board with the lies that poured out of my mouth on Friday evening. We headed off to Jenny's parents, who lived on the New Dunstable Road, a tree-lined avenue in the posh end of town, only a short drive from Jenny's flat.

"Mum and Dad are pleased I have a man to bring home to them. Mum said it's about time, *'Jenny, you don't want to get stuck on the shelf'*, she said."

"Oh, well, I hope they approve of me."

"They will. They're so easy to get on with."

"Well, they would be for you … they're your parents. I'll be on show and scrutinised."

"No, you won't. They're so modern. Mum and I are like sisters, and we often go to concerts together. We saw The Beatles twice."

"Yeah, really modern." It was odd, I was twelve years older than Jenny, but in reality, she was thirty years older than me, and Jenny's parents were more of my grandparents' generation. Christ, it was confusing, but it made me smile to think of anyone being born in the '20s as modern.

"It's so sad that your parents are both gone. You must miss them terribly."

"Yes, I do." However, I missed Joan and Neil, who had died twice, not Mary and Arthur, the couple who *other* Jason had known and presumably loved.

Turning into the gravel drive of her parents' home brought a halt to the conversation about dead parents. The nineteen-thirties, three-storey, detached house with a white wooden porch, framed by a climbing rose that had now come to the end of flowering but must have looked stunning a month ago, offered a slightly ramshackle appearance. I parked in front of the black, wooden, garage doors, noticing the driveway was empty, so I assumed their car must have been in the garage. That would be a rare thing in my old world because most garages were piled high with stuff, most of which no one needed.

"Come on." Jenny grabbed my hand and skipped to the front door, where her parents stood arm in arm.

Her father, John Lawrence, a tall chap with blond hair and a stature that afforded him the look of a retired police chief inspector that he was, offered out his hand. Dressed in jeans and a white shirt, I thought the denim was an odd choice in this era for a man in his late fifties, although he didn't look it – in fact, I thought he looked a similar age to me. I hoped her parents didn't consider me too old for Jenny. Also, I didn't look my best, with my nose still mashed up from my beating on Monday.

Frances Lawrence offered her cheek to Jenny, who kissed it, then she did the same to me. She was as stunning as Jenny: long, auburn hair and emerald green eyes. I could see how Jenny said they could be mistaken for sisters. As with Jenny's father, she didn't look her age of forty-eight, and had maintained her youthful looks. She took my arms and leant back to study me, swishing her long, flowing black and white, squiggly patterned dress from side to side.

"Yes, very handsome, very handsome indeed, even with a bruised nose." Jenny had inherited her smile from Frances. "Lovely to meet you, Jason. My daughter has been rattling on about you for a few weeks, did you know?"

"Oh right, well, I hope it was all good," I chuckled. "Pleasure to meet you too, Frances."

"Come on, you two, we have some cocktails ready," stated John, whilst offering his arm to Jenny.

With a crazily decorated cocktail thrust into my hand, we moved through to a huge Victorian conservatory filled with tall green plants and high-backed wicker chairs. I wondered if I'd stepped onto the set of the erotic film *Bilitis*.

"Hope you like Tequila Sunrise, Jason. Frances and I always enjoy these at the weekends."

I could honestly say I didn't think I'd ever had one before. I'd never been a cocktail man unless you call tequila-slammers cocktails, which I'd experienced on many a drunken occasion.

"Sorry to hear about that incident on Monday. A mugging in Fairfield in broad daylight … shocking. I think I got out of the Force at the right time. There does seem to be no limits to what criminals will get up to these days. Although, to be honest, I've had my fair share of incidents up at the Broxworth."

"Oh, it wasn't much. I'm sure I'll be fine. Never liked my nose much anyway," I jested.

Frances nestled up to me on the wicker sofa. Perhaps a little too close, invading my personal space, "Tell me about South Africa. It sounds so exciting. And diamond mining … such a flamboyant job, almost like James Bond. We loved that film we saw a couple of years ago. What was it called, Jonny?"

"Diamonds are Forever, dear."

"Oh yes, and that Shirley Bassey song." Somewhat bizarrely, Frances decided to offer her rendition of the film's title song. Although her singing performance was quite good, I felt a little embarrassed and was starting to wonder if this tea party was down the rabbit hole.

"Oh, Mum, please, Jason doesn't want to hear your singing," Jenny blurted out, laughing at her mother's performance.

Thankfully, she stopped singing but placed her hand on my knee. "Did you bring any big diamonds back with you? Maybe a big one to sit on Jenny's finger?"

"Mum!" exclaimed Jenny.

"Well, he is a handsome man, and you're not getting any younger. You need to grab him now, dear."

"Jason, forgive my wife. She gets excited easily. Don't you, dear?" John said, shooting her a wink and a boyish cheeky grin.

"Dad!" exclaimed Jenny.

"Jonny, you're a naughty boy; now, top up my cocktail."

"How is the new job going, Jason? Wouldn't mind betting you're finding it a real change from diamond hunting?" John threw in as he refilled her glass.

Frances accepted her drink and dramatically blew her husband a kiss. "Oh, yes, Jenny said you have an engineering degree and a teaching qualification. That's very impressive, I must say," she said, patting my knee again. This was not normal behaviour. Jenny smirked, presumably enjoying the show and my bemused expression.

"Roy Clark is the Head at your school, I believe? He's a member at my club, you know … bloody good chap. I understand you were school chums together?"

"Your secret club that women are not allowed at, Jonny? God knows what you all get up to in there, I'm sure, but I expect it's virgin sacrifice and all-night orgies," Frances blurted out with a laugh.

"Mum!" exclaimed Jenny – again.

"Wouldn't you like to know, my dear? If you play your cards right, you might find out later."

"Dad!" exclaimed Jenny – again.

"I couldn't deal with all those kids every day; well done to you. Alan is seventeen and fast becoming a bit of a rotter, to say the least," Frances squeezed out between gulps of her orange cocktail.

"Did Jenny tell you that he listens to that new dreadful music? Well, it's not music, it's more like delinquents screaming. What do they call it, Jenny?"

"Punk Rock, Dad."

I couldn't get a word in edgeways, but listening to them both was somewhat entertaining.

"Oh, yes, I hope it's a phase he'll soon grow out of. I thought Gary Glitter was bad enough, but he's a saint compared to this lot." Little did he know, I thought.

"They're not The Beatles, darling, are they? We love The Beatles. I would leave you for George Harrison. Wow, he is so sexy."

"Mum!" exclaimed Jenny – again!

"Do you like The Beatles, Jason? Jenny and I used to see them together, didn't we, Jenny?"

John chipped in. "More of a Jazz man myself. Miles Davis sort of stuff. Bloody good, you know. I saw him live a few years ago at the Royal Festival Hall. Of course, I didn't tell the Force I was going to see him. I'm not sure my Super would have approved. Anyway, come on, my lovely, let's get tea sorted and give these two love birds a moment."

Jenny moved over to the wicker sofa and squeezed up to me. Taking my hand, she smiled, "Sorry, Jason, you didn't get a word in, but I said they are modern in their ways, didn't I?"

"They're great, really great, Jen, so refreshing. Who would have thought your mum having a crush on George Harrison?"

I thought of the conversations I'd had with Lisa's parents, thirty years in the future, and it was as if they should swap eras. Her parents had an archaic attitude to music, décor – well, everything. But Jenny's parents were mad, raving mad, in a super cool way. Although I did think I was slightly too old to say *cool*, even if I was talking to myself.

"Sit yourself down, Jason. It's Italian food. I don't know if you have had it before, but we love it, don't we, Jonny?" Frances gestured her hand across the table.

John poured a large glass of white for Frances. I suspected she'd be pissed before we started eating. "Wine, Jason? We have red and white. Although I think they say white goes better with pasta, but have what you want, or both," he chuckled.

Recalling the disaster at Lisa's parents', I initially decided to steer clear of the wine in fear of referring to Jenny's great tits after too many glasses. However, for the first time that evening, I managed to get a word in edgeways. They must have thought I was a mute, so I took my chance when it came.

"Frances, the food looks fabulous, and John, thank you for the offer of wine, but I won't as I'm driving. Oh, and thank you for making me so welcome. Just to add, although you already know this, your daughter is truly amazing."

"Oh, Jason, that's lovely, so lovely. Jenny darling, you should marry him." Frances stood and clapped her hands like a toy monkey playing the cymbals, before whizzing around the table to hug me.

John picked up the bottle of red wine. "Bollocks to protocol of white or red with whatever food, have a glass of this red, it's delightful. You don't need to worry about driving because Frances has a room made up for you both, so drink up, and enjoy."

"And, you two, try not to make too much noise in bed because Alan's bedroom is next to yours. I know he knows what goes on, but he will be listening. Especially to you, Jenny," slurred Frances, whilst sporting a wicked grin.

"Mum!"

43

12th September 1976

eBay

"Jenny, can you answer the phone? I'm upstairs at the moment."

"Yes, will do," Jenny called back.

Saturday evening had been surreal. I'd enjoyed the company of Jenny's parents. She said they were modern, and indeed they were. There was an openness between Jenny and her parents, which was rare. Even if my parents had lived, I doubt I'd have enjoyed that kind of relationship with them. Jenny was incredibly blessed to have two parents with such unique liberal attitudes that would also be classed as modern in 2019.

Frances dabbled in painting large abstract canvases, selling them to private collectors. Although they were not my type of thing, even to my untrained eye, I could tell they were to a high professional standard.

The woman could only be described as an outrageous flirt – which I bore witness to. I know I said I was useless at picking up the flirtatious signs from women, but she was flirting – although I suspected it was alcohol-induced, and not an attraction to my ears. I enjoyed a fat cigar and a brandy with John, listening to his exploits in Spitfires during the war. It was fascinating, and I could have listened to his stories all night. I liked John, and I believed we could become friends. That would never have happened with Lisa's father but, on reflection, I didn't think that was entirely his fault. I'd changed over this past month, which was a change for the better.

Beth, who was now at the forefront of my mind, was about to be born – assuming there was no timeline shift. Of course, I had no idea what time on the 12th of September she'd entered this world. It could have been one minute past midnight whilst I was enjoying another glass of wine and having my bottom patted by Frances in her art studio, or it could have been one minute to midnight tonight. I suspected it must be how an expectant father would feel, a feeling I would probably never know.

"Jason, that was Don on the telephone. He said that Carol's in labour and went into hospital at nine this morning. He thought he would let you know and said he would go up to see her later."

"Oh, okay," I shouted down the stairs. "Is he still on the phone?"

"No, he just said to give you the message."

The timeline had stayed true, and hopefully, my best friend was about to be born. One thing is for sure, I'd have no idea if this baby was Beth. As I'd discussed with George, they all looked the same. What if it was a boy and not Beth, and Beth was never born or just didn't exist in this new timeline? What if it was a girl and still not Beth? How would I know, and when would I know? I didn't meet Beth until we were both aged eleven on the first day of school, and I wasn't sure if I could remember her that well at that age, or could I?

I tried to remember her face that day when old Bummer had bellowed at me to sit next to her, but I couldn't. I had a clear picture of her at the age of fourteen but not at eleven, so maybe I would have to wait for at least fourteen years before I would know if it was her. If I persuaded Jenny to get Beth – or this newborn – adopted by a caring family, could I be ruining Carol's life? She'd had her son taken away, and now I wanted to remove her daughter. What if I was wrong?

I reminded myself of the timeline of Beth's abuse, and even if it wasn't Beth born today, I still had to act. Carol was a drug addict, and whoever this child was, Beth or another, I would have to ensure that child's safety and away from Carol, and eventually

David Colney. Rather than pace around like an expectant father, I joined Jenny in the kitchen, keen to push her for information on Carol and assess how my plan was working.

"Jen, I know you can't say because it's confidential, but I think Don will be concerned about Carol and the new baby. I know he's grown fond of Carol, but he'll be worried about a baby being brought up by a woman who is using."

"What do you mean, 'using'?"

"Using drugs."

"Oh, yes, well, I will be bringing her case up at our meeting on Monday. Carol has been an issue for some years, as I'm sure living next to her you could see for yourself. It was heartbreaking taking that boy away, and Lexton House is no place for a child, but children can't remain in an unsafe situation."

"No, it must be difficult and upsetting when you have to make those decisions."

"Yes, it is, but we do have to have all the facts, and then a court order has to be obtained to remove the child. It takes a long time, even in extreme cases like Carol's. It can even be hard when the child is in immediate danger, and we then look to see if the family can take responsibility for caring for the child, but usually that isn't a suitable option either."

"Oh, right, how long can it take?"

"I have known some go on for years, can you believe?"

"Do you want a coffee, Jen? I will put the percolator on." Christ, I missed Beth's Nespresso machine. Perhaps I could invent one … hmmm, no … I was crap at practical stuff.

"Yes, please. You know Mum and Dad loved you yesterday, don't you?"

"Oh really? Well, it was a lovely evening, and you're right, they're so modern."

"Mum said you were a real lush and I must get on and grab you." Jenny had moved behind me and wrapped her arms around my middle as I made the coffee in my retro percolator.

"I couldn't believe how open they were about everything – I mean, even you-know-what."

"You-know-what, are we talking condoms again?" she giggled.

"Ha-ha, no, I meant, you know."

"Do you mean thingy?"

"Yes, Jen, I mean thingy."

"Oh, yes, thingy, as in what you do in bed, and I don't mean sleep."

"Yes, Jen, that's what I was saying. They were so open. If they were alive, I couldn't imagine my parents ever saying anything like that."

"Well, they were a lot older, darling."

"Well, no, oh … err … yes," I stuttered, again forgetting she was talking about Mary and Arthur, and I was thinking of Joan and Neil.

"Do you think Carol's case review will be a long one? Like you said, some can take up to a year."

"Hmmm, I don't think so. As we've already obtained a court order for the boy, it won't take much to get one for the new baby. Especially if the evidence suggests the child is in danger. Although, I know courts don't like to issue orders to remove a child from their mother. So I suppose it's complicated. That's what I'm saying."

"Yes, I can see that. Guess you will have a long meeting about Carol on Monday then?"

"We will. Sad as it is, she will be one case of many we have to discuss."

"Yes, you're right, all very sad. Anyway, there's something for you in the under-stairs cupboard."

"Oh, a present?" She proceeded to jump up and down, all excited like a four-year-old at a birthday party.

"Have a look," I said, pouring out the coffee.

Jenny stopped jumping and rushed over to the cupboard, yanking open the door to grab her surprise. "Oh, you've bought a HiFi system, very posh, but why is it in the cupboard?" She turned around to look at me, hands on her hips, sporting a quizzical look.

"It's for you," I said, now a little concerned I'd cocked-up.

"Oh, that's lovely, but I have one at my flat. Well, it's not a flash one like this, but it's a good one."

"It's not for the flat. It's for here."

"So I can play some records when I'm here?"

"Well, yes, look in the big Andy's Records bag."

Jenny pulled the bag out and delved inside, pulling out the records. "Oh, Jason, The Beatles, loads of them, but you're not keen on The Beatles."

"They're not for me … they're for you, Jen."

She continued to pull out the records, laying them on the carpet, shooting me a confused look. "Helen has all these at the flat; I could just borrow them when I want. These probably cost a fortune."

I knelt beside her, cupping my hand on her chin. "Jen, this is my stupid way of asking you a question."

"What is? I'm a bit confused."

"Well, the HiFi is for you, well, us, and the records are yours, so you have the full collection … to have at home."

"At home?" Jenny quizzed, starting to look slightly frustrated.

"Yes, Jen, at home," I nervously chuckled, wondering when the penny would drop.

"Jason, do you mean here, at home?" Hallelujah, the penny had dropped.

"Yes, Jen, I mean here at your home. I hope I'm not jumping the gun, and I know you were worried we were moving too fast, but I want you to live here with me. Have I made a mistake?

Have I got this wrong?" I winced, concerned I'd ballsed up. However, Jenny wrapped her arms around my neck.

"Mr Apsley, are you asking me to move in?"

"Jeeesus, I thought I was the dumb one. Yes, I am! Is that a yes, Miss Lawrence?"

"Hmmm, let's see, do I want to live with you? Your ears do stick out a bit." She flicked my left ear with her finger.

"What?"

"Yes, of course I want to, darling."

"That's a relief. Otherwise, I would have to put that record collection on eBay."

"On what?"

"Oh, it's just a selling magazine like Exchange and Mart." Another time-travel fuck-up. Hopefully, Jenny wouldn't now be nipping into WHSmith's and asking for the eBay magazine.

The phone rang.

"Leave it, Jason … whoever it is can ring back … we're going to be otherwise engaged."

"Are we?"

"Yes, we are … I want thingy."

44

She's Back

The phone rang again about an hour later. I made sure that I got to it this time.

"Jason, it's Don."

"Hello, Don, everything alright?"

"Spoke to your lovely lady this morning. Did you get the message?"

"Yes, I did, thanks. Is everything okay?"

"Yes, I've been up to the hospital. Poor girl, she's all on her own, you know. I know she's a lost cause, but I do feel sorry for her."

"Yes, I do too. Is everything okay, Don?" I asked again, as I felt he was starting to hold out on me, and now I was becoming concerned.

"Oh, yes. Damn good job she went in when she did because she had the baby at a quarter-to-ten this morning. She will be in for a few days, but everything is fine, and they let me see her because she has no family."

"What did she have, Don?"

"A baby."

"Yes, I know, Don, but—"

"Oh, yes," he chuckled. "She's got a lovely little girl, and she's already named her … Amy Elizabeth."

"Thanks, Don. I'll ring you in a couple of days. Oh, and take care on that estate, won't you?"

"Don't worry about me, son. I fought in the Great War; I can handle myself."

"Okay, bye, Don." My eyes were already watering.

"Bye, son."

I nipped up the stairs and locked myself in the bathroom, plonking down on the toilet seat. Then, dropping my face into my hands, I burst into tears – tears of relief. My best friend, my only true friend, that pillar of my life – she was back.

Part 3

45

13th September 1976

The Hatton Garden Job

A month had passed since I'd sat in that kitchen at the flat when writing the list of what I needed to do in this new strange world I'd landed in. There wasn't a day went by without me half expecting to wake up back in Beth's spare bedroom, and the last five weeks to have been some figment of my over-active imagination. I still harboured that niggling worry that I would be somehow catapulted back to my previous life, thus find myself in a hospital with limbs removed and the prospect of an even worse life ahead than it already had been.

I lived with a frightening concern that my new life was fragile and ready to crumble at any given moment, similar to that precious sandcastle you construct as a kid, which always got washed away. Perhaps your dad had spent hours with you building it on a hot summer's day – upturned buckets of wet sand decorated with seashells, a masterpiece – but the threat of that incoming tide is always present. I needed to hold the tide at bay or reinforce my sandcastle with concrete: preserve and secure it.

I was now getting the hang of this teaching game, and what surprised me was I enjoyed my work. Every day, the sense of purpose was hugely fulfilling, and I was making a positive difference to the pupils. For sure, teaching would have been at the bottom of my career choices in my old life. Roy kept reminiscing about the old school days, and I'd fallen in to a routine of adding vague add-on-bits of information to which he often said – *'Oh yes, you're right, I had forgotten that,'* – which was frankly ridiculous as I'd just made it up. But he enjoyed talking about those school days, and I think what I added got newly built into his memory.

I was keen that the school progressed ahead on computing. No one in this era could foresee the need to ensure the next generation was computer savvy. Well, yes, there was one person – me. Although no computers were available at this point, there were computers at the school in my day. However, frustratingly, that was more than ten years in the future.

Roy agreed that I could complete some research and was open to introducing computer lessons for interested pupils. I wasn't a computer whiz, but I had reasonable computing skills, so I planned to set up the computing department by funding the purchase of a computer myself. This was exciting, but the first task of securing a computer would be challenging.

There was always excitement in classes when I talked about computers and my predictions for the future. Hands would shoot up at the start of class, pupils almost standing to get their fingertips higher than the others hoping I would pick the pupil with the tallest finger to ask a question. I amused myself talking about what I called my predictions for the future – although they were facts – causing ripples of laughter as I loosely described what was normal everyday life for me back in 2019. Would they recall those lessons when my predictions came true? Would they remember their old teacher fondly, as a forward-thinking genius?

"My old school teacher back in the seventies used to predict that we would have an iPhone and that my Tesla car would exist – he was a great teacher – it's impressive how he could predict the future, God knows how he thought this stuff would happen."

~

The lunch break afforded me forty minutes to whip into town to the bank. That key had been burning a hole in my pocket since the conversation with Dennis on Saturday. Notwithstanding the excitement of what I would discover, I harboured concerns, and a certain amount of trepidation about what I might find in that safety deposit box.

After locating a parking spot on the main High Street, I studied the parking meter. The charge was twenty-pence for an hour, so I slotted in two ten-pence pieces and the dial duly moved around and started to tick back.

Earlier that day, when I'd phoned the bank, the clerk advised that I didn't need an appointment to open my box, just my key and passport for identification. There would be documentation to sign, of which I would get a duplicate copy, so it all seemed relatively straightforward.

With the formalities completed and furnished with my small, slim metal box, the clerk ushered me into a wooden cubical similar to a voting booth. It sported a half-height privacy curtain covering the top half. However, the bank clerk waited for me about two metres away, so not strictly private. I tentatively lifted the lid and peered inside.

No gun, collection of passports, or a stack of banknotes, just a large brown folded envelope with two small black silk pouches on top – and that was it. Taking hold of one silk pouch, I loosened the strings apart and tipped the contents into my hand. Out rolled twelve stones. I don't mean pea shingle, although the size of each stone was similar, but actual diamonds, each one huge – I just stared at them. I was no expert on diamonds, but the one in Lisa's engagement ring was a quarter of the size of any of these stones, and that ring cost over two grand. I had at least fifty times that amount lying in the palm of my hand. Now living forty years in the past, they wouldn't command the same value, but it was all relative. These were worth a fortune assuming they were real, but they must be – no one would put glass beads in a safety deposit box – and if they were real, had I acquired them legally? Was I a criminal and on the run? I pondered that might be the case and was the reason I left South Africa. My hands started to shake as I fumbled whilst trying to open up the second pouch. Out dropped a diamond ring, the diamond, at least twice as large as any other in the first pouch, and was centred around a halo of sapphires.

"Fuck me," I exclaimed.

"Is everything alright, sir? Everything in order?" the clerk behind me asked.

"Yes, fine … I won't be a moment."

"No rush, sir. Please take your time."

Plucking up the envelope, a quick look inside revealed the content was paperwork. Due to being short of time to properly scrutinise the documents, I decided to take the envelope with me. I reopened the silk pouches and removed the ring plus one of the stones before slotting them into the half-used packet of cigarettes. Paperwork signed and carbon copy returned to me by the bank clerk, I ventured out onto the street. Four doors up stood Maypole Jewellers. Not that I'd ever bought anything there, but it had been in the High Street for years. It still exists forty years in the future, with generations of the same Maypole family running the business.

The shop could be described as a bygone-age kind of store, double-fronted, with both display windows crammed with jewellery – you literally couldn't stick a pin in a spare space. The hand-written price tags attached to each item appeared faded, rendering them illegible. As I pushed open the heavy door, an antiquated bell clanged to denote my arrival. Three glass-topped, wooden display cases, set in a horseshoe formation, offered jewellery chaotically presented on faded velvet and were all as equally rammed as the display windows. An array of clocks and silver photo frames covered every inch of the walls.

An elderly gentleman stood waiting for a customer or God. It was debatable who would come first, but luckily for him, I had entered the shop, so God would have to wait.

"Good afternoon, sir," said the elderly gent with his hands rammed in the pockets of a well-worn cardigan.

"Good afternoon. I have a ring and an unmounted diamond that I am looking to get valued. Do you do valuations? The only problem is I'm a little tight for time."

"Yes, sir, we can do that. I'll need a few moments, that's all. However, it will only be an approximate value, and I can't guarantee it will be accurate as I don't buy second-hand jewellery."

I passed the ring across the counter. "Yes, that's fine. Just a rough idea of value is all I'm looking for."

"Good grief, sir, there's nothing rough about that ring," he chuckled, plucking it up and holding it to the light.

He pulled out a drawer that held an array of eyeglasses, all set neatly on more purple velvet. Selecting one, he scrunched it into his eye socket, and with his head down, he examined the ring. I patiently waited – the shop deathly quiet, apart from the out-of-sync ticking of those outdated clocks.

I glanced at my watch, becoming concerned that I needed to get going. I coughed as if this would speed the process up, but all I was getting was mutterings from whom I assumed was Mr Maypole.

At last, he looked up, with the eyeglass still scrunched in his eye, giving the appearance of a massive eyeball protruding from his head.

"Well, sir, stunning … just stunning. I don't get the pleasure of handling stones like this very often, I can tell you."

"What is it?" I demanded, taking another glance at my watch.

"A diamond set in a halo of sapphires."

"Yes. And?" I prompted, slightly exasperated.

"Sir, this is an F1, Jager, Emerald cut. Very unusual indeed."

"Oh great, sorry, I'm no expert, but what does that mean?" I assumed that F1 had nothing to do with motor racing.

"Right, yes, let me explain what those terms mean. It's not complicated, although you just need to understand diamond grading, and then it's extremely simple, sir."

"Yes. And?"

"And what, sir, may I ask?"

"What does it all mean?" Bloody hell, this was taking forever – all I wanted was a straight answer.

"That is what I was coming to, sir."

"Great. And?" I was close to strangling him, and then God would be his next customer.

"F1 is flawless. Jager is the colour, which means no colour, the best you can get. Only one per cent of all diamonds fall into this category, and it's five-point-five carats set in a platinum band. The halo is pretty, but the stones are small, amounting to two carats … totally stunning."

"Right, how do you know how many carats it is by just looking at it?"

"Sir, I have been looking at diamonds for fifty years. I can measure by eye quite accurately."

"Right, and value?"

"Oh yes, alas, not as valuable as a pink or red diamond, you see, now they are of an exceptionally high value. I've not had the pleasure of seeing one of those for many a year. However, as clear diamonds go, this is pretty good. So, I would estimate … but it is only an estimate … let's say … fourteen thousand."

"Pounds?" I questioned, slightly stunned.

"Yes, sir. Pounds."

I closed my eyes, trying to work out how much that was in this time. *Other* Jason had paid thirteen and a half grand for my house on Homebrook Avenue. Christ, it was worth the same as a house.

"Shall I take a look at the unmounted one, sir?"

"A quick look, please," I said, handing him the diamond and taking another glance at my watch.

"There is no difference from a quick look to a long look, sir. It takes as long as it takes." Head down again, he studied the

280

diamond. I checked my watch for the fourth time in as many minutes, concerned that I needed to return to school. Mr Maypole looked up, fortunately, this time he'd removed the glass from his eye socket.

"The very same, sir. Stunning stone, Emerald cut, flawless."

"Value?"

"It's three carats, so about six-and-a-half thousand, and as per the last one, that's in pounds. I shall give you a small box to put them in because I think this is rather a lot to carry around in your pocket with your loose change, sir."

"Brilliant, thank you. How much do I owe you?"

"Nothing, sir, absolutely nothing. It was a pleasure to see the stones, so I should be thanking you for bringing them in."

I snatched up the small black ring box containing twenty-thousand pounds worth of diamonds. "Thanks," I threw over my shoulder as I hot-footed out of the store, somewhat shocked at the valuation received.

"Sir, sir … hello, sir." Mr Maypole stood at the door waving the folded envelope I'd left in the shop. I jogged back, thanked him again, and then focused on returning to school before the afternoon lessons started.

Parking back at school, I securely stowed the folded envelope and ring box in the spare-wheel compartment and dashed in with a few minutes to spare.

With the class studying their textbooks, I couldn't help thinking of the events of this lunchtime. Mr Maypole had said the diamonds were flawless – the insignificantly small stone in Lisa's engagement ring was about as bad as you could get.

We'd nipped to London for the day, shopping up the West End. After traipsing around umpteen clothing boutiques, Lisa advised me that she fancied a trip to Hatton Garden. I just agreed, moping along, wishing the day to end so we could go home. It was easier to comply than protest after I'd already suffered four hours of painful shopping – moaning would only drag the day out and prolong the pain. Unaware that Hatton Garden wasn't a park but rather the go-to place when shopping for jewellery, I recall becoming slightly uneasy regarding the reason for this add-on to our planned trip.

Lisa studied the window displays of each store in turn, showing a relatively uninterested me the lovely engagement rings on offer. I was reasonably confident I hadn't proposed unless I'd blurted something out during a night of passion or when I was pissed, but I couldn't remember it. Somehow, we found ourselves sitting opposite a young sales assistant wearing white gloves, slotting different rings onto Lisa's finger. The fourth finger on her left hand.

"Oh, Jason, this one is lovely, and it's only four thousand."

"Four grand, bloody hell, I want the whole fucking shop for four grand!" I blurted.

Lisa outstretched her arm, admiring the ring, "You should spend three months' salary on an engagement ring … everyone knows that … so four thousand is a bargain."

"It's a good quality diamond, sir, a full half-carat and set into a beautiful white gold band. We can offer finance," the white-gloved sales assistant stated.

I turned and whispered to Lisa. "Lisa, I can't afford four grand. I don't have the money!"

"Well, how much can you afford?"

"Well, about a grand … if pushed."

"Oh." Lisa looked forlorn.

"Alright, two grand," I relented.

"Can we see something slightly cheaper, please?" I asked the sales assistant, who looked disapprovingly at me. I expect she would have liked to advise Lisa to dump me.

"We have this one, which is nice." She handed Lisa a ring as she returned from rummaging out the back. The word nice, I suspected, meant the opposite.

"Now, yes, this is lovely, and it's still quite big." Lisa looked surprised but pleased.

"Yes, it's still a full half-carat, although it has a high number of what we call inclusions, so the quality is lower; well, a lot lower."

"Oh, well, it's still really nice, and it fits. Jason, do you like it?"

"How much is it, please?" I asked, wincing, waiting for her reply.

"That, sir, is two-thousand-two-hundred."

"Wonderful, we will take it, and I will wear it now as it fits perfectly," Lisa stated, swivelling around and kissing me. "Thank you, honey."

I went begrudgingly on a clothes shopping trip, came back over two grand lighter, engaged to be married, and I wasn't sure how that had happened. I do remember Beth telling me I was a cheap-skate and to be thankful that someone wanted to marry me because I was a miserable ton of shit.

With some quick decisions made, I scooted back to Maypole Jewellers as soon as my school day had finished, just getting there in time before the shop closed up for the day.

Pushing open the door, Mr Maypole appeared to be standing in the same position as earlier, hands still stuffed in his cardigan pockets. I suspected he'd not served any customers since my visit at lunchtime.

"Hello again, sir. Have you acquired more diamonds for me to look at? Did you rob a bank?" he chuckled.

"No, not quite. Actually, I'm looking for some advice."

"Yes, of course. How can I help?"

"I want to sell the ring, but I understand you don't buy second-hand jewellery, and I don't know where to start."

"No problem, sir. I know enough people in the trade, so I should be able to secure a sale for you. I'll give you a receipt and hold it in my vault, then let me get to work on moving this on for you. With my connections, I'm confident that I can find a buyer. I know it's a precious ring, so are you comfortable to proceed on that basis?"

Based on the fact I knew the shop still existed in forty years, I presumed I could trust him, so I decided to proceed with his offer.

"Also, I'm in the market for a picture frame. From memory, it needs to be eight inches by ten inches. What do you have?"

"I have a selection of silver-plated and two that are solid silver, but they are obviously extremely expensive."

"Great, I will take the most expensive one you have. There's a picture of a lovely lady called Peggy that needs a frame."

46

16th September 1976

Second Chance

We'd planned Saturday as the moving day for Jenny. Her father and I would help move all her belongings, whilst a friend of John's, who owned an old Commer van, would assist with the few pieces of furniture. Although pleased for Jenny, Helen was upset to be losing her flatmate. She'd phoned me on Tuesday to advise me quite clearly that I'd better look after her otherwise she'd remove my testicles with a rusty saw and shove them down my throat. Of course, I assured her I would because I also valued my testicles.

George and I met for a pint on Tuesday evening, where we discussed the content of my safety deposit box. At that point, I remembered the envelope I'd left in the spare wheel compartment of my car, which I planned to review later. I had a clear idea of how to use the ring money and, on a positive note, George agreed with my plans. However, unsurprisingly, he wouldn't accept any money to support bringing up Stephen.

I had asked Jenny about the meeting she attended regarding Carol Hall but, frustratingly, she'd stated the decision regarding Beth had been deferred. Jenny was planning a visit on Thursday with a nurse because Carol would be home with the baby by then. It did concern me that her department was procrastinating, but they didn't know what I knew.

Wednesday morning, Mr Maypole left a message with Miss Colman for me to call him. Returning his call later that day, he relayed the good news that he'd secured a buyer for the ring at fourteen-and-a-half-thousand pounds. A cheque was duly being prepared, and he would broker the deal if I wanted to proceed. Now, all I needed to do was invest the money, but I already had a cunning plan on that front.

With school finished for the day and a quick wardrobe change, I adorned a trilby hat I'd purchased from Dunn and Co. a couple of weeks ago. Although I'd have preferred a baseball cap, unfortunately, no shops sold them. Leaving the car at school, I walked the entire length of Coldhams Lane to the Broxworth Estate. I'd phoned Don earlier to check he was home, which I knew he would be, and told him to let me in as soon as I arrived. After my beating, I couldn't risk being seen by the Colney clan – my nose couldn't take it.

My disguise consisted of a scarf around my neck and the trilby, although it certainly wasn't cold enough for either, and I probably stood out like a vicar in a brothel. Fortunately, although the labyrinth of concrete alleyways oozed with a mixture of unruly kids and wretched drunks sleeping off their daily intake, no one gave me a second look. I guess Don must have been standing by the door waiting for me as instructed because I was in after a quick tap on his door.

"Alright, son, good to see you, but did anyone else see you?"

"Yes, loads of people. Although, in this get-up, I hope no one recognised me and informed the Colney clan. I'm hoping they're busy peddling their drugs somewhere else."

"Right, come through. I'll get that kettle on."

A strong cup of coffee in hand, I spotted the frameless picture of Peggy poked behind the clock on the mantelpiece, relieved I'd purchased the correct size.

"So, what's happening next door, Don?"

"Well, your lass came this morning with some nurse, a big buxom woman. She could handle herself, reckon she was hand-picked for coming to the Broxworth. They were here about thirty minutes or so, and since then no one has come around, which is good. I've heard the baby crying a few times, though. These bloody walls are paper thin."

"No sign of the Colney brothers, then?"

"No, nothing. Someone probably clocked your lass all official-like, and they've given Carol a wide berth today. What do you think will happen then? She ain't fit to bring up a child, you know?"

"Yes, I think we both know that, for sure, but to be honest, I don't know. Apparently, these things take time, like everything."

"Bloody ridiculous, if you ask me. They let that little lad suffer from all the comings and goings; it was that fight of yours that was the final straw. He should have been taken from her years ago … could have been given to a nice couple that would bring him up proper."

"You heard from your girls recently?"

"Nah, nothing. They're all too busy with their lives. I suppose I wasn't the greatest father, and I'm being repaid for that now … with silence. Would break my Peggy's heart, it would."

I glanced at her picture. "Yes, I'm sure it would. That's a lovely picture you have, you know?"

Don plonked himself on the sofa, his tartan slipper-covered feet landing on the leatherette pouffe, "Yes, my favourite, that's how I remember her just before we got wed."

I plucked up the picture. "Not thought about getting it re-framed?"

"Yes, I should, but I don't want any old frame out of Woolworths, and the pension only goes so far, even less and less now. Did you see they said inflation is at seventeen per cent, and the bloody pension's not rising at the same rate?"

"Look, Don, please accept this gift. A little thank you for being my chief intelligence officer." I handed him the silver frame as I removed it from its black presentation box.

"Oh, son, that's bloody lovely, and it's the right size. But you didn't need to do that. I enjoy keeping an eye out and don't need payment."

"Don, I'd like you to have it."

"Son, that's smashing. Thank you … thank you. 'ere pass me Peggy's picture; let's get her in there right now."

"Don, there is something else that I'd like you to consider. I think I know you'll say no, but hear me out," I said, passing Don the picture.

"That's all a bit cloak and dagger, but go on, son, I'm all ears."

"Look, my parents have passed, and I've no family to speak of. To be honest, there are times in my life when I haven't been the nicest kind of bloke, so I'm trying to change all that, and I could do with your help."

"Go on."

"I have a bit saved up, and I'm looking to invest in property; can't go wrong with bricks and mortar." Well, you could if you bought in the late '80s because there were so many people in negative equity. However, in the '70s, no one would ever have thought that could happen.

"So, I'm considering buying a couple of three-bedroom semi-detached properties up on the new Bowthorpe Estate. It's that new development on the east side of town, and it looks a good investment." What I also knew was that in forty years, it was still a reasonably desirable place to live with good schools and other amenities.

"Good idea, son, you should get a good return on those houses. That will be your pension for the future. Bloody wish I had the foresight at your age, but realistically, every penny I earned went on keeping Peggy and the girls. But how can I help?"

"So, this is what I would like to do, and it's not charity. It's about me, Jason Apsley, just becoming a better person. I'm going to rent them out when I've purchased them, and I'd like you to be one of my tenants. What do you say?"

"Son, I would like that, but the rent on my flat is about as much as I can afford. I couldn't afford a house like that."

"Yours will be rent free."

"You can't do that! That's madness, total madness." I'd feared this response.

"No, it's not. Look, my parents have passed, and I enjoy your company and, as I said, I want to be a better person. Another thing, I can't enjoy your company whilst you live here."

"Son, I don't take charity. I've worked all my life, and I'm not going to take handouts. No, sir, I have my pride, son. Thanks, but no thanks."

"Don, meet me halfway, one-pound-per-week rent, then. They will have a garden. You said before how you missed having a small garden to muck about in. Well, this will give you one, and the walls will be thicker than paper."

Don pondered for a moment, looking down at the newly framed picture of Peggy, which was still firmly in his grip. It was a good sign. I knew this was going to be a bloody tough sell, but the silence suggested he was thinking about it.

"And Don, you hate it here. You have said so many times. Come on, are you really going to stay here and then regret not having this opportunity when it's your time to depart this world? Your girls are not in touch. I don't know your business, but kids should help out their parents in later life. So, treat me as the son you didn't have if that's not too presumptuous?" I was piling on the pressure. "The rent agreement will all be above board, and only you and I will know the terms, no one else. Come on, Don, help me out."

"No charity. I pay four-ninety a week for my flat, but that's cheap, would you believe?" He waved Peggy in my direction. "I'll pay you the same as I do for my flat."

I grinned ear to ear – I'd got him. "One-pound-twenty-five."

"Four-pounds-fifty," Don replied.

The bargaining continued until we agreed on two pounds and shook hands to seal the deal.

"Well, son, I really don't know what to say … I'm dumbfounded."

"Well, I've got to buy them yet, but there was a big full-page advert in the Chronicle this week. I enquired and have two houses reserved. I've just got to pay a deposit this week, and then it should be sorted. With a bit of luck and a fair wind, we can get you in before November."

Don was an elderly gent, and I could see he was a little watery-eyed. Seeing this was an opportunity to give him a private moment, I took my leave.

"Don, I'm going next door to say hello to Carol. I'll be back in a little while, and you can make me another drink – strong one though, two heaps of coffee." I patted him on the shoulder, opened the front door a crack, checked the landing was clear, then scooted out and knocked on Carol's door. No response, so I hammered a little harder.

"Fuck off!" boomed the response. Unperturbed, I continued to give the door frame some welly. Eventually, the door flung open. Carol didn't look her best, her clothes and hair in varying states of dishevelment – but who wouldn't when caring for a new baby. I had no experience, but I guess it must be exhausting.

"What the fucking hell, I've got a baby, and you've just woken the bastard up, you fucking git."

"Oh shit, sorry, Carol."

"Oh, fuck, it's you. You better come in … word is you're not welcome around 'ere."

"Thanks."

I followed her in, unsure whether to wipe my shoes on the doormat or defer that task until I left – the place was a shit tip. With the overwhelming stench of cigarettes and stale sweat, I felt the need to cover my mouth. Beth was screaming her head off – it was ear piercing – I was surprised a tiny baby could make so much noise. Carol closed the bedroom door, but that didn't dull the noise. She strode to the kitchen, plucked a cigarette from a packet of No.6 and lit up – Beth was still screaming.

"Fucking little shit won't shut up, and that ginger bitch was around earlier, reckons I needed to clean up a bit with a baby in the flat. Fucking bitch, who does she fucking think she is … she's got no fucking idea. No kids of 'er own … reckon she might change 'er fucking tune if she had one of 'er own."

The rant stopped so she could drag hard on her cigarette, then blew out a long stream of smoke towards the ceiling.

"Do you need to see to the baby?"

"You fucking do it … she's getting on my fucking tits."

I entered the bedroom. There, lying in a small dirty wicker basket, was Amy Elizabeth. I knelt to pick her up, shaking as I'd never picked up a baby before and, therefore, frightened of hurting her. I gently lifted her but hadn't supported her head – she was so delicate. Repositioning my hand, I lifted her in my arms. Christ, this was difficult. Kneeling on the floor with tense arms, I cradled her whilst she continued to scream.

"Hey, Beth, how are you? Long time no see. What you been up to since I died? Did you miss me? 'Cos I bloody well missed you. I'm having to make decisions all on my own without your support. Yeah, I know it's amazing, and I've made some really good ones, without cocking everything up like I usually do. Yes, Beth, I know it's unbelievable. I've met someone … you'd love her. Oh … well, funnily enough, you've already met her this morning. She's the real deal. I'm actually doing fab at the moment, not depressed, and I don't feel anxious about anything, which is bizarre. Yes, that sounds mad, I know. Jason Apsley positive, who would have thought, eh?"

Beth had stopped screaming, but I hadn't noticed at first. She just looked at me with her blue eyes.

"Trust me, Beth, I'll get you out of here, I will. You won't have to suffer as you did, I promise."

Laying Beth down, I gently placed the blanket loosely around her. I held the tip of my middle finger in her hand, allowing her to grip it whilst those blue eyes held my stare. I stayed in that position until the kneeling had drained the blood from my lower limbs, causing a wave of pins and needles. Then, stretching out and releasing my dead legs, I kissed Beth on the forehead before returning to the kitchen to find the chain-smoking Carol.

"What you do, kill 'er? I can't get 'er to shut the fuck up."

"You coping, Carol? Do you need anything?"

"Don't need do-gooders like that bitch from the Council, and you're starting to sound like 'er."

We both remained silent whilst Carol continued pushing smoke at the ceiling. I leaned against the sink, the rancid smell from the drain permeating the air, although slightly masked by the fog of cigarette smoke.

"Look, sorry, Jase, I know you meant good. It's just fucking tough at the moment."

"You okay for money?" I asked, although concerned if I gave her any it wouldn't be spent on keeping Beth, but provisions that Paul Colney could supply, which isn't the stuff you get from the supermarket. I didn't wait for a reply, thumbing out two fivers from my wallet. With her cigarette clamped between her lips and left eye closed, avoiding the smoke that wafted across her face, Carol grabbed the cash.

"Carol, I better go … as you said, I'm not hugely welcome around here. Make sure you look after the little one, as well as yourself. If you need anything, Don knows how to get hold of me."

"Okay, cheers, Jase."

Back in Don's flat, I was aware that I'd potentially put both Don and Carol in danger by just turning up, so I said goodbye after checking he was still okay to be my tenant, which he was.

"Son, you said you wanted to be a better person. Well, I think you're a bloody superstar, and I would be proud to have you as a son, I really would."

I'm not sure anyone has said that to me before. I seemed to be doing the right things now. Perhaps I had taken this second chance given to me, making the most of it and becoming a better person.

47

17th September 1976

Tipp-Ex

The future events that I knew were coming were always in the back of my mind, along with that conversation with George. He was right, of course. I couldn't change the world. Evil things would happen, even if I devoted time to change them or ensured that they could be avoided. As with the death of my parents, bending time or steering it to take another route wasn't easy. The laid down path of the future fought hard not to be altered.

I still couldn't remember any facts from the book Lisa bought me that Christmas. Would the Ripper strike soon, and how would I feel about sitting on my hands?

Whatever I planned to do, obviously, it would have to be anonymous. I couldn't have the scrutiny of the press or media if I were suddenly exposed as a remarkable psychic. It would be a circus, and a circus that I didn't want to join.

I lacked the knowledge of how police investigations worked but believed DNA identification was not available in this era. However, I presumed the authorities could trace a typed letter back to the exact ribbon and typewriter upon which it was produced. Certainly, handwriting a letter was a no-no, but I needed to ensure any typed letter wasn't traced, which would prove difficult.

The easy answer was to use the typewriters at school. The main secretarial training room had at least twenty, and any number of people could have used them. It was the era when girls, and it seemed only girls, could take the Pitman Secretarial training, forming the central part of their education. I guessed it would have seemed odd to have a male secretary in the '70s, but it still seemed strange to me, and I was surprised the typewriters weren't pink coloured.

Not having ever used a typewriter, I settled down at the end of the school day and inserted the paper. The QWERTY keyboard was the same as my Apple-Mac, so this wouldn't take long. I typed—

To whom it may concern:

The Yorkshire Ripper is—

No.

I ripped out the paper, scrunching it up into a ball and lobbed it, basketball slam-dunk style, into the bin. Then, realising that I couldn't leave it there, I scrambled across the room and retrieved the paper, flattened it out, and secured it in my pocket.

Think Apsley – think, I started again.

To Whom it may concern:

I urge you to read this letter and take the content seriously. I can guarantee you that if you don't, and you fail to act now, in a few years, you will realise you should have, and you will never be able to live with yourself.

Over the last twelve months, two young women were brutally murdered in the Leeds area. If you look at vicious attacks over the previous years, you will be able to link these to the same assailant as the two murders.

The man you need to investigate is Peter Sutcliffe. He lives near the Bradford or Leeds area and will kill again soon. He is responsible for those two murders.

I appreciate that you may often receive letters of this nature. However, there is nothing more I can say, but you will live to regret this if you do not act.

I have copied this letter to four national newspapers and the Yorkshire Post, asking them to use this in the future to prove that this letter stated the truth. This is not meant as a threat, but I hope just a nudge for you to act, and act now. Many lives depend on what action you take.

Once the letter was completed, I nipped down to the main office to bang out enough photocopies for what I needed.

"Hello, Miss Colman. Can I use the photocopier?"

"The what? Oh, you mean the Ditto Machine," she questioned, pointing to what looked like a printing press from the Victorian era, although a small machine with a crank handle.

"Oh, right, err …" I hadn't considered that photocopiers were not yet commonplace in all offices.

"Leave it with me, Mr Apsley, and I will get it done for you tomorrow. How many copies?"

"Five," I replied, still trying to get my head around that contraption.

"Oh, well, yes, I can do that, although using carbon would have been easier." She stretched out her hand to take my letter. I almost handed it to her before snatching it back.

"Err … no, it's okay, no worries." I threw back, already swivelling around to return to the typewriter room.

"No worries indeed." I heard the reply from Miss Colman as the door swung back behind me.

When bolting back up to the typewriter room, I decided I must use the same one as before, rather than a second one, because I believed they all have their own '*fingerprint*'. However, as I stood in the doorway, I couldn't remember which one I'd used – Bollocks. I slowly crept around the room, trying to imagine where I was when lobbing my first draft into the waste bin and thus pinpoint the right machine. After some calculations, I settled on the one with the warm chair.

Carbon paper inserted, I started again and retyped the letter. Thank God it wasn't that long. When completed, I noticed that the carbon was the wrong way around – *oh, for fuck sake*.

Starting again, this time with the carbon paper inserted correctly, I bashed out my letter. Frustratingly, I spelt Sutcliffe with one 'f', so I wrestled the paper out whilst momentarily considering throwing the typewriter out of the window, then restarted what was becoming an absolute ball-ache.

The level of verbal obscenities now pouring from my mouth could have filled my grandmother's swear box, which Stephen and I had to add fifty-pence to when we uttered a bad word, like *bugger*. If we'd have said *fuck,* well, the fine could have run into thousands. Fortunately, neither of us uttered that word in her house. Well, not in her earshot. I gathered my things and left the typing room – Jesus, I missed my Apple-Mac or even a bottle of Tipp-Ex.

I'd addressed the envelopes to the newspapers and the critical one to the Chief Constable of West Yorkshire Police. Although I wasn't confident I had the correct police force, it was my best guess. Now I had to wait and hope – that finger and toe-crossing stuff. At this stage, I had no idea what my next move would be if the letter were to be ignored.

48

18th September 1976

Fast Food

Jenny officially moved in Friday night, although we would be collecting her possessions on Saturday. She was bouncing around the house like Tigger again, all excited and totally out of control. The sex that night had an animal intensity to it; we ravaged each other.

It hadn't occurred to me that moving your girlfriend in was considered taboo. However, in this era, it was all the wrong side of the blanket, so to speak. Fortunately, John and Frances held attitudes beyond their time. Their whole mantra was about being happy and not conforming to the rules of society. Jenny believed that her father developed this attitude precisely thirty-six years ago over the skies of the English Channel, every day, not knowing if each day would be his last. As for Frances, she was a free spirit, perhaps a product of the sixties free love. Express yourself, go with the mood attitude. Fair to say, George didn't think it was the done thing, and Ivy would have looked very dimly on this sort of goings-on.

By early afternoon, we'd moved everything from her flat. Helen and Jenny had a tearful cuddle, and I made it very clear to Helen that she was always welcome at our house whenever she wanted to visit. I think I had started to thaw her out, and baring her Rottweiler teeth firmly a thing of the past.

Frances had joined the party, so to speak. I guess checking up on where her daughter would be living, and she seemed to approve. Thank the Lord she avoided my bum this time, but insisted that we come around later for tea so we didn't need to worry about cooking.

I left Jenny to it for an hour, saying I needed to run some errands in town, and Jenny was more than happy to start nesting. It was heartbreaking that the nest would be childless, but we had each other, which was a huge step up from my old life. Although it hurt Jenny, she had come to terms with never having children – it was a '*gravity issue.*' Bloody hell, I hated that phrase, another one of Gary Oxney's favourite sayings.

The bell gave its now-familiar ring and, as per my previous visit, I was the only customer. However, today Mr Maypole wasn't behind the counter. In his place, a young girl looked to be holding the fort. I instantly recognised her from school. Oh hell, this was a bit embarrassing.

"Hello, Mr Apsley. What are you doing here?"

"Hi Sarah, I could ask you the same question."

"This is my Saturday job. I've only been here for two weeks, but it's nice to work in a jewellery shop. Have you come to buy something?"

"Not quite. Is Mr Maypole in?"

"Mr Apsley, good to see you. Come through." Mr Maypole had poked his head around the door and beckoned me through to the back of the shop.

"Thanks, Mr Maypole, much appreciated."

"Terry," he said, as he extended a hand.

"Jason," I replied, and we shook hands.

"Take a seat."

I struggled to see a chair, let alone any recognisable furniture, as tools and equipment covered every conceivable area.

"Ah, let me move these boxes; there is a chair under here somewhere," Terry chuckled, as he shoved two brown boxes to the floor, revealing a brown leather swivel stool. "So, Jason, I have a cheque for you, for the small sum of fourteen-and-a-half-thousand pounds. You can cash that on Monday, and it should process through the clearing banks by Friday. Then I can release the ring to my contact. How does that sound?"

"Brilliant, thank you."

"The cheque will take a few days to clear, but my contact is good for the money. I like to work the old-fashioned way. Hopefully, that's agreeable?"

"Yes, I'm more than happy with that. What do I owe you for acting as the broker?"

"Not much, as it was only a couple of calls, so shall we say sixty-pounds. Is that acceptable?"

"Absolutely, yes, but I would like another favour if you can do it?"

"Go on … I will see what I can do."

"How long will it take to set my three-carat diamond in a platinum ring?"

"Err … once you have the ring, I could set it in … say, in a few days."

"Right, I thought you would say that. Hmmm, if I make it worth your while, could you do it quicker?"

"In a hurry to get your girl, Jason?" he chuckled, whilst shoving his hands in the pocket of his well-worn cardigan.

I gently closed the door that separated the back area from the shop because young Sarah had crept up to ear-wig the conversation.

"Look, Terry, I was hoping you could source a platinum ring that will hold the diamond and get it turned around in, let's say, an hour?"

"What … an hour? No, that's not possible." His hands shot out of his pockets, now positioned like an evangelist preacher praising the Lord.

Reaching into my pocket, I produced a cheque for five hundred pounds and slid it over the workbench, tapping the cheque to highlight the amount. Terry swivelled his eyes downwards whilst maintaining his raised hands in that preaching formation.

"That's for you. I don't think sixty pounds for selling my ring was enough, but also, I would like you to set this diamond in an hour. Can you do it?"

Old man Maypole continued to stare at the cheque. Finally, he dropped his arms and rubbed his chin, grinning in thought, weighing up the possibility of my request.

"Plain platinum band, high set, five clasp, what size?"

I slid across a silver-coloured ring with a large green stone centred on top, costume jewellery borrowed from Jenny's jewellery box.

"This size."

Terry slid it on a mandrel that he plucked from the workbench.

"J, thin finger."

"You can do it?"

"Okay, the band will have to be reasonably thick, and the clasp will need to be wide as that's a big stone. If you let me crack on, yes I can do it, but I will need some help from you, my friend."

"Anything."

"Young Sarah has only been here two weeks, a pleasant girl but very young, so I need someone to mind the shop while I work."

"Deal, thank you."

"She must be special, your lady?"

"More than special ... a lot more than special."

I moved back to the shop, leaving my diamond in Terry's capable hands – I hoped.

"Hello Sarah, Mr Maypole needs some peace and quiet to do a piece of work for me, so I'm going to stay in the shop and help if you get any awkward customers, and well, you know, need a bit of support, not that you would I'm sure, but you know, a little moral support." I seemed to be babbling, and I'm not sure why.

"Oh, okay," responded Sarah, as she stared at the front door, the opposite direction from me.

The poor girl had to put up with me all week and then, come Saturday, had to spend the afternoon in my company as well. I bet I would be the subject of some school gossip next week. I assumed this wasn't the busiest of shops in the High Street and therefore doubted that another customer would come in and break the silence, so I decided to strike up a conversation.

"Do you like working here?"

"Yes, it's okay, I suppose."

"Do you get many customers?"

"No."

"What's your favourite thing in the shop?"

"Nothing, really. It's all a bit old-fashioned."

Christ, this was riveting. Apart from teaching these kids, I clearly lacked the social skills to engage in a conversation with a sixteen-year-old girl. I checked my watch. Only three minutes had passed. Bloody hell, it was going to be a long hour.

"Mr Apsley?" Sarah turned to face me.

"Yes, Sarah."

"I'm sorry about listening at the door earlier. I do realise that was very rude of me. Please, could you not mention it to Mr Maypole if you haven't already? I honestly didn't hear much, but I don't think Mr Maypole would be thrilled with me. I don't want to lose this job."

"Let's do a deal. I'll keep quiet, and you say nothing at school next week about my meeting with Mr Maypole."

"I wouldn't!"

"Really?"

"Well, maybe I would have. It's a deal, thank you." Sarah flashed a thin smile and flushed bright red.

"Good, a deal."

Silence fell again. I shoved my hand in my trouser pocket to grab my phone and check the BBC Sports website for the latest football updates. Something I would do when sitting outside ladies' changing rooms, waiting for Lisa whilst she tried on umpteen dresses. I'd be stuck there for hours, and then she would re-emerge, saying they were all horrible. But of course, there was no phone, but the habit of reaching for it would take a lifetime to stop, and when they were invented, I would probably have just got out of the habit.

"Oh, Mr Apsley, there's a group of boys outside the shop. I don't want them in here."

Peering through the window, I spotted six teenage boys standing about five feet from the shop front, all smoking and spitting mouthfuls of Coke at each other for some reason. I recognised one of them.

"Sarah, they're not coming in here. They're just messing about on the pavement. Do you know them?"

"Only one of them, David Colney. He was in our class. Well, you know that."

She had a worried look on her face, a look that she genuinely was concerned about these boys, or boy.

"Are you concerned about David Colney?"

"He's evil, pure evil. He frightens me."

"Why? He's moved schools, so you don't have to have anything to do with him now."

"He does things he shouldn't."

"Like what?"

"Oh, I shouldn't say." Sarah screwed up her face as if remembering what she declined to disclose.

"Sarah, like what?"

Sarah shook her head and looked away.

"Okay, you don't have to say, certainly not to me, but you should talk to your parents."

"He touched me," she blurted.

"Can I ask where, if that's not too uncomfortable to say?" Sarah dropped her head again.

"Where you shouldn't be touched," she whispered.

"And I'm sorry to ask, but you didn't want that?"

"No! Of course not. He forced himself on me."

"Sarah, this can't happen. Have you told your parents?" She shook her head again.

"Do you think you could tell them? It's important."

"No." Her voice was so low I could hardly hear her.

"Do you want me to talk to your parents, or if not me, Jayne Hart from school could?"

She chewed her lip, picked at her fingernails, huffed, and then looked up. "I don't know."

"When did this happen?"

She dropped her head again and continued to pick at her nails. "Last year."

"Sarah ... Sarah, look at me." She slowly lifted her head, teary-eyed and still chewing her lip. "This can't be ignored, and I think you should talk to your parents."

"Do they have to know?"

"Well, I think they should. Talk to your mum tonight. You might be surprised how supportive she is. I know parents seem old, but you would be surprised how empathetic they can be. Give it a try."

What the fuck I knew about parenting you could list on the back of a postage stamp in large font, but this was further confirmation about David Colney and the path he was going to take. Sarah was legally classed as a child a year ago, so he'd committed child abuse even before he got hold of Beth. I had a plan to save Beth from him, but that didn't help anyone else. He had to be stopped, but how I could do that apart from borrowing George's antique Luger pistol, I still had no idea.

The rest of the hour passed with relative silence, only broken by an elderly couple who entered the shop asking Sarah to show them some bracelets which they didn't buy.

Terry poked his head around the door, looking rather pleased with himself. He didn't say anything – he didn't need to. I zipped into the back office to find him holding up the ring, appearing rather smug. The diamond, now set, appeared twice its size. Apart from the one I'd sold, I had never seen anything like it – it was fabulous. I just hoped the stone wasn't too big, if that were possible. The larger the stone, the more chance people would think it was fake, as if it had dropped out of a cheap supermarket Christmas cracker. I didn't want that for Jenny.

"Terry, it's stunning."

"Yes, it is, if I say so myself."

"And you did it in an hour."

"Yes," he chuckled. "You know, I think I'll start up a fast-jewellery shop like those new fast-food restaurants!"

"Terry, I don't think that idea will catch on."

"No, I agree. Neither will those fast-food restaurants either."

"Terry, I wouldn't be so sure … I wouldn't be so sure."

49

Miss Pontins

Jenny had been super busy, as most of the furniture was now placed in a different position when I returned from my visit to Maypole Jewellers. This pleased me; evidently, she'd settled into our new home, which was now our home, not my house with my live-in girlfriend.

Although you are always confident that the outcome will be what you expect on a done deal, there is that slight chance it can go wrong. As I'd never proposed marriage before – well, as I said, I couldn't remember it, and certainly couldn't remember a response from Lisa – this was the first time, I think. I was crystal clear about Jenny and, although it was whirlwind stuff, I was ninety-nine-point-nine per cent sure she felt the same about me. The fly in the ointment would always be her parents. I'd expected many hurdles to overcome before meeting Frances, and I could imagine her mother saying:

"Jenny, what are you thinking? Have you lost your marbles? You've only known him for five minutes, and he's twelve years older than you! When he retires, you will still be in the prime of your life. Anyway, does he know you can't have children? Does he accept that, or will he stray when he's bored? Hmmm, sweetheart, I don't think you have thought this through – yes, okay, you're thirty, and you feel that you want to settle down, but not with the first man that gets on one knee! Come on, dear, think about it. You could choose anyone. Really think about this, Jenny. Remember, act in haste and repent at your leisure."

But no, her parents were not the concern that I thought they would be. In fact, last Saturday, Frances had practically ordered me to marry her daughter. So, with no hurdles laid out on the proposal-to-Jenny-track, I had a clear run.

I just hoped I'd not miscalculated and hit the nought-point-nought-one per cent chance that she'd say no.

"Oh, Jason, how sweet. No, I don't want to marry you. I just want to live in a lovely house and for you to regularly screw my brains out."

I was sure that wouldn't be her response, but I would cross my fingers and toes just in case.

Frances calls it tea, I call it dinner – however, I guess it amounts to the same thing. Now we'd finished our meal, we all ferried the plates to the kitchen for the washing up. We'd all completed this together last Saturday, and it was enjoyable to be together doing a mundane task. Yes, I know it was only washing up, but it allowed the flow of the dinner conversation to continue.

"John, take Jason for a cigar in the conservatory. Us girls can do this. It will be good for you two men to have a chat."

"Not going to argue with that, my lovely. Come on, Jason, we'll also have a small brandy."

"Jason?" Frances called out.

I turned and looked at her. When fixing her stare on me, she nodded and smirked. Does she know? Can she read minds? Or was the ring box making an unmistakable shape in my trouser pocket?

John handed me a brandy. "Never seen Jenny this happy in years. I don't need to say, but you will look after her, won't you? She is very precious to us. Please don't think I'm interfering, but you know father and daughter stuff and all that, but to me, she's still my little girl."

"I will, John, I promise. I know my age will be a concern—"

John interrupted me, waving his hand as if swatting a wasp away, causing a large blob of ash from his cigar to fire off. "No, not at all. I'm nine years older than my wife. Frances and Jenny are very similar. They both get easily excited, if you know what I mean. They both need a strong man, a man to guide them, a proper man, if you get my drift?"

It was the first time I'd seen or heard anything from John that fitted the generation he came from, a very antiquated point of view, but I understood what he was saying, and I felt confident it wasn't meant in a male chauvinistic way. I needed to get around to the question. John had set it up perfectly, but I seemed to be a little tongue-tied. In my era, there wasn't the requirement to ask the father for permission, that decision was between yourselves, and then you just informed everyone else.

When Lisa and I informed her parents, our news wasn't met with the greatest response. But to be fair, I'd given a competent performance of how to be a complete tosser on several occasions, so who could blame them for being concerned about Lisa's choice. Lisa had removed her ring before we went around to tell them, so they didn't notice it before we spilt the news. Lisa and I both knew it would be a tough sell, not that we discussed the fact, but we knew, and Lisa was on edge all day before we arrived at her parents.

We all stood having a coffee in her parents' kitchen. Lisa announced that we had something to tell them and then looked at me. Again, nothing was discussed, so I wasn't prepared for the baton-swapping to happen. I had just assumed Lisa would do the talking, and there would be some 'Ohs' muttered by her disappointed parents, and that would be that. I had underestimated their displeasure;

"You haven't got her pregnant, I hope," Lisa's father bellowed.

"Oh Christ, Lisa, you're not going to have his child," her mum followed up.

"No," Lisa threw in, and again looked at me, eyes bulging.

"Well, Jason, what?" her father countered.

"Um, err, it's like this, um, well." My usual useless non-assertive dickhead self, managed to mumble.

"Well, what, spit it out, man," her father shouted and stretched out his arms as if about to take a large painting off a gallery wall.

"We've got engaged, Dad," Lisa jumped in.

"Oh, for Christ sake, Lisa, don't be so ridiculous. You can't want to marry this idiot," her father responded, shaking his head.

"Oh, really, Lisa, why?" her mum added, with a real lack of enthusiasm and a hint of sadness.

Come on, Jason, this is different. You're not old Jason anymore, so just get on with it. The voice in my head guided my brain to engage my tongue. "John, I have something to ask—"

"Shall I make it easy for you, Jason? The answer is yes, I do give you permission. Does she know?"

"Err … no, she doesn't, but how do you know I was going to ask?"

"Been there and done it myself, and as Frances was only eighteen and pregnant at the time, not that her father knew, I went through hell with this very same conversation."

"Right, well, thank you."

"Jason, we've only spent a few hours together, and I like you. Also, some people I know have done some checking, and you came up clean."

"Oh," I responded, relieved because that checking must have been about *other* Jason.

"Don't be disappointed. You want to take my little girl from me, and I have the connections."

"No, no, I understand."

"But more to the point, Frances is the best judge of character I've ever met. She sees things others don't … a sixth sense … and I've never known her to get it wrong. She thinks you're spot on."

"Right." I was a little lost for words. "Actually, although you've made it easy for me, I still think I should ask. Nothing is worth having in life if it comes too easy."

309

"Well said."

"John, can I have your permission to ask for your daughter's hand in marriage?"

"Yes, you can." And with that, I thrust out my hand with confidence.

"Welcome to my family, Jason, welcome." John shook my hand and slapped my back, nearly knocking the cigar clean out of my mouth.

"The only hurdle I have now is getting your daughter to say yes."

"That won't be a problem, I promise you. As I said, I can't ever remember her being so happy. So, when are you going to ask her?"

"Will it be okay to do it after the washing up?"

"Perfect. Now, let's enjoy these cigars whilst the girls finish up. It would be a shame to go in too early and have to pick up a tea towel."

Frances and Jenny entered the cigar smoke infused conservatory. "Johnny, I'll have a Martini, please."

"Jenny?" he asked.

"Same please, Dad, but only a small one. It's been such a busy day, and there's lots of house sorting to carry on with tomorrow. I'm so tired," Jenny huffed, plopping herself on the wicker sofa beside me.

"So, what have you boys been gassing about in here?" Frances asked, sporting a cheeky grin, looking directly at the small, black ring box I'd placed on the mahogany coffee table right in front of where Jenny was sitting.

"High-level man conversation, dear," John offered over his shoulder as he prepared two martinis.

"Frances, would it be okay if I say something?"

Here we go.

"Of course. To my daughter or me?" she smirked.

"Ha, well, yes, your daughter." John handed out the drinks and stood by Frances's chair, his hand on her shoulder, allowing Frances to place hers on his. Then, clearing my throat as if preparing to make a speech, I faced Jenny, taking her hands in mine.

"What's going on? You all know something I don't," quizzed Jenny.

"Right, well—"

"Oooooo, what's that?" Jenny exclaimed, looking at the ring box. She tried to release her hands from mine, but I held on tight.

"Jenny, in that box, is something I hope you will wear and, to do that, you will have to say yes to my next question."

"Well, it's a small box, so I assume it's not a dress or coat?" she chuckled.

"No, it's not, and you have to wear it on this finger," I smirked, tapping the top of her fourth finger on her left hand – Jenny grinned. I thought at this point I was safe, and she would say yes. I picked up the box, but before I could open it—

"Yes. Yes, I will."

"Yes, you will what?"

"I will marry you."

"I haven't asked you to … yet."

"Yes, but you're about to, aren't you?"

"Yes, I am. Jenny, will you marry me?" I asked, opening the box.

"Yes, of course, darling. Oh my God, it's huge!"

"Oh, Jenny, that's enormous! Try it on," blurted Frances, jumping up from her chair and helping Jenny put on the ring.

"There, told you, Jason."

"Told him what, Dad?"

"That you would say yes."

"Oh, did you, and how would you know that, Daddy?" Jenny said, flashing her wonderful smile.

311

"Because, young lady, your mother and I have never seen you so happy since you won the young Miss Pontins competition on our summer holiday in '58."

Jenny beamed that smile, the same one I couldn't take my eyes off when she knocked on my flat door a month ago. Our relationship had progressed at warp-factor speed, but the feeling that I was capable of genuinely making someone happy was new to me, and I loved it.

50

19th September 1976

Thick as Thieves

I was never one for car cleaning. Although a petrolhead, cleaning cars was a pain, and anyway, that's what the rain did, didn't it?

Occasionally, I would nip the Beemer down to the local car wash, where an army of efficient Eastern European chaps would swarm over it, and it would emerge washed with shiny tyres in no time. What was clear in my new life was that car washing was considered a man's job to be performed at the weekend. There was an old conveyor drive-through car wash at the Esso petrol station on the other side of town – it was still there in 2019, but no one used it. Standing on my drive that Sunday morning and peering up the road, I spotted about ten blokes doing the same thing. The lifting of the hose-pipe ban appeared to have spurred the street into action.

Our first full day of our engagement fell into domestic bliss. Jenny planned to cook a proper Sunday lunch whilst I offered to clean her car and, as it turned out, mine as well. After bashing out the rubber car-mats against the wall of the house, I thought I would tackle the boot, which had turned into a mess after moving Jenny's stuff yesterday. Tucked in the spare wheel compartment was the brown envelope – shit, I'd forgotten it.

Pulling the content out, I laid it across the boot. Birth Certificate confirming I was born on the 30th of March 1934, and not next year, and the Last Will And Testament of Jason Apsley. Why I had a copy in my safety deposit box, God only knows, as no bugger would find it there as I would be dead. That sounded familiar, being dead. I pondered for a moment – was I dead? Shaking my head, it was a question I just couldn't fathom, like trying to imagine nothing existed – no world, no universe – you can't, it was just impossible to do.

I read on, the usual legal jargon blah-blah-blah, then the next paragraph sent the hairs on the back of my neck bolt upright and a shiver across my body. I glanced up to see if Jenny was looking at me; no she wasn't, no one was. I reread it to ensure my eyes were not imagining the text.

I leave my entire estate to my daughter, Jessica Rose Apsley, born 17th June 1956.

Oh hell, I have a daughter. Well, I don't actually, well, I do, but don't. Well, *other* Jason has, but that was me, kind of, and she was aged twenty. Fucking hell, and what about her mother? Was that my wife? More to the point, where were they? Why were they not in *other* Jason's life, that was now my life? Evidently, they hadn't been for some time thinking of Annie. *Other* Jason had lived in South Africa for nearly fifteen years, although I'd not experienced any of that, so what was happening at the time of my daughter's birth? Christ, if she walked up to me now, I wouldn't know who she was. I had no photos of her and didn't possess any pictures of Jason's life pre South Africa. Leaning up against the car boot, I lit up a cigarette and drew heavily. "Sorry, Jason, for taking your life," I muttered, and it wasn't the first time I had uttered that phrase.

"Whose life have you taken, darling?"

I leapt into the air and spun around. Attempting to remove the cigarette from my mouth, but saliva had welded the filter to my lips, resulting in my fingers running down the cigarette to rest on the lit end. "Fuck, fuck, that hurt."

"Jason, quiet. Your language is awful."

"Sorry, Jen, I just burnt my bloody finger!"

"I made you jump, sorry, darling. You were daydreaming about me, I hope." We kissed as she leant against me. Behind me, with my right hand, I discreetly folded the paperwork and stuffed it into my back pocket.

"Let's go up to the Three Horseshoes tonight? I would like you to meet a close friend of mine," I suggested, keen to deflect the conversation away from Jenny's question.

"Yes, okay, is that your friend, George? But we can't be late. We both have to be up for work in the morning."

"Yes, that's him. Talking of work, what's happening with that Carol Hall? I know Don will be calling this week, telling me all sorts of tales about her goings-on."

"I'm due to visit her tomorrow. When I visited last Thursday, I wasn't happy with how she was looking after her baby. So, I want to check that she is doing the things I asked her to do. Your old neighbour, Don, seems very protective of her, doesn't he?"

"Yes, he is. I think it's a combination of loneliness and missing his daughters."

"Yes, that is truly sad."

I realised I'd put myself in an awkward situation if Carol was to mention that Jason, her old neighbour, visited last week. I wanted to come clean with Jen, but it seemed impossible. Adding further complications, I now had the Jessica Rose problem to consider. Life was becoming incredibly complicated, a feeling of being backed into a corner. I wasn't really lying, just withholding information, but the more I did this, the tighter hole I was being squeezed into. I felt like I was sinking into quicksand.

I called George to see if he was going to the pub. He confirmed he and Ivy would be popping down, as Vera next door was going to mind Stephen for a little while. Obviously, the conversation couldn't be as per our regular planning meetings. Still, it would be enjoyable to spend time with him and see my grandmother again.

~

315

"Park there, darling,"

Jenny pointed to a parking space at the back of the car park. The pub was always busy, but tonight it looked packed. I took Jenny's hand as we entered the lounge bar. George always preferred the lounge as opposed to the public bar, which had a pool table and was usually full of younger punters, many of whom I suspected were underage. However, in the '70s, no one gave a toss. We were a little early, George and Ivy hadn't arrived, so we grabbed a couple of barstools and ordered our drinks. Jen had a Dubonnet and lemonade, whatever that was, but the bar staff seemed to understand, so all was good.

Dawn swivelled around on her personalised barstool. "Hello, Jason, is this your lovely lady? Where have you been hiding her? You're gorgeous, my dear."

"I'm surprised you can even lift your hand … that must weigh a tonne," chuckled Dennis, his eyes bulging as he pointed to Jenny's ring.

"Hello, Dawn, evening, Dennis. This is Jenny, my fiancée." I waved my hand around as part of my introduction.

"Well, Jason, you're a lucky chap, I'd say. And Jenny, my dear, you've got a good one there. He's a lovely lad, isn't he, Dennis?"

"It is lovely to meet you both. So how do you know Jason?" Jenny asked.

"Oh well, my dear, we occasionally pop in for a drink and met Jason here," replied Dawn.

"Dennis, your wife is drunk, occasionally pop in … oh no … you practically live here," Brian, the landlord, interjected, as he placed our drinks on the bar.

"Evening, George. Oh, and Ivy, too. Nice to see you both. Usual?" Brian added, raising an empty pint mug in George's vague direction.

George's favourite bay window seat had already been taken, so we grabbed a table at the other end of the lounge and settled in for a pleasant evening. I'd forewarned Jenny about their daughter's death, just managing to hold back from telling her that she was my mother, and we kept the conversation light.

"George, another port and lemon, and please excuse me, but I must powder my nose," said Ivy.

Jenny jumped up as well. "Good idea. I will come with you."

"Delightful lass, Jason. It's all gone rather quick though, don't you think? You've only just met her."

"Yes, it is quick, but I'm sure. Look, George, I need to talk to you, but we only have a few minutes." I recounted the concerning discovery in my will, also mentioning that David Colney assaulted Sarah when she was fifteen.

"Bloody hell, lad, you've got yourself in a right pickle. One thing is for sure that Colney rotter has got to be stopped sooner rather than later."

"Yes, I know, but what the hell can I do that's legal? And what if I'm married already? I've just got engaged, for Christ sake!"

"Lad, for now, deal with what's in front of you. Look after your new young lady, and let's think about this Colney chap. The daughter bit will have to wait."

"Oh, bollocks. What a mess," I muttered, before gulping down my beer.

"Lad, this daughter of yours – or his – hasn't appeared during the last six weeks, so I suggest you forget about her for the moment. But that Colney chap has got to be stopped. It's not right him doing these things, and what you say he does in the future is, I believe, certain to happen again."

"Yeah, I know you're right. It's great that women take forever in the toilets, but they will be back soon, so we can't talk. Can we meet for a pint after work tomorrow?"

"Not tomorrow, lad, but Tuesday will be okay, usual time," George replied, and, as predicted, the ladies returned.

"Did you forget the drinks, George?" Ivy asked, taking her seat.

"Christ, yes, I will get them now."

"No, stay there, George. I'll get them. I must nip to the little boys' room on the way."

"I'll come with you, lad. It seems the beer is running through me tonight."

"You two are as thick as thieves. Are you planning a murder?" Ivy joked.

"Yes, my love, we are," George chuckled.

"Not you, George Sutton. You wouldn't hurt a fly."

Neither could I – that was the problem. George and I weren't the Kray twins, although it was someone like them that we needed to put a stop to David Colney. I'd dismissed the idea of using George's Luger and didn't think hiring a hit-man was on the cards, even though I could now afford it.

51

20th September 1976

Super Mario

"Mr Poole, is Sarah Moore in today, as I haven't seen her this morning?"

"No, Mr Apsley, she hasn't come in today, but I haven't had a chance to check with Miss Colman if there is a message from her mother. I'll check right now."

"No, that's fine. Leave it with me."

That was odd, as I believed Sarah had a full attendance record. She was a very focused student and always worked hard to get her grades. I guess we all get ill from time to time, but I had a niggling concern in my mind after our conversation on Saturday.

"Good morning, Miss Colman. I trust you had a good weekend?"

"Oh yes, Mr Apsley, it was lovely, thank you, really lovely."

"Really, that sounds exciting. What did you get up to?"

"Nothing, Mr Apsley. Well, nothing in particular." Clearly Miss Colman could have a fantastic weekend doing nothing.

"Did you have a good weekend? What did you do, Mr Apsley?"

"Nothing, really. Oh yes, I got engaged to be married, but nothing else," I grinned.

"Mr Apsley, congratulations, that is wonderful news. Who's the lucky lady? Do we know her?" She'd bent forward with her hands in the praying position, almost as if offering a polite oriental greeting.

"Jenny, no, she works for the Council, but thank you. Just a quick question. Has Sarah Moore or her mother called in today, as she is not in school?"

"Haven't you heard, Mr Apsley?"

"Heard what?"

"Well, I shouldn't say, as it's not my place, but Mr Clark has two plain-clothed policemen in with him at the moment. They're detectives, I think, and they're investigating what happened yesterday, but I'm not one to gossip, as you know."

I leaned forward and whispered, "I can keep a secret. What's going on?"

Miss Colman leaned further forward, did the furtive sideways glance, left and right, and then blurted it out; she couldn't help herself.

"Sarah's father was stabbed yesterday during an altercation on the Broxworth Estate. Rumour has it that he went up there to see the Colney family and got into a bit of a set-to with one of the Colney boys … Patrick, I think. He was one of the old boys here, a rough boy like the rest of the family. So anyway, Patrick got arrested, and Mr Moore is in the hospital with multiple stab wounds."

"Oh hell, that's horrendous. I hope Mr Moore will be alright, but why are the police here to see Roy?"

"Well, apparently—"

Abruptly, Miss Colman stopped talking and blushed as Concorde Waite nosed in to the office. I reckon his nose was in the door a full few seconds before the rest of his body followed in.

"Hello, you two. This all looks a bit clandestine," he grinned, as we quickly parted, establishing a normal distance between us.

"Morning Jon, Miss Colman was just giving me a run-through on the Ditto Machine." I could see that Jon didn't believe that for one moment.

"Ah, I see. Well, I just need some textbooks, then I'll leave you both to it," he replied with a raised eyebrow, before rummaging through a large wooden bookcase, occasionally glancing over at us whilst we stood awkwardly waiting for him to leave. When he finally left the office, it was nose first, body second.

Miss Colman and I resumed our positions. She performed the old 'one-two', left and right, and continued. "Well, as I was saying, the altercation had something to do with an incident between Sarah Moore and David Colney some time ago. I think the police want some background information on both students. Such a shame because Sarah is such a lovely girl … lovely girl."

"Miss Colman, can you show these two gentlemen out, please?" boomed Roy, as he flung open his office door.

"No need, sir. We can find our way out. Thanks for your help. We'll be in touch," stated one of the officers.

"Morning, Mr Apsley," Roy conveyed to me, then disappeared back into his office. No small talk today, as he appeared burdened with issues.

Armed with this new information, I felt the need for a cigarette, so I nipped along to the staff room. It was safe to assume, after our chat on Saturday, Sarah had informed her parents as I suggested, resulting in her father now fighting for his life in a hospital bed after presumably barrelling up to the Broxworth Estate to deal with David.

So, had I now altered history? Perhaps I should have kept my mouth shut because if Mr Moore dies, that will be my fault.

This sobering episode reminded me that my actions could have both positive and negative effects. Of course, saving Stephen had been positive. However, I was oblivious to any ripple effect on other events on time, and the Sarah incident was a negative because her father might lose his life. I now wondered what the impact of meeting Jenny was. Who would she have met if I hadn't turned up, or would she have met *other* Jason, and the same story played out anyway? There was the possibility that she carried on seeing that Tom bloke and maybe married him.

I stubbed out my cigarette after using it to light another. "Christ, I'm chain-smoking," I muttered. I had to stop these 'what ifs and buts'. I was here, *other* Jason wasn't, so I just had to live my life. Maybe by persuading Sarah to say something, the police would thoroughly investigate and David Colney would come on their radar now and not in four years' time. Therefore stopping some other young girl from having to suffer his abuse in the future.

I decided I'd done the right thing, and only good could come from it. I just hoped Mr Moore would be okay. Of course, there was a chance that Sarah would look to blame me for her father's injuries, sucking me into the investigation if she spilt the beans about our conversation on Saturday afternoon.

I thought yesterday life was complicated, but today it had moved up a level. I felt my whole existence was like a game of Super Mario – master this level and then move on to the next much harder one. The question was, which level was I now on, and how many levels were there to complete?

The feeling you get when coming home to the person you love can't be underestimated. The first time I'd returned from work when Jenny was home, our home, made me feel sad for Don, who missed Peggy so much. Old Jason had been a bloody island, continually pushing people away, presumably because I thought I could face the world on my own. Now older, with the experience of the last five weeks, at last I valued the connection with others, the friendships I was developing and the love I received from Jenny. The thought of losing that loved one was, if I'm honest, frightening. So, I made a point of giving Jenny a big hug when I arrived home.

"Well, hello you. That was nice, fiancé," Jenny cooed, as she stood preparing vegetables.

"You had a good day?" I was fishing for information without sounding too bloody obvious.

"It was a tough one, to be honest. I had to go up to Lexton House this afternoon for a meeting. It's such a ghastly place, so grey and imposing, it gives me the creeps. I wish we didn't have to send children there; it's so horrible."

"Yes, I know the building you mean. It looks pretty grim. That's where Carol Hall's little lad is, isn't it?"

"Yes, we have temporarily housed him there. Either he will go back to Carol, or, if not, we'll follow the adoption process. He's too young to stay at that home, but we're short of foster carers at the moment. Well, no, we're always short of foster carers."

"He's not likely to go back to Carol, is he? She can't look after the baby, let alone her son as well. Her place is a shithole, stuff everywhere."

"How would you know that about Carol's flat?" Jenny quizzed, frowning, the vegetable knife now pointing in my direction as she waved her hand in the air.

"Oh, you said something about it yesterday," I'd ballsed up again, digging a hole for myself.

"No, all I said was that I was concerned and asked her to complete some actions before I return on Monday. I didn't say it was a shithole."

"Oh, well, it must have been Don who said it when I spoke to him on Friday." Phew – crawled out of the hole.

"I hope you didn't go and see Don on Friday after what happened to you last week. Did you?"

"No, of course not. We spoke on the phone." Well, technically not a lie – I visited Don on Thursday, not Friday. No, I was kidding myself. I was lying and getting good at it. However, soon I was going to get caught out, for sure.

"Good, I don't want you anywhere near that estate. Your nose has only just started to heal. There is little chance of Christopher returning to Carol, and I have spoken to her today about whether she can cope with the baby. Finding foster parents for a baby is easy. When they get older, it becomes more difficult."

"Right, that sounds a good move. How did she react?"

"She scrunched her face up. You know, like those old men that gurn, called me a ginger bitch and told me to fuck off. Really nice, I thought."

"Jesus, that's horrible, Jen. I hope you don't have to put up with that kind of language often?"

"Only when I'm with you, darling, your mouth can be like a sewer."

"Sorry, too many years working in an all-male mining industry. I will work hard on reducing my 'fs'." More lies flowing effortlessly from my mouth.

"You know I shouldn't be telling you all this stuff. It's supposed to be confidential."

"Yes, of course, Jen. I wouldn't say anything, I promise."

"I know, I know you won't. Just saying that's all. When I left Carol's flat today, I was concerned because a vile-looking bloke was walking up the landing. When I turned and looked back, he was banging on Carol's door," Jenny said, as she forced the knife through a potato.

"What time was that? I could ring Don … he would give me the low-down on who it was and if you should be concerned." Bollocks, that was Paul Colney visiting. I had to get Beth out of that flat, but I knew apart from kidnapping her, the only way was to convince Jenny to act legally and remove her.

"Actually, darling, could you? You could have a casual chat, and without directly asking him, he might tell you. It could really help. I think at some point soon we'll have to remove the baby, and that's not easy without a lot of evidence to back up the removal order."

Early evening, I sat on the stairs and phoned Don. I made a mental note to get the phone moved into the kitchen.

"Evening Don. Are you well?"

"Evening, son. Yes, I'm okay, thanks. Son, you know what we discussed about the house—"

"You're not backing out on me, are you? A deal's a deal! We had a gents' agreement ... we shook on it."

"No, not at all. I was just checking it's still going to happen, and I didn't dream it."

"It's still going to happen, Dad. Oh, err ... sorry, so sorry, Don, I apologise. I don't know why I said that ... a slip of the tongue."

"Son, I liked it. I would have loved to have been your father, although I expect he was a splendid fellow."

"Yes, Don, he was. He was a very fine fellow indeed. Well, Don, I would like to apply for the position of the honorary son of Donald Nears."

"Your application has been successful. You have the position, son."

"Great!" We both chuckled. However, I got the sense it was important to both of us.

"Dad, did Carol have a visitor today?"

"Yes, your lovely young lady, but I expect you know that and then straight after, Paul Colney. He stayed about twenty minutes, but I couldn't hear much apart from the young baby crying; it cries all the time, you know."

"Do you think he was peddling drugs?"

"I would say so. Reckon he might also have had a quick one, if you know what I mean."

"Yeah, I think I do. Look, I'll give you a call later this week. I'm hoping to have moved forward on my purchases by then."

"Great, thanks, son."

"Thanks, Dad." We both ended the call laughing.

Don had supplied some valuable information, which Jenny thought could be helpful when building the case to remove Beth to a safer environment – my plan was working.

52

24th September 1976

Four Candles

Every day for the past week, I'd bought the Daily Express, one of the recipient newspapers of the letters I posted last Friday. I scoured every page to see if there was any mention of the anonymous letter I'd sent. Unfortunately, as I expected, I found nothing. What the West Yorkshire Police had done with it was anyone's guess, but only a week had passed, and I surmised the policing-wheels moved slowly. Perhaps my letter got dumped and treated as a crank letter sent by some ex-friend of Peter Sutcliffe. Although, fortunately, there were no more reported murders, I feared he would again strike soon.

The cheque had cleared, inflating my already healthy bank balance by fourteen-and-a-half-grand, and the purchase of the two houses on the Bowthorpe Estate was progressing. It appeared the process of buying a house was similar to the process forty years from now – excruciatingly slow.

Sarah returned to school on Wednesday. Although still in the hospital, her father would make a full recovery, which was a huge relief. Sarah and I avoided each other, which seemed the best policy due to that particular level of the game of life was difficult enough without adding extra complications.

I'd met George for a pint on Tuesday evening, and we discussed again what we had in the beer garden nearly a month ago. However, as expected, neither of us had any ideas regarding how to stop David Colney. I wasn't keen on the killing idea for three reasons. Firstly, I was too scared to do it. Secondly, I wasn't a murderer. And thirdly, if I got caught, I didn't relish spending my life in prison. So, the upshot was we enjoyed a beer and a catch-up but achieved bugger-all.

Without the Internet, it was a merry-go-round investigating Jessica Rose and any potential wife still lurking in the background. The good news was that there were no records of Jason Apsley ever being married in the UK. The mother of Jessica Rose was Jennifer Redmond, which was spooky, another Jenny, and I remember the elderly lady living near Beth had the same surname – weird!

Anyway, this woman with whom *other* Jason had a child was born on the 22nd of March 1936, so she was twenty when she gave birth to Jessica. As for their whereabouts, I'd not been able to glean that information, but neither were dead, as no records stated that. I decided to take George's advice and ignore that problem for now. As I didn't appear to be already married, I wasn't about to commit bigamy – what a relief.

On Thursday, Jenny revisited Carol to discover she was high on drugs. So, with the aid of the courts and the police, Jen obtained an immediate removal order, and Beth was duly placed with foster parents. Whilst I was delighted that Beth was safely away from Carol and the future threat of David Colney, I now didn't know where she was. Although I was slightly concerned about not knowing, Beth was now safe, and that's all that ultimately mattered.

Don informed me that the word on the street was that Patrick Colney had been remanded in custody and charged with the attempted murder of Mr Moore, so with the Colney clan weakened, I felt comfortable visiting Don. After school, I applied my previously used disguise and marched up to Broxworth Estate, this time taking the long route to avoid the block that housed the Colney clan. I zipped up the concrete steps to the second level and, as I was about to turn the corner, I bumped straight into David Colney, who was running and poised to leap

328

down the steps. We bounced off each other as we collided. I steadied myself whilst Colney fell straight on his arse. For a brief moment, we just glared at each other.

"Apple, you wanker, you're not supposed to be on the estate."

"It's Apsley, and Mr Apsley at that."

"Fuck off! I don't go to your school anymore. I'll call you what I fucking like, you knob."

"David, look, I'm aware they've arrested your brother, and I know why, because of that fight with Mr Moore. You're heading down the wrong route, and you're also going to end up in prison along with your father if you don't change your ways. Can't you see that?"

"Don't you fucking talk about my old man. He's one of the most feared men in this town. You can't touch me ... he knows people."

David stood leaning against the concrete landing wall and then gobbed a huge phlegm at me that fortunately missed, hitting the wall to my right. I glanced at it stuck to the wall, then turned to see him grinning – I wanted to kill him.

"What you going to do, Apple, take a bite at me? Bet you're mad to the core," he immaturely laughed.

"David, what you did to Sarah was wrong, you know that. If you carry on like this, you'll get caught. When you turn eighteen, you'll be classed as an adult, and you'll end up in prison. I can assure you sex offenders don't fare well in those places."

"Fuck off! You don't fucking know what you're talking about. Anyway, that bitch was begging for it."

He pushed himself off the wall, stepping to within a few inches of my face. Although shorter than me, he appeared menacing, probably benefiting from the training received from his brothers, the great role models that they were. He repeated himself with spit shooting out of his mouth.

"She was begging for it, okay?"

With that, he pushed past me, vaulted down the concrete steps, turned at the bottom and glanced back up. "Fuck off, Apple, you're a total prick."

~

I updated Don regarding the progress of the house purchase and, although a little early for me, I joined him for a small whisky to keep him company before taking great care when exiting the estate. I'd had enough of the Colney family, and unquestionably, any idea that I could make an impression on David Colney on how he could change his ways wasn't a possibility. There would be no bending of that time-path, so as long as Beth wasn't returned to Carol, she was safe. However, although now confident regarding Beth's safety, that didn't alter the fact that there would be other girls who would suffer and women who would die forty years from now when he progressed to become a serial killer. Therefore, the problem hadn't changed, and my solution was still the same – no idea.

Jenny was enjoying a girls' night out with Helen, so I had the house to myself. Although I was generally okay with my own company, tonight I wasn't. My mind and I were not getting on too well together. I found myself talking to myself as I pushed through the stuff in my head.

I wondered about Beth. Although my life was so much better now, I missed her. What had happened after my crash? Had time been eradicated, therefore nothing had happened after the 12th of August 1976? That couldn't be right, but I had time travelled and had no idea how it worked. Had there been a funeral for me in 2019, and did many mourners turn up? Beth, probably Lisa, and that would be about it. What had happened to *other* Jason? What had happened to Martin, sitting next to me as I ploughed the Beemer in to that white van? Had I killed him in the crash, or had he escaped with his life? Maybe he went to my funeral as well. That would have made three – almost a crowd.

I assumed my actions had now changed Beth's time-line so David Colney would not have the opportunity to abuse her. But what effect did those actions have on future events? Maybe Beth would no longer attend the Fairfield City School, resulting in Cindy and Barbie being able to avoid having to perform their nude run.

Turning on the TV and pouring myself a large whisky – which I was now getting the taste for – I was treated to an episode of The Two Ronnies' show. I settled down to watch the re-run. Well, a re-run for me, but the first airing of the show for everyone else, unless there were more time-travellers sitting in their living rooms watching The Two Ronnies at the same time – unlikely, I thought.

My mind drifted whilst Ronnie Corbett, in his leather chair, recounting one of his shaggy-dog stories, which I found mildly amusing, only for my interest to become piqued by a sketch set in a hardware shop – the hilarious Four Candles sketch. Although I'd seen it a million times, as we all have, well, in my old life we all had, it still made me laugh, bringing tears to my eyes.

The Two Ronnies successfully dragged my mind from its melancholy state. I realised I had everything you could ever want: a lovely house, not massive, but big enough, financially stable, and friends. Yes, I was starting to make friends: George and Ivy, a bit odd as they were my grandparents, and Don, my new honorary father, because time had cruelly stolen mine – twice. And then there was the new job that I was starting to love. For the first time in my life, I looked forward to going to work. But to top it all, Jenny had agreed to marry me. "You lucky bastard. Get a grip, man," I muttered.

As George had counselled me on several occasions, I had to move on because I couldn't manipulate *time* to change in every situation. What was going to happen was going to happen – time to move on, enjoy my new life and take hold of this second chance.

53

25th September 1976

Curiosity Killed the Cat

Jenny snuggled up to me. I was in that half-awake state, those moments when you know you're still asleep but about to wake up to a new day.

"Morning, future husband."

"Good morning, future wife. You look particularly sexy this morning."

"Why thank you, Mr Apsley, very nice of you to say so. I may look particularly sexy, but also, I'm particularly thirsty."

"Is that a hint?"

"Uh-huh."

"Okay, I'll make a drink in a minute."

"Shall we go to the football this afternoon and then see Mum and Dad tonight? But only if you want to. I know Mum and Dad love seeing us, and they have asked Alan not to go out so early with his mates so that he can meet you."

"Yes, okay, let's do that. I take it you mean West Ham?"

"Yes, silly, no other team has Frank Lampard, do they?"

"Oh, yes, I forgot there are three of us in this engagement … you, me and Frank."

"Don't be silly, but he is good looking, and I think he looks like you."

"Ha, that's a bit tenuous."

"No, you're right. You're much better looking. Oh, and by the way, I'm still thirsty."

"Okay, flattery will get you everywhere." I kissed her gently before I exited the bed and plodded down to the kitchen. My mood had significantly improved after giving myself a bollocking last night.

I enjoyed going to football. In my era, it was impossible as you had to have a season ticket, and if you didn't, the next option was to sit on the phone for hours trying to get any spare ones. And if you weren't a member, well, forget it. But today, all we had to do was turn up and pay the entrance fee. But that was the only improvement, as my memory of the last game concerned me. How people weren't regularly injured every week was a bloody miracle. I knew events were coming where injuries and death would happen. There was the Hillsborough tragedy, another event that I knew was going to happen. And this particular one, I knew the exact date – could I prevent it? I shook my head. That's a decade away. No, we would just enjoy the game, whoever they were playing. The phone rang. I padded my way through to the hallway and caught it on the fourth ring.

"Son, it's Don."

"Morning, you okay?" I asked, a little concerned at the sound of his shaky voice.

"She's dead, son, she's bloody dead. I know she's a rum-one, but the poor girl is dead."

"Don, who's dead? What's happened?"

"Carol next door … she's dead."

"What do you mean, dead?"

"Well, she's gone … you know what dead means."

"Yes, but what happened?"

"Son, it's all kicked off. Last night, there was an altercation between Carol and Paul Colney. I could hear it through the walls. Anyway, that soon ended, and he left the flat. It's happened many times with Carol, so I thought, oh well, you know, just another episode in that sad girl's life. But this morning when I popped my head out of the door to grab my paper, her front door was open, which I thought was odd. So, I nosed in and called out her name. There was no reply, so I stepped inside and there she was, lying in her bed, stone-cold dead."

"Jesus, how did you know she was dead?"

"Needle sticking out of her arm. I've seen enough dead bodies in my time, son. She was dead."

"Oh my God, that poor girl."

"Police have been here and removed her body. Of course, that lot will chalk it up as just another druggy who's overdosed. But that evil Colney bloke gave her the drugs … he killed her. As I said, son, that Colney lot are evil, and it's so sad Carol has lost her life at such a young age." I thought he sounded distressed. He'd seen a lot in his life and so much sadness in recent years.

"Oh, that's terrible. I'll pop up and see you around mid-morning."

"No need, son. Best you keep away from here."

"Okay, Don, but I will give you a call later and just catch up. But thanks for letting me know."

"That's okay, son. And don't worry, I'm fine. You have a nice day with your young lady … you have to cherish every day you have. You know that girl of yours fits into two categories … good and happy. She probably saved that baby's life by getting her removed from next door. Your job, my boy, is to ensure she stays happy."

"I will, Don, I bloody will."

Time had bent again. Back in 2019, I didn't know what happened to Carol as Beth never talked about her. Carol had let her boyfriend abuse Beth, so she blanked her mother out of her mind. However, Carol was alive in 1980 in that world, and now she was dead in 1976 in this world. The act of Beth's early removal had changed the future. I now wondered if I had caused Carol's death, or premature death, by my intervention and the alteration of time. Climbing back into bed, I relayed the telephone conversation to Jenny.

"Oh, that's awful, but thank God we got that baby removed this week. Lord knows what would've happened if she was still there."

"Yes, it is, but I wonder, did she take an overdose because now both her children have been taken into care?"

"I had to do my job, Jason. The child comes first, and there's no way I could leave that baby there."

"No, I didn't mean it was your fault. Of course, you had to take the baby away, absolutely, but I gave you cause to go there again with the information from Don. I now feel guilty."

"No, the baby is safe, and that's the important thing." Yes, thank God, that intervention had probably saved Beth.

"Also, Jason, Carol chose to take the drugs. No one forced her, did they?"

"No, I guess not."

But that wasn't quite right because the circumstances of Carol's life had pushed her into drugs. Maybe one mistake shoved her down that road, and that decision led to her pregnancy at the age of sixteen. What would have happened to Carol if she had said no and didn't get pregnant whilst still at school? A different life, perhaps. I also considered whether she injected herself or Paul Colney injected her, purposely delivering a fatal dose. Again, I was going down that route of 'ifs and buts', but it filled my mind.

"Penny for them, darling. You're in a trance."

"Oh, sorry, Jen, I was miles away. I was just thinking about Don." Another lie.

"When can you get him out of that flat?"

"It will be a while yet, as the houses are over a month away from completion, but hopefully soon."

"You are such a good man, Jason. You don't know Don that well, but letting him have one of those houses for a meagre rent

335

is a wonderful thing. Most people are out for themselves to get what they can, but not you. You think of others and how you can help. You're a good man, a caring man, and I feel lucky to have you." She cuddled up to me, her head on my chest – perfect.

A good man? I certainly hadn't been a good man – no, I'd been selfish and sad. Don had the four categories that he liked to pigeonhole us all in to. The *'good'* change things for the better – they counterbalance the *'evil'* – was that true? I didn't know, and was I *good* for escalating the death of Carol Hall? I didn't know that either.

"Don was quite upset on the phone."

"Well, he would be. It's not every day you find your neighbour dead. It must have been quite a shock."

"Yes, you're right, but he's seen enough in his life to take scenes like that in his stride. In the First World War, he saw horrible death every day."

"Yes, but that was a long time ago." Jen twiddled the ring on her finger, something I'd seen her do often that week.

"Think I might nip up and see him this morning. Check he is okay. He doesn't have anyone else."

"Okay, do you want me to come with you?"

"No, I'll just nip up there and be back before we go out."

"Okay, but please be careful. I hate that estate. I don't mean to sound callous, but I'm glad I don't have any other cases up there at the moment."

"So am I, Jen. I don't want you up there either."

We stayed in bed and enjoyed our Saturday lie-in. I left to see Don at ten o'clock, leaving Jen tucked up in bed. I would rather have stayed where I was, but something drew me to check on him. Perhaps it was the threats that Paul and Patrick Colney had made when they gave me a beating. They said that Carol might be persuaded to kill herself if I returned. Christ, I now hoped my last two visits weren't the reason the poor woman was now dead.

I started to think that my meeting with David Colney yesterday had been the catalyst for Paul Colney to see Carol, then kill her and make it look like a suicide. Also, there was the threat that Don may have a fall. Had I set the wheels in motion for that to happen and, if I go there, will they hurt him, or worse – kill him?

As I drove across town, I considered that perhaps the sensible course of action was to go home and thus avoid placing Don in danger. However, for some reason, I kept going.

What was the saying? Oh yes, 'curiosity killed the cat'. Let's hope that cat had nine lives – well, I was already on my second.

54

Dead Junkie Whore

I parked in precisely the same spot I had thirty-odd years in the future to collect that rubbish wine rack. This time, no gang of youths appeared, and the wall that most of them had sat on hadn't received its full-sleeve tattoo of graffiti yet.

The estate was busy, which I thought was better than quiet. I could mingle and not stand out, although I wished my designated car wasn't bright yellow. I elected to stay in the car for a few minutes whilst I surveyed the landscape. Thankfully, I couldn't see any of the Colney clan. There were mostly kids on bikes and skateboards, probably the same ones that had blocked my path so the Colney boys could dish out my beating – for sure, my nose would never be the same.

Again, I considered this was potentially a bad idea, fearful I'd be spotted, and they'd inform someone higher up the food-chain that I was on the estate again, which could put Don in danger. Starting the engine, I slammed the car into reverse and backed up a few feet, turning the wheel, preparing to pull out. I should abandon this trip and call Don later, as I'd said I would. Yes, that was the right thing to do.

I held my position for a few minutes, although unsure why I hadn't moved and what was stopping me. The decision was made – just go home – go and enjoy the football and then another surreal evening at Jenny's parents. That was the decision I made yesterday – live my life and stop trying to intervene in everything – but no, I was still parked and not moving.

Ramming back into first gear, I re-parked, killed the engine, and removed the key from the ignition. I still couldn't put my finger on it, but something was telling me that I needed to go and see Don. Like a sixth sense – something nagging at me, that little voice on my shoulder whispering in my ear – it was persistent. There was a reason, what that was, I didn't know, but there was, and I needed to go and scratch that itch.

I had another scan around, looking out of all the windows and checking the mirrors. Those kids on skateboards were still there, a few adults walking with shopping bags, and a couple of youths leaning against one of the stairwells smoking, but no one was looking at me. I was just another bloke parking up on the estate. I exited the car and locked it, still scanning around and seeing who was about. Then, with my head down, I marched towards Belfast House. I arrived at Don's door without incident, passing the youths smoking by the stairs, but they hadn't looked at me, and David Colney hadn't appeared as he had yesterday.

The lack of police crime-scene tape across Carol's front door and no police officer on sentry point guarding the crime scene suggested Don was right – this was just a druggy death – case closed – no one cared. No one, and probably no one ever would, except Don and myself, and it was questionable how long we would be thinking about her in reality. Carol had a short life, which produced two children, and then she departed. I hoped to a better place. I knocked on Don's door.

"Hello, son. I didn't expect to see you today."

"I thought I would just nip up and check you are okay after this morning's horrible discovery."

"Yes, son, I'm fine. Nice of you to check on me, though." Don shuffled back to the kitchen and lit the stove, ready to put the kettle on.

"Well, that's what a son should do for his father," I chuckled.

"Ha, yes, my honorary son, and I do appreciate it. Pity the girls can't be bothered."

"I see nothing is happening next door."

"No, they took her body away this morning and just closed the flat up. One of the officers asked me how I found her, but that was it … they didn't ask anything else. I told them about Paul Colney visiting her last night, but they seemed uninterested. It was just another dead body that had to be dealt with."

"Do you think she overdosed by accident, or Paul Colney had a hand in it?"

"I don't know, son. I can't see why Paul would risk getting involved in killing her. But at the end of the day, who knows? Maybe she didn't pay for her drugs or was too much trouble, so he decided to end it for her. No one will ever know, I suppose."

"Yes, you're right, I guess. Bloody hell, what a mess."

"There you go, coffee. Yes, as I said, good job your lass got that baby out of there this week."

"Thanks, Don." I took a slurp of strong, black coffee.

"You feel safe here until we can get you moved?"

"Yes, son, I'll be alright. I'm just some old git that no one cares about … no one is going to harm me."

"I care."

"Yes, son, you do, and I am so grateful, but no one cares about me up here. I'm one of those invisible people." I hoped he was right about that.

"If needs be, I could put you up for a few weeks until we get you into the new house."

"Well, son, that's really good of you to offer, but no, you are just starting your life with your young lady, and I'm not playing gooseberry."

"You wouldn't." Although Christ knows what Jen would have said.

"Ha, yes, I would. No, I'm fine, honestly, son. It's only a few weeks, and I will be out of here. I've been fine for several years, so a few more weeks won't change anything."

"Okay, if you're sure, but the offer stands."

"Thanks, but I'll be okay."

We moved into the sitting room. It was great to see the framed picture of Peggy in the centre of the mantelpiece and not tucked behind the clock.

"You want a biscuit, son?"

"No, you're alright, Don," I replied, not wanting to repeat the Wagon Wheel experience.

"I will get the removal firm sorted for you when the time comes. Sharps moved my stuff okay. Is that alright?"

"Yes, son, that will be good. Thank you. I will sort the money out with you at the time."

"Yes, fine," I said, not intending to take any money.

The yellowing net curtains that covered the windows still provided a clear view of the corridor. I could see how easy it was for Don to keep track of comings and goings, even with the nets in place. Whilst taking a sip of my coffee, out of the corner of my eye, I saw a figure trot past – David Colney.

I sprung from the sofa, pulling the net curtain up to peer along the landing. Why was David Colney up here? He didn't live in this block, and he was here yesterday. I slapped my head against the glass to see, which reminded me of the times I used to spy on 'Tits-out-Amanda'. That was a different time, a different life, and I felt quite embarrassed thinking about it.

David had stopped at Carol's door. Although I couldn't quite see what he was doing, I guessed he was up to no good. As I strained my neck against the window, I spotted he'd placed something on the floor whilst holding a paintbrush – I presumed he wasn't decorating.

"Wanker! I've had enough of that shit-head," I shouted, before slamming my coffee down, hot-footing my way down Don's hallway, and ripping open the front door.

"Son, what's going on?"

"Colney, stop. Stop now!" I bellowed. He looked up, brush in hand, with white paint dripping from the end. He appeared shocked by my outburst.

Daubed on Carol's door, in white paint that was starting to run legs from every letter was—

Dead Junkie Whore

I moved forward towards him. "You fucking shit, I've had enough of you,"

Colney pointed the dripping brush at me as if wielding a knife. "Fuck off, Apple." He looked nervous, probably because of my outrage, and I must have appeared quite menacing.

Don had poked his head out of the doorway. "Son, stop. Don't get involved."

I reached out to grab David's arm, but he swiped the brush at me. As I involuntarily jumped out of the way, the paint sprayed in an arc across the gap between us. Lobbing the brush at me, he turned and bolted down the landing to the stairwell. Hopping over the paint tin, I hurtled after him and leapt forward, attempting to grab his jacket as he bounced up the concrete steps to the next level. Vaulting up the steps, I continued to give chase, not sure why or what I was doing, but I was so angry. Not that I knew Carol that well, but she'd just died and this shit-head thought it would be fun to paint that on her door – I was furious.

We reached the top of the block, bolting out of the service door that accessed the flat roof. The distance between us was the same as when we started the chase, but now there was nowhere to go. Colney realised he'd made a mistake going up and not down. If he'd gone down, he could have outrun me, but now we stood looking at each other, feet apart like two sumo wrestlers preparing to start their bout.

Colney glanced from side to side, weighing up his options. "What you going to do, Apple?"

"I'm going to drag you down those stairs, and you can get that paint off that door. That's what I'm going to do."

"Fuck off, the whore is dead, and pity the bastard baby isn't as well. I'm not going nowhere with you."

The mention of Beth from this evil boy's lips enraged me as I closed the gap between us. He backed away; the confidence I witnessed in him yesterday seemed to have evaporated. I sprung forward, attempting to grab his jacket again but missed as he ran backwards, stopped only by the low perimeter wall that knocked in to the back of his knees. Reaching out again, I grabbed his arm, but his backward force whipped him over the wall, causing him to disappear from view. As I clung to his arm, the force of gravity hurtled my body forwards, slamming my torso onto the edge of the wall.

A terrified-looking David clung to my arm. The five-storey drop below him with only my arm holding him from certain death. Although his weight would surely rip my arm from its socket, I hung on.

"David, look up, hold my arm, look up." David stared in to my eyes. He was terrified, a fear I'd never seen before.

"David, swing your other arm and grab my hand," I shouted, offering my arm over the wall. I wedged my knees to brace myself from falling over the edge, thus avoiding both of us dropping to our inevitable deaths.

"Mr Apsley, hold me, please. I can't hang on. I'm slipping."

"Give me your other hand. I've got you … I won't let go of you. I've got you." David swung his left arm and grabbed the same arm with which I was holding his right hand. I groaned as my shoulder screamed with pain. Then, swinging my right arm, I managed to grab his hand. We now had all our hands linked, and I started to pull as every muscle in my body popped with the strain.

"David, I've got you … I've got you."

"Please help, help," he cried, tears streaming down his face.

Using my knees to gain purchase against the wall, I started to pull him up, confident I would be able to drag him back over the edge.

"Stop, son!" Don had joined us and stood to my right, peering over the edge of the wall.

"Don, help me, help me pull him up," I shouted through my panting.

"Son, do you want to do that?" Swivelling my head, I stared up at him, struggling to understand what he was saying.

Don placed a hand on my shoulder. "Son, there are good, evil, sad, and happy people in this world. What do you reckon he is?" He pointed at David, swinging from my painfully outstretched arms. "I think we know which category he's in, don't we? He falls into the evil category."

"What?" I bellowed. "Christ sake! Stop yakking and lend me a bloody hand! Don, for fuck sake, give me a hand before I drop him."

"Mr Apsley, I can't hang on. Please, please."

Don turned to face me. "Jason, look at me."

"Don! Help me!" I screamed, turning my attention from this lad's pleading eyes and back to Don.

"Son, let him go … let him go."

The last six weeks flashed around my head. The conversations on how to save Beth, the long-term issue of how to stop the fifty-nine-year-old David Colney from becoming a serial killer, and here I was, arms aching, trying desperately to save his life. Human instinct had taken over, and I was a good man. I had to save him. I wasn't a murderer, but this teenager hanging on my arm for dear life, pleading to be saved, was, or would be in the future.

55

Deaf and Blind

I let go.

David didn't cry out. He drifted from my hands and started his fall to the concrete floor below, his eyes fixed on mine as he descended, our visual connection held until he became too small in my sight as the distance increased. He landed with a thud, back first, head second, a pool of dark blood seeped out from the back of his head that must have cracked open like an egg.

I stared down at his prone body. "Oh God, what have I done?" I muttered as I closed my eyes, frightened to reopen them, praying when I did, it would erase that vision of David's body. I cracked open one eye – nothing had changed except the increased size of the pool of blood around David's head. Don placed his hand under my right armpit, which suggested that I should stand. However, I couldn't move, the sight of David's body had transfixed me.

"Son, I need you to stand now, and I need you to walk with me." His voice was direct and solid.

I looked up at him. "What?"

"Stand and walk with me now." It was an order, a direct order.

I stood, my arms and knees screaming in pain as they started to recover from holding David. Don led me by the arm back to the service door on the roof. All I could see was the ground, my shoes, and his tartan slippers shuffling forward. I don't think we met anyone on the way back to his flat. Don guided me through the open front door, removed his hand from my arm, and shuffled back to Carol's front door. He calmly dipped the brush in the paint and methodically painted over the daubed words before collecting the brush and the tin of paint and stepping back into his flat. He calmly closed the door and shuffled through to the kitchen.

Still standing just inside the door, I had an empty feeling. I was a murderer, or was I, or was it manslaughter? I didn't know, but I'd just killed a child.

Don returned from the kitchen holding two glasses of whisky clasped between his thumb and finger. He grabbed my elbow and led me into the living room, coaxing me to sit before handing me a glass. "Drink this," he commanded.

I downed it in one. Don took the empty glass and handed me the other. "Drink that one as well."

I peered up at him like a child taking orders from their father.

"Drink it, son," he once again commanded before shuffling off towards the kitchen.

Don returned with the bottle and another glass, refilling mine and slopping in a considerable measure in the other, gulping it down before sitting in the chair opposite. "Right, son, you hear me?"

I nodded.

"I want you to listen and listen good."

I nodded.

"I've killed plenty of men. Yes, okay, they were German soldiers, but they didn't deserve to die. They were good men forced to be in trenches in France like I was … it was them or me. David Colney was evil, from an evil family, and you made a good decision. He was evil like his brothers, and you will have stopped bad acts he would surely commit in the future."

I nodded.

"I'm going to call the police and say I heard a disturbance. You just sit there and drink that whisky. You're in no fit state to

346

drive home at the moment. He fell off the back of the building that faces the open fields, so no one saw what happened, only you and me. This stays between us and never gets mentioned again … ever."

I nodded.

"In a minute, you're going to gather yourself together and ring your young lady and say, in a solid, convincing voice, that I'm in a bit of a state over Carol's death, and you need to keep me company for a while. She will understand. Then you will sit here while we let the police and the people of this estate do what they will do. After that, you're going to drive home, tell that lass of yours that Don seems to be okay now, and apologise for ruining her weekend. You will kiss her and act normal. You will not mention what happened."

I nodded.

"You're a good man. You did what needed to be done, and that's that. Do you understand?"

I nodded.

"Son, do you understand?"

"Yes, Don, I do," I croaked out, finally finding my vocal cords.

I gulped down the rest of the whisky whilst Don made his call. Then, stretching the phone from the telephone table through to the lounge, he placed it on the arm of the sofa. "You ready, son?"

I nodded and dialled the number, my hands shaking throughout the process.

"Hi, Jen."

"Hello, darling, is everything alright?"

"Yes, yes, err … Don is a bit cut up about Carol's death … think I might need to stay a little while longer with him. Is that okay? I know we will miss the football. Sorry, Jen."

"Oh, alright, darling. Yes, it doesn't matter. You will be home later though, to go to Mum and Dad's? I said we would be there at seven at the latest."

"Yes, of course. I won't be that late."

"Oh, good. You are okay, aren't you?"

"Yes, why?"

"You sound a little strange, almost distant."

"Ha, no, Jen, I'm fine. Sorry again about the football."

"That doesn't matter, darling. Try not to be too long."

"I won't. Love you."

"Love you too."

I replaced the receiver. Another lie; it was lie, after lie, after lie.

"Well done, son." Don placed a hand on my shoulder, then padded up to the window and peeked out.

"What's happening?"

"Nothing, as it's all at the back of the building, but I can see three police cars in the square and an ambulance."

"An ambulance!" I exclaimed, springing to my feet.

"Son, sit down! I don't want your face seen at the moment." Don was in complete control and very direct. "Stay where you are and let me do my usual … being nosey."

"Is he still alive? If an ambulance is here, he might be alive." I had shifted from remorse to worrying about my own skin. If Colney were alive and could talk, I would be arrested within the hour – arrested for attempted murder.

For the next half an hour, Don kept me abreast of the activities he could see whilst peeking through the net curtains. Finally, Don spotted a body covered with a blanket being stretchered to the ambulance by a couple of medics – David was dead.

Don turned to face me. "Son, the police are going door to door. Are you ready? Are you going to be able to handle this? We both go to the door, and you say nothing apart from confirming what I say. You got it?"

"Should I just hide in the bedroom?"

"No, son. After they are gone, you're going to leave the flat and go home in full view of the police. You can't be seen sneaking off … it has to all look normal."

"Right, okay."

"Can you do it?"

I took a deep breath, closed my eyes, exhaled, and nodded.

Don grabbed my arm and looked into my eyes.

"You trust me, son?"

"Like a father."

"Good, come on, and put your jacket on as if you're about to leave."

We stood in the hallway for what seemed a lifetime. I was about to scream with anticipation when two dark shadows moved in front of the obscured glass. I noticed I'd crossed my fingers and, scrunched up in my shoes, my toes had joined in as well.

The glass rattled. "Hello, this is the police. Can you open up, please?"

Don looked at me, and I nodded.

One of the officers was good-old Frenchie, buttons amazingly still on her tunic – she must have welded them on.

Frenchie opened up the conversation. "Hello, sir, I'm aware you live here. It's Mr Nears, is that right?"

"Yes, that's correct."

"And you are Mr Apsley. You live two doors down, correct?"

"Well, I did, but I moved out a few weeks ago. So I'm just visiting," delivered with a surprising amount of confidence. However, having Frenchie asking the questions felt less intimidating.

"I see. Well, there's been an incident at the back of the block. Have you been in all morning?"

"Yes, I have," replied Don.

Frenchie looked at me. "And you, sir, how long have you been here today?"

"Oh, I've been here since early this morning, just been helping Don with some legal paperwork," I replied, fully in my stride, and the lies pouring out – effortlessly.

"What kind of incident? I'm a nosey old git. I did see the police vehicles, but up here, seeing your lot isn't that unusual."

"I'm afraid a youth has fallen from the top of the building, and we're enquiring to see if anyone saw or heard anything."

Now I was starting to sweat and, like a guilty person, felt the need to say something. "Oh, that's awful. Who was it?" Don shot me a look, which I took as an instruction to shut up.

"I'm afraid I can't say, sir," replied Frenchie, as she shifted her sizeable chest in my direction, which I suspected must have taken a fair bit of muscle power.

"Were they hurt?" I asked, ignoring Don's second glance at me.

"Yes, sir, one youth is dead, fell from the top level. We believe he died on impact."

"Oh, hell."

"Did either of you see or hear anything in the last couple of hours that might seem unusual?"

"Nothing is unusual on this estate, miss, not even the death of that lass next door," Don interjected before I could open my mouth.

Frenchie raised her eyebrows, "No, quite … so nothing, then?"

"No," replied Don.

Frenchie looked at me and raised her eyebrows again.

"No," I replied.

"We received a call this morning about a disturbance on the estate. Did either of you gents make that call?" Frenchie asked, her eyes flicking back and forth between us.

"No," replied Don.

"Right, gents, thank you." Frenchie and her side-kick moved on, past Carol's door, not noticing the wet paint, and knocked on the door of flat one-two-one.

Frenchie turned to her partner. "No one saw or heard anything. Everyone on this estate is the bloody same, deaf and blind. This is a waste of time."

Clearly, Frenchie's comment wasn't meant for our earshot. She looked back down the corridor at us both, peering out of the door. "Thank you, that will be all, gentleman," she shouted back, waving her arm, gesturing we should close the door and go back inside.

Don closed the door and grabbed my arms. "Well done, son," he whispered. I guess years of living here he knew, oh so well, how easily any noise travelled through the walls. "Are you ready? Be as confident as you just were, and go nice and slow, normal pace back to your car. Act normal and go home. Make sure you prepare yourself to talk to your young lady and start to forget this. I mean it, son. Start to forget it."

I took hold of his hands. "Thanks, Dad."

56

Four Months Later

Oh Bollocks

My most brilliant achievement was to persuade my wife to marry me, a quote from Winston Churchill.

I had to agree I couldn't think of a better achievement I would ever accomplish. Jenny and I married at Fairfield Registry office. Jenny wasn't that fussed about a church wedding, and I'd not enjoyed my previous excursions there: marriages and funerals. We enjoyed an elaborate reception at her parents' house, which Frances and Jenny planned to perfection – a Christmas wedding on the 30th of December 1976.

I had two best men, which I know was strange, but I couldn't choose between them. George Sutton and Don Nears. One knew the truth of who I was and where I'd come from, and the other knew what I'd done. They were my closest friends.

We honeymooned in Belgium, of all places. Well, we couldn't go for long, so we opted for a short trip abroad. I insisted that a young couple walking along the seafront in Ostend take our picture whilst we perched on a wall looking out to sea – yes, that wall. That wall and that picture of Mum, Dad, Stephen and me, which every day I was struggling to keep clear in my memory.

Nothing came of David's death. Each day after that fateful day in September, I stopped looking over my shoulder one less time, until it got to the point that I would go a whole day without thinking about it. The newspaper report in the Fairfield Chronicle stated the coroner's court had recorded a verdict of misadventure, and that was that.

Following the explicit instruction from Don, my new honorary father, I never told anyone what had happened that day. George thought it was fate and a stroke of luck that David Colney had fallen off the roof of the flats, and that's how we left it.

My letter to the West Yorkshire Police had achieved nothing, but neither had the Ripper, so I prayed that in this new world, time had changed, and he didn't go on to kill numerous other women.

Jessica Rose hadn't surfaced, and I hadn't looked. Legally, she was my daughter, but not *my* daughter, she was *his* daughter, and I felt it best left until I had to deal with it – if ever.

Don moved into his new home in early December. Seeing him pottering about in his new shed was a wonderful sight. He looked younger, a happy man, the sadness had started to ebb away.

I'd now been teaching for six months and looked forward to school every day; I'd found my vocation. Roy stated that the deputy head position would be available and urged me to apply. However, I wasn't sure; we didn't need the money based on the content of my safety deposit box, and if it meant less time teaching and more time completing administration, then I wouldn't want the progression. Nevertheless, I said I would think about it.

In her role at Fairfield District Council, Jenny had connections, and connections were beneficial. The saying '*It's who you know, and not what you know*' is so true. On the 11th of January 1977, we adopted two children: Christopher William Hall, aged five, and his half-sister, Amy Elizabeth Hall, aged four months. Stephen became part of my life again, and he and Christopher became close friends. Having my older five-year-old brother as a regular visitor was strange. However, now I could ensure we stayed close, albeit with a very different relationship.

We needed a bigger house, and I'd lived in Homebrook Avenue with too many memories from thirty years in the future. A local building firm had secured a piece of land to build a small development of five-bedroom houses on the north side of town. Beth and I knew it well, but this Beth had never seen it. The last time I saw it, on the 12th of August 1976, it was a hot summer evening, and that piece of land was full of swaying, late summer corn.

We secured number eleven, the house Miss Redmond owned with the stupidly named dog, Frank. I silently apologised to Miss Redmond for buying her home before she could – she would have to buy a different one. But she would never know that she should have purchased number eleven, and I think Frank, the Labradoodle, would be happy in any house. Anyway, it was the best house on what would be Winchmore Drive, with a large corner plot, and it would be ready to move into by the early summer.

My mental health had significantly improved, which was odd, as the events of the last six months theoretically should have made it worse. However, now I had a sense of purpose, my family and friends, and, of course, my students. My old life was a distant memory, and that debilitating OCD was glued together with old Jason forty years in the future. As for the constant need to lie, although it made me uncomfortable, I came to understand that it was a necessary evil that I would have to live with.

One Saturday evening, after the kids were tucked up in bed, Jenny and I sat late in to the night with the lights off and curtains open, watching the beautiful white flakes of snow float down. On Sunday afternoon, we spent an hour in the garden after lunch. Christopher and I built a snowman whilst Jenny gently rocked Beth in her pram. It was a lovely, sunny, but cold January afternoon.

The doorbell rang.

"I'll get it, darling. Can you keep an eye on Beth, please?"

"Okay."

"Darling, there's some bloke called Martin at the door. He asked if Lisa lives here and said he knows you from Waddington's Steel. I have no idea what he's talking about, and what's Waddington's Steel?"

Bewildered and concerned my world was about to collapse, I mooched my way towards the front door. This couldn't be – it must surely be some mistake. With great trepidation, I opened the door – my jaw dropped, now sporting that open-mouthed, gormless expression I'd perfected some time ago.

"Oh God, Jason, it's you. What's going on? Jesus, mate, I think the whole world's gone fucking mad." He raised his hands in the air and continued with his verbal tirade. "I thought I'd lost my fucking marbles, but thank God you're here. Who the fuck was that woman who answered the door, and where the fuck is Lisa? Anyway, what are you doing here? I thought you and Lisa split up?"

"Martin, is that you?" It was him, but how could it be?

"Yes, of course it fucking well is. Who do you think I fucking am? It's me, Martin! Jason, what the fucking hell is going on? Where is everyone else? And why has every fucking nutter I have met today told me it's 19 fucking 77?"

"Oh, bollocks."

The End … Hmmm, well, is it?

What's next?

Jason returns in ***Ahead of his Time***, where the arrival of Martin sends his perfect world into a spin!

Can you help?

I hope you enjoyed this book. Could I ask for a small favour? Can I invite you to leave a rating or review on Amazon? Just a few words will help other readers discover my books. Probably the best way to help authors you like, and I'll hugely appreciate it.

Free book for you

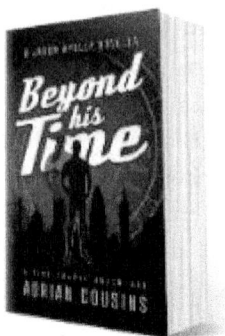

For more information and to sign-up for updates about new releases, please drop onto my website, where you'll get instant access to your FREE eBook – Beyond his Time.

When you sign up, you get a no-spam promise from Adrian, and you can unsubscribe at any time.

You can also find my Facebook page and follow me on Amazon – or, hey, why not all three.

Adriancousins.co.uk
Facebook.com/Adrian Cousins Author

Books by Adrian Cousins

<u>The Jason Apsley Series</u>
Jason Apsley's Second Chance
Ahead of his Time
Force of Time
Beyond his Time
Calling Time
Borrowed Time

<u>Deana – Demon or Diva Series</u>
It's Payback Time
Death Becomes Them
Dead Goode
Deana – Demon or Diva Trilogy Boxset

<u>The Frank Stone Series</u>
Eye of Time
Blink of her Eye

Acknowledgements

Thank you to my Beta readers – your input and feedback is invaluable.

Adele Walpole

Craig Larner

And, of course, Sian Phillips, who makes everything come together – I'm so grateful.

Printed in Dunstable, United Kingdom